D1353465

Bournville Lane B30 2JT
TEL: 0121-464 1534

Loans are up to 28 days. Fines are charged if items are not returned by the due date. Items can be renewed at the Library, via the internet or by telephone up to times. Items in demand will not be renewed.

Please use a bookmark

Date for return		
1 9 MAR 2012	0 5 FEB 2013	
	0 8 APR 2013	
	3 0 APR 2013	
	0 8 JUN 2013	
0 7 APR 2012	2 0 FEB 2016	
0 MAY 2012		
1 6 JUL 2012		
2 4 MAR 2013		

Check out our online catalogue to see what's in stock, or to renew or reserve books.

www.birmingham.gov.uk/libcat

www.birmingham.bov.uk/libraries

 Birmingham City Council

Birmingham
Libraries

56567

"The baby's mine?"

Callie might have expected this. She swallowed past the lump in her throat, hurt that he'd even asked. "Yes."

Tagg inhaled sharply. "You were ticked at your father and you what? Seduced me in order to defy him?" He turned to her then, his eyes black with fury.

"Tagg, listen. You're wrong. I can explain."

"I don't think so. It all makes sense now." He spoke with conviction as if nothing in the world could change his mind.

"I mean that was only part of the reason." What could she say now, that she'd come face to face with her fantasy man? That she'd seen an opportunity to finally take something she wanted, to go for broke, to do something wild and so out of character for her?

How could she tell him that? How could she tell him she loved him?

Dear Reader,

Have you ever met your fantasy man? Someone that is so perfect for you, deadly handsome and honorable with charm to burn, that his very perfection makes him unattainable in your eyes?

Lucky for me, I married my fantasy man, but that's another story for another day, so I figured why couldn't my heroine, Callie Sullivan, finally meet the man of her dreams?

Enter Taggart Worth, ex-rodeo rider, rancher, businessman and the owner of Callie's heart. The Worths are her father's fiercest competitors and all her life she's been forbidden to associate with any of them. But a chance encounter with Tagg and a heart full of yearning has Callie going for broke with her sinfully sexy fantasy man.

Welcome to Red Ridge, Arizona, and Worth Ranch, where skies are blue, the land is vast and mountaintops shine deep crimson.

I hope you enjoy Tagg and Callie's story!

Charlene Sands

CARRYING THE RANCHER'S HEIR

BY
CHARLENE SANDS

Published in Great Britain 2011
by Mills & Boon, an imprint of Harlequin (UK) Limited,
Eton House, 18-24 Paradise Road, Richmond, Surrey TW9 1SR

© Charlene Swink 2011

ISBN: 978 0 263 89085 3

51-1111

Harlequin (UK) policy is to use papers that are natural, renewable and
recyclable products and made from wood grown in sustainable forests. The
logging and manufacturing processes conform to the legal environmental
regulations of the country of origin.

Printed and bound in Spain
by Blackprint CPI, Barcelona

Award-winning author **Charlene Sands** writes bold, passionate, heart-stopping heroes and always…really good men! She's a lover of all things romantic, having married her school sweetheart, Don. She is the proud recipient of a Readers' Choice Award and double recipient of a Booksellers' Best Award, having written twenty-eight romances to date, both contemporary and historical Western. Charlene is a member of Romance Writers of America and belongs to the Orange County and Los Angeles chapters of RWA, where she volunteers as the Published Authors' Liaison.

When not writing, she loves movie dates with her hubby, playing cards with her children, reading romance, great coffee, Pacific beaches, country music and anything chocolate. She also loves to hear from her readers.

For fun stuff, contests and more, you can reach Charlene at www.charlenesands.com, Goodreads, Facebook and Twitter too!

To my dear friends and high school buddies, Mary,
Robin, Allyson, Pam, Denise, Susan, Cindy and Kathy.
Girls who know a good "crush" when they see one!
Our friendship has aged well and I love you all!

A special thank you to Charles Griemsman, my stellar
editor, for his wonderful insights on this story!

One

The subtle sound of hooves pounding earth and good-natured snorts usually put a smile on Taggart Worth's face.

But not today.

Today, his gut was in a twist as he leaned on the corral fence drinking coffee, watching his three prize mares trot around the circular arena, the slight Arizona wind sweeping their manes. Once again, Worth Ranch had lost out on a lucrative cattle deal to Big Hawk Ranch. Hawkins Sullivan had outbid them and won.

Sullivan.

He was their neighbor and a big thorn in Tagg's side. Though Worth Ranch held its own with their biggest competitor, Tagg hated losing this last deal. He'd been led to believe it was a sure thing.

Tagg took a sip from his coffee mug. The thick brew had grown as cold and bitter as his emotions. He splashed the remaining coffee onto the ground and set the empty cup on the top of the rail post. His thoughts strayed to the one-night stand he'd had with Sullivan's daughter Callie last month in Reno. For weeks now, she'd been on his mind and that wouldn't do for the chief financial officer of Worth Enterprises.

While he should have been outsmarting and outbidding The Hawk, as he was known in the cattle business, Tagg had been thinking about Sullivan's daughter instead. The devil in him wondered if Hawkins had sent her to that Reno rodeo deliberately to distract him and throw him off balance. Sullivan was known to be ruthless in business but even he wouldn't go that far—sacrificing his daughter for a cattle deal. Callie didn't strike him as the type of woman who could be easily manipulated, either, but then Tagg had been wrong before when it came to women.

He'd known Callie as a child. Their ranches bordered each other, but he hadn't seen her in years until she'd pulled him off that bar stool in the Cheatin' Heart honky-tonk and dragged him onto the dance floor.

That night had been wild.

"Dance with me, cowboy. Show me your moves," she said as she slid her arms around his neck and cozied up real close. Long dark waves fell in a tangle onto her back. She shimmied her body and sent him a smile that beckoned.

"Can you handle my moves?" He spread his hands on her hips and drew her tight against him. She felt like heaven, warm and willing. He was one whiskey away from pure misery—rodeos did that to him. Made him remember what he'd lost. All-grown-up Callie had caught the brunt of his dangerous mood.

"Oh, yeah, Tagg. I can handle any move you want to make on me." Breathless, her lips angled up to his, so close, so tempting. She stared into his eyes with unmistakable invitation. *Take me,* she had said with that look, tearing his waning willpower to shreds.

Rational thought had escaped him then. He'd been without a woman for months and Callie seemed to want the same thing as he had, a night of crazy-wild sex. She'd seemed eager for it and Tagg hadn't an ounce of self-control left. He'd grabbed her hand and taken her to his hotel room, no questions asked. They'd barely made it through the door before they'd tossed each other's clothes off.

"She's a fine-looking filly."

Tagg turned to find his older brother standing at the corral fence three feet away from him. Tagg and his two brothers owned seventy-five thousand acres of prime ranch land in Red Ridge County—land that had been in the Worth family for generations. Clay lived at the main house, and Jackson spent most of his time in the penthouse, while Tagg lived up in the hills on the site of the original Worth cabin in a newly built ranch home.

"Trick?" Tagg nodded, glancing at the youngest of the three mares, a dappled gray. "She's from good healthy stock. The other females have taken to her just fine."

"You named her Trick?"

"Long story, but she wasn't easy to acquire. In fact, it was damn tricky. I had to do some fast talking."

They watched the horses settle down on the far side of the corral, the two older mares sandwiching Trick between them, mothering her.

"It's been a while since you've come down to the main house." Clay tipped his hat back to look at him directly. "When I drove up you looked deep in thought. Everything okay?"

Tagg wasn't the kiss-and-tell kind of guy. He felt guilty about skipping out on Callie that morning, leaving a note on the hotel bed in his wake. He'd never done that to a woman before. But he wasn't going to discuss that or the loss of the cattle deal to Sullivan with Clay this morning.

It was his problem and he'd deal with it.

Tagg liked his privacy and thanks to modern-day inventions like computers, the internet and iPhones, he didn't have to venture too far to conduct ranch business these days. Clay dealt with the ranch employees and Jackson took care of the other Worth holdings in Phoenix. All three of them didn't mind getting their hands dirty and working the land.

"Everything's fine. Just been buried under a pile of paperwork. How about you?"

"Busy with Penny's Song. The construction is almost complete. Our first young visitors are due to arrive in a few weeks."

"That's good. I'm planning on lending a hand. Anytime you need it."

Penny's Song was Clay and his estranged wife's brainchild, named after a local child who'd died from a debilitating disease at ten years old. With the Worth money and name behind it, the facility built one mile into the property would honor her memory and provide a safe haven for children recovering from life-threatening illness. From the get-go, it was designed to help mainstream those recovering kids into society in a dude ranch-type setting.

"We're counting on your help."

"I'll stop by later today and check out the progress."

Clay nodded and took a step toward his truck, but then turned and stared at Tagg for a moment.

He lifted his brows, curious at Clay's expression. "What?"

"It's been four years, Tagg."

Tagg took a quick pull of oxygen. Noting the concern on his brother's face, he tempered his impulse to lash out with careful words. "I know how long it's been. No one has to remind me."

"Maybe it's time you gave yourself a break."

He watched Clay turn around and get into the cab of his truck. The engine roared and red dust kicked up a fuss as he drove off, leaving Tagg alone with his thoughts. The way he wanted. The way it had to be. He'd lost his wife, Heather, four years ago and nothing would make it right. Giving himself a break wasn't on his agenda.

Ever.

Callie Sullivan stood in the shadows of the Red Ridge Mountains, just steps from Tagg's front door. A tremble pulsed through her body. She recognized it as anticipation and not fear. She couldn't wait to lay eyes on him again even knowing he wouldn't be glad to see her. Even knowing that he'd never called, never tried to get in touch with her again after the night they'd spent together.

She strode up the porch steps and pulled the note he'd written to her on hotel-room stationary out of her jeans. She'd taken it out and read it so many times the paper had worn ragged and thin. She remembered how she'd felt when she'd woken up to find *it* and not Tagg in the bed beside her that morning. She knew the words by heart now; she didn't have to see them.

Callie,
It was great. Heading home early. Didn't want to wake you.
Tagg

As far as notes went, it wasn't much. Tagg wasn't a verbal man, but he'd sure made up for his lack of social skills in the bedroom. Callie had no regrets about that night. She'd been restless, frustrated and unhappy during that trip to Reno until she had spotted Tagg sitting on a bar stool all alone. Something short of crazy clicked in her head and told her to go for what she wanted. She'd always wanted Tagg.

Callie, this is your chance.

She'd taken that chance and that night her "Tagg fantasy" had come to life.

She stood on his doorstep and knocked, the note tucked safely into the back pocket of her jeans.

Silence.

Callie knocked again.

Still nothing.

She stepped off his porch and with a hand above her brows she scoured the property, squinting against the afternoon sun, looking for some sign of Tagg.

His sprawling one-story home sat atop a hill and afforded a panoramic view of the Red Ridge Mountains. The picturesque scene reminded Callie why she loved this part of Arizona so much. More than an hour away from the bustling city of Phoenix with its legendary historic districts, sports centers and trendy shopping, Tagg's ranch home seemed far removed from that life.

It's the way he wanted it, she thought. Everyone knew his past history. The bronco champion married to the rodeo queen. It had all been so perfect. A real fairy-tale ending.

And they lived happily ever after.

But they hadn't. Because Heather Benton Worth had died in a small-plane crash on an airstrip on Worth land and Tagg's life had been engulfed with grief. The details of how it had all come about were sketchy and if anyone knew, not a soul in the county spoke about it. It had been a tragic end to a beautiful life. And it had been as if Tagg had died that day, too. He'd quit the rodeo, leaving his friends and his career behind to build a modest home in the hills. Callie's father had said that Clayton Worth made Tagg the CFO of the company to pull him out of his grief, and his solitary life on the ranch had begun.

Off in the distance, Callie spotted a lone rider coming in from the range. She took a few steps forward to be sure. Her heart sped. Emotions washed over her. She hadn't seen Tagg in five weeks. Five weeks too long. She held a secret close to her heart. One she wouldn't yet share with him.

Long and tall in the saddle, Tagg was just as much a cowboy as he was CFO of Worth Ranch. He wore tan leather chaps over Wranglers and a blue work shirt. Dark Ray-Bans blocked the penetrating sun. As he rode his mare up the dirt path to the barn her breath constricted in her chest. Every nerve ending pulsed.

If Tagg seemed surprised to see her, he didn't show it. He kept his expression blank as he swung his leg up and dismounted the gorgeous bay mare; her coat was glistening with sweat. Callie put a hand on the horse. "You're such a pretty girl," she said, taking hold of the bridle and stroking the mare's forelock. She had a soft spot for all animals, but she loved horses and considered herself an expert horsewoman.

Tagg stood several inches taller and she had to look up to see his face. He folded his arms across his body and leaned back. "I could say the same to you."

She couldn't see his eyes, but was fairly sure he'd just complimented her. "Hi, Tagg."

"Callie." He looked her up and down through his sunglasses, making her wish she'd worn something frilly and feminine instead of blue jeans. "You looking for me?"

"I am."

He rubbed the back of his neck and let go a deep sigh. "Listen, I'm glad you showed up here—"

"You are?" Callie couldn't help herself. She'd been afraid Tagg wouldn't want to see her again. So this was good news and she couldn't hide it in her voice.

He removed his sunglasses and dark silver-blue eyes narrowed in on her. Excitement raced in her veins. Those eyes had seen every ounce of her, had traveled over her body with admiration and desire. Callie would never forget the hot gleam and what it had done to her.

Growing up, Callie had been forbidden to have anything to do with the Worth boys. Her father's rules. The Worths hadn't been *worthy* of the Sullivans. In her father's mind, no one was good enough for Callie. But she'd known Tagg at school, had seen him around town and later had watched him bust broncos in the rodeo.

Simply put, Taggart Worth had owned her teenage dreams. She'd thought the sun rose and set on his broad shoulders— the chisel-jawed, dark-haired, handsome neighbor boy she wasn't allowed to get to know. Six months ago, when she'd returned home from Boston to care for her father after a slight heart attack, nothing had changed except that Callie was her own woman now. And her father's staunch restrictions no longer applied.

"Yeah. I've been thinking about you."

Callie held her breath and on to the hope that surrounded her.

"You have?"

He wrestled with his words. "I'm…sorry. About Reno. Shouldn't have happened."

She deflated faster than a birthday-party balloon. Her stomach clenched tight and a slow burn began inside her belly. She'd been bold with Tagg that night. She'd never be sorry for taking what she wanted. For giving Tagg all she had to give. She'd relinquished more than her body in Reno. And now he was apologizing? Telling her it shouldn't have happened?

Pride and anger replaced her disappointment.

"I don't walk out on women like that, usually."

How many women? How many one-night stands? She wished they'd woken up in each other's arms that morning and declared undying love for each other. But she wasn't foolish enough to believe that would happen between them.

"You left a note," she reminded him in a tone that made him wince.

His look of deep, honest regret overpowered her. He regretted everything while she held close to her heart those wonderful memories.

"I should have stayed and explained."

"Nothing to explain, Tagg. We both got what we wanted."

Tagg shook his head. He didn't believe it.

Unable to stomach his remorse another second, Callie looked away, glancing at the mare. "Are you going to comb her down? She's breathing hard."

Before he could answer, Callie took the reins and walked the horse inside the barn. "Come on, girl," she cooed. "Let's get you out of the hot sun." The familiar musky scent of straw, feed and dank earth wafted in the air. She'd grown up around those barn smells.

Tagg stood there a moment watching her, his expression tight, giving nothing away. Then he strode into the barn behind her. Callie had never felt so raw inside. So unnerved. But she came here to tell Tagg something and she wouldn't leave until she did.

She took off the mare's bridle while Tagg began removing the saddle.

"You don't have to do that," he snapped.

She'd annoyed him. Good. "It's second nature with me. I grew up on a ranch, too." She shot him a smile.

"Kind of hard to forget our biggest competitor."

She set the bridle on a hook and grabbed a grooming brush. "Is that the problem? I'm The Hawk's daughter?"

Tagg's mouth twisted. "No."

She handed him the brush and their fingers touched. Briefly. For a split second. It was electric, a jolt that tingled down to her toes. She saw a flicker in Tagg's eyes, a gleam that lit up before fading into his unreadable expression once again.

"I wasn't expecting flowers and candy," she said quietly.

"You got less than you deserved." He set the brush on the mare and began grooming her with long sweeping strokes.

"I knew what I was doing, Tagg. It was…pretty amazing. Are you going to deny that?"

Tagg stopped brushing the mare and turned to her, his eyes dark and hard. "No, I won't deny that, but it can't happen again."

"I don't want it to," she said quickly, her pride taking hold. "Just so you can get your ego through that barn door, I'd better say what I came here to say. I thought you'd care to hear this from me rather than from your brother. You're going to see me around Worth Ranch from now on. I'm volunteering at Penny's Song. It's a worthy cause that I'm fully behind and I can't wait to get started working with the children."

"You?" Tagg silently cursed. Callie Sullivan was the last person he wanted to see on Worth land day in and day out. He couldn't believe she'd shown up here today. He'd been thinking about that night in Reno for weeks now. Remembering how good it was with her. His blood pressure escalated the second he'd spotted her on his property. And in that instant when they'd touched, memories of hot sweaty mind-numbing sex had rattled his brain.

"Yes, me."

"Why?"

"I told you. I want to work with children. I've got a degree in psychology and I know I can be an asset at the facility. Clay thought I'd be perfect, since I'm good with horses, too."

Clay? He was going to have to talk to his brother. Never mind that Callie Sullivan was Hawkins Sullivan's daughter and they'd already beat Worth Ranch out of one big cattle deal this year, Tagg didn't need the temptation Callie posed to him.

He resumed brushing down the mare. Clay had no clue about Tagg's one-night stand with Callie and he wasn't going to bring it up. If word got out, the family would try their hand at matchmaking. Lord knows, they'd tried before. But Tagg wasn't shopping for a relationship and he'd made himself very clear. "Well, thanks for telling me."

"It's a pretty wonderful charity. Your brother is a good man for doing this."

"Uh-huh."

"I told him to forget I'm The Hawk's daughter while I'm on the ranch. My focus will only be on helping to get Penny's Song off the ground."

"I'm sure he appreciates that." He patted the mare's rump then turned to fill a steel bucket half-full of oats. He'd ridden the horse hard while on the range.

Before he could get the oats to the mare, Callie stepped up, bumping him slightly. He caught a whiff of her perfume—flowery but earthy, as if she'd stamped her own unique scent on it. Memories flooded back instantly. That sultry dance in the bar. Her long black hair flowing wild and free. The way her moist skin tasted when he'd kissed her.

"I bet she'll like this more." Callie reached into her front pocket, coming up with half a dozen sugar cubes. She opened her palm to the mare. A pink tongue came out to lap up Callie's treat. She slid her hand along the mare's mane. "Are we friends now, girl?" Her tone was soft and soothing, as if they'd just shared something intimate. "Yeah, I think we are." She turned to Tagg, her eyes bright. "What's her name?"

Tagg set the bucket down in front of the horse and moved to the wall to hang up the brush, leaving Callie and her tempting scent behind. "Russet."

Callie smiled wide. "That's perfect."

Tagg nodded, watching Callie interact with his horse. She wore jeans and a soft cotton shirt, nothing daring, nothing that would raise a man's temperature. Except that he knew what was underneath her clothes: soft creamy skin, hips that flared slightly and perfect breasts that when freed of constraints could bring a man to tears.

She knew horses. Knew how to talk to them, how to treat them. That didn't surprise him as much as please him. He leaned back against the wall watching her until Callie realized what he was doing.

Her brows lifted, a question in her expression as she looked at him.

"Why'd you do it, Callie? We barely knew each other. Why me?"

Deep in thought, she studied him, and Tagg wondered if she would tell him the truth. A moment ticked by and then she tilted her head slightly. "When I saw you sitting on that bar stool...you looked how I felt." She stood with set shoulders near his mare. "Lonely. Disappointed. Wishing things in your life were different. I thought we needed each other. That maybe we could help each other."

Tagg hadn't expected that much honesty. Callie had looked

into his soul and really seen him. He never spoke of Heather to anyone. It was as though if he didn't say the words aloud, they wouldn't be true. They wouldn't hurt as much. Except now, with Callie, he felt a need to explain, if only this one time. "It was the anniversary of my wife's death. She was *everything* to me. I went to Reno on the pretense of business, to forget."

Callie cast him a sympathetic look, her eyes filled with understanding. "I'm sorry."

"No sorrier than I am." He looked away, gazing out the barn doors to the land that had belonged to the Worths for generations, not really seeing any of it. He pushed images of that fiery split-in-two plane on the tarmac out of his mind. He'd seen it enough in his nightmares. He turned to her then, looking deep into her pretty brown eyes. "When I said that night shouldn't have happened, I meant it. Nothing's gonna come of it, Callie. It'd be best if we put it out of our heads."

"Agreed," she said instantly, her eyes firm on his. "Like I said, I'm here to break the ice. In case we should bump into each other at Penny's Song. I'm not good with awkward."

Tagg smiled. "Me, neither. Never had any social skills."

She chuckled deep in her throat and nodded in agreement. He almost took offense but then Callie's lips parted slightly and she spoke soft words that couldn't be misconstrued. "You make up for it in other ways."

"Do I?" Always nice to know a female companion had no complaints when he took her to bed. Tagg's mind drifted to the beautiful brunette with soulful caramel eyes moaning his name as he drove deep inside her. Oh, man. He shook those thoughts free before Callie caught a hint of what he was thinking.

He wondered what she needed to forget. What kind of loneliness and pain had she been clinging to that night? But

Tagg wasn't going down that road. He didn't want to know. He didn't want any more involvement with Callie Sullivan, pretty as she was.

Callie pursed her lips and nodded. They stared at each other silently.

"I should go."

"Probably should."

"Okay, then." She walked out the barn door and Tagg followed quietly behind her.

But then she stopped, turned on her heels abruptly and he nearly mowed her down. Their bodies connected; his chest knocked her backward. On impulse, he shot both arms out to keep her from falling. "Damn, woman. Give a man some warning."

And there he was, holding soft, pretty Callie Sullivan in his arms. Her hair fell back, and when he righted her, the shiny strands came forward and tickled his fingers.

She blinked. Looked up into his eyes. "Thanks."

"Why'd you stop so quickly?"

"I had something else to say."

"Say it." That musky flowery scent invaded his senses and reminded him once again about their night together. He released his hold when he was sure she was on level footing. Callie set her hands on her hips, the exact place where his hands had been. It was an unconscious gesture on her part, but one that tugged at his cold heart.

"I don't usually pick up men in bars." She shot him a bold look that dared him to doubt her.

Tagg arched his brows.

Color rushed to her face. "I mean to say, I've never had a one-night stand before. It's not my—"

"Got it." He wanted out of this conversation and the reminder of that night.

"You do? You believe me?"

"Doesn't make a bit of difference if I believe you or not, but yeah, I do believe you. I may not have social skills but I've got good instincts."

"It makes a difference to me. I'm glad you believe me. I mean, since we'll be seeing each other from now on. Your opinion matters."

It shouldn't, he wanted to say, but kept his lips sealed.

His cell phone rang and he was glad for the interruption. Callie had a vulnerable expression on her face and Tagg was a sucker for a female in distress. He lifted up the phone. "Gotta get this."

She smiled weakly and nodded. "Goodbye, Tagg."

He watched her walk to her car and get in. Once she started the engine and circled around to the gravel road, he answered Clay's call. "What in hell were you thinking hiring on Sullivan's daughter?"

"I'm so glad you called, Sammie. I really needed to hear your voice today." Callie leaned back on her bed, resting her head against the daisy pillow sham, speaking on the phone with her best friend and onetime college roommate.

Her bedroom on Big Hawk Ranch looked the same as it did when she was a child. The pale yellow and cornflower blue walls spoke of a brightness that Callie didn't feel these days. She'd come home from Boston because her job there had ended just about the same time her father's health had taken a turn for the worse. She felt the timing was right. She'd missed living in Arizona. She'd missed the ranch. But once she'd returned, she'd found that while everyone else had moved on with their lives, Callie's life had remained stagnant. The room her mother had decorated when Callie was just a girl was one of many perfect examples. The Hawk never wanted the room changed and Callie had acquiesced.

"Yeah, you sound down this morning. There's something wrong. So what's going on?" her friend asked.

"I…I just miss you."

"I miss you, too," Sammie said. "And you know there's nothing holding you there. You can come back to Boston anytime. I've got an extra room in my apartment that has your name on it. But, hon, I know that missing me isn't what's putting that tone in your voice. What's up?"

"You know. The usual. My father."

"The Hawk? He's at it again? What did he do this time?"

"It's a little complicated right now."

Callie wasn't ready to share everything with Sammie, especially the guilt she felt about her secret. But she could tell her the most basic truth, which was that she'd reached her boiling point with her father last month. She'd thought that having a college degree, having lived off the ranch for several years and having reached her twenty-sixth birthday would have made a difference with her father. But she'd come to the bitter realization that he would never change. Oh, she did love him. In many regards he was a good father, but his need to control the outcome of her life had gotten out of control lately.

"You know I was dating a man named Troy, right?" she asked.

"Right. The tall, blond carpenter." He'd come to the ranch to build a new pool house and Callie had hit it off with him. "I thought you were *still* dating. I mean, the last time we talked you didn't say you weren't."

"I didn't tell you what The Hawk did because I was so furious with him, I needed some time to let it sink in. My daddy just doesn't get that I can make decisions for myself.

He can't see it as a control issue. He thinks he's looking out for me the way a father should."

"He's overcompensating for you not having a mother. Trying to be both parents at once."

"I've always understood that. I cut my father slack because I knew he grieved for my mother. But Mom's been gone eleven years and instead of him moving on with his life, he tossed all of the love he had for her onto me. I'm on the receiving end of a doting, controlling, overpowering father. Lucky me."

"Oh, Callie. Sorry. I thought he'd lighten up after you got home from Boston."

"Just the opposite. He wanted me to work for him when I got home. Laid the guilt on pretty thick too this last time. The Sullivan legacy will die if I don't take the reins at the ranch. All that he'd built up will go to ruins. The sky will fall and crush everything he's worked so hard for. Finally, I gave in. I worked with him for months. And I tried, Sammie. But The Hawk and I just don't see eye to eye on things."

Which was a nice way of saying her father was too ruthless a businessman for Callie. She had strong professional ethics that he didn't understand. They'd butted heads over business decisions constantly. "I finally told him no, not at this time. I want to work in the field I'm interested in, the field I studied for four years. And he backed off, a little. And then he pulled his Hawk maneuver with Troy."

"What did he do?"

"Troy's a really great guy. I liked him, but it wasn't earth-shattering or anything." Nothing compared to how she felt about Tagg Worth. Especially now, but she had to hold those feelings close to her heart for the time being. She was purposefully deceiving Tagg with a sin of omission, but it couldn't be helped.

Restless, Callie rose from the bed. She moved over to the

window and smiled when she looked down from the second story to find her palomino, Freedom, prancing around the perimeter of the corral. When her mother was alive, living on Big Hawk Ranch had given Callie so much joy. She still loved the ranch, but couldn't abide her father's way of doing things.

"I'd only dated him for a month. Daddy kept asking questions, hinting that Troy wasn't good enough for me, just because of what he did for a living. Apparently, blue-collar workers aren't good enough for a girl raised on a cattle ranch," she added with sarcasm. "I was really beginning to like this guy and then he stopped calling. I couldn't reach him by phone, so one day I stopped by his office trailer outside of town and asked him what happened. And you know, I have to give Troy credit for telling me the truth."

"Which was?"

Before Callie could respond, Sammie sighed. "Oh, your father threatened him?"

Callie turned from the window, tempering the anger she felt at her father's manipulation. "No, no…nothing that blatant. He offered Troy a lucrative job doing a remodel for a friend's ranch in Flagstaff. Would take about six months at the very least. The only stipulation was that he break off all contact with me." Callie laughed without humor. "Can you imagine? I about died of mortification and whatever I had building with Troy had been sullied, ruined by The Hawk, even though Troy had turned my father down flat."

"Oh, wow, Callie. That's too bad."

Callie thought so, too. After that humiliating experience, Callie had packed her bags and driven to Reno to blow off steam. Her cousin, Deanna, lived there and she had an open invitation to visit. For the first few days, Callie could barely see straight for the anger and humiliation she'd felt and she vented to her cousin, who'd lent a responsive ear. She was on her way back home when she'd stopped at the Cheatin' Heart and spotted Tagg sitting on that bar stool.

Callie's fantasy man.

And her father's worst nightmare.

Callie took the opportunity presented to her. No, that wasn't entirely true. She had to be totally honest with herself—she'd *made* things happen with Tagg. Because she wanted him and because she'd been sorely exasperated with her father. She wasn't sure if one or the other alone would have sparked her bold move, but the combination of both was too tempting to resist. She couldn't possibly have predicted how that night would end.

Because Callie hadn't *planned* on falling in love.

Or conceiving Tagg's baby.

Yet, both had happened.

Callie finished her conversation with Sammie and placed the receiver back onto its cradle. With a hand to her belly, she marveled about the new life growing inside her, wondering whether it was a boy or a girl. Wondering if the baby would have her brown eyes or Tagg's beautiful silver-blue ones. Would the child have a golden bronze complexion like the father or be fair-skinned like Callie?

In only her most selective, perfect fantasies did she entertain thoughts of a future with Taggart Worth. She wouldn't use the baby as bait to lure him into a relationship. She wouldn't trap him into marriage. Yes, he had a right to know about the baby, but not yet. Shoving aside the guilt that burdened her by not revealing the truth to him, Callie held firm to her convictions. She needed a little time and a chance to win him over. She'd fallen in love with him and wanted nothing less in return. *Before* she told him she carried his child.

Callie had set the wheels in motion. Tomorrow she would begin working with the Worths at Penny's Song.

Two

Tagg's eyes nearly crossed as he stared at the computer screen. He'd been intent on doing an inventory of Worth Ranch holdings and had spent the better part of the morning staring at numbers.

Tagg's office space, which was an appendage of his main house, consisted of three rooms. The room where Tagg would conduct business if need be, he had designed himself. Rough wood beams angled across the ceilings, wall-to-wall walnut bookshelves and cabinets spread across the entire perimeter, and his wide desk faced the door. The other two rooms were smaller with walls painted in rustic gold. One he used as a makeshift lounge area, complete with a wet bar, built-in refrigerator and a chocolate leather sofa. The other room was where he kept old file cabinets and outdated equipment. All of the Worths' business machines and electronics were state of the art now, upon Jackson's insistence.

"Enough," he muttered as he shut down the computer. He

squeezed his eyes closed for a moment. At the age of thirty-one he was too damn young to be feeling so weary before noon.

"You're doing too much," his brother Jackson said as he walked into the office. "Why the heck don't you break down and get yourself some help? A secretary, for Pete's sake. You know, someone who can answer phones and file, crunch those numbers you're staring at too long."

"When the hell did you get here?" Tagg asked, baffled. He was concentrating so hard on his work, he hadn't heard Jackson drive up and walk into his office.

"Don't change the subject. You know I'm right."

Tagg glared at him. His brother was two years older and a whole lot more polished than Tagg. He wore six-hundred-dollar snakeskin boots and dressed like a fashion model for *Cowboys & Indians* magazine. He operated the Worth offices in downtown Phoenix.

"I'm thinking about it." He hated to admit it. His brothers were always on his case about hiring someone to help out. The trouble was that Tagg liked the solitude of the ranch. He liked keeping his own hours without answering to anyone. He liked being alone with his thoughts. An employee would cramp his style.

In his younger days, he'd spend all-nighters with the rodeo boys, drinking whiskey until the sun came up without one iota of sleep. But his eyes never burned like they did now, spending hours in front of the computer screen. Of course, after a long bender like that, he'd felt no pain anywhere on his body.

Tagg smiled thinking about his crazy rodeo days and the friends he'd left behind. But then, dark memories immediately flooded in, reminding him why he left the rodeo.

"Well, I'm glad to hear you're thinking about it," Jackson

remarked. "I can have Betty Sue take a look at the list of résumés we have at the main office. That woman is great at hiring the right employees for the company."

Tagg waved him off. "Maybe. But not now."

Jackson persisted with a coaxing smile. "There's no time like the present."

Tagg rose from his seat and shot his brother a look. "Give it a rest. I said I'll think about it."

Jackson took Tagg's suggestion and shrugged with nonchalance. "Fine with me. So, are you helping this afternoon with Clay's project?"

"Yeah, I'll be there. He wants me to pick out the right horses for the kids coming to the ranch. You going?" He gave the tailored suit his brother was wearing the once-over.

"Not today. I have a meeting in the middle of the day. Gotta get back to Phoenix."

"Something important?"

"Maybe. I'm thinking the Worths should get into the restaurant business."

Tagg shook his head. "What?"

"Could be a really sweet deal. We could franchise, eventually."

Tagg shook his head. Jackson was the go-getter in the family and had done very well for himself outside of Worth Enterprises. He had a gift when it came to making money. "That's out of our comfort zone a tad bit, isn't it?"

Jackson smiled wide. "Nah. I'm thinking it's time to broaden our horizons."

"Cattle, land development and now restaurants? You've got too much time on your hands, Jack."

"Not true, I'm busier than ever."

"Then maybe you need some outside interests that don't include work."

"Look who's talking," Jackson said with a grin. "This, coming from a man who doesn't step foot off Worth land. Maybe you need to get a life."

"I've got a life, right here. I'm not a recluse. I go out." Rarely. But he did venture out on occasion. The last time he left town, he'd gone to Reno and had a sizzling hot night of sex with a sultry brunette.

"Okay, whatever you say. You got some time to feed me before you head over to Penny's Song?"

"Yeah, I think I can wrangle us up some lunch."

An hour later, Tagg got into his Jeep Cherokee and drove over to the Penny's Song site. He had to hand it to his brother. Clayton Worth, country-western superstar, had retired from singing at the ripe old age of thirty-seven to live a simpler life on the ranch. Along the way, he'd had the inspiration for Penny's Song and was making it a reality. All three brothers had pooled their resources and invested in its development. But Tagg felt close to this project for his own reasons.

He climbed out of his Jeep and studied the construction site. At least a dozen workmen applied their trade, though most of the major construction was complete. Shingles were being nailed down, barn doors were being set on hinges and new buildings forming an old-town-style street were wet with paint announcing Sheriff's Office and General Store. The Red Ridge Saloon had an attached kitchen where the meals would be served. The bunkhouse where the kids would sleep would be run by well-screened volunteers.

"It's coming along," Clay said, walking up to him. He pushed his hat back on his head.

"It's looking better than I imagined. The kids are gonna love it."

"That's the plan."

Tagg captured his brother's attention. "So, no hard feelings about the other day?"

Clay chuckled and shook his head. "You mean when you barked at me for not turning down The Hawk's daughter? Nah. No hard feelings. I've never held Callie responsible for her old man's doings. Even after you explained he'd just beaten us out of a big deal, I can't fault her. She's capable and more than qualified. Our mama didn't raise no fool," he said with a grin. "I know a good thing when I see it."

Tagg held his tongue as Clay continued, "Fact is, she came up with a great idea for the general store. The kids are gonna get tokens every time they complete a chore. And then they can barter them for something in the general store. She's donating little prizes and gifts to put in there."

"That so?" Tagg had to admit it was a good idea. What child wouldn't feel a sense of accomplishment being given a little reward for a job well done? His own father had instilled in all three of his sons the idea that hard work paid off. If you do a good job, you reap the benefits. "You should've thought of it."

Clay's eyes gleamed. "Maybe, but I was smart enough to hire on a pretty gal who knows child psychology. I'm taking full credit for that."

Before Tagg could respond, his thoughts were interrupted by a burst of laughter coming from behind him. He turned around to find Callie Sullivan in the midst of a group of workmen by the barn, her head thrown back in amusement. All of the men in on the joke had their eyes on her, laughing along with her.

Something churned inside his gut. Seeing her again, smiling and happy around the crew, put him in a foul mood. She looked beautiful, even in faded jeans and a soft plaid work shirt with her hair pulled into a ponytail. She didn't need frills to get him hot and bothered. Didn't need her hair wild and loose to remember how soft those strands felt falling through his fingers.

She turned her head and caught him staring, then smiled wide, her dark eyes still glistening with mirth. She lifted her hand in a slight wave.

"There she is," Clay said. He immediately gestured for her to come over. "I was darn surprised when she landed on my doorstep the other day inquiring about Penny's Song. I hadn't seen her in years." Clay narrowed his eyes and shot a glance Tagg's way. "But then, she stopped by your place, too, didn't she? Enough to get you riled."

Tagg bit his tongue. He'd seen enough of Callie Sullivan to occupy his dreams. "She didn't rile me," he said through tight lips. With Callie fast approaching, he couldn't say much more to his brother.

"Hi, boys."

Callie smiled at him then focused her attention on Clay. A piece of straw was stuck to her hair and Tagg had an uncanny urge to pluck it free. He focused on that strand of gold sticking out while Callie engaged in conversation with his brother.

"I'm so proud to be a part of this, Clay. Don't forget, I'll be happy to help with fundraisers, too. I've got some ideas that might bring the community together on this."

"That's real thoughtful, Callie." Clay reached up and pulled that piece of straw from her hair. Tagg ground his teeth, watching Callie touch her hair and smile at his brother, like he'd just cured world hunger.

"Oh, thanks."

Clay nodded and continued, "We're depending on volunteers right now, but eventually, if all goes well, we'll need more funds and have to hire on permanent help."

"Keep me in mind."

Clay smiled. "I surely will." He turned to Tagg. "Actually, I'm glad you're both here. I've got a job for the two of you."

Callie shot Tagg a quick look then focused back on Clay. "Okay, I'm ready for whatever you have in mind."

"We need to decide which horses will work best for the kids. Their ages range from six to thirteen. We need the tamest of the string, the horses with the most patience. We can't afford to give up too many of our own trained cutting horses, but if you could select a few for now from our stables then we'll go from there."

Tagg could do this with his eyes closed. There was no need to involve Callie.

"I'd love to," Callie said immediately.

"I can get this done, Clay," Tagg stated. "If you need Callie for something else."

Callie turned his way and he sensed her stare. He kept his gaze trained on his brother, not willing to see the recrimination in her eyes.

Clay shook his head. "No. I need you both for this. You each know horses, but Callie's worked with children. And since none of us Worths have been around kids much, the two of you will make a good team."

Tagg shrugged, giving up. Wasn't as though he couldn't spend an afternoon with Callie without jumping her bones. "Fine. We'll pick out a few gentle mares from the string."

Clay glanced at his watch and winced. "I'm running late. I'm gonna have to leave the crew in your hands today. I've got an appointment in town. Tagg, keep those boys in line for me. Seems every one of them is already smitten with Callie." Clay winked at her and the sound of her sweet throaty chuckle set Tagg's nerves on edge.

"Something tells me Callie can take care of herself."

Clay narrowed his eyes and the conversation quickly died.

After a few seconds of silence, Callie chimed in, "Now, don't you go worrying about me. Those boys are treating me just fine."

"Glad to hear it." Clay darted them each a curious look as if trying to figure out something.

Tagg set his jaw, waiting for his brother to leave.

"I'll be in touch," Clay said finally, then bid them fare-well.

Tagg stood alone with Callie in front of the general store. They stared at each other for a few uncomfortable seconds until Callie's smile brought him up short. "Well, I'm glad I stopped by your house the other day to break the ice. Because *that* wasn't awkward."

Callie's remark broke the tension. Tagg relaxed and sent her a smile. "Do you always blurt out whatever's on your mind?"

Callie smiled back and her caramel eyes lit up. "Yeah, most times I do."

"What about those other times, when you don't? How does that work for you?"

Callie thought about it for one second then replied, "It works fine. When I keep my words in check, it's usually to keep the peace with my father."

"The Hawk," Tagg bit out.

"My *father*."

"Are you afraid of him?"

"Heavens, no. Let's just say it's usually easier to deal with him without hysterical drama. Which is what it would be if I really let loose on him."

"So you hold back."

"I deal with him in my own way and, most times, I'm suc-cessful at making my point. What about you, Tagg? Do you always hold in your feelings?"

Tagg didn't like speaking about feelings. What man did? "What feelings are you talking about exactly?"

Callie got a distant look on her face and then blinked it away. "Scared feelings. Like leaving a girl a note on the hotel bed instead of facing her."

Tagg wasn't going there. He chose to ignore Callie's comment. It was safer that way for both of them. He put his hand to her lower back and applied slight pressure. "Let's get to those horses. I'll drive."

They strode toward the Jeep in silence, Tagg aware of Callie right beside him. Her unique scent wafted up to tease his nostrils and remind him of things he wanted forgotten. His foul mood kicked up a notch. When they reached the vehicle, he opened the door for her before he walked to the driver's side and got in. He turned the engine key and gave it gas, but didn't put it in gear. Hesitating, he stared out the dashboard window.

They'd both entered into the one-night fling. Callie wasn't completely off the hook. She'd done her part in tempting him beyond his willpower. But Tagg never shied away from his responsibilities. And he had felt responsible for what had happened between them because he knew going in that Callie Sullivan was off-limits for more than one good reason. She was the daughter of his biggest competitor. She was his neighbor and a woman he'd be bumping into at times. But perhaps most importantly, Tagg knew Callie wasn't the one-night stand kind of woman. She didn't play loose and fast, which was the only kind of woman Tagg ever got involved with these days.

After mulling it over in his mind, Tagg figured an explanation was exactly what was needed. Basically, he was an up front kind of guy. He liked to lay things on the line. "Callie,

I wasn't afraid of anything. I had to leave and didn't want to wake you. That's the truth."

"The whole truth?" she asked.

With an inward sigh, he rested his arm across the steering wheel and turned to probe deep into her eyes. "Look, I don't want to be a jerk about this. But that night wasn't about feelings."

"That's a lie."

"Okay, it was about feelings, but not my feelings for you."

"I know that. You were hurting."

"Yeah, I was and you were there. *Easy. Convenient. Beautiful.*"

Callie's eyes grew round with stunned surprise and then they squeezed shut. "Oh."

Tagg cursed under his breath.

She squeezed her eyes even tighter as if to ward off the pain he'd just caused. When she opened them she nodded quickly. "Got it."

"I didn't say that right." He felt like a heel and hated every second of this conversation. Moments like this one were the reason he didn't get involved with women anymore.

"Oh, no. You made yourself perfectly clear."

Callie refused to look at him. She stared straight ahead, her body as rigid as an ancient statue. Tagg put the Jeep in gear and drove toward the Worth stables. About five minutes into the ride, Callie shocked him when she began making small talk, seemingly fully recovered from his callous words. "You know I went to Boston College for four years. I only came home for short summer stays and holidays."

"Yeah, I know." He glanced at her. She appeared more relaxed and looked him square in the eyes.

"You know?"

He shrugged. "Nothing's a secret in a small town. We all thought The Hawk's only child couldn't wait to get as far away from him as possible."

"He's not that bad, Tagg. He loves me. And I love him. But I really liked having a life without a lot of meddling."

"Can't imagine he could do too much meddling from over two thousand miles away."

"He managed some, but overall my stay in Boston was wonderful. It's a very quaint city in many regards."

"So why did you come back?"

"I missed Arizona. I missed the ranch. Silly me, I'm not a city girl after all. And my father had a little health scare. He's really the only family I have. Except for my mother's side. I have an aunt and a cousin who live in Reno."

The Jeep barreled over some rough patches in the road and tossed them both forward. On instinct, Tagg threw his arm across Callie's body to keep her from hitting the dashboard. The back of his hand connected with her chest as he pressed her back to safety. His knuckles grazed her breast and met with resistance, the contrast of firm giving way to soft, so female, so Callie, that his blood pressure elevated. Instant images flashed in his head of touching her there, pressing his lips to her perfect pink tips and filling his mouth with her taste.

He swallowed down and slid her a glance. "You okay?"

Her lips curved up in a soft smile that unnerved him. A smile that seemed to suggest *touch me anytime, take me anywhere*. "Yes."

He turned to face the road and kept on driving, obliterating that memory, denying the inviting look on her expression and refusing to acknowledge that he was damned attracted to Callie Sullivan.

Three

Callie bounded out of Tagg's vehicle, keeping her spirits up. Tagg's cutting words a few minutes ago had hurt, but she couldn't let them discourage her. She'd known Tagg was a loner when she'd approached him that night. She'd known about his past heartache. She couldn't expect him to claim undying love for her at this point, not when he'd been wallowing in grief for years.

They'd had a great night of sex in Reno. But she also believed that it wasn't just sizzle between the sheets. Tagg had been sweet and thoughtful during that time and they'd talked and shared intimacies that she'd always remember, in between their bouts of lovemaking.

She hadn't planned on conceiving his child that night. But she'd never say that her baby was a mistake. She wanted this child, now more than ever. She knew she was on shaky ground at the moment. The quake that was Taggart Worth could topple a less determined woman. But Callie had nothing to lose and everything to gain so she wouldn't allow Tagg's sharp tongue to stop her.

Once they arrived at the stables, just a stone's throw from the Worths' main house, Callie got out of the car and crossed to the corral to take a look at half a dozen horses.

"Not those," Tagg said. "They're too high-strung."

Callie could tell that already, just by their stance, the way they held their heads and the way they seemed too aware of their surroundings. Like they were ready to bolt any second. Callie nodded. "They're spirited."

"Our best cutting horses," Tagg said, nodding in the direction of another corral behind the stable. "Over here."

Callie followed Tagg as he marched over to another fenced-off arena. He opened the gate and entered. At least six horses were scattered about. He waited for Callie to walk through the gate and then closed it behind her. Upon entering, a few of the horses lifted their heads, giving them a casual perusal before going back to grazing. The others didn't seem to notice them, or if they did, they didn't seem to care.

"I think we've found our candidates," Callie said, approaching a light chestnut mare whose coat gleamed under the afternoon sun. The horse looked healthy and didn't seem to spook easily. Callie knew enough to move slowly, especially when advancing on an animal that didn't know you. "Hey, girl," she said. "What's your name?"

Tagg strode to her side. "This here is Sunflower. She's done her part on the ranch."

Callie studied the horse. She had kind eyes. "She's what, ten or eleven?"

Tagg nodded. "She's eleven."

Callie stroked along her nose, all the while looking into Sunflower's eyes. "She might be a good choice. She's not too tall, either, and she's a good age. I'd like to spend some time with her. Maybe take her for a ride. See how she does out in the open."

"Good idea." Tagg nodded. He walked toward a black gelding with four white socks and a long white stripe along his nose. "This here is Tux."

She grinned and acknowledged, "Because of his black-and-white coloring."

Tagg stroked the horse's mane. "Yeah. He was so fine in his day. He's about twelve now. I used to ride him when I came home from the rodeo. He's got a lot of life left in him."

Callie walked over to Tux, admiring him. "Do you trust him?"

Tagg looked the horse over and nodded. "About as much as I trust any one thing. Which sometimes isn't all that much. I want to take him out and see how he does."

Callie wondered about Tagg's comment. Was he only speaking about horses? Or did he have other issues with trust. "Today?"

Tagg glanced at her. "No, not today. Since Clay's put me in charge, I'd better get back to Penny's Song before too long. We'll have to do it another day."

"Okay." Callie glanced at the rest of the horses in the corral and found some to be far too old and lazy, some to be a little bit too jumpy. Tagg agreed, doing a calculated assessment, much the way Callie had.

"Let's take a quick look in the stable," Tagg suggested. "Might as well see them all while we're here."

Callie followed behind Tagg and wished she'd been a little quicker in her stride. Because the view from here was too darn good. His dark hair, jutting out from under his hat and curling at his nape, made her wish she had free reign to run her fingers through those thick strands. Wide shoulders tapered down to a waist that accented slim hips and a perfect male butt. Taggart Worth fit into his jeans like nobody's business.

With an unsteady breath, Callie sighed as she moved from bright sunlight to near darkness inside the stable. It took a while for her eyes to adjust. Once they did, she spotted Tagg inside a stall beside an old mare. She looked gaunt and weary. "This here is Sadie. She was…mine."

Tagg looked at the mare with admiration and devotion. Something soft and warm tugged at Callie's heart. She'd never seen Tagg's emotions so raw, so real. His eyes gleamed with pure love. He spoke softly to the mare, stroking her, and Callie kept her distance for the time being, allowing the two of them to reconnect.

After a moment, Tagg added, "She'd probably be good around children. She'd welcome the attention and I think the kids would love her."

The way you do, Callie wanted to say.

"She's not too long for this world." The horse nuzzled his neck playfully, looking more alive.

"She heard that. She's gonna prove you wrong."

He glanced at the mare. "Maybe. We'll try her out and see how she holds up."

Callie stepped closer to Tagg, removing the distance between them. "The horse I had growing up is gone. I wish I still had her."

"Oh, yeah?"

Callie spoke softly. "I was only eight when she was born. I watched her birth. I'd seen other mares foal, but this time it was special for me. I knew the little filly entering into the world that day would be mine. My daddy promised and I had to swear to take care of her myself. I was eager to do it. When she struggled up on those skinny little legs to take her first steps in the barn, I cried. It was love at first sight." Callie smiled and glanced at Tagg.

He'd moved closer to her, too. She saw another gleam in his eyes. This time aimed at her. Sadie moved back a step but the slight rustling of straw didn't interrupt, didn't suspend the intense look on Tagg's face. It didn't stop his approach. "Tell me more."

"Her name was Jasmine. Named after the fairy-tale princess. I had visions of flying off on a magic carpet with her."

Tagg smiled. "Or she'd fly you around on her back."

"A little girl's daydreams can't be messed with." She relished the smile Tagg offered her. He was so darn handsome…still her fantasy man.

The light was dim in the stable and cool enough when she'd first walked inside, but now the stable heated up and familiar musky scents of earth and straw closed in on her. She stood toe-to-toe with Tagg. "I don't suppose you had daydreams."

Tagg seared her with a hot glance and arched his brow. "I'm having one now."

She looked at his mouth with longing. She wanted him. She always had. "So am I, Tagg," she said, breathless.

Tagg reached one hand out and pulled her close. She flowed easily toward him. His mouth came down on hers in a rush of heat. Instantly, she wrapped her arms around his neck and put everything she had into returning the kiss. Weeks of yearning, desire and uncertainty all rolled up into one ignited when his mouth met hers. A deep rugged groan escaped Tagg's throat and fueled those flames as their bodies brushed. The magnetic pull was something neither could fight. It was just there, driving them closer.

Tagg deepened the kiss, opening his mouth and wetting her lips with his tongue. She parted for him immediately, inviting his tongue inside her mouth. Holding her breath, she prepared for the onslaught, the intense mating that swept fiery heat through her body.

Tagg pulled at her hips, jutting them up against his. His erection pulsed between their clothes, solid and strong.

"Oh," she moaned, barely able to breathe. She gave herself up to him, to the power of his kiss. She went weak-kneed and Tagg's strong grip was all that held her upright. He put his arms around her waist and then in one quick move, removed the rubber band from her hair. The strands were released, and he shoved his fingers through, spreading her hair out.

She thought to do the same to him, remembering her wish of just minutes ago. She grabbed his hat and tossed it aside, garnering a deep-rooted chuckle from him. Then, as he continued to kiss her, she ran her fingers into his long dark locks, playing with his hair just as she'd fantasized.

Callie pulled back just enough to catch her breath. "Easy?"

Tagg's lips curled up. "Anything but."

He continued to kiss her.

She pulled back slightly one more time. "Convenient?"

Another chuckle. "You've got to be kidding." He swept his tongue one last time inside the hollows of her mouth before breaking the kiss and flashing her a sincere look. "But beautiful is a fact."

Callie smiled and breathed out, "Thank you."

Tagg reached for her again, but voices from ranch hands approaching outside stopped him. Instantly, he stepped away and grabbed his hat from the ground. With a look of regret, he darted a glance her way and plopped his Stetson onto his head. The ranch foreman appeared in the sunlit line of vision from the wide stable door and Tagg cleared his throat. "Let's get out of here," he said, keeping his voice down.

She saw him reach for her hand and then think better of it.

With their arms to their sides, they walked out of the stable together and got into the Jeep. Tagg waved to the men who'd returned to the stable area without stopping to talk.

They drove back to Penny's Song in silence. She was grateful for the quiet ride. At least Tagg wasn't telling her how that kiss shouldn't have happened. At least he wasn't denying that something drew them together like a force of nature.

Callie could only hope that she was making headway with Tagg.

She'd caught him in a weak moment, is all, Tagg thought as he pulled up to Penny's Song. One minute it had all been about Clay's request to find horses. Then he'd seen Sadie and gotten sentimental. There was nothing worse than having a woman see you when you're vulnerable. And then Callie's soft looks of understanding and commiseration did him in.

The kiss just happened. And he wasn't going to apologize for it. He wasn't going to deny it was good. Hell, it had been great. But Callie was a dangerous woman to be around and the one thing he swore he wouldn't do was to get involved with her. He wouldn't forget who she was, or who *he* was. He'd already had his one chance at love and had blown it.

He climbed out of the vehicle and walked around to the other side, but Callie had already opened the door herself. She got out and they looked at each other. Tagg spoke first before she said something he didn't want to hear. "I'd better check on the workmen. See if they need anything. Are you sticking around here?"

"For a little while. I have some things I want to finish up."

"Okay, then. I'll let you get to your work. See ya." He tipped his hat.

He'd only gotten a few feet away before Callie called him back. "Tagg?"

He turned around, bracing himself for what she had in mind. He didn't like to analyze things the way most women did. He'd kissed her. It was great. Period. He doubted it would ever happen again. "Yeah?"

"I think we did a good job picking out the horses today."

"Yeah. We did."

"I'd still like to ride Sunflower. I'll ask Clay if I can do that tomorrow."

Tagg scrubbed his jaw. "Don't think I can make it tomorrow."

She frowned and shook her head. "I'm not asking you on a date, for heaven's sake. I can ride the mare without you and make a determination on my own."

He held his expression blank to keep from blinking his surprise. Callie had put him in his place. "Okay, the sooner we accomplish that, the better."

"That's what it's all about." Tousled, well kissed and rosy cheeked, she faced him from a few feet away. He'd put that look on her pretty face. Sensations whirled. Unsettling possessive instincts took hold in his gut. He stood there for several minutes, well after she'd turned on her heels and walked away.

Jed Barlow rode up on his horse and dismounted just a few feet away. "Hey, Tagg. I'm glad I found you here. Clay thought you might be available for the game tonight. Diamondbacks are playing. Then after the game, we'll be happy to take your money at the poker table. We need to fill a seat. Brett Williamson's daughter is getting married, so he's out of commission for the week."

Baseball and poker were just what he needed to take his mind off Callie for the night. He wasn't a regular, but when the boys needed a substitute, Tagg didn't mind filling in. "Sure. Why not?"

"All right then. We'll see you at seven." Jed led his horse toward the stable, but turned after taking just a few steps. "Hey, was that Callie Sullivan I saw you jawing with just a minute ago?"

"Yeah, that was Callie."

"Never thought I'd see her around here."

Jed had gone to the same high school as the Worths. His father owned a small ranch ten miles north of their property. After years of struggling, unable to compete with the bigger ranches in the area, Kent Barlow quit the cattle business. The Worths had always liked the Barlows and Clay hired Jed straightaway. He knew ranching like the back of his hand. He'd been a trusted employee going on five years now. "That makes two of us," Tagg answered.

"She sure is pretty."

Tagg nodded. He didn't need a reminder.

"I remember a time when I liked her, back in school. She was book smart and I was flunking out of English. I must've been sixteen or so. She offered to help with my homework one day and I showed up at Big Hawk Ranch." Jed stopped talking to shake his head and grin. "I think I had a death wish or something. I didn't get one foot on the porch when her daddy comes up behind me holding a big ole shotgun, telling me Callie wasn't seeing any visitors that night. He told me if I knew what was good for me, I'd turn around and keep on going."

"Had you shaking in your boots, did he?"

"Had me pissing in your boots was more like it. That man was mean."

"He never scared me."

"You ever try to date his daughter?"

Tagg shook his head. What had happened between him and Callie couldn't be called dating. "No. She was younger. I barely knew Callie in school."

"Good thing, too. The Hawk's got no use for the Barlows, or the Worths, either, I hear. Callie once told me she wasn't allowed to speak to any of you. Looks like that's changed."

"She's volunteering here, going to work with the kids at Penny's Song. I don't think her father has much say in what she does anymore." Tagg didn't know why he felt the need to explain that to him.

"She married?" Jed searched the area, presumably to catch another glimpse of Callie.

He shook his head. "No."

"Okay, then." Jed got a big smile on his face. "Maybe I'll just reacquaint myself."

Tagg watched him enter the stable, tempering his irritation and talking himself out of being angry at Jed. He had no reason to be annoyed. What Jed did in his spare time wasn't any of his business. What Callie did in her spare time wasn't, either.

But later that night, Tagg got immense enjoyment out of cleaning Jed's clock at the poker table. The victory gave him such great satisfaction that he wouldn't allow himself to believe it was motivated by anything more than his strong competitive drive.

"Hi, Daddy." Callie kissed her father on the forehead before taking a seat adjacent to him at the dining room table for dinner. Her father insisted on taking his meals in the formal room rather than breaking bread in the kitchen. He said he paid a cook and housekeeper good wages to keep the house and he damn well was going to enjoy it. Before her mother died, they used to eat breakfast and lunch in the kitchen. So

Callie had a feeling it was less about formality and more about not dealing with the memories that drove her father.

"Callie, honey. Where've you been lately? Seems I got a ghost instead of a daughter. I only hear you rattling around. You're up and out early every day."

It had only been three days since she'd begun working at Penny's Song. "I'm home every night for dinner," she reminded him. "And you promised me you'd give me some space."

"Space," he muttered, reaching for a glass of iced tea. "You and your psychology mumbo jumbo. I've been letting you do what you want, haven't I?"

"Dad, I'm nearly twenty-seven years old. I'd hope so by now."

"You're still mad about that Troy fella." He forked a bite of his salad, swallowed and made a sour face.

Callie smiled inwardly. She'd been harping on her father for months to eat better. He hadn't known what a green leaf was until Callie came home and insisted he lose weight. He wouldn't agree until she played the orphan card. He didn't want to die and leave Callie without a father, did he? He knew he hadn't been eating right and even though he griped about the food she'd introduced, he had finally relented. And Callie even believed he'd enjoyed it somewhat, but more because she cared enough about him to want to keep him healthy.

"You have no right interfering in my private life. You know how I feel about that. And another thing, if you don't want me changing my room, I won't. But I will be moving into another one. One I can decorate myself. I'm not twelve anymore, Daddy."

"You got that right. You never sassed me like this when you were younger."

"I'm not sassing you now. I'm just telling you how I feel."

"If decorating your room will keep you at home more, fine. Change the room any way you want."

Callie knew her father ached inside with loneliness. He'd always been overbearing, but her mother knew how to temper him. With her gone, Hawkins had become even more demanding. She reached for his hand and covered it with hers, squeezing gently. "I won't change my room. I'll do up another one."

He glanced at her with those big brown eyes that she'd inherited and nodded. "Whatever makes my little girl happy."

Oh, if only that were true.

"So, where have you been off to every morning?"

"I've been volunteering my time for a worthy charity."

Hawkins stared down at his bland broiled chicken, unable to work up any enthusiasm for the fare. He'd been eating fried chicken and mashed potatoes topped with sour cream and gravy until Callie had come home. She had to stifle a chuckle seeing him look like a little boy who didn't want to eat his vegetables. He set his fork down and glared at her. "That charity have a name?"

"Penny's Song." The entire community knew about Clayton Worth's pet project. He'd started it on his own, but when the news got out, he'd received a good deal of support and a long volunteer list from the town.

Her father frowned and narrowed his eyes at her. "You mean to tell me you've been going over to the Worths every day?"

She wasn't nearly as intimidated by him as he wanted her to be. She reminded herself that she was living here to make sure he didn't dig himself into an early grave. She could move out anytime she wanted. She didn't have to put up with his ruthless, conniving ways. But he was her father and she loved living on Big Hawk Ranch.

"Yes, that's what I'm saying, Daddy." She kept her voice calm. She wouldn't argue the point. "I'm going to work with the children that come there. I hope to make a difference in their lives."

"The Worths aren't—"

"It's not about the Worths. It's about the children and what I want to do."

"You'd rather go there and give away your services for free than work beside your own father?" He raised his voice with condemnation.

"That's your point of view, Daddy. Not mine. I'm—"

He slapped a hand down onto the table and it shook. "This ranch is your legacy, damn it."

Callie didn't jump at his theatrics. She cut into her chicken and took a bite.

He pushed away from the table, his face flushed with anger. "You can't be going over there. I'm forbidding it. You know those Worths, they'd do anything to put me out of business. Been trying to for years."

"What I'm doing has nothing to do with the cattle business." Callie took a steadying breath, determined to get through this meal without a fight. At least, on her part. Her father was chomping at the bit, ready to argue his way through their fruit salad dessert. "And you can't forbid me to do anything anymore."

"Callie," he warned in a tone that used to make Callie cringe. He rose from the table. "You know how I feel about those Worths."

She looked up at him. "I never understood that, Daddy. Yes, you're competitors but you're neighbors, too. And neither one of the ranches has been hurting. You've managed to keep

Big Hawk Ranch on top. There's room for everyone, isn't there?"

"With thinking like that, you'd have us in the poorhouse before I turned around."

Callie tried a smile. "So maybe it's best I don't work for you."

Her father's face flushed with even more color. "Callie, you're trying my patience."

"Daddy, I don't want to fight with you. Sit down. Eat your meal."

He glared at the food on his plate and wagged his finger. "You call that a meal? That's horse feed."

Callie closed her eyes. Frustration mounted. She thought about the baby she carried—a Worth. She didn't even want to think about her father's reaction when he found out about his grandchild. But it wasn't the right time to tell him. Tagg had to be the first to know. She hadn't told a soul yet and it would have to stay that way for now.

Callie rose, her appetite gone. "Well, then, we'll have some really *healthy* horses in our stables. Because *they* know what's good for them. *They* won't be dying of a coronary anytime soon."

She walked past her father and out the front door.

Before she was out of earshot, she heard her father call to the cook. "Mattie, make me a steak. A big, fat, juicy one and I want gravy to go with it!"

Callie inhaled a sharp breath and got into her car.

She revved the engine and drove off, happy to be away from Hawkins Sullivan. Happy to be anywhere but on the ranch she loved so much.

Callie stood with Jed Barlow by the Worth stables the next morning combing down Sunflower in the shade of a mesquite tree. "It was a good ride. I think Sunflower is tame enough for children. I just had to be sure."

"The same goes for Tux. He's pretty gentle," Jed said. "I'm glad I was able to take the ride with you this morning."

Callie smiled at Jed. They had been friends in school once, but she hadn't seen him since she'd returned to Red Ridge. She brushed the mare's mane while Jed combed down Tux. It was nice taking the horses out together before the heat of the day. Since her return to Big Hawk Ranch she hadn't had a riding partner. She'd wanted to ride out on the range with Tagg today, but he'd flat-out refused. Maybe he really did have plans this morning. It wasn't like he didn't have a job. He ran the Worth empire from his house. He had responsibilities.

"It'll be real nice getting to know you again, Callie." Jed smiled.

"Same goes for me. I haven't reconnected with too many people since I've been home. Some of my high school friends moved away and some are married and have their own lives. So this is great."

"I think so." He stopped brushing down Tux to look at her. "You know I had a crush on you back in high school, don't you?"

She furrowed her brows. "No. I didn't think boys got crushes." Jed was tall and blond and relatively nice looking but Callie didn't like where this conversation was headed.

"We do. Uh, did. But we're always too macho to admit it. Your daddy took care of that, though."

Callie rolled her eyes. Everything always went back to her father. "How?"

"He ran me off your property once. You'd offered to help me with my studies and I came over."

"Shotgun?"

Jed got a startled look on his face. "You know?"

"It's a wonder I didn't run away from home. He chased off quite a few guys that way."

"I was a little young to know he was bluffing."

Callie laughed and put her hand on his arm, shaking her head. "The sad part is, he wasn't bluffing. He's fiercely protective of me."

He glanced at her hand and smiled. Callie removed it instantly, self-conscious. "Even now?"

"I try not to let him get away with anything anymore," she offered, feeling sorry for Jed. Maybe she would have liked dating him back then. She could only imagine how her father had intimidated him. "Sorry. I didn't know. Of course, my father kept that from me."

"So maybe we could make up for that. Would you like to go out sometime? Maybe Saturday night?"

Callie hadn't entirely seen this coming. She'd been so wrapped up in her feelings for Tagg that she'd mistaken Jed's friendliness. Oh, God, what to say? How to answer without hurting him or making him feel foolish?

"She's not available," said a voice from behind them.

They turned and found Tagg leaning against the shade tree, arms folded. "Tagg, what are you doing here?" Callie asked.

"Hey, Tagg." Jed looked confused, darting them both glances.

"I came to ride Tux," he said to Callie, giving her a recriminating look.

But that didn't stop her heart from fluttering like a trapped butterfly. Just one look at him standing there, despite his sullen expression, and she was toast. He was handsome times ten. The whole cowboy getup wasn't outdated on a man like Tagg. He wore his chaps well.

"How long have you been here?" she asked, wondering if he'd overheard their conversation.

"Just got here."

She thought that was a lie. Tagg looked too comfortable against that tree to have just walked up.

"Looks like Jed beat me to the ride."

"Hell," Jed said, "at least I can beat you at something. You wiped me out last night."

"Wiped you out?" Callie shot them both a glance.

"At poker. Remember, when I bumped into you? I was on my way to meet up with Tagg and the boys for a card game."

"You bumped into her?" Tagg asked, his gaze focused on Jed.

Jed nodded halfheartedly. "Well, not like that. I was driving down the road and she passed me in her bright red convertible. She was barreling down the highway at eighty miles an hour."

"I was not," she defended herself.

"You were," Jed said with a big grin. "Lead foot, my mama used to say. And then all of a sudden she stopped the car by the side of the road."

"I would've never seen that downed calf if I was going that fast, Jed," Callie pointed out. She turned to Tagg. "It looked like the calf got tangled up in some broken fencing. Jed stopped his truck and helped me get her on her feet. She turned out to be all right."

Jed shrugged. "Callie's got a soft spot for animals."

Tagg didn't seem pleased with either of them. Callie recalled what he'd said when she'd first spotted him.

She's not available.

Not that she wasn't glad to see him. He'd interrupted her

having to refuse Jed's offer for a date, but her curiosity got the better of her. "Why am I not available?"

Tagg moved away from the tree and approached her. He stopped when he got close enough for her to see the quicksilver surrounding his blue eyes, the ticking of his jaw. Ignoring Jed, he peered at her. She swallowed and met his gaze. "Because we have an appointment to look at some horses on Saturday."

"Ah, well, that's okay," Jed said, with his good nature. "It won't take all day."

Tagg slanted Jed a quick look, then focused back on Callie. "In Las Vegas."

Four

Callie's mouth dropped open. She stared at Tagg. *"In Las Vegas?"* She shook her head, trying to understand. Endless possibilities entered her mind. "Why there?"

"I have a friend who's offering us the pick of his string for the charity. They're thoroughbreds and mustangs that have served him well but are a bit older, like Sunflower here." Tagg stroked the horse gently. "All we have to do is choose the ones we want and arrange transportation. He's giving us a dozen horses."

Callie immediately thought of how the children would benefit. She pictured a dozen children riding the mares with smiling faces. "That's fantastic. Are you sure you need me to go?"

Tagg glanced at Jed, then redirected his gaze back to her. "Clay wants you in on this."

What about him? Did he want her in on this? The idea of spending alone time with Tagg appealed to her on so many levels. But was his disgruntled mood because Clay had insisted Tagg take her along? Or was it something else?

"We've got plans to discuss, Jed," Tagg said. "Suppose you could see to the horses? I'll walk Callie back to her car."

"Sure," Jed said, looking at Callie. There was no disputing who the boss was here. The employee had just been ordered away.

"Bye, Jed," Callie said with a smile.

"See ya, Callie." He swatted each horse's rump and they trotted into the stable. Jed followed behind.

Callie ran a hand through her hair and inhaled deep. Tagg had just saved her from an awkward situation with his ranch hand.

"Were you going to go out with him?" he asked, gesturing toward the stable.

"Jed? Uh, no. I wasn't." She lifted her chin a notch. "Not that it's any of your business."

A spark of mischief entered his eyes. "Granted. None of my business."

"I don't have too many friends around here. Jed and I used to be friends in school. It's nice getting reacquainted."

"He had it bad for you." Tagg smiled.

"You *did* hear! You were listening to our conversation!"

"It was fascinating. I didn't want to interrupt."

"But you managed to. The minute Jed asked me out." She looked at him with suspicion.

"Don't pretend I didn't save your butt just then. You were stumbling…looking for a way out."

Callie opened her mouth to protest, but Tagg was right. And he'd recognized her dilemma. "True." Though she hated to admit it.

"Then it's not a problem going to Vegas?"

"You mean I have a choice?" She sent him a teasing smile.

"You don't have to go. But you are the 'kid expert.'"

"So, it's a request?"

He nodded.

"From Clay?"

Tagg shifted his gaze to the ground. He scratched the side of his cheek. "I haven't told Clay about this yet."

"But you made it seem…" Callie stopped for a second and eyed him. Could it be possible that Tagg wanted her to go? That this was all his idea?

"We need to leave by five tonight."

Callie blinked. "We're leaving tonight?"

"John's an old rodeo buddy. He invited us to dinner. Under the circumstances, I couldn't refuse. Are you in?"

Yes! "I'm in. I'll be ready at five."

With bells on.

"You are one lucky girl, Callie Sullivan," she muttered later that afternoon as she packed. She folded her jeans and a plaid no-nonsense blouse into the suitcase before closing it shut, grateful that her father had left for Houston that morning. There would be no arguments about where she was going and no repercussions when she got home. If she were really fortunate, she'd return before her father this weekend and he'd never have to know she'd been gone.

Fate had a way of looking after her. At least, this time. When Tagg had called a few hours ago arranging to pick her up at home, she'd been happy to inform him that her father wasn't around and it wouldn't be a problem.

"You mean, I won't face a shotgun?" Callie had laughed at his joke, though she'd never have let Tagg on Sullivan property to face her father's wrath had he been home. She would have made other travel arrangements to save them all a nasty confrontation.

In truth, Callie had been looking forward to having the house to herself for the entire weekend. But nothing topped this turn of events—even if it was just an overnight business trip.

Because she'd be with Tagg.

Callie zipped up her suitcase, leaving it on the bed and strode into her walk-in closet, searching for just the right outfit to wear tonight. She came up with a black dress that crisscrossed over the chest but wasn't too revealing. The dress hit her knees in a flow of material and gathered at the side with a bit of rhinestone bling. It was appropriate for a dinner invitation and yet nothing too provocative.

She'd tossed ankle-high boots in her suitcase for tomorrow. For tonight's dinner she chose a pair of strappy black heels.

Callie combed her hair, applied light makeup to her eyes, glossed her lips and then slipped into her dress. She was ready by four-thirty.

At exactly five o'clock, a black Lincoln pulled up to her front door. She watched from the window as Tagg got out of the backseat and straightened next to the limo. Her breath caught and she whispered, "Oh, wow," grateful he couldn't see her initial reaction.

He looked deadly handsome wearing a white shirt under a stunning black suit coat with wide Western lapels. A dark felt Stetson sat low on his head and his jeans were brand new. He strode up to the front entrance and knocked.

Callie opened the door. "Afternoon, Callie," he said.

He looked even better up close. A whiff of his cologne wafted over to her. His scent alone was enough to send her over the edge but the whole Tagg package got her heart pumping hard and heavy.

She smiled tentatively, realizing this was her big chance to dazzle him. She wanted to be smooth and elegant tonight. She wanted to know the right thing to say, to keep him intrigued and interested.

Then the reminder came.

They were checking out horses on a ranch.

Not having a romantic rendezvous.

Tagg looked her over, his gaze resting on her hair, which she'd put partially up and away from her face. Loose tendrils flowed down her back. A gleam of approval shone in his eyes. Then his gaze shifted down to her neckline and even farther down to her chest. Her nipples hardened under his scrutiny and she wondered if the arch of his brow meant he'd noticed. He finished his perusal by checking out her legs and then returned to her face with a slow nod. "Nice."

Inside, she sighed with happiness. "Not so bad yourself, cowboy."

"Are you ready?" he asked.

She nodded. "Yes, I'll just get my—"

"Got it." Tagg reached past her to pick up her overnight case. He clutched it easily and glanced inside the house before turning around. "Anything else?"

"No, that's it."

"Then let's go."

Callie locked the front door and moved silently alongside Tagg as they strode down the inlaid stone pathway leading to the car. In many ways Big Hawk Ranch was situated the same as any other wealthy ranch, including the Worths'. The sprawling two-story ranch house that glistened with pristine paint and wood sidings was the centerpiece. A barn, stable, bunkhouse and storage buildings made up the backdrop of eighty thousand acres of prime grazing land. Cattle roamed off in the distance and the slight sweet scent of wildflowers and tall grass mingled with earth and cattle smells.

A chauffeur stood waiting by the passenger side of the car and Tagg handed him the suitcase. "Thanks, Emmett."

Tagg allowed Callie to get into the car first, then climbed in after her. It was spacious in the backseat with room to stretch her arms and legs. Yet she couldn't mistake Tagg's formidable presence inside the car. He took up space with confidence, as if he had a right to it. The door slammed shut from the outside and the driver got behind the wheel. "I'll get you to the airstrip in good time, Mr. Worth." And soon the car was moving off Sullivan land.

Tagg the CFO was just as formidable as Tagg the rodeo champion and equally as cool and distant. Callie wondered if she could penetrate the walls he'd erected. She wondered if Tagg would ever let her get close enough to try. Before she had to tell him about the baby. Keeping her secret from such a man could prove dangerous, and she prayed every day she wasn't making a colossal mistake.

She slid a glance his way and caught him looking at her legs. When their eyes met, he smiled then turned away to gaze out the window at the passing scenery: miles and miles of the same, pastures and cattle, horses and fences.

She hated that his smile alone could wilt her.

He's your fantasy man, she reminded herself.

Hang in there, Callie.

Tagg didn't like airports. He didn't like flying. But he never let that stop him from getting where he needed to go. It wasn't fear, but a deep-rooted loathing of anything related to planes. Heather's crash came too easily to mind when he was near a small airstrip. After that fateful day, he'd stopped taking the Worth family jet and, shortly thereafter, his brothers had decided to close down that piece of land in his wife's memory.

They boarded a commercial airliner at Sky Harbor International Airport. Tagg made sure they had secluded seating in first class. He didn't want Callie to be cramped or uncomfortable. And he wanted her to have a good time, but he wouldn't delve too deeply into why that mattered to him.

Once they were settled and the plane had taken off, Tagg unfastened his seat belt and turned to Callie. "I get how you know horses. You pretty much can't *not* know about them growing up on a ranch. But I'm puzzled. How are you an expert with children?"

He watched as she tried to undo the seat belt, her slender fingers fumbling with the stubborn latch. "I, uh, oh, this is really impossible," she said, her mouth creasing down.

Tagg grinned. "Here." He leaned over and worked the clasp. Without the slightest resistance, he managed to free her. He was close, leaning in so that his shoulder brushed hers. The subtle female scent he'd resisted while on the drive over invaded his nostrils and he breathed her in fully. Was it her hair, her skin, her perfume that made her smell so damn good?

Tagg slid her a glance and looked into her soft dark eyes. They glistened like melting caramel as she met his gaze softly. "Thank you," she said.

Tagg looked at her for another second before righting himself and leaning back in his seat. "No problem."

She relaxed a little, the frustrated frown gone from her face now. "To answer your question, I went to Boston College. I earned my degree in psychology and I worked for some time for the Department of Social Services. It was dry, boring work, not what I really wanted to do. But then something happened to me. I got…mugged."

Tagg blinked. That was a word foreign to small towns and big ranches. "You got mugged?" he repeated.

"Yeah, I did," she said, and then her expression turned soft. Almost dreamlike. "It was sort of strange. I couldn't believe it was happening."

"Did he hurt you?" Tagg asked. He didn't understand her wistful expression.

"Oh, no, nothing like that. And it wasn't a he. It was a she. And she was all of eleven years old."

"A little girl mugged you?"

"Yes. I could hardly believe it. One minute I'm walking down a crowded street in an upscale part of town, and the next, I feel my purse being yanked off my shoulder. She caught me so off guard that even as I watched her run away, I didn't understand what had just happened. She was so young and obviously neglected. I could tell from her clothes and the way her hair spiked in ten different directions, like she hadn't seen a bath in weeks."

"Did you call the police?"

"No. I ran after her."

Tagg narrowed his eyes. "You?"

"Of course me. Hey, I was raised chasing dogs and riding horses. I climbed fences with the best of them. And there was something so...I don't know...so vulnerable and almost apologetic in that girl's expression that I knew I had to find out more. I had to catch up to her and, well, I had to get my purse back."

"And did you?"

Callie smiled quickly. "Yes. She led me on a wild goose chase for blocks and blocks. I ended up in a bad part of town. Rundown buildings and all. Finally, she stopped and turned to me and we stared at each other. Both of us were completely out of breath. She flung my handbag at me and told me to take my dumb stupid purse.

"When I thought she'd run away, she started sobbing big, uncontrollable tears."

Callie shifted in her seat and faced him. "Her name was Amber. And she had a little brother named Georgie. Her mother had been ill for a long time and they had very little money. Amber told me she'd never stolen before and I believed her."

Callie went on to explain how she'd gotten Amber's mother the medical help she needed. And how she'd begun working at a foundation for underprivileged children in her spare time. Amber and Georgie were the first of many children she'd counseled at the foundation. "From then on, I knew I wanted to work with children."

"But, if you loved it so much, why did you come back?"

Callie smiled. "I never intended on living back East. I'm really a country girl and when my father had a scare with his heart, I knew it was time to come home."

Her lips pulled down and she spoke with frustration, "But nothing I do seems to matter. He's like a tornado. I can't stop him or slow him down. And he thinks he knows what's best for me. Even now."

From her tone Tagg could tell it was a sore subject. He didn't want to get into a conversation about Callie's old man, so he let the subject drop.

The plane landed right on time and the taxi drive to the hotel took less than fifteen minutes.

Callie turned to him when the taxi pulled into a long driveway on the Las Vegas Strip. "The Bellagio? I assumed we'd stay with your friend at his ranch."

Tagg shrugged. "We own a suite here. On the top floor. I like to stretch out when I'm in town."

"Okay." Her eyes flickered over the length of him but he couldn't tell what she was thinking.

Stretching out was the very least he wanted to do tonight. And he'd finally admitted that to himself when he saw Jed drooling all over Callie today. He'd declined John's invitation to stay at his house in North Las Vegas. He wanted Callie. Alone. If she was willing. He was through denying it.

"Do you come here often?"

"A few times a year. On business and for the rodeo finals."

Tagg helped Callie out of the taxi and with a hand to her lower back he escorted her through the lobby. As they strode toward the elevator, Tagg gestured to the ceiling adorned by a chandelier sculpture made up of thousands of multicolored glass flower blossoms catching and reflecting light. "I always get a kick out of those petals up there. Feels like a scene out of a fairy tale," he said.

Callie stopped and lifted her gaze. "They are sort of surreal. I've heard about them. Seeing them is something else."

"So, you've never stayed here?"

She shook her head. "No, never. I've only been in Las Vegas for the rodeos, but not for years."

They rode the elevator to the top floor and Tagg walked her to the Worth suite. It was an indulgence, something his brothers had wanted, and now he was glad they'd insisted upon it. He opened the wide door and let her enter first. She walked in slowly, glancing about. The square footage of the suite was bigger than some people's homes. Roomy and elegant with richly appointed furniture. The view from the expansive window looked down onto the Strip.

"This is nice, Tagg. I see what you mean about stretching out."

"The Worth men like space."

Tagg showed the bellboy where to deposit the luggage, directing Callie's bag to the master suite and his to the bedroom beside it. Then he glanced at his watch. "We have just enough time to get settled before dinner."

Thirty minutes later, they arrived at a small hole-in-the-wall Italian restaurant that only the locals knew about off the Las Vegas Strip. The second Tagg walked in, the rich scent of olive oil and garlic and freshly baked bread perked up his appetite. John had raved about the food and Tagg was grateful to get away from the crowd of tourists in hotel row.

He found the Cosgroves sitting in a corner booth lit with candles and decorated with a flower arrangement. Tagg made the introductions and helped Callie to her seat before taking his. John Cosgrove and his wife, Sadie, were in their early sixties but could keep up with anyone half their age. Tagg had always considered John not only a friend, but also a mentor back in his rodeo days.

They talked horses and rodeo and Penny's Song. Callie and Sadie had both grown up on a cattle ranch, so they had a good deal in common.

"Not only is John a horse rancher, but he owns his own rodeo," Tagg said to Callie.

"That's how I met Tagg here," John said. "He busted a few of my prize stallions in his day. He knows horses. And what about you? How did you get involved with this guy over here?"

Callie's face colored. "Oh, uh..."

Sadie sent her husband a warning look. "John."

"Callie is a neighbor. She's Hawk Sullivan's daughter," Tagg announced.

John grinned. "Is that so?" He darted a glance at both of them.

Callie nodded. "Yes, that's right," she said, then turned to glare at Tagg.

He returned her look with a simple smile. He liked honesty. He wasn't into pussyfooting around an issue.

Callie cleared her throat. "I've just returned home from going to school and working in Boston. I found out about Penny's Song and knew I wanted to be a part of it. Tagg and I, we are…are working together on the project."

"I've had some dealings with your father," John said, catching Tagg's eye before focusing on Callie. "He's a smart negotiator."

Callie blew out a breath. She was uncomfortable talking about her father. "Thank you for that. I know you're being kind."

Sadie steered the conversation back to a more amiable subject. "Tagg, did you know that Blue Yonder sired a stallion? I hear he's a beauty, too."

"Is that so? I bet he's spoken for already." Tagg inhaled deep. He'd wanted to buy that Arabian for the past three years, but the owner wasn't selling. The stallion had pure bloodlines and ancestry that could be traced back to Spain. "The Kents refused to even talk to me. Can't say as I blame them. If I had that horse, I wouldn't let another horseman get within a hundred yards of him."

"There's a list a mile long and an acre wide bidding on the foal."

"What'd they name him?"

"Wild Blue," John said.

Tagg pursed his lips. "Great name. I guess that ship has sailed. I'd bet my last dollar they keep him themselves."

Sadie shook her head. "You never know."

Tagg shrugged it off. He didn't think so, but he wouldn't argue with her.

The food was delivered to the table—pasta with scallops and shrimp and about a dozen other things in a lemon wine sauce. There was no shortage of garlic, either. Tagg couldn't remember eating a better meal.

He glanced at Callie. She'd ordered an antipasto salad that overflowed the plate. He was glad to see she'd eaten more than half of it already. She wasn't shy when it came to eating, but she did tend to eat lighter fare. And she'd refused the red wine that flowed into everyone else's glasses.

He watched her sip a glass of water carefully, then say something to Sadie. Callie looked elegant tonight. Dressed in black, her creamy skin glistened under candlelight and the play of light skin against dark hair and eyes made him stir with desire. He remembered how she looked minus the dress. It was a memory never far from his mind—a memory he'd like to duplicate.

After dinner the Cosgroves drove them back to the hotel and bid them both good-night. They made arrangements to see the horses after breakfast the next morning.

He entered the penthouse suite after Callie and walked straight to the bar. "Are you tired?" he asked.

"Not really." She set her purse down on the sofa and looked out the window to the bright lights below.

He remembered Callie had been drinking rum during that time in Reno, so he poured her a rum and cola and spilled two fingers of whiskey in a tumbler for himself. He brought the drink over to her. "You should be. It's been a long day."

She turned from the window and stared at the tumbler in his hand. "Oh, no. No, thanks. I'm not…thirsty." Her shoulders stiffened.

Tagg raised his brows. She seemed pensive and nervous for some reason. "Okay." He set the drink down on the cocktail table behind him and when he turned back to Callie, she was staring out the window again. "Everything all right?"

She nodded.

He edged up beside her and glanced out the window, sipping his drink. "You're not drinking tonight. Is that because you don't want a repeat of Reno?"

She turned to him, her gaze warm and soft. "I didn't sleep with you because I'd been drinking. If that's what you think."

He furrowed his brows. "Seems I wasn't doing much thinking that night at all."

A low self-deprecating laugh escaped her throat. "So I've been told." She turned back to the window, her arms folded around her middle. "You've made that very clear," she said quietly.

Tagg grinned. "That wasn't an insult, Callie."

"Was hardly a glowing review, either."

He set his glass down and walked in front of her, blocking her view from anything but him. He lifted her chin with his thumb and gazed into her beautiful eyes. She flinched, not in fear but with surprise, then lowered her arms to her sides. The anticipation on her face gave him pause. She blinked and inhaled a sharp breath.

"It was a compliment."

She searched his eyes. "How so?"

"You made me forget things I'm damned determined not to forget." He glanced at her mouth and saw her tremble. "Why are you so nervous?"

"I'm not," she blurted, lifting her chin up and taking a step back. "I have nothing to be nervous about." She turned then and reached for her purse sitting on the sofa. "You know, I think I am tired. I'm going to bed."

Tagg reached his arm out and snaked it around her waist,

pulling her close. Her intoxicating scent destroyed his patience.

"What are you doing?" she whispered.

"Are you really tired, Callie?"

She shook her head no. Then gazed deep into his eyes.

He set both hands on her waist, enjoying the lush feel of her hips in his outspread palms. Silence filled the room. Fading dusky beams of starlight filtered through the window to cast them in shadows.

He angled his head and moved closer. His legs met with her thighs. An ache of need began growing. He gave in to the sensation and brought his mouth down on hers. She froze, her lips refusing to respond for a second, and Tagg was ready to back off, lest he seduce an unwilling woman. But then she moved closer, wrapping her arms around his neck, crushing her breasts to his chest. She gave into the kiss then with effort and passion, the way he remembered her. The way they'd kissed before.

She was sweetly alluring, tentative yet fiery. Tagg relished having her in his arms.

They came up for air a full minute later, both breathing hard. Callie reached her arm around to move her hair to her right side, the locks falling freely on one nearly bare shoulder. It was a reflective move, one to give her time to think, he surmised. Their lips still close, she softly spoke. "I didn't think you wanted this. You said it would never happen again."

Tagg closed his eyes briefly. He had said that. And he'd meant it at the time. "I guess I was fooling myself."

She shook her head slightly, her eyes questioning. "What changed?" she asked.

You, he wanted to answer. *Or rather my perception of you.* He'd gotten to know her, and liked what he saw. She loved horses. She loved Arizona and small-town life. She even begrudgingly loved her miserable father. Her story about Amber and Georgie tugged at something primal and protective in him. But he wouldn't tell her that. He wouldn't tell her that she'd gotten to him. That maybe meeting up with her in Reno had been the best thing that could have happened to him.

There'd be no purpose in that. He had no place in his heart for another woman. He'd closed himself off emotionally. There was no going back. So he told her a half truth and one she would understand. "Jed."

Her eyes snapped up. "Jed?"

"He was panting after you, plain as day." He lifted a curl that rested on her chest, watching it fall from his fingertips. "I came to the rescue."

"And you stepped in to *save* me?"

Tagg looked away before peering into her eyes. "Yeah, something like that."

She seemed a little baffled. "Were you jealous?"

"No," he lied. He'd seen more green than his pasture after heavy rains.

She narrowed her eyes, a skeptical look on her face. Then with determination, she moved closer to him and brushed an air kiss to his mouth. His groin tightened. "Not even a little?"

He shook his head, keeping his eyes trained on her mouth.

She came even closer, until their mouths were almost touching again, then licked at his lips with her very skilled tongue. "Are you sure?"

Tagg smiled. This was the bold, sexy woman he remembered from Reno. They'd done wild things together. "Callie," he warned and then didn't give her a chance to protect herself.

He hauled her hips into his, making his point with one flush move against his straining erection. His hands went into her hair and he planted his mouth on hers in a rough, desperate kiss that brought a soft moan of pleasure up from her throat. Their openmouthed frenzy sped his heart rate, and when Callie whimpered again, it was all he could do not to rip her dress off. They fought with each other's clothes, unfastening, unbuttoning, unzipping, hands clumsy but efficient until she was naked in his arms and he was almost there. He picked her up, carried her to the master bedroom and set her down on the oversize bed. He took a minute to look at her, beautifully bare, her hair spreading out like a glorious fan around her upper body. Her breasts round and full enticed him with two inviting upturned peaks.

She smiled coyly and turned on her side, her hip curving up from her waist, shadowing the V between her long shapely legs. He rid himself of his briefs and Callie beckoned him with a look at his manhood, her gaze bright with anticipation, ready for their long sexy ride.

Tagg reached into the bedside drawer and came up with a condom packet.

A tremble ran through Callie's body. She stared at the silver packet as Tagg ripped it open. They didn't need protection. They'd already made a baby. But Tagg didn't know that and the cold, hard reality came crashing down on her. Guilt coiled in her stomach and pounded in her brain. What was she doing? She hated deceiving Tagg. Hated that the condom itself signified her deception. It was on the tip of her tongue to tell him. To lay out the truth, that she'd conceived a baby with him in Reno. That she'd been lying to him all along.

Could she be that brave? Could she ease her guilt and own up to her pregnancy? Tagg was going to be a father, yet she had withheld that information from him for weeks. One little mistake, one slip of the tongue and she could lose Tagg forever. If she told him now would it be all over between them, before it really had a chance of beginning?

She bit her lower lip and closed her eyes, wishing that everything would just turn out okay. Somehow. She needed a miracle, but she wasn't that big an optimist to believe she'd be granted one.

The bedsheets rustled and she sunk into the mattress when he lay down beside her. His warm breath caressed her cheek. "Callie? Did you go somewhere?"

He smelled of whiskey and lust and Callie's body reacted, her bare nipples pebbled at the sound of his voice. She opened her eyes. He was there, his beautiful face against hers, his nose in her hair, breathing in her scent.

"I'm here, Tagg," she whispered, losing her nerve. She couldn't tell him. She had to give them more time. It wasn't selfish on her part, she told herself. The baby's future was at stake. Was it so wrong to hold out for the brass ring? To hope that given time, Tagg would come to love her? Was it so wrong to hope for a happy ending?

He nibbled on her throat, his lips drawing moist circles all the way down to the hollow between her breasts. "That's good. Stay with me."

That's what she intended. To stay with Tagg. To be his for the rest of her life. But at the moment, the goal seemed out of reach and the guilt she felt also stayed with her. Even as he kissed her. Even as he ran his hands along her body, making her moan with pleasure. Even as he parted her thighs and stroked her with deft fingers, until her first orgasm slammed into her with enough force to make her cry out.

"You came so quickly," Tagg said with a note of male satisfaction.

Callie let go of her mental fight and gave herself up to physical bliss. Her remorse would have to wait. She was with Tagg, naked on his bed, and there wasn't anywhere else she'd rather be. She gave him a little shove and he fell onto his back, a deep chuckle coming up from his throat.

"You do that so easily to me," she whispered.

"You saying you're easy?"

Callie lifted up on her knees and straddled his lower legs. She took his penis in her hand. "Only with you."

Tagg gazed into her eyes. His were pure liquid fire as she stroked his erection. "Nice to know," he gritted out.

Callie loved bringing him satisfaction. Tagg's grunts of approval as she slid her hand up and down his shaft again brought shivers of heat to her body. She wasn't through with Tagg. She'd make love to him all night.

She watched his face twist and contort with pent up desire as her hand ran up and over the length of him, her thumb pressing the sensitive tip. A rumble emanated in his throat and Callie smiled. "Let's see how easy you are." She bent her head and licked the moisture off with long fluid strokes, circling the tip like she would an ice cream cone.

Then she took him into her mouth.

His body stiffened; his erection went rock hard. She set her hands on his thighs and drank him in. She sensed his eyes on her, watching. She remembered from the last time they'd been together that Tagg never closed his eyes during sex. He liked to watch. It turned him on. Through the curtain of her hair resting on his belly, she looked up and their eyes met for an instant. The delicious expression on his face stilled her. She loved him so much that she physically ached. All she could do was show him. She slipped his erection back into her mouth and loved him with her tongue. She stroked him with both hands until she knew the exact moment he was ready for release.

They were in sync that way.

She moved off him slightly. He grabbed the unnecessary packet, ripping it open and she helped him slide it down onto his erection. He reached for her then, lifting her up on her knees so that she was directly over him. With skilled hands, he guided her hips down and impaled her with his swollen shaft.

"Tagg," she breathed out. The first initial thrust filled the tip of her. She wanted more. She moved on him then, undulating her hips, grasping him, letting him fill her slowly, taking in one pleasurable inch at a time. He felt so good, so warm, so right. She'd dreamed about this, about having him inside her again, feeling his body rock under hers.

She heard him curse in a way that brought a smile to her lips. He watched her, she knew, and that turned her on as well. She sank farther down, taking him in fully, and moved without thinking now, lifting her hair off her shoulders and letting it fall back down again. His eyes followed the flow of her hair. And then she touched her breasts for him, cupping them slightly, fingering the pebbled peaks once, twice. His eyes glistened with deep hunger and his expression was pure sin.

She rode him hard, sinking and lifting, both of them uttering deep throaty sounds of pleasure. She moved faster now, with his encouragement, the pressure building inside her. He reached for her breasts and caressed her with his palms, rubbing the insides of his hands over her nipples. The contrast of rough to delicate sent shooting jolts of electricity through her body. She loved his hands on her. She loved him touching her.

"Stay with me, Callie," he whispered, barely getting the words out. "We're…almost there."

They were close. So close. "Hurry, Tagg."

It was all he needed to hear. Splaying his fingers out, he grabbed her waist and pushed her down onto his shaft harder than she could have alone. He filled her completely now and took control, thrusting up with potent, powerful force. It felt good to let go, to give in to him fully and take the sexy ride.

"I'm ready," she moaned, holding back the waves that wanted to shatter within her.

He lifted his body, coming half off the bed, and held her bottom with both hands, moving her forward and back hard, harder. Then with one last deep, powerful thrust, their release came, together, forcefully, each of them huffing out guttural sounds of completion.

He held her tight until the last shreds of pleasure were wrought out of both. It was beautiful and satisfying, but now that it was over, Callie couldn't look him in the eye for fear of him seeing her every emotion.

"Are you okay?" he asked.

She nodded, then swallowed, but words wouldn't come.

He kissed a path up her throat, working his way to her mouth. She kept her face turned away.

He put a finger under her chin and applied slight pressure to turn her toward him. She met his gaze finally. "Are you sure?"

She noted the concern in his eyes and managed to answer, "Yes."

He let go a relieved sigh, cradling her to his body. "That was pretty damn good."

She nodded again.

"Callie?"

"Just…good?" she blurted. She was in love with him and

had given up her head and her heart for just *good*. It wasn't about sex for her. It was about feelings and emotions and love. While she knew she should be thrilled and delighted that they'd made love, she only felt empty inside and guilty about her secret as well.

Tagg lay back, holding her as they fell onto the cool sheets. "Great. Awesome. Perfect. You don't disappoint, Callie."

"Neither do you," she said. She lay her head down, snuggled into his chest and closed her eyes. He stroked her head, running his fingers through her hair. "But do you think it was a mistake?"

The muscles of his arms tensed and he hesitated long enough to worry her. "I don't think I could've stayed away from you, so no. Not a mistake."

But he'd stayed away after Reno. He'd left her with a note and had gone home. And never called her.

"What about you? A mistake?"

She shook her head. "Definitely not." Being with him could never be a mistake. Callie knew men always said nice things after a satisfying night in the sack. After-sex talk was usually warm and cozy, until the light of day shined through and reality set in.

Tagg didn't want a relationship. And he was just trying to make her feel better. She also knew that men didn't like to analyze their feelings after making love. So she bit her tongue from saying anything else that would destroy the moment.

"Do you want anything? A drink? Something to eat?" he asked.

"No, but you go ahead if you want something."

Tagg chuckled and the muscles in his arms relaxed. "Really? I think what I want isn't in the kitchen."

Callie smiled and looked into his eyes. "And what is it that you want?"

"You, all night long." He kissed her then, a warm brushing of his mouth, less hurried, less frenzied than before. Callie returned the kiss, agreeing to his plan.

Tagg woke up before dawn, with Callie sprawled halfway over him. Her long dark hair rested in waves on his chest, her head tucked into his shoulder. The unique erotic mix of musk and flowers that he couldn't name drove him slightly insane as he breathed in. His hand lay atop the curve of her bare bottom, his palm filled with soft smooth skin. He'd convinced Callie not to put on her nightie last night. He'd wanted her naked next to him through the night and now he thought about the wisdom in that. He would have gotten a better night's sleep if he hadn't insisted. He'd woken up hard and ready twenty minutes ago. He wasn't going to wait much longer.

His erection pulsed and ached like a sex-starved teenager.

She moved on him, stirring a bit, her breasts crushing into his side.

He swore under his breath, wincing at the pain and wondering if he'd made a colossal mistake taking her to bed.

Sure as hell didn't feel like a mistake. It felt pretty damn amazing.

But he couldn't forget who Callie was. He couldn't forget that she wasn't a woman he could turn away after a night of wild sex. He'd done that to her once and had regretted it.

Callie stirred again and Tagg held his breath, waiting for her to awaken.

He wanted her. She was an indulgence he couldn't afford, yet one he couldn't seem to resist.

Her eyelids lifted and she looked at him with a sleep-hazy gaze, her hair in a tumble around her face, her lips parted.

Tagg claimed her mouth in a slow easy kiss. "Morning."

It wasn't quite. The early light of dawn hadn't stolen into the room yet.

"Morning." Her soft breath blew over his chest. She stroked her fingers into the scattered hairs there. "Did you sleep well?"

He ran his hand up and down the smooth sleek skin of her thigh. She cooed from his touch and his erection stiffened. "I've been awake for a while. Waiting for you."

Callie lifted her head to look at him. Her gaze drifted down past his waist. Her smile was sweet, her words a little sassy. "Not my fault. You asked me not to leave. Or put on my nightgown."

Stay naked. Sleep with me, had been his exact words. "Wouldn't have mattered." He told her the truth. "Just having you under the same roof is enough."

Callie nibbled on her lower lip and a mischievous gleam brightened her eyes. "What are we going to do about that?"

Tagg rolled her over and set her shoulders against the mattress. He rose above her, his erection pressing into her flat belly. "I have a plan."

Hours later, sated and holding Callie close, Tagg woke to dim sunlight pouring through the curtains. It was nearing time to get up and go about the business of the day.

Tagg could stay in this bed with Callie all week and that realization nagged at him. She was a fantastic lover, the best sex he'd had in a long time, if not ever. That worried him. He didn't have a plan for this. The truth was, he didn't have anything to offer her. Not a relationship. Not a courtship. He was done with those things.

So done.

And she was Hawkins Sullivan's daughter.

He wouldn't forget that.

When Callie stirred, Tagg draped his hand over her shoulder and rubbed her arms up and down. He felt her fatigue as her body went limp. "That feels…good. I'm…so tired."

He brushed a kiss to the top of her head. "Go back to sleep. We have a little time."

"I'm not going to wake up to a note, am I?" She spoke quietly, holding on for his answer before she drifted off.

"I'm here, Callie. I'm not going anywhere."

Five

Tagg glanced at his watch, a tic working his jaw as he paced the floor in Clay's parlor. He'd been waiting for fifteen minutes for a meeting he had with his brothers and Callie about fundraising for Penny's Song. The usual bustling ranch looked like a morgue today. There wasn't a soul in sight. Normally, Tagg liked solitude but now he was anxious.

Damn anxious. *To see Callie.*

Finally the door slammed shut and he recognized the sound of his brother's boots shuffling across the hardwood floor.

"Sorry, I'm late." Clay marched into the room and tossed his hat onto the sofa.

Tagg grunted.

"Jackson's not coming. He's tied up in town. You want a drink?" Clay moved to the bar in the corner of the room and poured a glass of iced tea for himself, then turned to Tagg.

"Nothing for me." He glanced at his watch again. It was

almost eleven-twenty. "What time did you call the meeting for?"

"Eleven."

Clay took a big swallow of his drink, then wiped his mouth with the back of his hand the way he had as a boy. "Where's Callie?"

Tagg shrugged. That's what he wanted to know. He'd dropped her off at Big Hawk Ranch after they'd concluded their business with the Cosgroves and said he'd call her. A couple of days slipped by as Tagg struggled with just the right words to say to her. Once he figured it out yesterday and had his speech all set, he'd called and gotten no answer. He'd left her two messages that she didn't return.

"Don't know. I haven't spoken to her since we got back from Vegas the other day."

"How'd that go? I haven't seen either one of you since you got back."

"Just fine. The Cosgroves let us ride a few mares and pick out the ones we thought best for Penny's Song. I'm arranging for their transport to the ranch. We should have them in time."

"Thanks. That's a big help." Clay downed the rest of his drink. "So you and Callie worked okay together?"

Tagg nodded. What could he say? That he and Callie wore out the bedsheets in the Bellagio suite? That she'd given him another night of great sex? And that he'd deliberately stayed away from her since that day because nothing was going to come of it? "We did fine. She does know horses."

Clay sat down on a wide wing chair and stretched his legs out. "I'm surprised she's not here. This meeting was her idea. Seemed eager about it. You sure you didn't do something to piss her off? I know you don't like her."

Tagg eyed his brother, his mouth tight. "Don't go putting words in my mouth."

"So, you do like her?"

"You hired her. I've got to work with her." Tagg clammed up after that. Fact was, he did like Callie. But that didn't change anything.

"Surly this morning."

"No more than usual," Tagg said.

He glanced out the window again. There was no sign of Callie. Where the hell was she? He hated to admit it, but he'd been looking forward to seeing her. He'd gone home to an empty house and while that usually comforted and put him at ease, he'd found himself restless and tense. He'd thought about having a short-term affair with her and wondered if she'd want the same thing. He'd been ready to broach the subject on the flight home, but Callie had rested her head on his shoulder and fallen into a deep sleep. Tagg had draped an arm around her and closed his eyes to an unwelcome sense of peace with her in his arms. He'd attributed his softening emotions to another satisfying night of sex. Period. And thought better of getting more involved with her.

"It's not like her to forget." Clay scratched his chin, contemplating. "I'm a good judge of character and Callie impressed me as someone you can count on. Don't suppose something happened to her father?"

"We couldn't get that lucky."

Clay grinned. "He's really got your shorts in a knot."

"He stole that Bender deal right out from under me. I still can't figure out how he did it. I thought I had it all tied up."

"That was a tough one to lose." Clay glanced at the antique walnut grandfather clock sitting catty-corner to the far wall. Another ten minutes had passed. "Well, looks like she's a no-show. Why don't you give her a call? I'll speak with Jed. See if we got our signals crossed. Maybe she's waiting over at the site for us."

Tagg got out his cell and punched in her number while Clay went into the other room with his phone. Callie's phone went straight to voice mail and her sweet, sultry voice came on the phone. "You know I'd answer if I could. I'll get back to you as soon as possible. Thanks for the call."

"This is Tagg, Callie. We're waiting for you over at the main house. We had a meeting at eleven. Clay wants to know if you're coming."

He'd spoken in his business voice, blunt and to the point. No sense getting Clay suspicious about the two of them. If his brothers got an inkling of what had gone on between Callie and him in Vegas, they'd be riding his case about it.

Clay walked back into the room. "Jed hasn't seen her. She was supposed to stop by the site this morning and bring some children's books to the bunkhouse, but she's a no-show there, too."

"Well, it's clear she's not coming." Tagg let out a frustrated breath. "I've got work to do. No sense waiting any longer."

"Yeah, so do I. I'll let you know if she calls."

Tagg strode to the front door and let himself out. A bad feeling churned in his gut and he didn't know what to make of it. But if he couldn't reach Callie by later today, he was going to get to the bottom of it.

One way or another.

By seven that evening after two more unanswered calls, Tagg stood on the doorstep of Big Hawk Ranch—this time without a limousine waiting, this time without anticipation of a weekend fling with his enemy's daughter. Tagg hated to admit it, but he was genuinely concerned about her welfare.

The housekeeper answered his knock and Tagg felt a

measure of disappointment not seeing Callie at the door. "I'm Taggart Worth. I'm looking for Callie. Is she here?"

"Callie is home, Mr. Worth, but she's not—"

"I'll take care of this, Antoinette" came a voice from behind her.

Immediately the woman stepped aside for her employer. "Yes, Mr. Sullivan."

Tagg now found himself face-to-face with The Hawk in the doorway. He narrowed his eyes. "I'm looking for Callie."

"So I heard."

"I know she's here. I'd like to see her."

The big man shook his head, his gaze raking him over with fire in his dark eyes. "I oughta toss you off my land."

"You gonna get your shotgun and chase me away?"

"After what you did to my daughter, I'm tempted to do more than chase you away."

Tagg hesitated. He'd seen Sullivan in a state before, but his reaction went beyond anything he'd ever witnessed. What had Tagg done to Callie? She was an adult. She knew what she was doing when they took that overnight trip. If her daddy disapproved, he'd just have to get over it. "I'd like to speak with her."

To find out why she won't answer my calls.

"Well, you're gonna speak with me first. I got something to say to you."

Sullivan backed away from the door and Tagg took the opportunity to step inside. The place was massive with dark oak floors and rich wood paneling. As he followed The Hawk through the house, he took in the beautifully restored antique furniture in the anteroom, the parlor and the study. He kept an eye out for Callie, but he suspected she was in another part of the building. Maybe she was up the long winding staircase that led to other rooms.

Sullivan closed the double study doors and didn't mince words as he sat down behind a rectangular mahogany desk. "You got my daughter pregnant."

Tagg stared at the older man. Then blinked, speechless.

"That's right. She's upstairs right now, sick as a dog. Puking up her guts. Can't keep anything down. I recognized the signs straightaway. Her mama reacted the same when she was with child."

This was the last thing Tagg expected to hear. He let Sullivan's words sink in. Callie was pregnant with his child? A dozen emotions rolled through his system. He wasn't sure which one would take hold. Denial, anger and disbelief were at the forefront and battled for dominance as he went over the facts. She couldn't have gotten pregnant in Las Vegas. Even he knew it was too soon for a woman to go through morning sickness after a couple of days. Which meant Callie got pregnant in Reno. Six, seven weeks ago.

Sullivan folded his hands together and set them on the desk as he leaned forward. A knowing smile creased his face. "You seem surprised. She didn't tell you, did she?"

He shook his head an inch. The older man gloated. Tagg summoned his willpower to stand still and not put a fist in his face. He braced his hands on the edge of the desk and leaned forward, his mouth tight as he finally managed to speak. "How long has she known?"

The man shrugged. "Does it matter?"

"Yeah, it matters," he gritted out.

"A month. Maybe more."

"And why should I believe you?"

"Callie likes to have a glass of wine with dinner. She stopped drinking weeks ago. Asking for lemonade, claiming the wine's been upsetting her stomach lately."

"Maybe it's true." Tagg voiced his thoughts aloud.

"It's bull. And you know it. Fact is, she ran off to Reno to see her cousin because I'd riled her. She was damn irritated at me for interfering with her love life with some low-life carpenter and what does she go and do? She takes you in her bed! A Worth. She did it out of spite. To get back at me. To show me that I couldn't dictate her life anymore. She knows how I feel about you Worths."

Tagg plagued his memory for accuracy. What had Callie said to him about that night? Then it came back to him with near haunting clarity. *"When I saw you sitting on that bar stool, you looked how I felt. Lonely, disappointed, wishing things in your life were different."*

It all made sense now. Callie had thrown herself at him that night for a reason—to get back at her father. He'd meddled in her love life and she wanted retribution. She'd come on to Tagg like her life depended on it.

Any red-blooded male would have given in to temptation, especially when she'd looked at him with pure sin in her eyes and she'd fit her body into his like they were two halves of a whole. She'd seduced him, plain and simple.

To spite her father.

She'd used him for payback. And now an innocent baby's life was at stake.

A surge of white-hot anger raged inside. Tagg had been played, and this time he couldn't blame the old man. It wasn't The Hawk's fault, though he had to hand it to Sullivan. He'd taught his daughter how to manipulate well.

"Where is she?" Tagg turned and headed for the door.

"Not so fast!" Sullivan's coarse voice stopped him cold.

Tagg turned and glared at him, his nerves ready to burst through his skin. "What?"

"Sit down, Worth. You're gonna listen to me." He pointed

to the seat in front of his desk. Tagg walked closer, but didn't sit.

"Say it and be quick."

Sullivan opened the top drawer in his desk and pulled out a thick manila folder. He glanced at it for a moment, then tossed it toward him. The file spun and landed on the desk facing him. "Look at it."

Tagg humored him, though he wasn't keen on doing any of Sullivan's bidding. He opened the file and raised his brows. "It's the Bender contract."

"That's right," Sullivan said, smug.

"So? You rubbing my nose in it?"

"No, I'm offering it to you. If you see there, the contract isn't signed. I'm holding off."

Confused, Tagg glanced at the man. "For what?"

"It's worth a small fortune. More than three million over two years, I'd say. If current beef prices hold and the cattle sale goes through without a hitch."

"Hell, I know that."

"I'll back out and Worth Enterprises can step in with your offer. All you have to do is walk away right now. Leave Callie to me. Let her have the baby and I'll find her someone suitable to marry. She doesn't need your money. You know that. Just tell her you want out of any obligation to the child."

Tagg stared at him. Was he a madman? Had he had one too many unscrupulous dealings in his past to believe Tagg would agree to this?

Tagg gripped the folder, his fingers curling around the edges. He spoke through clenched teeth. "Let me get this straight. You're offering me the Bender deal if I walk away from my child? I give him up? Lose all rights to him or her, and I get the contract?"

"That's the deal I'm offering."

"So, to put it another way, you're using your grandchild as a...*a bargaining chip?*"

"That's just one way of looking at it."

Tagg hissed through tight lips, "I don't believe this."

Sullivan's mouth turned into a grim line. "You don't want my daughter. Or the child she's carrying. And we have no use for Worths around here."

Tagg shook his head in disgust. "You think everyone's a ruthless bastard like you?"

Sullivan didn't back down. He gestured to the contract. "It's a damn good offer."

"Keep your friggin' deal." Tagg tossed the file down so hard, the papers caught flight and several sheets hit Sullivan smack in the face. Tagg found no enjoyment in that. He was beyond rage. "Go to hell, old man." He turned on his heels and strode out of the study. He took the steps two at a time as he raced up the staircase. "Callie!" he called out. "Callie!"

He saw her before he reached the top of the stairs. She was standing by a window, dressed in a long light beige nightgown with the fading sunshine behind her back. She would have looked angelic but for her pale drawn face and the lack of luster in her eyes. They stared at each other for several long seconds. Tagg thought he knew Callie. Thought he liked her. But he found he didn't know her at all and right now he detested anyone named Sullivan. "Get dressed. You're taking a drive with me."

She nodded, not saying a word. He glanced at her stomach, then met her eyes again. There was no need to ask about the pregnancy. Though her flat belly showed no signs yet, her guilty expression gave her away. She was carrying his child.

He didn't want Hawkins Sullivan anywhere near his kid. There was no way he'd allow his child to be influenced by him, much less grow up in his household. And there was only one way to ensure that. Callie had to agree. He wouldn't take no for an answer.

"Don't say anything, Callie. Not one word. Not until we're off this damn ranch."

He wouldn't look at her. He stared straight ahead, peering out the Jeep's windshield, shifted into gear and hit the gas pedal.

Callie's stomach churned at Tagg's tone. She didn't want it to be like this. She didn't want Tagg to find out about his child until she was sure he had feelings for her.

He does have feelings for you. He hates you.

Callie closed her eyes. She'd had a rough few days. The doctor said the morning sickness would subside but there was no telling when. She'd been sick for three days straight, almost from the minute the plane had landed back from Las Vegas. Initially, she had thought she'd picked up a virus, but her doctor confirmed what she was experiencing was first trimester morning sickness. For some women, it lasted only days, others weeks, and the really lucky ones were blessed with emptying their stomach contents for the majority of their gestation.

Please, no.

She laid a hand to her belly.

Tagg noticed. He turned his head and peered at her stomach. The hard glare in his eyes softened for a millisecond before his jaw set tight and his lips pursed again.

Callie leaned against the side of the cab and drew oxygen into her lungs. She felt better being out of the house and off the ranch. And crazy as it seemed, she felt better being with Tagg, even with him being as angry as he was.

She should have told him about the baby right away. She

should have been honest and let the chips fall where they may. She'd experienced enough guilt over this to last her a lifetime. It had all been so clear in her head when she made the decision to wait before telling Tagg about the baby. She'd wanted time. She'd wanted a courtship, to have a real relationship with him. She'd wanted a chance.

Instead, her father had witnessed her morning sickness and had instantly known that she was with child. He'd demanded to know whose child she carried and Callie hadn't any more deception left in her. Her body physically ached and she had little strength. In a weak moment, she'd confessed everything to her father, including blaming him for making her so darn angry that she felt she needed to defy him with Tagg.

But she never expected that Tagg would come over, and when she'd heard him arguing with her father from her bedroom upstairs, she was shocked. Then she'd taken one look at Tagg racing up the steps like it was an Olympic sport and knew he'd learned the truth and was furious with her.

After a ten-minute drive at seventy miles an hour on the open highway, Tagg slowed down and turned down a long winding road. They drove through a cropping of tall cottonwoods and farther on to where green meadows filled the panorama with colorful wildflowers nurtured by spring rain. Elizabeth Lake came into view, and as they approached Callie saw the reflection of dark blue waters glistening under diminishing sunlight.

Tagg parked by a shallow embankment. His mood seemed calmer now, the planes of his face more relaxed. She hoped her optimism wasn't merely wishful thinking. He bounded out of the cab and strode around the front of the vehicle to open the passenger side door. "Take a walk with me." She slipped her hand in his and he helped her climb down.

Her fingers tingled from his touch. But Tagg dropped her

hand as soon as she was on solid ground. She'd been wrong. His anger hadn't subsided—he'd just masked it better now. A tic worked in his jaw. His eyes on her were cold and hard. A bad sign.

He led her to where long grass cushioned the lake bank. "Let's sit."

Tagg waited for her to drop onto the grass, then he lowered himself down beside her. He stared out across the lake. "The baby's mine?"

Callie might have expected this. She swallowed past the lump in her throat, hurt that he'd even asked. "Yes. You're the only man I've been with since Boston."

"What about that carpenter? The one you'd been seeing?"

Callie winced. It seemed her father had told him everything. She shook her head. "The relationship never got that far. I… Troy was…it never got physical," she said quietly.

Tagg inhaled sharply. "You were ticked at your father and you what? Seduced me in order to defy him?" He turned to her then, his eyes black with fury. "He never let you near a Worth. You weren't allowed to talk to any of us. So, you saw me that night, looking…lonely and vulnerable, and you thought to yourself, if I hook up with Tagg, I'll finally get payback. Even if your father never found out, you'd know. You'd have that satisfaction. You settled the score by screwing my brains out. It was a hell of a ride, Callie."

"No! It wasn't like that."

"Defying your father must have been so damn sweet."

"Tagg, listen. You're wrong. I can explain."

"I don't think so. It all makes sense now." He spoke firmly, with conviction, as if nothing in the world could change his mind.

"I mean that was only part of the reason." What could

she say now, explain that she'd come face-to-face with her fantasy man? That she'd seen an opportunity to finally take something she wanted, to go for broke, to do something wild and so out of character for her? How could she tell him that? How could she tell him she loved him?

It wouldn't matter. He wouldn't believe her.

The darkness in his eyes went deeper. "You got pregnant on purpose, Callie. The ultimate revenge. To have a Worth bastard. When were you going to tell me?"

"No! Tagg, I didn't. You can't believe that."

"Hell, I don't know what to believe." He turned away from her, his face contorted with disgust.

"Please. I'm sorry I didn't tell you sooner. I was waiting for the right moment. I never thought I'd get pregnant. Never. You have to believe me. I'm not…ruthless."

Tagg shot her a look. "You're a Sullivan."

And that said it all. Callie's eyes filled with tears. "I'm not my father, Tagg."

"Then why didn't you tell me? Vegas would have been a good time. We were alone together, going at it all night long. You might have slipped in, 'oh, by the way, Tagg, I'm carrying your baby.'"

"I…couldn't." She felt drained and exhausted. As if she'd been in a fistfight and had gotten worked over pretty good. Her body sagged in defeat. She had no energy for this battle. Not tonight. "I should have. I'm sorry."

"You deceived me. I've got to admit you sure had me fooled. I've never been this blindsided by anyone. Not even by your unprincipled father. But you," he said, jabbing his finger toward her, "you didn't feel any compunction about lying to me. You played me, Callie."

"Tagg, please—"

"Doesn't matter. None of it. Because I don't want my child

anywhere near Hawkins Sullivan. That man will have no influence over our baby. None."

"Why are you so angry at my father?"

"He's truly a bastard, Callie. I never knew how much until today."

Tagg picked up a large pebble and hurled it into the lake. The stone slid over the smooth water, dimpling the surface several times before making its descent. Both of them watched until the last wrinkle in the water smoothed out.

"He offered me the Bender contract, a multimillion-dollar deal he'd stolen right out from under me, if I'd give up all rights to the baby. He tried to bribe me to stay away from you and my child. Claimed he'd find you a suitable husband to marry."

Callie's mouth dropped open. A tiny moan of mortification slipped out. "Oh, no."

"Oh, yeah. It turns my stomach that he used an innocent child as a bargaining chip. My child. Did he really think I'd give up my own flesh and blood for a contract? He made it clear he doesn't want you to have anything to do with me."

Callie's stomach, already going through a war zone this week, turned over again. "Tagg, I didn't know he'd react this way."

"Like I said, it doesn't much matter, Callie. Because you're gonna marry me and I'm going to raise my child at Worth Ranch. The old man is out of luck."

He glared at her, defying her to refuse him.

Callie's heart took a tumble. As far as proposals went, it was just shy of horrible, but it was all she was going to get.

He rose up then and reached for her hands. He helped her to her feet, but when he let her go, her knees buckled and her head spun. "Oh, I'm not…"

Tagg scooped her up in his arms. She felt small and fragile…and safe. "Hold on to me, Callie."

That's what she intended to do.

He strode to the Jeep and gently lowered her into the cab. Once her seat belt was fastened, he leaned against the passenger door and met with her eyes. "What's your answer?"

Callie blinked, clearing her mind. Her answer? Did he think his demand of marriage warranted an answer? What were her choices? She loved him, but ultimately, this was about the baby and what was best for him or her. Tagg would be a loving father. The baby would have his name and his protection and after what her father proposed, Callie would never raise her child in the Sullivan household. Even if she wanted to, which she didn't, Tagg would never allow it. She had other options, she knew, but only one felt right. She made the decision that would change her life forever.

His lips tightened. "I'm waiting for your answer."

"Yes, Tagg. I'll marry you."

He nodded an acknowledgment. And shut her door.

It was hardly the way she'd imagined in her fantasy.

And maybe this time, the end didn't justify the means.

Tagg watched his brother Jackson get out of his sleek black car and stride over to the corral fence, dressed as if he'd just finished a photo shoot for some trendy magazine. The only thing that spelled cowboy on Jackson was his black felt hat and jewel-studded bolo tie. "You just come from a funeral or something?"

Jackson grinned wide, showing off a perfect smile that melted female hearts. "Just a regular workday, bro. I just finished up a meeting in town. Drove all this way because you needed to see me in person. So what's up?"

"Clay will be here shortly. It'll keep a few more minutes."

"Suit yourself." Jackson glanced in the pen and watched the mares. "You gonna breed them?"

"I'm hoping to." Tagg knew cattle ranching, but he loved horses. He'd like to breed a string of purebreds someday, but that was the furthest thing from his mind now. Last night, he'd mulled over different ways to tell his brothers about Callie, but in the end decided they needed to hear nothing but the truth.

A part of him didn't want them to judge Callie too harshly. He felt an uncanny need to protect her. She carried his child. And whether or not he liked it, Callie would become part of the family. After their talk last night, he'd driven her back to Big Hawk Ranch and told her that wasn't her home anymore. She'd be living on Worth Ranch as soon as they tied the knot. He wanted that wedding, sooner rather than later. Just to protect his child from Hawkins Sullivan. No telling what extremes her father would go to in order to win. This time, the old man wasn't getting what he wanted. Tagg would make sure of that.

Clay pulled his truck up to the house and parked. Tagg and Jackson strode in his direction, heading toward the house.

"Let's take this party inside." Tagg walked past Clay and opened the door for his brothers.

Tagg caught Clay and Jackson exchanging curious looks before entering. All three took their hats off and hooked them on a ledge Tagg had made special for the Worth boys, reminiscent of his father's hat rack back at the main house. Three hats, three brothers. Tagg wondered if another hook would have to be added soon, for his son.

Or maybe his daughter.

The thought made him smile for a brief second.

Until he thought about how his wife died. How he'd failed as a husband.

"Okay, I wasn't going to say it," Jackson stated, once he settled in a wing chair, "but you look like *you've* just come from a funeral. You got bad news, just say it. We lose another cattle deal or something?"

Clay took a seat as well and left Tagg standing over them. "Something."

His brothers glanced up and waited for more.

Tagg paced back and forth. He took a deep calming breath. "I'm getting married."

Both brothers rose from their seats.

"What?" Jackson and Clay said in unison.

"You heard me." Tagg glanced from one brother to another.

"I didn't know you were seeing anyone," Jackson said.

"I wasn't. I mean…it's Callie Sullivan. She's…we're having a baby."

Jackson smiled. "You don't say? You're gonna be a papa?" He walked over and shook his hand. "Congratulations."

"Thanks."

Clay appeared confused. "You went away with Callie last weekend. How did she get…uh, this is real quick, Tagg. And you weren't thrilled when she volunteered for Penny's Song. I recall you bawling me out."

"I know. Believe me, none of this was planned." Tagg explained the situation to his brothers, giving them the truth but leaving the details out. They didn't need to know specifics. But he made sure they knew about Hawkins Sullivan's proposition to buy him out of his child's life. He made sure his brothers knew that Sullivan was not to be trusted and why he felt he needed to rush into marriage with Callie.

"Congratulations, Tagg," Clay finally said, once he understood. "It's not ideal, but you're doing what's right. I'm behind you all the way. We'll make Callie feel welcome. She's having the first Worth heir. That's something to celebrate."

Tagg didn't feel like celebrating. He didn't trust The Hawk or his daughter. She'd been needlessly deceptive, in his opinion, but Tagg had no choice in the matter. For his baby's sake, he'd have to marry the enemy's daughter.

Six

One week later, Callie stood in Tagg's guest room staring into a cheval mirror. She wore her mother's wedding gown, a mermaid design of white lace and pearled sequins that hugged her body and flared out slightly below the knees. The dress fit her without exception and she sent up a prayer of thanks to her mother. She'd curled her hair and pinned it up. A few strands fell in wisps around her face. In place of a veil, she wore a narrow rhinestone and pearl headband.

"Cinderella has nothing on you," Sammie said, after she'd finished her primping.

"Well, I am getting the handsome cowboy prince, but I'm afraid that's where the fairy tale ends."

"Don't think that way. Tagg is lucky to be marrying you. You'll make a good wife, Callie. And a terrific mother. I just know you will."

Callie hugged her best friend tight. "Thank you for saying that. I really need you today."

"I wouldn't have missed it." Sammie's lilac satin dress rustled as they broke their embrace.

"You came all the way from Boston. I know you moved heaven and earth to get here yesterday. I can't tell you how much that means to me. Especially since I have no family here."

"What about Deanna and her family?"

Callie shook her head. "I couldn't ask them. It would be too…awkward, not having my father here. It's best to keep the wedding small. It's what Tagg wanted."

Sammie took her hand and squeezed. "I know that's rough. Even after all your father did, you'd still like to have him here."

"If things were different, of course I would. But he can't be reasoned with when it comes to the Worths. He went semiballistic when I told him I was marrying Tagg. We argued and he made threats and demands. I let him rant, but in the end nothing he could say or do would change my mind. I told him I loved him very much and I wished he would understand. I really hated to see him so upset, but I've never been angrier with him in my life for what he proposed to Tagg. I had to get out of there, so I moved into Red Ridge Inn."

"I'm sorry, Callie."

She shrugged. What could she do? Her father wasn't going to change. Most young girls dreamed of having their father walk them down the aisle on their wedding day, but Callie had resigned herself to this. Callie was furious with him for what he'd suggested to Tagg, but she had to keep his heart condition in mind. She knew moving off Big Hawk was the only way to keep some semblance of peace. If she stayed at home, her father wouldn't give it a rest. And he'd been stubborn enough not to go after her.

She squelched her sadness and focused on the good things in her life. She was marrying the man she loved. Her morning sickness had ebbed to bouts of infrequent queasiness and her baby was thriving and healthy. "I'll be okay. I've got you here."

"And I'm going to be the best darn maid of honor that walked the planet." She adjusted the sparkling headband on Callie's head. "You can count on me."

Callie smiled and moisture reached her eyes. "I know I can. I couldn't do this without you."

"Don't you dare spill those tears. You'll smudge my expert makeup job."

Callie straightened and set her shoulders. "You're right. No tears. This is my wedding day."

"That's my girl."

Someone knocked on the door. "You ladies ready?"

"That's Jackson," Callie said, gesturing for Sammie to open the door.

"If he's half as handsome as your fiancé, I'll faint." She feigned a swoon, buckling her knees and throwing her hand across her forehead.

Sammie opened the door to Jackson's back. When he turned to face her, dressed in a black tux and spit-shined boots, all silliness drained from her face. They stared at each other a second without saying a word, then Sammie shot Callie a you've-got-to-be-kidding look. Callie laughed. "Jackson Worth, I'd like you to meet my best friend, Sammie. She flew in from Boston to be here."

Jackson smiled his deadly smile. "Nice to meet you, Sammie."

"Same here." To anyone who didn't know her, Sammie's

expression would appear flawless, but Callie recognized her friend's body language. She was completely bowled over.

Jackson came to stand in front of her. "You look beautiful, Callie."

Callie spun around and curtsied. "Thank you, sir."

He laughed and his eyes twinkled. For some reason, she felt comfortable with Jackson. He had a winning personality and a great sense of humor. She'd come to know him a little from working at Penny's Song. Of the three brothers, Jackson put her the most at ease.

"Tagg is one lucky guy."

"Thanks for saying that, but we both know why we're getting married."

Jackson studied her. "Answer this for me, where did he propose to you?"

Callie glanced at Sammie, and her friend gave her an encouraging nod. "Not that it was much of a proposal—"

"More like a demand?" he interrupted.

She nodded.

"That's Tagg for you. Okay, where?"

"He drove me to Elizabeth Lake, to talk."

Jackson grinned. "And he asked you there?"

"Yes, but it's—"

"It's where every single one of the Worth men has proposed to his wife since my great-great-great-granddaddy's day. Chance Worth named the lake after his wife Lizzie back in the 1800s."

Callie's mouth dropped open. "Really?"

He smiled. "I wouldn't lie to you. Now, are you ready, ladies?"

He moved between them and offered each woman an arm. With Sammie on the right, Callie on the left, handsome, charming Jackson Worth proceeded to escort them to the top of a hilly rise that offered a panoramic view of the Red Ridge Mountains.

Where Taggart Worth and Callie Sullivan would exchange their vows.

"Here comes your bride," Clay said from his place beside the minister.

Tagg stopped pacing the hilltop and cursed under his breath when he spotted Callie walking toward him, holding one long-stemmed calla lily. He barely noticed her friend Sammie or his brother Jackson; his gaze was focused solely on his soon-to-be wife.

Tagg shuddered at the thought. He never thought he'd be in this position. He'd vowed to never marry again. Yet circumstances couldn't be ignored. He'd gotten Callie pregnant and he was doing the right thing.

"She looks pretty," Clay said, once Tagg took his place next to the minister.

Tagg had insisted on a quiet ceremony with only family and a few close friends in attendance. The hilly rise beyond his home had long been his favorite retreat, a place to come to gather his thoughts and stare out at the stunning Red Ridge vista.

Now, he stared at another stunning vision—Callie. She looked beyond pretty, but he wouldn't correct Clay.

Jackson stopped to give her a kiss on the cheek. Her friend did the same, then they left her side to come and stand beside Pastor McAdams.

Jed strummed the guitar with an acoustic version of "Here Comes the Bride."

Callie stood alone now, staring at Tagg, her hands trembling, her caramel eyes nearly liquid with unshed tears. She took the steps necessary to reach him, her smile tentative.

For a split second, Tagg thought he should have given her a proper wedding with vows spoken in a church and then had a reception with all their family and friends present.

A mental battle raged inside his head and finally he let go of his anger to savor the moment. Callie would be his wife now, and he couldn't deny his attraction to her. He relished the thought of making love to her at night and waking up with her every morning. She carried their unborn infant. She would help him raise the child on his land and he or she would become the first Worth heir. He had to respect that, and Callie for bearing his child. He hung on to that thought when he took her hand in his and faced the minister.

They spoke their vows quietly, and Tagg felt a stirring in his heart. He didn't take marriage lightly, and this ceremony meant something to him. Despite his anger at Callie and his disgust at her father, he was going to try to make this marriage work. His child deserved as much.

"I now pronounce you man and wife." On the minister's bidding, he faced his new wife and lifted her chin to brush a soft kiss to her lips. She responded with a little purr of pleasure that seared him like a hot poker. His new wife could easily get under his skin if he wasn't careful.

"Ladies and gentleman, let me introduce you to Mr. and Mrs. Taggart Worth," the pastor said, his voice jubilant.

The guests in attendance whooped and applauded, his brothers the loudest of all. It annoyed him how his brothers accepted Callie into the family without qualm.

The fact remained, Tagg had married Hawkins Sullivan's daughter.

He was her husband now. She'd move into the house he'd built as a widower, the house that had granted him solitude. It had been just him and his horses up until now, but Callie would soon change that. She would disrupt his quiet life.

Hell, from the moment she'd approached him in Reno, she'd disrupted his life.

"Congratulations, Tagg," Jed said, offering his hand.

"Thanks." Tagg shook his hand.

Jed stared at him, then peered at Callie, who stood just a few feet away, garnering hugs and kisses from every man in attendance. "She's something."

Tagg didn't disagree as he watched her gracious smiles and heard her heartwarming laughter.

After all was said and done, the wedding party moved down the hill to feast on a sumptuous dinner at the main house upon Clay and Jackson's insistence. Sammie sat between his brothers and was thus occupied while Jed and the minister struck up a conversation along with the other guests.

Tagg and Callie sat at the head of the long linen-draped table. Tagg's appetite hadn't waned. He was famished and ready to consume a good hearty meal. He'd been served a good portion of braised beef, roasted potatoes and asparagus tips topped off with home-baked bread that had his mouth watering. After taking a few bites, he glanced at Callie's full plate. She hadn't touched a bite.

"You're not eating?"

She shook her head.

"Not hungry?"

"No. I…can't eat, right now."

Her face, so bright and vibrant during the ceremony, appeared pale under the glow of candlelight.

Tagg put his fork down. "Are you going to be sick?"

Her hand cradled her stomach. "I'm trying not to be." She peered into his eyes. "I don't want to be. Not on our wedding day."

"Can you control those things?"

"Not usually. The queasiness comes and goes. And it's coming now, but I can deal with it." She sent him a quick encouraging smile that didn't fool him. He could see her struggling to keep up appearances.

He rose and took Callie's hand. "We're going to have to say good-night to you all. But please, stay and finish the meal. You'll kick yourself in the behind if you miss the dessert."

Everyone laughed. He glanced at his brothers. "Thanks for all you've done today. It's time we went home."

Home.

Even as he said the words, they sounded surreal in his mind.

Callie rose from her seat and he tightened his grip on her. Wouldn't do for the bride to keel over in front of their guests.

"Yes, thank you all for coming. It was wonderful to have you here. Clay and Jackson, the ceremony, the dinner, everything was more than I could've hoped for."

"You're expectations are kinda low, Callie," Jackson said with a devilish grin.

"Yeah, you married our brother." Clay winked at her.

Tagg didn't comment. Normally, he wouldn't let his brothers get the best of him, but today wasn't a normal day. Today, he had a wife and baby to think about and right now, getting Callie away from here was his first priority.

He kept close to her as they said their goodbyes with another round of embraces and handshakes. Callie told Sammie she'd see her tomorrow and Tagg thanked the minister one more time.

Once they were out of the house, Tagg put a hand to her back and guided her to the car. "The fresh air's got to help, right?"

Callie nodded. "Yes. Sometimes it does, but…right now I'm still feeling…queasy."

Queasy. That wasn't a good word. It was neither here nor there, sort of like being in limbo. Tagg figured he couldn't much stop nature from calling if necessary. But he'd do what he could to make Callie comfortable. "Then let's get you home."

Callie's stomach twisted and turned. Part of the problem was her pregnancy but the other part was her situation with Tagg. Her nerves rattled and worry lines dug their way through her twenty-something forehead. She'd vowed before God to be a good wife and she fully intended to be, but her fears stemmed from thinking that Tagg would never love her. He was a widower, a man who'd married and lost, in death, the love of his life. He'd been shattered when Heather died. Did he still love her? How could Callie compete with the haunting memories of his first wife?

Tagg stopped the car in front of his ranch house and turned to her with concern in his eyes. He was so drop-dead handsome, Callie wanted to cry. He'd taken his tux jacket off, loosened his bolo tie and unfastened the top buttons of his shirt. She couldn't take her eyes off his throat and the scattered hairs peeking out from his collar.

Moonlight streamed in through the window. The familiar scents of horses and cool earth filled the air. He spoke quietly in the intimate confines of the car. "We're home, Callie."

She looked into his eyes and wanted to tell him once again that she hadn't planned for any of this to happen, but she lost her nerve. She didn't want to mar the day with accusations and denials. Tagg had been cordial today, his usual anger toward her gone. Maybe things would get better.

"This is not what either of us wanted," he began. "But I'm gonna try, Callie. That's the best I can offer you."

He was going to try? To do what? Tolerate her? Live with her? Was the thought of having her as his wife so unpalatable that he had to force himself to *try?* Callie's heart bottomed out then. His big confession hurt her on so many levels, her stomach squeezed tight.

Her hand covered her belly to ward off the pain. She felt faint.

Tagg was out of the car in no time, opening her door and lifting her into his arms. He strode with stealthy steps to the front door and kicked it open. "Hang on," he said as he carried her over the threshold.

Callie savored the moment, even in her despair, as her husband brought her inside his home. He lowered her down and she clung on, fearful to let go. "Lean on me, Callie." And when she did, he cradled her in his arms and held her very still. "Let me know when, if, you need to—"

"I'm feeling better now, Tagg."

"Are you sure?" He pulled back from her a little to gaze into her eyes. "You're not queasy anymore?"

"No, not at the moment. Just a little tired."

"It's been a long day."

"You carried me over the threshold." She smiled.

Tagg looked back at the opened door and then moved to shut it, a slow smile emerging on his face as well. "I guess I did."

And he had proposed to her in the place where all Worth men proposed to their wives. That had to mean something. Or was Callie grabbing at straws?

She continued to smile at him while she removed the rhinestone headband from her hair. "Oh, that feels better."

She shook her hair loose and the curls fell down onto her shoulders.

Tagg's gaze lifted to her hair. She witnessed him take a deep breath. "You should get to bed."

She arched her brow. "What about you?"

"I'll come to bed later. You go on. Get acquainted with things around here. I'll bring your bags into my room."

"But they're already in the guest room. Sammie and I brought them over earlier today."

Tagg strode past her and moved down a long hallway. He walked into the guest room and Callie followed him. "You unpacked in here?" He whirled around on her, his face unreadable.

"Well, I wasn't sure… I mean, under the circumstances, I didn't know what to expect—"

Tagg leveled his gaze on her. "You're sleeping with me, Callie. In my room. Every night."

Was this his way of *trying?* She didn't know what to think, but she darn well knew she didn't like his demanding tone. Whether she slept with him or not was her decision to make. But who was she kidding? She wanted to sleep with him. In his room. Every night. She'd prayed he would want her, hoping beyond hope that he wouldn't banish her to his guest room. "Is that an order?"

Tagg's face contorted and he truly looked puzzled. "What?"

"I mean, I'm your wife now, Tagg. You can't order me around like an employee or something."

Tagg took a measured breath. "Exactly. You're my wife now. And wives sleep with their husbands. At least Worth wives sleep with their husbands. So that's how it's going to be."

"Ordering again." Callie stood her ground, hoping she wasn't pushing her luck.

Tagg's silver-blue eyes narrowed on her. "Turn around."

"What?"

He repeated with practiced patience, his voice softer now, coaxing, "Turn around."

"Why?"

"Just do it. Trust me."

Trust him? That was never an issue. She did trust him. She met his eyes one last time before she slowly turned her back on him.

He stepped closer, his warm breath on her shoulders. He whispered, "You'd never get yourself out of this dress alone."

She felt the material of her gown shift and then part as Tagg unfastened one pearl button after another at the back of her dress. His fingers slid over her skin and tiny pinpricks of pleasure tingled throughout her body. His presence behind her gave her a thrill; the slip of his finger down her back excited her even more. She breathed in his earthy scent as she held her dress to keep it from falling.

"Let it go, Callie," he said softly.

And Callie allowed her mother's wedding gown to slip from her hands and puddle in a luxurious silk mess at her feet.

Sorry, Mama.

She stepped out of her dress and turned to face Tagg wearing only a pure white pair of silk panties.

Tagg looked his fill, his gaze roaming over her near-naked body with hot hungry eyes. "You're going to be the death of me, Callie Sullivan."

"Callie Worth," she corrected.

Tagg raised a brow, then swung her up into his arms. Her

arms automatically circled his neck. "Oh!" She hadn't seen that coming. "I should be used to this by now. Big man. Carry woman."

Tagg laughed and strode to the master bedroom. Faint hallway light guided their way and once they reached his room, she glanced down at his massive bed. He pulled the deep blue covers back and lowered her down until her head hit the pillow and her body dented the firm mattress slightly. "Get some sleep, Callie. It's been quite a day."

Callie grabbed the coverlet and pulled it up to her neck, shielding her body from view. The rejection she should have felt was overcome by something else—the comfort of Tagg's big bed. It drew her down with cushiony softness and she felt every single one of her muscles relax. "Are you coming?" she asked, as she felt the fingers of fatigue pull at her.

"Later."

"Uh-hmm," she muttered, faintly hearing Tagg's retreating footsteps right before she entered into a deep, deep sleep.

Sunshine poured into the room and heated Callie's face. She rebelled against the light, refusing to open her eyes. She gave her pillow a soft punch and bunched it under her head, enjoying the first waking minutes in the most heavenly bed she'd ever slept in. She lay there for long moments wishing she could sleep away the entire day. It was the best sleep she'd had in months.

Her eyes snapped open.

She'd married Taggart Worth yesterday.

Then memories flooded in and she turned to the other side of the bed. Tagg was gone. But the indent in his pillow and tangled sheets told her they had spent their wedding night together. Just not together in the way a normal couple would have spent their first night as husband and wife.

Callie hinged her body forward and sat up. Her stomach seemed happy this morning, no queasiness to speak of, so that in itself made it a good day. She swung her legs around and planted them on the wood floor. She'd never really gotten a good look at Tagg's room last night. It was spacious with tall walls and thick wood beams connecting with the ceiling. The bed took up half the space and what there was of furniture was equally large. A chest of drawers, two night tables and a wide-screen television made up the decor. The room was distinctly masculine with dark wood tones and light coffee-colored, textured walls. An archway inside the room led to two walk-in closets and a dressing area outside the bathroom.

Callie rose from the bed and walked over to one of the closets where Tagg had set her bags down. He must have repacked her suitcases and moved her things from the guest room into his room this morning. Or maybe he'd done it last night while she'd slept.

Staring down at her bags, she thought about how she'd left Big Hawk Ranch. And her father. It had been the best way to handle the situation and not give him an outlet for his tantrum. With her gone, his ranting would cease and, hopefully, he wouldn't end up in the hospital with heart palpitations. It hadn't been easy for Callie, but she'd stood her ground against her formidable father.

Her father was alone now. It was his own doing, she reminded herself. He'd manipulated her one too many times. But that didn't stop her from loving him or from worrying about his health.

The Brooks & Dunn tune "Cowgirls Don't Cry" blasted from her handbag on the floor of the closet. Callie sighed with heaviness in her heart as the ringtone went on. She knew who was calling and finally decided to pick up her phone. One quick look at the screen confirmed that it was her father.

He'd already left her three messages on her voice mail.

"How dare you walk out on me!" had been the gist of the first one on the night she'd left home.

"You're gonna regret marrying a Worth" had been the second pearl of wisdom she'd received while at the hotel room.

"Callie, you ungrateful child. You call me, right this instant" had been his message on his third and final call before her wedding.

Callie stared at the phone ringing in her hand. She couldn't bring herself to answer the call. She couldn't talk to her father. Not yet. She had a husband now and a baby to nurture, and that would take all her concentration today.

But once the phone stopped ringing, Callie felt a measure of guilt. Maybe her father needed her. Maybe he'd taken ill. Tears welled up and her chest grew tight with regret. Why couldn't she have an ordinary, regular, everyday kind of relationship with her father like other girls had? Why couldn't her father's love have manifested in ways that supported her instead of tearing her in two? Why were things always so hard with him? Callie knew better, but she had to hear her father's message. She had to know he was all right. She punched a button on her phone and listened to the voice mail he'd just left her.

"Callie, honey. You looked so beautiful in your mama's wedding dress. I watched you from a distance. I saw you speak your vows. Seems one of those damn Worths has some compassion, after all. One of them let a daddy watch his little girl walk down the wedding aisle."

"Oh, Daddy," she whispered.

Her body shook. Tears spilled down her cheeks as she realized her father had been there. He'd witnessed her marriage to Tagg. Callie sunk down to the ground in a heap of emotion as she listened to her father's parting words. "You know I love you, Callie, but nothing's changed. You shouldn't have married into that family. Soon as you come to your senses, you come on home."

Callie had been brokenhearted when she'd put on her mother's gown, realizing that her father wouldn't see her wearing it. He wouldn't guide her down the aisle, head held high and proud as he handed her over to her would-be husband with his blessing. Secretly, she'd hoped her father would soften to the idea. Secretly, she'd hoped he'd come around and accept her decision to marry. He'd seen her get married, but it hadn't mattered. Hawkins Sullivan was too stubborn and prideful to let her have a blissful wedding day. His hatred of the Worths ran that deep.

Her heart breaking, she sobbed and sobbed right there on the hardwood floor until her tears dried up. Long minutes passed as she sat like a statue, trying to compose herself, trying to block out the words that tore at her heart.

One of them let a daddy watch his little girl walk down the wedding aisle.

Someone stuck his neck out for her father and had risked Tagg's ire. Had it been Clay, who seemed levelheaded and decent. Or maybe it was Jackson? His actions didn't seem to fit into political correctness—he seemed to do what he wanted, damning the consequences. But whoever it was, Callie would be eternally grateful. At least she'd had that much.

When she heard Tagg's boots slide across the hardwood floor in the hallway, Callie jumped up and ran straight into the bathroom, closing the door and locking it. She turned the spigot in the shower on and as she waited behind the bathroom door, she glimpsed her reflection in the mirror. Big mistake. She groaned silently. She was a total mess. Her eyes were swollen. Her face was beet red and her nose beamed brighter than a spunky reindeer on Christmas Eve.

Callie cringed when she saw the doorknob twisting. "Callie?" Tagg called from behind the door.

She bit her lip. She didn't dare answer. She couldn't let him see her like this. He'd ask her what was wrong and she couldn't tell him the truth. That her father had been on Worth land, *his* land, yesterday and witnessed their marriage. Callie didn't want to start her married life by lying to her husband. So she let him think she was showering.

And to make her lie less culpable, she removed her clothes and, quiet as a mouse, opened the shower door again and got inside.

Half an hour later, after a good hot rinse and a cleansing of her soul, Callie felt much better as she strode into Tagg's kitchen and found him at the table drinking a cup of coffee.

"Morning," he said, looking up from the newspaper. "You sleep okay?"

"Yes, I did. Your bed is pure heaven."

He smiled. "Glad you got some rest. Help yourself." He pointed to the coffeepot.

"Oh, um, I can't have leaded coffee. It's not good for the baby."

Tagg folded the newspaper and peered at her. "Guess I've got a lot to learn about babies." He glanced at her belly, still flat in her jeans.

"We both do. I guess…we'll learn together."

He nodded and the conversation died.

"Uh, I'll make breakfast. What would you like?" Callie walked to the refrigerator to see what Tagg had on hand. To her surprise, the refrigerator was well stocked. "Looks like there's eggs, bacon, bread, veggies, pancake mix, milk, juice.

I'm impressed. Most guys don't have anything but beer and jam in their refrigerators."

Tagg eyed her. "I'm not 'most guys.'"

No, he wasn't. That was an understatement.

"And Clay's housekeeper, Helen, does my shopping for me once a week."

"Oh, okay." That explained the cream cheese and bagels, cupcakes and five-pound bags of sugar and flour. "Well, what can I make you?"

Tagg stared at her for a moment as if she was invading his territory. Which in essence, she was. He clearly didn't want her here. "Toast is fine. Thank you."

"Just toast?"

He nodded.

"I can manage that." But Callie felt awkward in his home and so out of place that she burned the toast on the first try. Ultimately, she managed to butter two pieces on the second try and slide them onto a plate. "Here you go."

"You eating?" he asked.

"Uh, yes. I think I'll have the same."

She sat with him and they ate in silence, Tagg having a second cup of coffee and Callie nibbling on her too-light-to-be-considered-toast bread. The toaster definitely had issues about evenness in heating, but the rest of the good-size kitchen was state of the art, with black granite countertops, stainless steel appliances, a wide double-door refrigerator and cognac-colored wood cabinets. The home was modest in size for the Worths' millions, with its four bedrooms, a study and game room to go along with a parlor and dining room. Callie liked that it wasn't palatial like her father's house at Big Hawk Ranch. Nor was it modern rustic, like the main house that Clay lived in. For Callie, Tagg's house was just the right size to make it a home.

"What are your plans today?" Tagg asked. He rose from his seat to splash the remaining coffee into the sink. Then he leaned against the counter and braced his hands behind him on the edge.

Callie was caught by surprise. Most newly married couples would be on their honeymoon by now without a plan or care in the world but to be with each other. She could only hope Tagg had something wonderful up his sleeve for them to do today. "Why, what did you have in mind?"

He stared at her and scratched at the day-old stubble on his jaw. Tagg's morning look, with rumpled hair and a scratchy beard, made her heart twist with desire. "Sorry, but I've got work to catch up on in the office."

"Okay," she said, her rising hopes vanquished. "In that case, then I'd like to spend some time with Sammie before she leaves the ranch."

"Fine. Well then, have a nice day with your friend. I'll see you later."

With that, Tagg left the kitchen and walked out the side door that led to the office attached to the house.

Callie closed her eyes. "O-kay." So that's how he was going to treat her, with measured tolerance and sickening politeness. Was that Tagg *trying*?

Callie left the kitchen and headed for her phone. She needed to see Sammie to say goodbye to her good friend, but first she had to call her father back.

Too bad neither of those two options would grant her any peace.

Callie's emotions lifted and dipped as the day forged on. She drove to Clay's home later that morning where she had lunch with Sammie. They sat outside on the Worths' covered veranda overlooking miles and miles of grazing land. Close to the house, an enormous pool with a rock waterfall and stone decking that could accommodate at least a hundred people ate up the width behind the long ranch house. The grounds surrounding the backyard were meticulously groomed and edged with an array of colorful pansies, white lilies and baby roses.

Sammie seemed unusually quiet. They both had a lot on their minds.

"I wish you could stay longer, Sam."

"I wish I could, too, but I'm just in the way here. You've got a new husband and I've got a lot of work to do when I get back."

"You could never be in the way, so don't even say that. Clay likes having you here as much as I do." Callie bit down on her lower lip to hold back tears. She'd already cried enough for one day. "I don't think I could have done this without you. Having you here meant everything to me."

Sammie took her hand and squeezed. "I know these are unusual circumstances, but you're married to a good man and you'll be a great wife. And remember, I'm coming back when the little one is born."

"You better! You're the godmother." She smiled but sadness gripped her heart. Callie's lips trembled. "I'm going to miss you, Sammie."

Sammie leaned over the untouched salad plates and looped her arms around Callie's shoulders. "It's all going to work out. I just know it."

"I hope you're right." They broke their embrace and Callie ducked her head when she gave her confession. "I called my father this morning. I know, I know. I said I wasn't going to for a while. But he left me quite a few messages. I couldn't ignore him."

Sammie's expression softened even more. "I know he's a hard man. But he's your father. Did you have a good talk?"

Callie thought about their conversation. She knew her father had tried to be civil, but he couldn't help being The Hawk. He'd given her a lecture and demanded that she come see him. "It was brief. I can't shut him out of my life, Sammie. But he'd almost destroyed everything with Tagg. And it's not just about me anymore. I have to protect our baby, too. We're going to be a family and I can't be torn in half anymore. I told Daddy that. He has to accept my decision and support me."

"I imagine that didn't set well with him."

"You imagine right." Callie cracked a smile then and Sammie laughed. They shared a light moment and it felt good to be able to smile about something.

Callie glanced at her watch. "Well, I hate to say it, but if we don't leave now, you'll miss your flight."

"You don't have to drive me, Callie, but you're a doll for offering. Jackson is having a car pick me up."

"Jackson, huh? You two were getting friendly last night at dinner."

Sammie shrugged. "He was being cordial since I didn't know anyone at the wedding but you. I think he took pity on me."

Callie laughed. "Jackson? Take pity? No, if he paid attention to you, it was because he liked you."

"So, what's his story anyway?" Sammie asked in a casual tone, yet Callie got the impression her friend was more than mildly interested in her answer.

"Well, all I know is that he runs Worth Enterprises from offices in Prescott and Phoenix. He keeps his private life private, but I know that he was in love with someone and she broke his heart."

Sammie nodded and then sighed with understanding as

if Callie's reply made all the sense in the world. "Well, you married into a good family. The Worth men are worthy." She grinned. "I should get so lucky."

"You will, one day," Callie said, more sure of that than of her own marital situation at the moment.

When the car arrived to take her friend to the airport, it was hard for Callie to say goodbye. Sammie had been her support, her rock of stability and sanity when Callie had had doubts. She'd given her encouragement over the past three days. Though they'd both promised not to, their farewell was wrought with numerous hugs and mutual tears.

Callie left the main house and decided to head home—it would take some time to get used to calling Tagg's ranch house her home—but she needed to get settled. She had yet to fully unpack. Then there was the matter of getting the rest of her things from her father's house.

Baby steps, Callie.

She'd deal with her father some other time.

As she pulled up to the house, she noted Tagg walking out of the stable, leading one of his prized mares by the reins, his black Stetson tossed over the saddle horn. She walked toward him as he readied the horse, adjusting the saddle cinches.

"Hi," she said. "How was your day?"

"Busy. Not too bad, though. I usually break up the day with a ride."

"Oh?" Callie would love to join him. She knew his horses needed exercise daily. She waited for an invitation that never came.

"Did you spend time with your friend?" he asked, straightening the bridle. It was obviously a chore for him to make conversation with her, but she wouldn't let that deter her.

"Yes. We had lunch at the main house. It was good of her to come to the wedding. I don't know how I would—"

Tagg shot her a look, his silvery eyes piercing.

Never mind, she thought. She shrugged it off. "Sammie's on her way to the airport. So I thought I'd come back and unpack my things."

"Sounds like a good idea." Tagg grabbed his hat from the saddle and plunked it on his head. She'd always loved how his hair fanned out from underneath his hat. It brushed the collar of his shirt.

"I don't know all the names of your horses," she said.

Tagg put his boot in the stirrup and swung his leg wide, mounting the mare. "This is Starlight."

The mare's black coat was marred by one star-shaped white marking on her forehead. "Hi, Starlight," she said, stroking her mane. "You're going to have a good ride, I just know it."

The mare turned to give her a look then faced the pasture ahead.

"We always do." Sitting atop the mare now, Tagg put his sunglasses on. A cowboy in Ray-Bans.

She nodded. "After I get settled, I might go over to Penny's Song for an hour or two. See if I can lend a hand, but I'll be back for dinner."

Tagg smiled. "I'll look forward to it. See you later, Callie."

"Okay." She watched him ride off until he disappeared from her view.

And she felt more alone now than at any other time in her life.

That afternoon, Callie finished unpacking, filling just half of the dual walk-in closet with her clothes and shoes. She set her toiletries in the bathroom on the large marble countertop that, since it had been cleared off, seemed designated as her side. Perfumes, body lotion and hair mousse filled the space now.

Tagg liked to keep things orderly. Everything in the house was clean and free of clutter. He'd been alone in this house for four years and now Callie was here, tilting his perfect world and setting it on edge.

She arranged everything as neatly as she could, so as not to infringe on his goodwill too heavily. The last item she set out was her toothbrush. She plopped it into the holder right next to his. She liked seeing those toothbrushes together. It gave her a certain sense of belonging, as if to say, I'm here. I'm your wife now. Deal with it.

Callie smiled and walked into the bedroom. The comfortable bed beckoned and the temptation was too great to ignore. Newly pregnant women had a right to nap in the middle of the day, didn't they? She pulled the covers back, took off her jeans and climbed in, changing her mind about work at Penny's Song today.

It wasn't too long before sleep claimed her.

Half an hour later as she mildly dozed, she heard the back door open and then shut. Tagg's footsteps resounded louder and louder as he made his way down the hallway. When she heard him stop, she opened her eyes partway to find him standing in the doorway with a tentative look on his face. His shirt and boots were off. He probably left them in the mudroom at the back of the house.

"I'm not sleeping," she said.

"Looks like you were. Did I wake you?"

"No. I'm just taking a rest. This bed is too comfortable." She noticed his muddy jeans. "What happened to you?"

"Starlight decided she wanted to swim. There's a stream about two miles out she likes to tap-dance in. Guess we both got carried away. She got her bath. Now I need mine."

Callie smiled. "Have at it. Don't let me disturb you."

He glanced at her and nodded, then strode the rest of the

way into the room. Without qualm, he sat down on his side of the bed and removed his jeans and boxers. "Go back to sleep. I'll be quiet."

Callie gulped oxygen, gazing at the smooth tanned skin on his back. She itched to touch him there, to run her hands along his broad shoulders and slide them down to his trim waist. When he rose, she watched him move through the room, buck naked. Every lazy muscle in her body jumped up in jubilation and she was consumed with raw overpowering lust.

Tagg entered the master bath and she heard him turn on the shower. She lay on her bed imagining him with water raining down, his body slick with soap. "Yummo," she whispered.

And then she was out of the bed, shedding her blouse as she entered the bathroom before good sense stopped her. On a deep breath and a wave of insanity, she opened the shower door. If she was going to tilt his world on edge, she might as well enjoy the process.

She met Tagg's eyes. A look of confusion crossed his features. He was wet and soapy from head to toe.

"I'm feeling a little grimy." It was her lame explanation.

He stared at her in her bra and panties. Then he pointed with his finger. "You coming in with those on?" he asked.

It was all the encouragement she needed. She shook her head and unfastened her bra, releasing her swollen breasts from their restraints. Tagg looked on as hot moist steam filled the room. Next, she bent to pull her panties down and when she came up, Tagg's arm shot out and she found herself being yanked into the shower stall. "You know how this is going to end up?" Tagg asked, his voice a low growl. He pressed her against the cool marble wall and trapped her with his arms by the sides of her head.

"We'll save on the water bill?"

Tagg grinned. "That, too."

And then he kissed her—a serious kiss that told her all games were over. Tagg pressed his hips to hers and she closed her eyes. He was hard already and wanting her. She couldn't think of anything she craved more than being with Tagg in this moment. She wrapped her arms around his neck and kissed him back, licking at his lips and mating with his tongue, the shower stall a thick cloak of steam.

Tagg bent down and spread her legs, holding her thighs in his grip. He brought her to instant climax with slick moist strokes of his tongue. Her legs nearly gave way from the sharp, powerful contractions that racked her body. Her immediate orgasm brought him up, his erection pressing against her belly, demanding release.

He lifted her body and set her down on his thick shaft, impaling her with a fluid thrust that had them both raising their voices, their cries echoing against the walls.

"So good, Callie," Tagg uttered, his strength bringing her down onto him again and again. Her hips gyrated in his rhythm. She pushed when he pulled and she wrought out every thrust, every inch of him, straining to give him everything she had.

The release shattered them both, the pleasure unmatched.

They stayed entwined until their breathing steadied. Tagg shut off the spigot and the rain stopped. He spun her around to hold her against him. She leaned back into his chest and let his strength keep her upright.

He caressed her breasts and kissed her throat from behind, his nose nuzzling her dripping hair. "Thank you."

She smiled. She should be thanking him. She'd never known sex could be like this. That love had something to do with it, at least on her part, heightened the feelings, the emotions and the pleasure all at the same time.

She knew Tagg didn't love her. But they'd consummated their marriage today and Callie felt glorious about that.

"You're welcome," she whispered.

"It was hard keeping away from you."

His confession brought mixed emotions. He didn't want her here. Didn't want to be married. Worst of all, he didn't trust her. But they had this…and maybe they could build from here. "Then don't keep away, Tagg."

Seven

Callie spent her days working at Penny's Song, putting the finishing touches on the bunkhouse with a few items that would remind the children of home. She had photo frames set up on each of the side tables for them to add a picture of their family or a special friend to keep them company during their one-week stay. Small compact alarm clocks shared the table space. The children would have to set them at night so they wouldn't be late for the breakfast call in the morning.

She kept thinking of how to occupy the children's time in the most beneficial ways possible. She set up a library area in the far end of the bunkhouse and was in the process of collecting books that would be of interest for the appropriate age range. She'd kept busy this past week, finding and buying books to add to the library's collection. She'd stocked fun, light stories and songbooks for the younger children, teenage novels for the ones a little older. For all, she'd supplied an array of books on horses, cattle and ranching.

Setting up the general store gave her the most joy. She'd written up a list of daily chores the children would have to accomplish in order to earn tokens toward something they wanted to buy. For some who'd been ill a good deal of their life, this would be their first paying "job" and a positive motivation after their arduous recovery.

She'd had the list printed professionally in Stagecoach font on yellowed parchment paper and had burned the edges with a match to attain a true rustic look. Just minutes ago, she'd taped it to the front window. She stood back a few feet to admire it.

"Mucking the stalls is only worth ten tokens?" Tagg came up from behind and startled her. She jumped at the sound of his voice and he laughed, wrapping his arms around her waist to brace her. He tucked his head on her shoulder as he read the list. "That's a mighty gruesome job. Should be worth at least twenty-five."

Callie leaned against him and smiled. It wasn't often Tagg got this close. He'd been trying, she knew, but he still kept his distance during the day. He still took solitary rides every afternoon. He worked long hours in his office, and she often wondered if she was the reason he stayed away every evening until just before dinner. Their meals were usually quiet, quick affairs with Tagg offering to help with cleanup.

She'd been married to Tagg one week now and while she would like to have seen more progress during the days, she had nothing to complain about during their nights. Tagg made love to her as if every time were their first time. And if Callie was too exhausted or had a bout of queasiness, he would simply hold her in his arms, making her feel safe and cared for before she fell asleep, like a regular, newly married bride.

"Are you doubting my pricing skills?"

She turned to face him, meeting his unique silver-blue eyes. She'd seen those eyes darken with desire and light with amusement. She'd seen fury in those eyes, too, when aimed at her, but each time she peered at him, no matter the mood or circumstance, her heart did a little flip.

"No, ma'am, only saying I remember mucking stalls as a boy. My father made all us boys do every one of the chores on the ranch. Didn't matter to him that we were Worths, we all pulled our weight. Made his employees respect his work ethic even more."

"I never got away with skipping it, either. The Hawk insisted that I do it if I was going to be a rancher one day. My daddy—"

Tagg's smile disappeared. He let go of her and she felt his absence both physically and mentally.

They stared at each other. "Sorry, Tagg. But he's my father. I can't ignore that."

Tagg backed away and nodded. "No, you can't. But neither can I and I can't pretend otherwise."

Callie stood facing him, her emotions in turmoil. She'd been happy moments ago when Tagg had actually acted like a husband to her. He'd seemed genuinely glad to see her, but the moment was lost when she mentioned her father's name. "I'm not asking you to do that. Just judge me for myself."

"You lied to me, Callie."

"I didn't lie. I just didn't jump at the first chance I had to announce my pregnancy to a man who'd told me that being with me had been a big fat mistake."

"You got pregnant that night."

"It takes two to make a baby."

"I'm not sure it wasn't deliberate on your part."

She didn't know how to make Tagg see the truth. He had a stubborn streak for one and her father's unscrupulous proposition hadn't helped her cause. Tagg believed the apple didn't fall far from the tree. But in her case, it did. It had fallen miles and miles away.

She planted her hands on her hips, fighting not only for herself but for the family they would become soon. "Tagg, look at me. Really, really look at me. Do you think I'd do that? Do you think I would use an innocent baby to get revenge on my father? Granted, I was really angry with him at that time, but I'd never do anything that hurtful just to prove a point. And I think you know that about me. I think deep down, you know the truth."

Tagg set his jaw and looked away. She watched him take a deep breath, his expression tight. Finally, he turned to face her again. "Maybe I'm beginning to. I want us to move forward from now on, Callie."

"I do, too."

He gestured toward the stables. "The horses arrived from the Cosgroves in Vegas. They're unloading them now. I thought you'd like to see them."

"I would."

"Okay, then let's take a look together." He reached for her hand and she took it as they headed that way.

The simple gesture touched a raw nerve and tears welled up. Maybe Tagg was really trying and maybe this was harder on him than she realized. Not only had he not wanted marriage, a baby or a family life, but she suspected he was dealing with something that plagued him much worse than losing a big cattle deal to her father. Something that had to do with his love for his first wife.

Tagg stood in the doorway watching Callie fuss around the kitchen, whipping up potatoes in a bowl and baking chicken for the dinner meal. She seemed comfortable in her surroundings, as if she belonged here and didn't mind his unadorned lifestyle. He had more money than he'd ever need, but he was the one Worth who didn't have his own servants, didn't hire out for chores on his ranch if he could do the work himself. He had a team of five part-time employees who took care of his prize horses and kept the stables running smoothly. Once a week, he paid Helen to bring in groceries. Tagg's lifestyle met his solitary needs. But did they meet Callie's?

She'd been raised in the Sullivan household on Big Hawk Ranch. Sullivan had a servant for every day of the week, it seemed. And Callie had grown up in luxury. She was heiress to her father's legacy.

"Hey, cowboy. Wanna help me with the salad?" Wire whisk in hand, she stopped cooking to send him a smile.

He walked farther into the kitchen. "I can do that."

She handed him a knife and slid the cutting board his way on the granite island. "Slice the tomatoes and cucumbers and I'll shred the lettuce."

Tagg picked up the knife and began cutting the tomatoes. "You know, if you need help around here, we can hire someone."

"Thank you, but I don't need help."

"You're busy at Penny's Song every day. It's only going to get busier when the children arrive next weekend."

"I know, but I don't mind. Makes the time fly by. Besides, you'd hate to have someone here, getting in your way."

He already did. Only lately, he'd been enjoying Callie's company a little too much. He'd been glad to find her at Penny's Song, wanting to share the arrival of the Cosgrove horses. But at the first mention of her father's name, Tagg's good mood had vanished.

"You might want help when the baby comes."

Callie smiled and her dark eyes softened. "We'll have to

see how it goes. While I was out getting books for Penny's Song, I bought half a dozen on pregnancy and baby care. I want to get it just right."

He finished cutting the tomatoes and moved on to the cucumbers. "I suppose we'll need to take classes or something, right?"

Callie laid a hand on his arm. "You'd go with me?"

He turned to her. "Did you think I wouldn't?"

"Well, I wasn't sure. I was hoping you would." She spoke quietly, her voice trailing off.

"I want to get it right, too." He glanced at her belly, something he was prone to do often, as if seeing the evidence of his child growing there would make it more real. But it was too early yet. The only sign he'd seen of Callie's pregnancy was the ripeness of her breasts. He couldn't help noticing they felt heavier in his hands, fuller, and were incredibly more sensitive to his touch. Callie's intense cries of pleasure when he fondled her had gotten him hot and ready in mere seconds. Just thinking about their nights of mind-sucking wicked sex tightened his groin to painful limits.

Tagg had to admit one thing: he enjoyed making love to his new wife.

"I'm taking the red-eye out to Tucson tonight."

Callie's brows rose. "Oh? You didn't mention it."

"It just came up. It's a cattle deal I've been working on. I've got a meeting first thing in the morning."

"Okay. Well then, I'll get dinner on the table right away."

Tagg looked at the chicken she'd just taken out of the oven, the mashed potatoes, creamed just the way he liked it and his gut growled with hunger. But not the kind food could satisfy.

Callie picked up two plates and Tagg stopped her, grabbing her wrist. "I'm not hungry for food."

He pulled her close and wrapped his arms around her waist.

"What do you need then?" she asked, breathless.

He filled his nostrils with her scent and nibbled on her throat. She always smelled so good. "You, Callie. I need you tonight. Before I leave."

"Tagg." Her voice was soft, her eyes even softer. "I need you, too."

Callie was always a willing partner. Tagg loved that about her. She'd never once denied him. He brushed a kiss over her lips and then another and another.

She responded with throaty little sounds that wiped away any thoughts of taking her slow. "We've never done it in the kitchen," he whispered, melding their mouths together.

Sinful laugher escaped Callie's throat. "You want *me* for dinner?"

He grinned between kisses. "You know it." But the granite island was full of hot food and Tagg didn't have time to waste moving it all away. "On second thought, let's have dinner in bed."

Tagg made a move to lift her, but Callie stopped him, setting her hands firmly on his chest. "Follow me," she said, taking his hand and guiding him into the bedroom. He liked it when Callie took the lead. He liked it even more when she shoved him onto the bed and undressed for him.

"What would you like for an appetizer?" she whispered and removed her chambray blouse.

"Unhook that thing and come over here."

Callie did his bidding and unlatched her white lace bra, freeing her breasts. She came down onto the bed, her legs straddling his thighs. Tagg reached behind her back and splayed his hands out, bending her to him until her breasts were inches from his lips.

He tasted her then, filling his mouth with one beautiful breast and making her purr with unabashed pleasure. "You taste good," he said, his voice hoarse. The need inside him grew more urgent. "But I need the main course. Right now."

Callie smiled and lowered down, helping him remove his clothes. His shirt went flying and he struggled out of his jeans and shorts. Once he was naked, Callie gripped his manhood. "Not yet. There's one more course to be served first."

She bent over him and took him for a ride with her mouth that if he lived a hundred years, he'd never forget. "You're good at that," he uttered.

She answered back instantly, "Only with you."

She'd said that enough times that he was beginning to believe her. Her eyes liquid with desire, her body poised over his, Callie was beautiful and eager, but he noticed something else—something powerful and genuine. Something he hadn't paid attention to before. But he didn't have the willpower to analyze it further. He was hot, hungry and ready. And for the next thirty minutes Callie helped him satisfy that hunger.

Shortly after, showered and dressed in Tagg's shirt, Callie followed him into his office. "I have an idea." She didn't come in here often, but she wanted to see him off tonight. She'd miss him the minute he walked out the door for his business trip.

"What's that?" He searched his desk, filling his briefcase with papers and folders.

"What if I helped out around here? I could be your assistant."

He stopped what he was doing to look at her. "You want to work for me?"

Callie grinned. "Sure. You work long hours. You do practically everything yourself. I bet I can cut your work time in half. You wouldn't need to be in this office all day long."

Tagg smiled and grabbed the lapels of the shirt she wore, pulling her up close. He looked into her eyes, slid a glance down her near-naked body and spoke with sincerity. "Honey, if you worked in the office with me, I guarantee you, we'd spend a helluva lot more time in here. *Not working*."

Callie wrapped her arms around him. "I want to help."

"You have your duties at Penny's Song." He brushed a kiss across her throat. His sexy aftershave tempted her senses with a rich combination of fresh mint and musk.

"I don't have to be there all day. I can split my time." The more she thought about it, the more the idea of working alongside Tagg appealed to her. Perhaps it would be one way to get closer to him. She knew asking this of him put him on the spot, but Callie had the advantage right now. Tagg was softening to her and she didn't want that to stop. She wanted to prove to him that she was a good wife. That she would support him and help him in any way she could.

"It might be too much, with the baby coming and all."

Callie wouldn't back down. "I feel fine. If it ever got to be too much, I'd tell you."

"I'm used to doing things a certain way."

"Jackson said you were thinking of hiring someone to assist you."

"Jackson has a big mouth. And he doesn't know what he's talking about."

"Tagg, why are you resisting this so much? I'm here. I know the cattle business. Wives help their husbands. I want to do that for you."

He stared at her and shook his head, hesitating to say what was on his mind.

"What?"

He glanced at his watch. "I've got to get going, Callie. Let's talk about it when I get back."

Tagg gave her a kiss goodbye and left. She listened until she heard his car pull out of the garage and power down the road, the crunch of gravel fading from earshot.

And then it dawned on her why Tagg wouldn't let her work with him. She let out a pitiful laugh. It all boiled down to Hawkins Sullivan. Tagg couldn't forget who she was. She hoped that wasn't the case, but deep down she feared that was still true. Yet, Callie didn't understand why her father treated the Worths like they were his mortal enemy. It was high time she got to the bottom of it and found out the truth.

The next day Callie sat at the Greenhouse Café in Red Ridge facing her father. When he'd first sat down, he had a sour look on his face, especially when he noticed the fresh turkey and veggie salad waiting for him on his side of the table.

"It's not that bad, Dad. In fact, it's delicious." Callie took a big bite to prove her point. She tried keeping her spirits up with her father, lest he see she was struggling in her marriage.

"Like the sole of my shoe," he grumbled, but he lifted the fork to his mouth and took a bite.

Callie smiled. He'd probably never change. It was too much to ask. "So, how are you?"

He set his hands on the table. "Fine. Just dandy. My daughter got married and I was allowed to watch from a football field away."

"Dad, when we agreed to meet for lunch, we also agreed not to argue. Let's just be happy to see each other."

He clammed up and nodded.

She saw more pronounced age lines around his eyes now. His ruddy face appeared more sallow. "I love you, Daddy."

"You have a funny way of showing it."

"Dad," she warned. In many ways, her father was like the child and she was the adult in their relationship.

"I love you, too."

She smiled. "I know." She wished he wouldn't love her so much.

"I need to know something, Dad. It's important. I'm married to Taggart Worth—"

"Don't remind me. My heart can't take it."

"You see, that's what I don't understand. You have other competitors in the area. Granted they're not as big as the Worths, but you don't seem to mind losing out to one of them."

"I mind. I just don't let it get to me."

"But you hate losing out to the Worths."

"Can't deny that."

"Why, Daddy? You seem to target them, time and again. Nothing makes you happier than beating them at their own game. And I would suspect you'd rather take a loss than let them win a contract. I just don't get it. You can barely stand to hear the Worth name. And it's always been that way."

He pointed his fork at her. "And you…you're having a Worth baby." He uttered *Worth* with enough venom to down an elephant. Callie had to find out why he hated them so much, but she also had to set her father straight.

"Our baby will be half Sullivan, Daddy."

"Humph."

"I want this baby."

"You've never known what's good for you."

"And thanks for asking how I'm feeling."

"I can see you're healthy. You've got the color back in your cheeks. You're eating and look pretty as a picture."

Callie smiled. "Thank you." She'd take a backhanded compliment from her father whenever she could get one. "But you're still not off the hook for trying to bargain the baby away from Tagg."

"Annoyed him, did I?" His eyes lit up for a moment before he took a bite of his salad.

"I'm in love with Tagg."

"He doesn't love you."

That hurt. Hearing her father voice her biggest fear dug a giant hole out of her heart. She couldn't deny it. She couldn't prove her father wrong. She wished she had Tagg's love. She wished for a lot of things, but she wasn't greedy. Right now, she'd settle for his trust. She'd come to learn that life was messy at times. And this was one of those times.

"Why do you feel such bitterness toward the Worths? I know it's something more than business. Please, Dad," she said, her plea grabbing his full attention. "Tell me. This isn't a joke. It's my life. And I'm being torn apart by two men that I love."

Her father's expression changed. The hardness in his eyes softened. A sad frown pulled at his mouth. "All right, I'll tell you. But this is only for your ears. You're never to tell another soul about this. Not your friends, not that miserable husband of yours."

Callie shut her eyes momentarily. She hated hearing her father speak so ill of the man she loved.

"I need your promise, Callie."

"I promise." Luckily, she'd picked a corner booth in the café for their lunch. The restaurant wasn't crowded and she was certain they were out of range for anyone eavesdropping.

Still, her father lowered his voice before he spoke. "And I'm only telling you this hoping to persuade you to leave your husband and come back home where you belong." He paused when Callie didn't respond to that. "It has to do with your mother."

"Mom?" Callie blinked. She wouldn't have guessed this in a million years. "What does Mom have to do with it?"

"She was in love with Rory Worth when I met her."

"Mom? And Tagg's father, Rory? But I never heard—"

"No one else knows this. Just me. And now you. Rory's dead and gone and good riddance to him. He never told a soul what he'd done."

Callie listened, part of her wishing she didn't need to hear this.

"He took your mother's virginity and got her pregnant straightaway. Catherine was only nineteen at the time."

No, she really didn't need to hear this, but she *had* to know.

Her father's voice grew quieter. "By the time your mother realized she was with child she went to Rory with the news. You can imagine how frightened she was. She'd trusted him and he'd played fast and loose with her. He told her he didn't love her. Told her he couldn't possibly marry her, because he was engaged to be married to another woman."

"Oh, wow." Callie couldn't believe what she was hearing. "That must have been Isabella Worth, Tagg's mother."

He nodded.

"It seems Rory and Belle had broken up for all of two weeks. But Rory hadn't grieved about the breakup. Instead, he'd gotten drunk one night—that was his excuse—and Catherine was in the wrong place at the wrong time. He'd charmed her into bed. Oh, she was head over heels in love with Rory. Had been for years. It broke my heart, because *she* loved him the way *I* loved her. And there she was, pregnant with Rory's child. It was my chance to make things right. I offered her marriage. She told me a part of her would always love Rory Worth. I understood that and hated it and, yet, I still wanted her. I wanted to love her and help her through it all. But she wouldn't marry me. She said it wasn't fair to me. But I hung in there. You see, I loved her enough for both of us."

Her father stopped talking, his voice hoarse and weary. He gazed down at the table in thought and then a smirk broadened his face. "I beat the crap out of that miserable Rory one night. He never knew what hit him, and no one spoke about it afterward. He knew why. And that was good enough for me."

"Dad, you?"

"I was in better physical shape then, Callie. Don't look so surprised."

"I'm…not." But she really was. "You said mom wouldn't marry you."

"No. Not right then. She lost the baby shortly after that and it devastated her. She went into a depression. Of course, those who knew her thought the baby was mine. And that was fine by me. I didn't want anyone thinking less of your mother and everyone knew I'd asked her to marry me about a dozen times. I guess I wore her down. She finally accepted my proposal."

Callie sipped her drink, the lemonade going down like acid. "I thought you two were happy."

He reached out for her hand and she clasped it. For a moment, Callie could see her father back then, young, vital and so much in love with her mother that he'd do anything to protect her. "We were. We had a good life. She never looked back after you were born, Callie. You made everything right. I guess that's why I dote on you."

Callie got that. She always had, but now she knew why. She knew the extent of the love her father had for her mother. And she understood why he hated Rory Worth. It must have been hard living in the same town, doing business, knowing that the woman he loved would always be in love with another man.

"So now you know why I never wanted you near a Worth," he said finally, after moments of silence.

Callie had to let it all sink in. "Yeah, now I understand your reasons." But it had nothing to do with Tagg and his brothers. Why couldn't he see that? Her father's way of getting back at them was to beat the crap out of them in business.

"You're wrong to hold what Rory did against his sons."

"You know what they say about the sins of the father," he replied stubbornly. "I'm not wrong."

Tears welled in Callie's eyes. Her situation seemed so hopeless. She loved Tagg with all of her heart, but he still saw her as the enemy. She would always be the daughter of his fiercest competitor. "Dad, you don't have any plans to retire, do you?" Was it silly of her to hope?

He looked a little baffled and shook his head. "Not a chance. Who would I leave my legacy to? You don't want it."

Oh, God.

Life just kept on getting more and more complicated.

Eight

Tagg walked through the door late that afternoon and Callie's heart beat a little faster when their eyes met. She left the paint chips and fabric samples she'd been carefully studying on the kitchen counter and walked over to greet him.

"How was your trip?"

Tagg pushed back his black felt hat and smiled. "It went well. I'm happy to be home, though."

"You are?"

"Yeah." He seemed a little surprised by his admission. "I guess I just realized that, the second I walked through the door." He leaned over to kiss her on the cheek—a regular, honey-I'm-home kind of kiss that brought Callie immense joy.

"I'm happy to have you home. Are you hungry?"

He shook his head. "No, but I could use a drink."

"Soft or hard?"

"Definitely hard."

"I'll get it for you."

Tagg followed her into the kitchen and tossed his hat on a chair. She moved efficiently, grabbing a tumbler from the cabinet and going into the parlor to retrieve the liquor. While she was gone, Tagg had moved to the granite island where she had samples all spread out. She poured his drink.

"What's all this?" He stared at the items on the counter.

Callie handed him the glass and stood beside him. "Don't think I'm silly, but I've been thinking about decorating the nursery. Colors and patterns have sort of been popping into my mind. So, on my way home from town today, I picked up some samples."

He studied the pastel paint chips and glanced over half a dozen squares of fabric she'd laid out. "Sounds like a good idea."

"It's a little early. But I'm kind of excited."

Tagg glanced at her stomach and his brows rose. He noticed the little bump expanding under her navel. Her jeans were fitting much tighter, so she'd put on a pair of black spandex that actually revealed her newly plump belly even more. "Maybe not too early."

Was there a hint of excitement in his voice? He came up behind her. His breath caressed her throat. And to her surprise his hand cupped her belly, ever so gently. She closed her eyes.

"Do you feel anything yet?" he asked.

"Only that my jeans aren't fitting right. The baby," Callie began, and for the very first time, she really felt pregnant with the reality of that little bump taking hold, "the baby is popping me out of my jeans."

Tagg stroked her stomach and she prayed he wouldn't disappoint her, wouldn't say something to spoil the moment. "I've only been gone overnight, but I can see the difference."

"It's strange, isn't it?"

"Not strange, Callie. Natural. And fitting."

Callie placed her hand over his and they stood there together, quietly enjoying the moment.

She spoke softly. "I missed you, Tagg."

He kissed her neck and pressed her closer to him, her back resting against his chest. "It was nice coming home to you, Callie."

Callie's lips trembled. She'd never thought she'd hear those words from Tagg. It wasn't an admission of love but was wonderful to hear nonetheless.

"Why'd you go into town?" he asked, breaking their embrace to sip his drink.

Callie stepped to the side of the counter, the pastel paint chips catching her eye. *Lie,* a little voice in her head begged. Lie and don't bring up The Hawk's name. But as she peered into Tagg's gorgeous eyes, she couldn't do it. She owed him and their relationship the truth. "I met my father for lunch."

Tagg took another sip of his drink and digested the information. He nodded and then dropped the subject. "So what color do you like?" He pointed with his index finger at the options on the counter.

"Oh, uh…I don't know. I think sage green is nice for a boy. But then, I'm a sucker for pink, if it's a girl."

Tagg picked up the cotton-candy-pink paint chip. "That would be a first in a Worth household."

"Awful?"

"Just different. I grew up in a house full of men. We didn't do pink."

Callie laughed, relieved that Tagg didn't get bent out of shape at the mention of her father's name. "I guess I jumped the gun. Can't really decorate the room until we know if the baby is a boy or a girl."

Tagg gazed at her stomach again. "When will we know?"

She shrugged. "In a month or two, I think."

"Well, in that case, maybe we should put our efforts into Penny's Song. I'm going to put on a little rodeo for the children when they arrive. You know, show them some roping and riding."

Callie liked that idea. "I was a pretty good barrel racer. Though I never did it for the rodeo, I can find my way around those barrels again."

Tagg shook his head. "No, Callie. I'd rather you not. It's too dangerous."

"Tagg, I'd only go through the motions. There's nothing dangerous about that. I'd set up the barrels and show them the ins and outs." She grinned at her little pun.

"You think you're funny." Tagg sighed and scratched his head, then gazed into her eyes. "Okay."

Callie felt she was winning small battles in her quest to gain Tagg's trust. After feeling her situation was hopeless this morning while speaking with her father, Tagg's change in attitude when he'd come home today had given her an inkling of hope. If she could build on that, then they'd have a fighting chance.

Brutal memories flooded his mind as Tagg tossed and turned in bed, his heart pounding, his body trembling. During the day, Tagg's head was crammed with enough Worth business to keep from remembering Heather's death. But nighttime was different. Often, the stilling silence while lying in the dark caught him off guard. Tonight was one of those nights when he couldn't push away those punishing guilt-ridden thoughts.

Tagg strode through the front door of the main house, eager to see Heather. He needed to hold his wife in his arms, to feel her golden-wheat hair slide between his fingers, to see the look of love in her eyes when they finally came face-to-face.

She was his solace. She was his peace. She made his life complete.

Tagg had never loved this way before. He'd taken one look at her and known the Rodeo Queen was going to be his.

He found her in the parlor. Sitting beside a man, their heads intimately close, their bodies nearly brushing. Tagg's smile vanished and he pursed his lips. He'd never seen this man before—a man who obviously knew Heather all too well.

He stopped short of entering the room, leaning against the door frame. "Heather?" She closed her eyes briefly and when she finally opened them to peer at him, a look of guilt crossed her features. She averted her gaze.

The man stood and crossed the room, offering his hand. "I'm Pierce Donnelly."

Warily, Tagg shook his hand. "Taggart Worth."

"I was just on my way out."

Tagg gripped the man's arm as he tried to brush by him. "Who are you?"

Heather rose from the sofa. "Let him go, Tagg. I'll explain everything."

Tagg released him and watched him walk out the door, then turned to his wife. Heather confessed to him that Pierce was her first husband. A boy from her past whom she'd married right out of high school. They'd been together for two months before they'd had the marriage annulled. Teary-

eyed, Heather explained to Tagg that she'd been keeping up correspondence with him, sending him money when he needed it and that she'd never wanted anyone to know she'd been married before.

Stunned by the news, Tagg cursed vehemently as he tried to comprehend why she'd kept this secret from him. He accused her of purposely betraying and deceiving him even as Heather denied it, crying her eyes out. Furious with her, he wouldn't listen to her explanations. He didn't care that she'd known Pierce from childhood and that he had a drinking problem and needed professional help. He didn't care that Heather didn't want to abandon Pierce fully and that he'd relied on her friendship. All Tagg cared about was that his perfect wife had intentionally lied to him over and over, shattering his image of her, of them.

She tried once more, "I was going to tell you…"

Tagg turned his back on her, refusing to look at her, refusing to accept her countless apologies. "You should have, Heather. You should have trusted me."

"I know, Tagg, I know. What can I do to make it up to you?"

He turned to her and shook his head. "I don't know." He was angrier with her than he'd ever been in his life. And hurt as hell. "I can't think straight right now. I need to get out of here for a few days to cool off. I'll go somewhere. I don't know…maybe to Jackson's place in Phoenix."

She put her hand on his arm, her teary eyes filled with sincerity. "No, Tagg. You shouldn't have to leave your home. I'll go. It'll give us some breathing room. I owe my mother a visit. I'll leave tonight for Denver and we'll talk when I get back. I promise I'll make this right." Tears spilling down her cheeks, her voice broke with deep emotion. "I love you so very much."

Tagg nodded, unable to manage even a halfhearted smile. He didn't say the words she wanted to hear. He didn't ask her to stay. He let his pride rule his heart.

Later that night, a firm knock resounded on Tagg's door. The shocking news was a blow that nearly destroyed him. "I'm sorry to have to tell you this, Mr. Worth, but you're wife was killed in a plane crash."

Tagg broke out in a sweat, his body shaking uncontrollably. This memory was too vivid, too real. He'd seen everything in color this time. His chest constricted and he had trouble catching his breath. He bolted up from his prone position on the bed and squeezed his eyes shut, trying to free his mind of the haunting memories and the mistakes he'd made with Heather.

Moonlight streamed into the bedroom and illuminated the woman lying next to him in bed. His new wife. Callie. She stirred restlessly, and Tagg didn't want to risk waking her.

Without a sound, he rose from the bed, testing his legs for stability. He was still shaky when he walked out the door and headed to the corral.

Princess lifted her head when he approached. She was the feistiest of his mares, the one who was always alert, always on guard. Trick, the filly, Russet and Starlight slept on the ground, the mares preferring the summer nights outside to the stable.

It was okay that Princess didn't approach him. He didn't want to disturb her. He didn't want to disturb anything. The open range and the vast starlit sky eased his mind, granting him a minuscule amount of peace. He stared out, grateful for the ranch and the plentiful land that had been in his family for generations.

He'd built his house on the very spot where Elizabeth and Chance Worth once lived, more than one hundred years ago.

He envisioned them here, starting up the ranch, struggling with drought, disease and rustlers, yet forging on despite their obstacles—their deep love and devotion getting them through dark days. They'd known their share of adversity and he wondered if the land, the Red Ridge Mountains and the infinite sky had brought them the same sense of comfort.

"Tagg?" Callie's sweet voice broke into his thoughts.

He turned and saw her step off the porch clad in a white nightgown that barely reached her knees. Her thick, dark hair framed her face, the curls bouncing against her chest as she moved toward him, guided only by the light of the moon.

Maybe it was the moment, or the mood he was in, but Callie's presence as she came to stand before him filled an empty hole inside him.

"Are you okay?" she asked.

A curly lock of hair had fallen forward onto her cheek and he reached for it, gently tucking it behind her ear. He traced his finger along the side of her face and down to lift her chin up and look into her pretty caramel eyes. "I'm fine."

"You couldn't sleep again?" Her voice held concern. "And you came outside for the mares to lend you comfort?"

He smiled. "Something like that. I'm sorry I woke you."

"I was worried."

He took her hand in his, skimming over her fingers gently. "I appreciate it, Callie."

Her voice was a soft whisper as she squeezed his hand. "I'm here for you. What can I do to help?"

He leaned closer and brushed a tender kiss to her lips, his mouth lingering near hers. "That'll help some."

"I'm glad."

They stood there for a few silent moments, gazing out at the night sky. When a chilly breeze made Callie shiver, he slipped his arm around her shoulder and walked her toward the house. "Let's go back to bed."

They entered the house quietly and climbed back into Tagg's big bed. He curled his arm around Callie and spooned her until she fell asleep. The weight of his burden had been lifted tonight. He grasped at the tranquility he felt and closed his eyes, finally free of the bad memories darkness usually brought him.

Tonight, Tagg forgot who Callie's father was.

Tonight, Tagg fell a little bit in love with his wife.

To his amazement, the notion didn't frighten him as much as it once would have.

Two days later, Tagg slammed the drawer in his office with enough force to rival an Arizona monsoon. The vibration shook the desk and echoed off his office walls. His coffee cup rebelled from the force and splashed liquid all over his files before dripping onto the hardwood floor in a muddy mess. He found no satisfaction in almost breaking the drawer. He slammed it again for good measure. Once again, the desk shook.

"Sonofabitch!" He spit out every other expletive he knew. Neither the slamming nor the cursing made him feel any better. He stared at the screen on his computer in disbelief and shook his head as he reread the email he'd received this morning from PricePoint Foods in Tucson. "I don't get it."

He'd practically had that contract wrapped up with a pretty baby-blue ribbon. And they didn't have the balls to call him with their decision. Instead, they sent him an email. "PricePoint is sorry not to be doing business with Worth Enterprises this time around. As a courtesy, a representative from our company will be in touch with you shortly."

"I won't hold my breath." But Tagg would. He had to get

to the bottom of this. It had to be Sullivan's doing. Big Hawk Ranch was the only other Arizona company large enough to accommodate such a lucrative contract. Their ranches were almost equal in size, steer for steer and acre for acre.

"Damn you, Sullivan."

Someone knocked on his door and before Tagg had time to react, the door opened and Clay stepped inside. He took one look at Tagg, removed his tan felt hat and sat down. "Morning, brother. What is it? What's put that piss-poor look on your face?"

Tagg reigned in his anger. He looked at the computer screen one more time then cast his older brother a baffled look. "Big Hawk Ranch beat us out of another deal."

"That so?"

Tagg rubbed his forehead and let go a heavy sigh. He had to deal with this rationally. "Yeah. What I can't figure is, I'm giving them the best market price I can. Any lower and we'd be losing money. I've worked on this for weeks, had our legal department look it over and flew to Tucson the other day to try to seal the deal."

"Are you sure it was Sullivan?"

Tagg nodded. "The contracts are supposed to be confidential, but PricePoint execs drop cow-dung-size hints. It's better for them to have their competitors in a price war. So, yeah, I know for a fact it's Sullivan."

"Not much you can do about it, is there?"

Tagg winced. Sullivan had beaten him twice at his own game and Tagg didn't like losing to Callie's father. He'd simply have to get him next time around. Not that Worth Ranch would go under without these contracts; they had their regulars who were loyal to the Worth name and reputation. It was a matter of pride and bragging rights now.

"How are things going otherwise?" Clay leaned back in the leather seat and crossed his booted ankle over his knee.

Clay was asking about Tagg's marriage in a roundabout way. He didn't usually talk about his private life to anyone, but he'd cut his brother some slack today because he needed the distraction. "Everything's fine. Callie and I are working up a little show for the kids when they arrive. I'll do some roping and riding. She'll show them how a barrel race works."

Clay's brows lifted. He shot him a curious stare. "So you and her, you're getting along?"

"We just about have to, don't we? We're married."

"Not all married couples make it," Clay said casually though it was evident he was talking about his own former marriage to Trish Fontaine. The subject of Trish was taboo and Tagg knew not to go there.

"We're having a baby, remember?" Thinking about the little mound spurting up from Callie's stomach put him in a better mood. "Callie's showing signs now."

"Really?"

"I'm doing *what?*" Callie stepped into the room holding a tray of freshly baked oatmeal cookies and two tall glasses of lemonade.

"Man, oh, man, those smell delicious. Hi, Callie." Clay sat up straight in his seat.

"Morning, Clay."

"She bakes?" Clay looked at Tagg.

"I bake," she said. "Never had much time before, but I'm enjoying the kitchen a little bit more these days." She set the tray down on the desk and then glanced at the halfhearted clean up job Tagg had done with the spilled coffee. "What happened in here?"

Tagg shot a warning glance at Clay. He wasn't ready to tell Callie about his latest loss, needing time to sort things out. Suspicion pushed through his mind about Callie and her father. The minute Tagg went out of town, Callie has visited with The Hawk. She had access to Tagg's accounts, his office and his computer. He didn't want to believe the worst about his wife, but how could he be sure where her true loyalty lay? Tagg had no proof, nothing to go on, so he shelved his suspicions. Though he wanted to trust Callie, he still wasn't there yet. "Had me a little spill, that's all."

She took a few napkins from the tray and did a better job of cleaning up his mess, never missing a beat. "Help yourself, boys. Whatever you don't eat is going to the crew at Penny's Song."

Clay grabbed two cookies and the lemonade. Callie handed him a napkin. Tagg took one cookie for himself. Both of them thanked her.

She leaned on the edge of the desk and looked from him to Clay. "So what is Callie doing?" She hadn't forgotten the conversation she'd overheard.

Tagg took a bite of the cookie. "These are good." He chewed and chewed, keeping his mouth full. Let Clay get out of this one.

Callie lifted her brows, waiting.

Clay cleared his throat. "Tagg was telling me you're starting to show, uh, the baby is, I mean."

Clay slid a quick glance at her stomach and Callie grinned. "I know. It's a little bump, but it's all baby."

"I can't see the bump."

"It's there," Tagg assured him. "But you don't get a closer look."

Clay sent him an eye roll.

Callie added, "And, thankfully, the morning sickness is all gone."

"Well, that's great news." He finished his cookie and

downed it with a gulp of lemonade. "Because I'm throwing a little party at the end of the week. For the crew and all the volunteers who helped out and especially for my family. It's my way of thanking everyone before our official opening. That's why I'm here. To give you a personal invite."

"That's a wonderful idea," Callie said. "Do you need any help with party planning?"

"I might, if you're up to it. Can I get back to you on that?"

"Sure, Clay. Anything you need." Callie offered him another cookie.

"It's black tie."

Tagg croaked out, "Black tie?" That physically pained him.

"Yeah, it means putting on your monkey suit." Clay winked at Callie.

"You'd think Jackson was putting this shindig on." Tagg scowled at his brother.

"Actually, it *was* his idea."

Tagg worked for the next few days putting together another proposal for a big beef conglomerate. He made plans to go to a cattle auction up Flagstaff way in three weeks and he called several of his regular clients. He wasn't used to having to schmooze to stay in business. It wasn't in his nature to make small talk and he was terrible at it. The conversations were stilted and brief and he hated every minute of it.

He set his phone down after his third and final call for the morning and stacked his file folders, making one neat pile. A swatch of fabric caught his eye, peeking out from under a financial report lying on the desk. Tagg moved the other papers away and picked up the soft piece of cotton. He held smiling monkeys, silly elephants and friendly lions in his hand. Stubby green-leafed trees and bamboo shoots filled the background of the material in soft tones. It looked like a happy scene from a Disney jungle movie. Tagg glanced down and found the paint chip that had been sitting underneath the fabric. He picked it up with his other hand. Green Earth had a sticky note attached on the back in Callie's handwriting and he read it out loud. "Great for a boy, don't you think?"

They were having a boy? Tagg felt a moment of excitement, but then he remembered that it was too soon to tell. Callie had said as much. They had an appointment with the doctor in a few weeks. Tagg still couldn't believe it. He was going to be a father. He'd never thought he'd be given another chance at happiness. He'd never thought he'd grant himself enough inner peace to let someone else get close enough. For years, he didn't think he deserved it. Had Callie changed that? Could it be possible that Hawkins Sullivan's daughter would be the one person who could see him through his grief and guilt?

He glanced at the evidence in his hands. A smile emerged. He wondered what Callie would pick out if they had a baby girl. Flying magical horses in pinks and purples?

He heard the distant sound of Callie's voice from outside and put down the items. He walked over to the side window and peered out. A horse trailer had pulled up and Callie was raising her voice above a palomino's whinnies.

Tagg plopped his hat on his head and marched outside, striding up to the bumper pull trailer, watching from the sidelines. He knew enough to steer clear of a skittish horse. Callie on the other hand, put herself right in the mix. "You need some help?"

She cast him a sideways glance and shook her head. "No. Freedom doesn't like the trailer is all. She's a bit high-strung." The golden horse backed out with Callie's soft urging. "Come on, girl. This is your new home now. Yeah, that's it. I sure did miss you."

Callie held a rope and eased the palomino out of the double hitch trailer. Once she was free of the drop down, Tagg glanced inside. "She did her best to destroy the kick walls."

"She does that." Callie held her rope tight and stroked the palomino's face. The horse lifted her head in rebellion. "It's all right, Free. Calm it down a little. No more bumper pulls for you."

"Does your father know you took her?"

She grinned. "Not yet. I made sure he wasn't home when I got her. I'll call and let him know later on."

"She's a beauty."

Callie smiled. "Thank you."

"I forgot she was coming today."

"I mentioned it last night."

Tagg vaguely remembered. He closed the gap between them and stroked the mare's mane carefully. He spoke into her ear. "You expect me to remember anything after last night? You drove every brain cell outta my head. I barely know my own name."

Callie shot a quick glance at the driver, who'd walked away to check the truck's engine. She sent her voice into a whisper. "Are you complaining?"

She knew he wasn't. Sex with Callie just kept getting better and better. "I'm no fool. I know a good thing when I see it."

She took her eyes off Freedom to take a leisurely tour of his body. She liked him in jeans and boots and made no bones about it. Her brow arched up in approval and she sent him a wicked look that shot straight to his groin. "So do I," she said quietly.

He could lead her back into the bedroom and…

"I'm taking Free out today," she announced, changing the

direction his mind had taken. "Let her see your land. Get used
the scent of the other horses."

"Sounds like a good idea."

"She's not going to like sharing the paddock with your
mares. She's pretty feisty."

"I can see that."

"But underneath it all, she's a sweetheart."

Tagg wondered if the same were true of her. "When are
you going for that ride?"

"After lunch."

"You want some company?"

Callie stared at him. "You want to ride out together?" A
familiar look of yearning crossed her features.

He nodded. "Sure, why not?"

He knew why Callie seemed surprised. He'd never invited
her before, even though he'd seen longing in her eyes and her
plea for acceptance on his ranch. He'd kept his afternoon rides
private so he could be alone with his own thoughts. But it was
also a way to drive some distance between them. To keep her
from getting too close and maybe to punish her for her past
mistakes. He hated to admit that, but it was solid truth. He'd
had to marry her and accept her into his home because of the
baby. He'd also had to tolerate her ruthless, immoral father.

"Because you've never asked me before. Why now?"

He stared at the little bulge at her waistband and felt a
sense of pride, but also a fierce sense of protectiveness. Callie
was an expert horsewoman, but her mare was jittery. After
seeing those knocked-in kick walls, Tagg didn't want Callie
riding out on his land alone with her horse. He worried over
his baby's safety, that was a given. But it surprised him how
much of his concern was aimed at his new wife.

He shrugged. "It'd be best if I went with you, is all."

"You're on, cowboy." Callie opened her mouth to say something else but seemed to change her mind.

And the she sent him a big, beautiful smile that spread warmth through his cold and distant heart.

Nine

"Your wife cleans up nicely," Jackson said, sipping wine from a cut crystal glass. He gestured to Callie, who was speaking with two crewman from Penny's Song under a tree wrapped with hundreds of twinkle lights on Clay's veranda.

Tagg glared at his brother.

"What? Just stating the obvious."

"Keep your eyes in your head."

Jackson smiled wide before taking another sip of thirty-dollar-a-glass Pinot Noir. "Just appreciating the best-looking woman in the place."

Tagg had to agree. He couldn't take his eyes off her, even though he'd seen her in the most intimate settings, touched every part of her body countless times and made her moan his name until the breath stole out of her lungs. Tagg still couldn't look away.

She wore her dark hair in an intricate pile atop her head with a few well-placed strands curling along her crown

and down around her neck. Rhinestones gathered her deep
crimson gown just under her breasts and flowed in soft pleats
all the way down to her sandal-clad ankles. Her eyes were
liquid caramel tonight under those sparking lights, her skin,
the smoothest cream. When Tagg first laid eyes on her as she
came gliding out of his bedroom dressed to kill, he'd dropped
the magazine he'd been reading in the parlor. He'd never seen
Callie look more beautiful. If he'd compared her to a Grecian
goddess, the goddess would lose out every time.

Clay walked up and stood beside them. He followed the
line of their attention. "She looks happy tonight, Tagg."

"For the moment," Jackson added.

Tagg blinked and sucked in a breath. His brothers wouldn't
let up. Since they found out about the baby, they'd been
painting a rosy picture about his marriage. Tagg resented it.
He needed more time. The feelings he had for Callie scared
the living hell out of him. He had niggling doubts that held
him back. He wasn't all-in yet and he didn't know if he ever
would be. "Why wouldn't she be happy?"

Clay scratched his head. Jackson polished off his wine.
They both stared at Tagg with raised eyebrows.

He grabbed a wine goblet from a passing waiter and
downed it in one long gulp. He knew why Callie wasn't happy
with him, but how did Jackson know? Had Callie said something or was his brother just being a pain?

Their one and only horseback ride hadn't gone well.
Freedom had been jumpy and Tagg had raised his voice
several times at Callie. They'd argued about horse tactics
and command and Callie ended up riding off in a different
direction. Tagg had only been worried about her safety. And
the baby's. Still, things had been tense between them since
that ride.

Clay was speaking, and his voice pulled Tagg back into

the conversation. "You got yourself a good wife. Don't blow it." Clay, usually the diplomat, shot him a cautionary look.

Crap, had Callie said something to both of them?

"You know, you're not all that," Jackson, his smart-ass brother added.

"I never claimed to be." He tightened his grip on the empty wine glass and cursed under his breath more from watching one of those workmen take Callie onto the dance floor than from his brothers' lame attempts to make him feel guilty. The minute the guy pulled her up close, Tagg's gut clenched.

"You're a little green, Tagg. Maybe it was the shrimp."

Jackson was getting on his nerves.

"No comment?"

He shrugged it off. He wasn't going to let his brother get the best of him.

"Maybe you should dance with your wife. Or maybe I will." Jackson made a move toward the imported parquet dance floor on the deck. Tagg blocked his passage with an iron arm. "Don't be an ass."

Jackson's usual smirk disappeared. His eyes darkened with concern. "I'm trying to keep you from being one. You're either stupid or scared. I know our gene pool. You're not stupid, Tagg. You're gonna lose her if you don't lighten up."

Tagg shot him a look. "What did she tell you?"

"Is there something to tell?" Jackson asked. "If there is, maybe you should be talking it over with her."

Neither Jackson nor Clay knew about his relationship with Callie. He couldn't explain it to them because, one, it was none of their business and, two, he couldn't really define it himself.

When the three-piece orchestra took a break, Clay took center stage. He'd outdone himself with this party. Not only had he invited family, workmen and volunteers, he'd invited the mayor and sheriff of Red Ridge, members of the city council and other townsfolk. Tagg's brother had been a star once, so he knew how to command an audience. But this event tonight wasn't about him or his onetime celebrity status, it was about giving thanks to the many who'd contributed their time and energy to the project.

Clay called the rest of the Worth family up to the stage to join him, where a crowd had gathered.

Tagg searched the area for Callie. He saw her slip into the background, standing behind one of those twinkle trees, sipping sparkling cider. He strode over to her. "Callie?" He offered her his hand. "You coming?"

Her gaze fell on his open palm, and she hesitated.

"We're being summoned."

"Tagg," he heard Clay say over the mike. "Get your pretty wife and come up here. Can't start without the two of you."

She darted a glimpse at Clay waiting for them, then with a tiny sigh, she nodded. She slipped her hand in Tagg's and he gripped her tight. He led her to the steps to stand beside Jackson, who grinned at her like a fool, and Clay, who gave them both a nod before he began his speech.

Tagg held her hand as Clay spoke to the group, giving thanks to everyone who'd taken Penny's Song to heart and singling out people who'd helped along the way. Clay had given him and Jackson credit for their part in the project, when, in fact, his two brothers had put the facility together without much help from him. Clay took a moment to welcome Callie officially to the family and commend her hard work and generosity, giving Callie a kiss on the cheek, which garnered a round of applause.

Callie found it necessary to let go of Tagg's hand when the speech was over to applaud along with the group.

"You haven't danced with me once," he said finally, after

leading her back to the cottonwood tree. His words came out sharper than he intended. He'd meant to sound nonchalant.

She faced him, finally meeting his eyes. "You haven't asked me."

He curled a strand of silken hair around his finger, his gaze lingering. "You've been busy."

"Clay asked me to be his hostess."

"Clay should get his own wife."

A tiny chuckle escaped her throat. "You're not jealous."

It wasn't a question but a statement of fact. Callie didn't know how jealous he was of every man who'd danced with her, every man who'd paid her attention, every man who'd been granted her smile tonight.

He brought her up close, wrapping his arms around her waist, holding her tight, his mouth just a breath away from hers. She smelled exotic, a rich blend of sexy and citrus. He inhaled deeper and his groin tightened. He'd gone without Callie too long. He wanted her. He wouldn't let her freeze him out. Her eyes sparked with defiance, but they held excitement as well. She'd never been able to resist him. He found that trait endearing. She wasn't all that angry with him anymore. "I'm jealous," he admitted.

Callie closed her eyes. "Tagg. This isn't a game."

He brushed a tender kiss to her lips. "I never thought so, Callie. Not for a minute."

Callie wasn't a quitter. As a child she'd never given up when she wanted something bad enough. Not the spelling bee championship when she was nine, not the Junior Miss Equestrian Pageant when she was fourteen and not the children who'd seemed lost and hopeless when she'd worked at the With Care Foundation in Boston. She'd stood up to her formidable father time after time and held her head high making something of her life that she could be proud of, despite her DNA.

And she wasn't quitting on Tagg now. She'd just needed a breather…

The old cottonwood tree held her upright as she watched her husband speaking with the mayor. Jackson had pulled him into the conversation and she could tell he wasn't thrilled to be there. Their eyes met from across the yard several times as he tried to focus on what Mayor Fielding was saying.

Tagg was deadly handsome in his Western tux, with dark strands of hair brushing the collar of his black jacket. His skin was bronzed from hours under the Arizona sun. She loved the way he moved, the confident strut of a man comfortable in his own skin. She loved the deep husky tone of his voice. There wasn't much she didn't love about Taggart Worth. Except the way he held her at arm's length. No, she didn't love that at all. He gave her just enough to make her wish for it all.

It had been exhausting trying to be a good wife when he gave little back in return. She was like a fountain that kept pouring out without any source of replenishment. His subtle and not so subtle emotional jabs were getting to her. She was made of thicker skin, she knew. She was, after all, a Sullivan by birth. But her changing hormones got in the way and made her feel weepy and filled with self-doubt. She'd had bouts of tears these past few days that she couldn't talk herself out of or seem to control.

It all had to do with Tagg.

There were times during the week when she thought marrying him had been a mistake. That maybe loving him wasn't enough. Sometimes, he'd open up to her, giving her a teensy inkling of hope, then he'd say something to wipe it all away. She felt like a nail being pounded further and further down. And her only recourse had been to sink inside herself, like a turtle hiding out in his shell. She'd needed the protection and the solace.

But she wasn't completely down-and-out and she wouldn't give up. Which probably made her a bigger fool than he was.

When the orchestra started playing again, Tagg begged off with Jackson and the mayor. He headed her way and her silly heart pounded in her chest. Once he reached her, he smiled and it was a killer. "Dance with me?"

"You just want a rescue from the mayor's rambling."

"I want to dance with the most beautiful woman here. And," he said with a wide grin, "you'd be saving me from the mayor's *incessant* rambling."

She gave him her hand. "In that case, consider yourself saved."

Her cold shoulder had melted the second he took her into his arms. Her breather was over. She'd missed Tagg.

They stepped to soft mellow music on the grass away from the dance floor, just the two of them with no crowds and no one looking on. It's how Tagg liked to operate. It was his MO. He was a loner and she had barged into his life, turning it upside down.

"I can't wait for this bash to be over." He nuzzled her throat.

Callie weaved both her hands through the bottom layers of his hair. It went thick and silky through her fingers. "People are starting to leave already."

"That's a good sign."

He touched his cheek to hers and brought her tight up against him, her breasts to his chest. They meshed like two parts of a puzzle. Everything below his waist was stiff and hard. Oh, how she'd missed him.

"I'm feeling tired," she said.

He pulled back, his eyes narrowing to slits. "For real?"

She shook her head and shrugged. "I could play the pregnant card to get us out of here."

"The way you've been playing it all week with me?"

"You deserved it."

Tagg heaved a sigh. "Maybe. But you're not getting away with that tonight."

He brought his lips down to hers and kissed her with enough tenderness to dissolve any remaining doubts she held inside. "This dress is coming off you by my hands tonight."

Callie tingled from head to toe. She couldn't wait. Her bones ached for him and other parts of her anatomy throbbed. "I'm feeling suddenly faint, Tagg."

"Then let's get the hell outta here."

He took her hand and led her to the car. He didn't give her a chance to say goodbye to his brothers. But Clay had seen them leave and so had Jackson, both of them watching with knowing looks on their faces as Tagg hightailed it out of the house.

"I'll buy you another dress, honey."

Tagg had been a little too eager to get her naked. He'd ripped the delicate fabric on her shoulder trying to shove it down her arms. The sound of tearing material only added to the thrill of making love with him again. The days apart, sleeping next to him and not allowing herself to touch him or be intimate with him had worn on her just as much as it had on him. The one thing that they had together, the one thing that never ceased to be fantastic, night or day, was making love.

Tagg never disappointed. He was a man who did things until they got done right. And he'd done it right twice tonight. She lay quiet and peaceful in the aftermath of their lovemaking. The intoxicating scents of man and sex filled her senses. She rested her head under Tagg's shoulder and ran her hands through the scattered hairs on his chest. An overhead fan circulated the warm pre-summer air, cooling the beads of sweat from their skin. Tagg tangled his fingers in her hair and absently stroked through the strands, his once heavy breaths slowing to a steady rumbling.

This was the time Callie liked best. The time when she felt like nothing in the world could separate them. The time when, after a satisfying night together, sharing bodies and souls, Callie found the most hope.

Tagg rolled her onto her back gently and came up over her. She looked into his eyes. They were so clear, so astonishingly blue-gray, a color unique to him. When she thought he'd kiss her again, he surprised her by touching a hand to her belly, just over the bulge that they'd both created. His fingertips swirled circles around and around her navel ever so tenderly, his eyes raking in her bare body but coming back to land on her stomach. "Do you think it's a boy or girl?"

"I don't know," she said quietly. "Either would make me happy. What about you?"

Tagg flopped back on the bed. He looked at the ceiling. "Doesn't matter." The careless words would have hurt, if he hadn't said them with such passion. Then he blew out a deep breath. "I just want a healthy kid."

Callie smiled. He'd been imagining the child in his life, the same way Callie had. A little girl, all ruffles and frilly lace, or a boy in blue with wagons and scooters getting into all kinds of trouble. Callie let out a little laugh.

"What?"

"Just thinking. What if we have a tomboy? What if she'd rather wear your hats and boots and ride your prize mares up on Red Ridge instead of scooting around on a hot pink tricycle with all the fancy bells and whistles?"

Tagg chuckled. "I've been imagining a lot of things, but that's not one of them."

Callie's throat constricted. She barely got out the words out. "You've been imagining our baby?"

Tagg didn't answer for a little while. Then on a long pull of oxygen, his throat tight with emotion, he confessed softly, "Yeah."

It wasn't just his duty anymore. It wasn't his honor at stake. It wasn't that he was protecting his child from the evil villain, Hawkins Sullivan. It was more. That one little word, that admission filled with a mix of wonder and excitement, told Callie something powerful. Something wonderful.

Tagg wanted this baby.

Tears welled in Callie's eyes. She'd been doing that a lot lately, filling up with tears, but this time it was different. This time, she had a good reason. She did a happy dance in her head. If it were possible, she fell even more in love with Taggart Worth tonight. And for the first time in a long time, Callie thought that just maybe her life would turn out all right.

Ten

Callie lay in bed at daybreak the next morning, drinking in the luxury of Tagg's comfortable mattress. She sank down into the softest pillows on earth and lay there, eyes closed, feeling good about the upcoming day. This was the best she'd felt since coming to Tagg's home. Something had changed between them last night, something remarkable. Something that gave her hope and she wanted to glory in it, to glory in the way her body ached in all the right places and the way she felt spent and satisfied and cared for.

Early morning sounds surrounded her. Birds chirped a melodious tune. The mares' whinnies and softly pounding hooves carried into the bedroom window. It was almost the launch of a new day, the dawn peeking on the horizon.

Tagg kissed her forehead when he got up. "Stay in bed and rest. I'm going into Phoenix. Be back later in the day."

She nodded, too tired to reply. The shower went on and off. She heard Tagg's quiet movements in the bathroom, but the temptation of catching his early morning ritual was too tempting to ignore. With blurry eyes, she watched him pad into the room, his bare body shimmering with moisture, his hair wet and slicked back from his handsome face. His chiseled jaw, set permanently tight since they'd married, seemed relaxed now, the expression on his face unguarded. He was strong where a man needed to be strong. Powerful muscles bunched on his arms and led to shoulders of steel. His slim waist and potent manhood left nothing to be desired. He had it all.

She hummed inwardly at his raw, sexual beauty and watched him turn to pull his briefs on. She said goodbye to his perfect butt as it disappeared into jeans and then he sat down and the mattress gave from his weight. She saw his back muscles work as he tugged his feet into boots.

When he rose Callie closed her eyes again, lest he find her ogling him.

Her fantasy man.

She held on to those thoughts as she drifted back into a peaceful sleep.

Callie woke and glanced at the clock on the nightstand. It was past ten o'clock in the morning. She rose from the bed, shamelessly guilty for sleeping so long, and scurried into the shower. She rinsed off quickly and dressed. The day had almost gotten away from her. She walked into the kitchen and made herself a cup of herbal tea and boiled some eggs. The baby needed protein. She had to eat a good breakfast— there'd be no skipping meals. And as soon as she was done, she would set her little surprise for Tagg in motion.

The idea had hit her this morning after Tagg kissed her goodbye. Once the notion entered her head, it took hold and wouldn't let go. Callie had to do this, or at least she had to try.

She stepped into Tagg's office and sat down at his desk. She cleared away a space, arranging his files in one neat pile, and set a notepad down. Then she logged on to the computer. Immediately, she tapped in her password for her bank balance. She had a hefty trust fund that her father could no longer lord over, the money having reverted to her no strings attached when she'd turned twenty-five. And she had a little savings account from her time working in Boston.

She'd already dedicated a portion of her cash to Clay's cause. She'd been buying books and gifts for the general store, but she'd also secretly given Clay a sizable donation to help keep the facility going until they could bring in more revenue from fundraisers.

She stared at the computer screen for a few minutes scanning over the numbers. Once she confirmed she was in good shape financially, she logged off the computer.

She had some digging to do, but she knew where she could start. She found Tagg's address book easily enough, in the drawer on the left side of his desk. She'd seen him use it many times. Once she found the number she needed, she dialed it on her cell phone. To her disappointment, no one answered. She left a message and then set her phone down on Tagg's desk.

Callie pulled out a few drawers in the file cabinets and looked through folders, but everything in there was related to business. Reports, more numbers than Callie would ever want to see, inventory files and ledgers. It wasn't what she needed. She glanced at the door that opened into the old storage room. "Maybe what I need is in there," she muttered.

She'd wished she'd been paying more attention to Tagg when they were in Las Vegas. The conversation had been short and if she'd daydreamed for a second during that dinner, she might have missed something important.

She turned the knob and the door creaked open. She'd never gone into this room before. She'd never had the need since Tagg hadn't accepted her offer to work with him. He didn't want her invading his space. He didn't want her to get too close. Callie hoped to change that. Excitement stirred within her. If only she could pull this off. If only she could do this for Tagg.

Callie strode inside too fast and the musty scent of old papers and dry Arizona dust hit her immediately. She sneezed and sneezed again. She waved her arms to circulate the air, but that only managed to give the dust more life. She turned to shield her face and saw something on a bookshelf that caught her eyes. She wandered over and sucked in a breath when she viewed the two photo frames sitting there. They were sandwiched in between Tagg's framed rodeo champion belt buckles.

One was a photo of Heather sitting atop her horse in full Rodeo Queen regalia wearing a shimmering Western blouse, a silver tiara on her head and a blue sash slanted across her torso. She rode a palomino, a little taller than Free, but not quite as blond. Heather was smiling, her face filled with joy. She was the woman Tagg had loved with his whole heart.

Callie picked up the frame and stared. She couldn't resent Heather. She couldn't, considering the tragic way she'd died. But she couldn't stop the envy that poured like hot liquid through her veins. She couldn't help but wish that she had been the woman who'd met Tagg first, the woman who would have stolen his heart. Her hands shook when she set the frame back down.

The other photo was of Tag and Heather together, his arm possessively roped around her shoulder in front of the main house. The happiness they shared in that image said it all. She'd never seen that expression on Tagg's face before. In all the time she'd known him, he'd never once shown her that one hundred percent megawatt, the-world-is-a-happy-place-and-I-love-life kind of smile.

Callie put her hands to her face. Tears spilled down her cheeks despite her valiant effort to stop them. Her heart broke and her envy dissolved in that moment. What she felt for Tagg was soul wrenching and overpowering. She felt his heartache in that smile. She felt his loss in the way he'd wrapped that protective arm around Heather's shoulders. She felt his *grief*.

She knew a little bit about grieving herself. She'd lost her mother at a young age and Callie had thought her life was over, too. Her *mother*—the woman who'd picked her up when she fell, the woman who'd smiled when Callie was sure she'd be angry, the woman who'd kissed away her little-girl troubles with love always in her eyes. Callie knew grief, and she grieved with Tagg now, for all the hurt he'd endured in his life. For losing the one person he'd loved beyond all else in the world. Callie's tears continued to fall and she didn't try to stop them. She needed to shed them for Tagg. Her body trembled, her head throbbed and when the well had finally emptied, Callie took a deep steadying breath.

She pulled herself together.

With a shake of her head she sobered.

Life pushed on.

Her mother's story had taught her that.

She'd thought the sun rose and set on Rory Worth's shoulders and he'd hurt and abandoned her when she'd needed him most. Her mother hadn't collapsed, hadn't given up. She'd been strong and brave. She'd given herself another chance at happiness and had moved on with her life. She'd had a good one, too, with her father. She'd loved him and she'd never looked back. That's what people did. That's what Tagg would do. And Callie would help him.

With renewed strength, she continued on with her search, her heart lighter, her hope brighter and more determined now than ever. Tagg would be thirty-two years old soon and she wanted to mark that day with a monumental gesture.

A booming voice startled her. She spun around abruptly to find Tagg in the doorway with a scowl on his face.

"What in holy hell do you think you're doing in my files?"

"Tagg? Oh, my God! You scared me!" Her back hit his gray metal filing cabinet with a thwack.

Of course she was scared, Tagg thought. She hadn't expected him home for hours. She looked guiltier than hell. "You didn't expect me home so soon, did you?"

"No," she said, her hand to her throat. She caught her breath. "I thought you went into Phoenix. You said you'd be gone most of the day."

His mouth curled down. "Honey, I'm home."

"Tagg?" She didn't miss his sarcasm and had the chops to look confused. "What's wrong?"

"What were you doing in here?"

"I, uh…I just came in here for—" Her face flushed and she looked away.

Tagg took her arm and led her out of the dusty room. He released her in the center of his office and pointed. "You've been at my desk? My files are out of order." He glanced around, noting the drawers in the cabinets weren't completely closed, either.

"Yes, I know. I was looking for something."

"You were looking for something?" He controlled his voice, holding on by a shred. "Did you find it?"

"No," she said with a shake of her head.

"I think you have."

"Tagg, what's this all about?"

She shot him an innocent look and did a damn convincing job of it, too. His fury built and he didn't know how long he could hold it together. "I think you know the damage you've caused."

Callie's face contorted and even with an unbecoming twist of her lips, she still looked beautiful. He cursed her for making him believe that maybe she could be trusted. For making him believe that what he was feeling for her was something more than mind-numbing sexual gratification. She'd proved him wrong on both accounts and made a fool out of him to boot.

"Wh-What kind of damage? Tagg, I've never seen you this way."

"You bring out the best in me, sweetheart," he countered through tight lips.

"Tagg?"

"I leave and come back early to find you sneaking around in my office, rifling through my files. Not too smart, Callie. You should have been more careful." Tagg walked around her, circling her, trying to see the real Callie and not the woman she pretended to be.

"I wasn't sneaking around."

"Weren't you?"

She closed her eyes briefly and then looked so damn guilty when she finally opened them, Tagg lost all of hope of being wrong. "Yes, I was being a little sneaky."

"You visit your father whenever I'm out of town."

"You know that I see my father."

"Have you seen him today?"

"No."

"So he hasn't told you yet?"

"Told me what?" Callie snapped. Her impatience was showing. Good. The real Callie Sullivan was finally coming out.

"Guess?"

She shrugged her shoulders, exasperated. "I have no idea."

Tagg sorted through the folders she'd gone through and came up with the Mosley Beef Conglomerate file. He shoved it under her nose, as if she didn't already know what he was going to say. He spoke quietly now, calming the firestorm brewing deep inside. "You had no idea that I lost this account this morning. To Big Hawk Ranch?"

"No, I… How would I know that?"

He tossed the file down and glared at her. "I was outbid. Again. By just enough to make sure I lost the deal. This was one of my biggest accounts."

She looked puzzled for a moment. "I'm…sorry." Her eyes downcast, she spoke softly, "I don't know what to say. I don't know how it happened."

Her apology meant nothing. She'd betrayed him and he wasn't going to let her get away with it. He kept an eye on her face, not letting up, not letting her off the hook, no matter how much she claimed innocence. "Don't you?"

It took a second, but her expression changed. She met his gaze finally as recognition dawned. Her eyes went wide. "You think I did this. That I—I—" she stuttered and couldn't finish the sentence. Tears welled in her eyes.

"Tell me he blackmailed you. Threatened to take your trust fund away."

Her head shook back and forth. "No. No, Tagg. My father didn't threaten me. He didn't blackmail me. Tagg, this is ridiculous. You can't possibly think that I had anything to do with it. You have to believe me."

He ignored her plea. "I meet you in Reno and the next thing I know, I lose three big accounts. *Three, Callie.* Right in a row. We play house and my company goes straight into the toilet." His body rigid, his heart frozen, he pointed his index finger at her. "I want to know, how did you do it? Did you spy on me? Listen in on my business conversations? Go through my files when my back was turned? Did you hack into my computer while I was sleeping?"

Her expression changed. She lifted her chin, her caramel eyes hard and hot as fireplace pokers. The tears were gone now. How easily she turned on and off the waterworks. "I didn't do any of that. And you know it."

Tagg didn't believe her. He wouldn't believe another word out of her pretty, traitorous mouth. "You know, you had me fooled. I was beginning to fall in love with you. You're good, Callie. You kept me entertained. Does your father know how good you are in bed? Does he pay you to distract me with down and dirty sex?"

She slapped his face. "You bastard."

Tagg's rage surfaced. He fisted his hands and backed away from her. "Don't ever do that again."

"I can't promise that," she spat out.

Callie's cell phone rang. She glanced at it on his desk, then locked eyes with him in a battle of wills.

Tagg's face stung from her slap. He wouldn't soothe it. He needed the wake-up call to see his wife for the manipulative little bitch she was.

The phone continued to ring. "It's your father, isn't it?"

Callie shook her head. "No, it's not my father."

"Answer the phone, Callie. Or I will."

"Fine, I'll answer it." Callie picked up the phone and seemed to recognize the number appearing on the screen. She spoke quietly. "Hello."

There was no mistaking a man's deep voice coming through the receiver.

"Yes, this is Callie."

Tagg took the phone out of her hand and put it up to his ear.

"Well, hello, Callie. This is John Cosgrove. I looked up Wild Blue for you. I've got the name of his owner here. He's thinking about selling. You could probably talk him into it if the price was right."

Shaken, Tagg stared at the phone. His stomach knotted. He turned toward Callie, confused, as if he were in a horrible, inescapable dream. "Were you trying to buy—"

"Happy birthday, Tagg," she bit out.

Tagg closed his eyes and cursed under his breath as he realized his mistake. Clay's warning hammered in his brain. *You got yourself a good wife, Tagg. Don't blow it.*

But it was too late.

Callie had dashed out the front door.

She was gone.

Tagg slumped down in his chair and nearly missed landing in the seat. He grabbed the arm for balance and hung on. What had he been thinking? Maybe he hadn't been thinking at all. Maybe he'd just been reacting to emotions he'd bottled up for too many years to count. Maybe he was too damn scared to face his feelings.

He'd treated Callie like a second-class citizen on the ranch. He'd kept her at arm's length and he'd done a good job of injuring her, time and time again.

She didn't deserve his brash treatment.

A flash caught his eye from his office window. He strode over to peer out. Callie had saddled up Freedom and had taken off at breakneck speed, leaning forward and low over the saddle, the palomino's mane slashing at her face. She headed north toward the rocky terrain of Red Ridge Mountains.

Tagg raced out the front door and around back, calling her name. "Callie!"

She didn't hear him. She was already only a tiny speck in his line of vision.

He stood there, for a moment. Defeated. Angry. Ashamed.

And then he thought of another argument he'd had. *Another wife.* And all those guilt-ridden memories came back more clearly now than ever. He'd let Heather go after they'd argued. He'd been stubborn and prideful and something terrible had happened. She'd lost her life. Because he hadn't backed down. He hadn't stopped her from leaving. He hadn't gone after her.

His thoughts flashed back to Callie and the terrible hurt he'd witnessed in her eyes. He'd accused her of sabotage and wouldn't let her explain. Her body had stiffened at his accusations and she'd looked so damn confused and innocent. At the time, he'd thought it an act. But the horrible joke was on him. He was the maker of his own tragedy. He'd been dead wrong about her. It shouldn't have taken a phone message from John Cosgrove to wake him up. He should have known. He should have placed more trust in Callie.

She'd been a good wife to him. She'd tolerated his moods and, Lord knows, he'd had more bad than good ones. He thought of the two children she'd helped in Boston and the foundation where she'd volunteered her spare time until she'd felt duty bound to come home and tend to her lonely, wretched father. And when she got to Red Ridge, she'd joined the Worths to help his family launch Penny's Song. She'd done all that without asking for anything in return.

She enjoyed making others feel good about themselves. Hell, she'd tried to do that with him. She'd tried so damn hard to cement their lives together so that one day they'd become a true family. It couldn't have been easy for her—both Tagg and her father had pulled at her from opposite ends. He wouldn't blame her if she wrote the two of them off for good.

He thought about the stone and stucco walls he'd built to wallow in solitude, to keep others out and hide away for fear of feeling something valid and meaningful from entering inside of him. It was just a house, not a home. A house without life. A house without joy. A house without *Callie*.

He didn't know if she would ever forgive him for the awful things he'd said to her, the appalling way he'd treated her. He'd been granted a second chance, a second wife in Callie and hoped it wasn't too late. He wanted her in his life. He *needed* her in his life. He'd been such a fool.

Without wasting another minute, he grabbed his hat and strode to the stables. He had a wife to retrieve and he saddled his fastest horse to bring her back home.

Callie slowed Freedom to a trot as they left the pasture behind. They headed east, climbing up the foothills with the sun at their backs. It had taken ten full minutes for her heart to stop bulldozing its way against her chest. The pounding finally relented and she was able to take normal, steadying breaths, yet she felt as if she'd been hit over the head with a sledgehammer, torn up, broken down and beaten.

She'd been unnerved by Tagg's accusations. They'd come out of left field and startled her. She'd never fully understood the depth of his hatred for her father and the residual effects it had on her until now. Tagg had never trusted her. He'd probably always suspected her of sabotage. That's why he'd kept her out of his office. Why he wouldn't let her work alongside him. Why he'd never allow himself to place any faith in her.

Callie tried being a good wife. *A wife Tagg never wanted,* she reminded herself. She'd done everything she knew to do to make him see her for herself and make him love her. But it wasn't enough. Nothing she'd done had been enough.

She rode into the canyon, her mare climbing up a plateau where the vistas were staggering. Off in the distance, white puff clouds in a summer blue sky touched the mountaintops, but the immediate view was just as breathtaking. Callie dismounted and let her mare graze. She looked out into the crimson hills and deep-cut canyons before her with a heavy heart. She couldn't truly appreciate the beauty here. Everything bright in her life had dimmed. Whatever was left began fading fast.

Exhausted and weary, she walked to a boulder flat enough to fit her bottom and sat down. She put her head in her hands and closed her eyes.

A few seconds ticked by before she heard the earth pulse beneath her, a subtle sound that she recognized from years of trail riding.

When he reached the ledge, she didn't look up. "If you're here because of the baby, you can turn around and ride back home. I know my limitations and I'd never push Freedom further than was safe. I'd never endanger my baby."

"Our baby," Tagg said tenderly. She heard him dismount and approach. "And I'm not here because of the baby."

"Go away."

"I can't."

"Taggart Worth *can't* do something? Now that's a first." She kept her head down and studied the red dirt encased on her boots. The sound of Freedom's breathing reached her ears. She'd ridden her mare hard.

"Callie, I'm sorry. I've been such a fool."

Callie peered at him finally, only to agree with him. "Yes, you have."

"I never meant to hurt you. I swear to you."

"You've never seen me as anything but the enemy's daughter. You've never given me a chance. I can't…do it anymore. I won't."

Tagg nodded. "I don't expect you to."

She looked away then, her heart aching with raw pain. She knew her marriage was over.

"Callie." He stepped closer, his voice so achingly gentle now that she steeled herself. She had to be strong and brave.

"What hurts the most is that you think my father actually needed my help to sabotage you. And that I would do it! He's been one-upping his competitors all of his life. But you've beat him many times, too, and don't forget I came to the ranch only after you'd already lost out to him once this year. Knowing me had nothing to do with that. Don't you know that he'd bribe, undermine, lose money and even pose subtle threats to win out against you? The Hawk doesn't play fair, but you're too honest and honorable to know that. You have principles. You'd never do something like that to a competitor."

Tagg lifted his beautiful lips. "You love me."

For all her little speech, he only got *that* from her explanation? Her dismay turned to anger. She rose from her granite seat. "Of course I love you, you idiot! Why do you think I slept with you in Reno? Why, Tagg? Did I just pick the hottest cowboy in the crowd and drag him off to bed? You…you were my fantasy. I'd only known you from a distance, but I'd seen you in school, seen you at the rodeo and when I saw you on that bar stool that night, looking like you needed someone to help you forget the pain, I took a chance on you. You were forbidden to me up until then. I chucked my father's rules and maybe now I wish I hadn't."

"You don't mean that." He came closer. Their eyes met. His presence unsettled her. She needed space from this man. She needed to push him away and keep him away. The hurt of losing him would nearly kill her. It *was* killing her.

She realized the implication of her last statement. Her voice softened. "No, I don't mean that," she admitted. She put her hand on her abdomen and felt nothing but love for the baby growing inside her. "I want this baby, Tagg. I want it more than my next breath."

Tagg exhaled and it came out as a deep sigh, "So do I. I want our family. I love you, Callie."

She shook her head, refusing to believe him. This would only hurt later and the wound would never heal. "No, no, you don't. You don't love me."

"I do, Callie. I've been fighting it. For so long."

Tears threatened to fall. She had to be strong. "How can I believe that?"

"You can't take me at my word?"

"Not this time, Tagg. You have too much at stake. I know you want to protect the baby from my father. I know you don't want me to move off the ranch."

"I love you, Callie."

She shook her head.

"I love you. I'll say it a thousand times if I have to. I'll say it until the day I die."

She gasped, wanting to believe him. Trying to believe him.

Tagg studied her, seeing her indecision. When she thought he'd give up and stalk away, he sucked in a breath. It was as though he fought a mental battle and the decision was made with a quick nod of his head. He met her eyes earnestly. "I know your father was at our wedding."

Was this another of his accusations? She retreated. "I had nothing—"

"Shh." He snaked an arm out to bring her close and pressed two fingers to her lips. "I know you had nothing to do with it. *I did.* I arranged for him to be there."

"You!" Callie couldn't believe it. Why, when Tagg hated her father so much, would he have allowed him on their property, much less to watch them take their vows. "Tagg, not you. You'd never—"

"I did and believe me, it wasn't for your father's sake. To this day, he doesn't know I was the one who arranged it. I did it for you. I didn't want you to regret marrying me. I couldn't bring myself to have The Hawk as part of the ceremony, but I knew one day you'd come to resent me for not having him there. And even then, as angry as I was with you, I wanted to give you that much."

"Oh, Tagg." How could she not love this man? How could she turn him away now?

"There's more, Callie. It's time I told you the whole truth. You have a right to know. To understand why I couldn't give you what you wanted. My first wife…"

Tagg's voice broke. Callie helped him along. "I know about Heather."

"You don't know this. No one does. I've kept this secret from everyone important to me. But now, you need to hear this as much as I need to say it."

"What do I need to hear?"

"The night Heather died, we had an argument. Fact was, Heather had been married before. It only lasted a few months and the marriage had been annulled long before I'd met her. Her ex showed up at our house and I found them together talking. Just talking. She tried to explain but I was too jealous, too angry to listen. It was something that I should have let go but the whole thing got blown entirely out of proportion. We'd never fought like that before. She couldn't take it anymore. She packed a bag and told me she was going to spend some time with her mother. I was…I was foolish enough to let her go. I figured I was right and she was wrong and she'd come crawling back to me when she figured it all out."

"Tagg, you couldn't have known…"

"I know that, but it doesn't help. If I'd called her back, she'd be alive today." Tagg's face twisted in pain.

"I'm so sorry." Callie ached for him, but she didn't have words to share in his grief.

He closed his eyes as if reliving it. Then on a quiet, barely audible breath, he said, "Heather was pregnant."

Callie stared at him. She shook her head. "Oh, no."

Tagg's voice took a self-loathing turn. "She hadn't told me yet. The doctor said she'd wanted to wait…until my birthday. She'd wanted to surprise me."

Callie gasped, unable to hide her shock. She cried inside for the loss of life, for the unborn child that had never stood a chance. For an accident that shouldn't have happened in the first place. Everyone knew about the plane crash on the runway, a takeoff that went very wrong. Everyone knew that Heather died that night. But to her knowledge no one knew about the baby. Tagg had carried his burden alone. He'd lost a child that night as well. The guilt and pain he felt must have been excruciating for him to bear. And he'd chosen to endure that all alone.

Callie couldn't miss the similarities to their relationship. The pregnancy she'd kept from him, the birthday surprise, the fight that they'd had tonight and her storming out, riding off the ranch on her horse. All of it seemed surreal now. "Tagg, I…" But she couldn't get the words out.

"I closed myself off, Callie. I refused to let anyone in. I'd already blown one relationship. I lost someone dear to me. I lost a child. It was my fault—all of it. I didn't want to feel anything for anyone ever again. I wouldn't let myself fall in love."

Tears spilled down her cheeks. Emotions washed over her at the utter pain she heard in his voice. "Oh, Tagg."

"I figured when Clay started Penny's Song I could contribute and, in some small way, I could make up for the child that I'd lost."

She wiped her tears away. "Because you're a good and honorable man."

"And a big idiot, too. You were right. I know I don't deserve you. I used you as a scapegoat. I blamed you for something you couldn't help. Your father has a vendetta against my family, but you have never taken part in any of that. What's important now is that you know that I'd move heaven and earth to earn back your love. Let me love you, Callie. I promise I'll do better. I'll make it up to you."

He took her hand in his and she felt her bruised heart healing. He'd confided in her something he hadn't told another human being. He'd trusted her with his truth. He'd opened up his heart to her and bared his soul.

She wouldn't tell him about his father and her mother. Not now. But maybe someday the two families could sit down together and talk it out, finally putting the past where it belonged. She would make her father listen to reason. And if she had to, she'd give The Hawk an ultimatum. If he didn't let the past go and accept Tagg on his own merit, he'd truly have no part in her life. Or her child's. Callie would make it right. She had to. She loved Tagg and her unborn baby too much and wouldn't be torn in two any longer.

Tagg got down on one knee.

Callie drew her lips tight. Her hands trembled and the rest

of her was a wobbly mess of nerves. "What are you doing?" she asked on a whisper.

"I'm proposing to you, Callie. The way I should have. Let me do this right."

He waited for her answer.

"Okay," she said ever so softly.

He took a moment to gather his thoughts and then began, "Callie Sullivan Worth, will you marry me? Will you let me love you and treat you the way you deserve to be treated? Will you let me be a husband to you, giving you all my faith, trust and love? If you give me this second chance, I swear to you, I won't ever disappoint you again. I promise you we'll have a good life together. I promise you, I'll love you forever and then some."

Callie's heart opened and a rush of tenderness flowed in. She melted with happiness. She forgave Tagg all of his bad moods, lack of trust and unfair accusations. She forgave him for making her feel like an outsider on the ranch. For pushing her away every chance he could. Seeing him on bended knee, professing his love for her, she could forgive him anything. All in all, she'd always thought him the perfect man. No, she amended that. He was the perfect man *for her.*

Tagg loved her. She repeated it over and over in her head. This wasn't a dream. *He loves me. He really loves me.*

She bobbed her head up and down and joyous tears trickled down her cheeks. "Yes, Tagg. Yes. Yes. Yes."

Tagg rose and she looped her arms around his neck, needing to touch him, to make sure all of this was real.

Tenderly, he wiped the moisture from her face. "I love you, Callie."

"I believe you."

"We'll be happy together."

"I know. We will be." She was certain of it.

He took her in a deep, soul-melding kiss that assured them both years and years of happiness. When they finally broke apart, Tagg stared into her eyes. And then something remarkable happened.

His lips curled up and he gave her his one hundred percent megawatt, the-world-is-a-happy-place-and-I-love-life kind of smile.

She knew she'd never love Tagg more than at this very moment.

He turned her and arm and arm they looked out at the majestic splendor of the Red Ridge Mountains. Together they witnessed their future on this land.

Callie sighed with immense delight.

She'd married her fantasy man.

How many girls could honestly say that?

* * * * *

"You won't need to worry about that in future."

Her breath stalled. "What do you mean?"

"We're getting married."

"Married?" She heard the words and thought she might faint. The minute he'd learned about their child, she'd thought it might come to this, but hearing it out loud hit her hard.

And yet...if she had her son, she had everything that mattered. "So you're *not* going to try and take Nathan from me?" she said weakly.

"No." He paused. "Of course, if you don't marry me I'll fight for custody. A child should have both parents. Even if we don't love each other."

Dear Reader,

Do you believe in love at first sight? How does someone know in an instant that they will love the other person for the rest of their life? And what if something happens and love turns to hate? I imagine it would be almost impossible to trust in your feelings ever again after that.

My heroine, Gemma Watkins, thought she'd found true love from the moment she met Tate Chandler—until he accused her of something she didn't do. As for Tate, he hadn't planned on "ever after" when he first met Gemma. He was only interested in an affair—until she betrayed him with his best friend. Gemma may have been in love, and Tate in lust, but both of them went from thinking they knew the other, to realising they couldn't rely on their own judgement at all.

And now there's a child involved, and Gemma and Tate have to put aside their differences and concentrate on what's important. Will the love for their son show their real characters to each other?

True love is exactly that—true forever. Nothing pulls it apart. This time Gemma and Tate have the chance to change their future together, but only by rising above their past.

Happy reading!

Maxine

SECRET SON,
CONVENIENT WIFE

BY
MAXINE SULLIVAN

Published in Great Britain 2011
by Mills & Boon, an imprint of Harlequin (UK) Limited,
Eton House, 18-24 Paradise Road, Richmond, Surrey TW9 1SR

© Maxine Sullivan 2011

ISBN: 978 0 263 89085 3

51-1111

Harlequin (UK) policy is to use papers that are natural, renewable and
recyclable products and made from wood grown in sustainable forests. The
logging and manufacturing processes conform to the legal environmental
regulations of the country of origin.

Printed and bound in Spain
by Blackprint CPI, Barcelona

This *USA TODAY* bestselling author credits her mother for her lifelong love of romance novels, so it was a natural extension for **Maxine Sullivan** to want to write her own romances. She thinks there's nothing better than being a writer and is thrilled to be one of the few Australians to write for the Desire™ line.

Maxine lives in Melbourne, Australia, but over the years has travelled to New Zealand, the UK and the USA. In her own backyard, her husband's job ensured they saw the diversity of the countryside, from the tropics to the Outback, country towns to the cities. She is married to Geoff, who has proven his hero status many times over the years. They have two handsome sons and an assortment of much-loved, previously abandoned animals.

Maxine would love to hear from you. She can be contacted through her website at www.maxinesullivan.com.

To Elvina Payet, and Bec and Scott Schulz
for their support and helpful advice with this book.
Thanks guys!

One

Gemma Watkins stopped dead as she stepped outside the hospital waiting room. A tall man was striding toward her along the corridor. His broad shoulders, his purposeful walk, reminded her of…

Please God, not Tate Chandler!

In that instant he saw her. His footsteps faltered just a hint, then increased pace until he reached her. "Gemma," he rasped.

His voice traveled under her skin like a shiver of apprehension. This was the man who'd once been her lover. The man she'd once fallen in love with. The man who'd cut out her heart almost two years ago.

She couldn't believe it was him. Tate Chandler was an Australian who'd taken his family's luxury watchmaking business to new levels and high international standing. He was a man suited to his surroundings, whether it was here in this large hospital close to the city, his well-appointed headquarters on the most prestigious street in Melbourne or his luxurious penthouse in one of the city's most affluent suburbs. He was a billionaire with a powerful presence that went beyond his supreme good looks. He had the golden touch...and his touch was golden. *She* knew that firsthand.

Gemma swallowed the panic in her throat. "Hello, Tate."

His blue eyes flicked over her blond hair tumbling to her shoulders, to the flush of her cheeks, as if he couldn't quite help himself, then as quickly his eyes narrowed. "I hope your being here is merely a coincidence."

It took a moment to actually absorb the words. Her brows drew together. "I'm not sure what you mean."

Skepticism crossed his face. "My family dedicated the new children's wing in my grandfather's name today. Surely you saw mention of it? It's been in all the media."

"No, I didn't." She'd been too busy working and trying to keep her head above water. "So your grandfather's... dead?"

"Three months ago."

"I'm sorry." Tate had been very close to him. "But you can't think I came here today to see *you*. I could see you anytime I like."

His lips twisted. "You think so?"

Her heart constricted. He hadn't forgiven her for what he saw as her betrayal. Had she expected he would?

And that brought her back to why she was at the hospital today. What bad luck that she'd decided just now to look for the nurse from the recovery room. She supposed she could be grateful that the rest of his family didn't appear to be anywhere in sight. "Well, I must—"

"What are you doing here then?"

She saw not one ounce of kindness in his eyes. "I'm with a…friend."

"Male?"

"Er…yes."

"Of course it's a male," he mocked. "Nothing's changed there, has it?"

Her hesitation made her look guilty, but he couldn't know it wasn't for the reason he thought. Realizing this was her "out," she lifted her chin. "This has nothing to do with you, Tate. Goodbye." She went to move past him, but he put his hand on her arm, stopping her.

"Does the poor sucker know he's one of many?"

"I—"

"You what? Don't care? Believe me, *I* know that more than anyone."

The words stung. She'd willingly given herself to Tate the day she'd met him at a party held by her architect boss. At the time, she'd wished she hadn't given away her virginity years ago to a boyfriend in high school. She'd fallen instantly in love with Tate and had known then what her mother had meant when she'd advised Gemma to keep herself for the man she loved. Gemma would have been proud for Tate to have been her first.

She could only thank the Lord now that she hadn't told Tate she loved him. Somehow she'd kept that secret to herself and had managed to keep some of her pride intact when he'd turned his back on her after a month-long affair. During their short weeks together, they'd barely left Tate's penthouse apartment. His best friend had been the only one to know about their relationship.

The memory of it all made her shudder. Their unexpected reunion today was so unfair, yet she couldn't tell Tate the truth. Not now. He might decide to—

"Oh, there you are, Gemma." A female voice a few

feet away from them made Gemma suck in a quick, sharp breath. She turned to look at the nurse from the recovery room. Oh, God, she'd almost forgotten.

"He's fine, love," Deirdre said before Gemma could ask. "And out of recovery now."

"Thank God!" Gemma forgot about Tate as intense relief washed over her. They'd said it would be a minor operation, but there were always risks with these things.

Deirdre's gaze dropped to Tate's hand on Gemma's arm, and she frowned slightly. Gemma knew she had to act quickly. From the depths of her being, she dragged up a reassuring smile. She didn't want any issues here. The sooner she got away from Tate, the better. "I'm coming now, Deirdre. Thank you."

The nurse paused a second longer, before seeming to accept there wasn't a problem. "I'll go tell Nathan that Mommy's coming then." She headed back to the recovery room.

Gemma didn't need Tate's tightening grip to feel the increased tension emanating from him. Her heartbeat thudded in her ears as she gathered the nerve to look into his eyes, torn between running to Nathan and staying here and standing guard.

"You have a *son?*"

Her heart quailed. How could she deny it now? "Yes."

His head went back, as if from a blow. Then, without warning, his expression changed, turned suspicious. "And his name is Nathan?"

She gave a quick nod.

"My grandfather's name was Nathaniel."

"It's a common enough name," she said, finding her voice, kicking herself now for allowing herself that one weakness.

All at once, he swore. Then he dropped her arm and strode past her.

Like a mother bear, Gemma jumped in front of him, putting herself between him and her son. "He's only ten months old, Tate," she lied.

He stopped. "He's not Drake's, is he?"

"No!" He'd never believed her innocent where his best friend had been concerned. Drake Fulton had made her uneasy, always being too friendly whenever Tate left them alone together, making it more than clear he wanted her. In the end he hadn't gotten her, but he'd made damn sure Tate hadn't held on to her either.

"So your son belongs to another man."

She dropped her hand. "Yes."

Him.

She prayed Tate would turn and walk away. Instead, he surprised her and moved ahead. She quickly caught up to him, frantic with worry. "Wh-where are you going?"

He continued toward the recovery room, purpose in every step. "You've lied to me before."

"I didn't. I—" She sidestepped a young couple walking down the middle of the corridor, then caught up to him again.

He ignored her as he hit a button outside the recovery room to open the electronic doors. She went with him as he entered the room, watched his gaze slice down the row of occupied beds. Past Deirdre now attending to one of the patients…past the nurse at her station…until he came to the crib set slightly away from the rest of the beds.

Time was suspended in the air.

Then, almost in sync, they both started forward, stopping only when they reached the small blond boy playing with his teddy bear. Nathan looked up, and Gemma held her breath.

Tate couldn't know.

He just couldn't…

And then Tate turned to look at her, his face white. His eyes skinned her alive.

She was going to pay dearly for this.

Tate felt the blood drain from his face the minute the infant looked up and caught him by the heart. Caught and grabbed and would never let go.

For just a moment, Tate almost wished that the boy *wasn't* his, that he could turn and walk away and never have to see Gemma again. He didn't want her in his life again.

But one look and he knew.

This was his *son*.

And Tate wasn't going anywhere.

Just then, the boy saw his mother. He dropped his teddy bear and threw his arms out to her with a cry, and Gemma gave a small sob as she ran to the crib and lifted him up and over the side. "Sh, darling, Mommy's here," she murmured, hugging him and soothing him.

Mommy.

Daddy.

His.

She leaned back to check the boy. It would have been touching if Tate hadn't suddenly realized something.

"What's wrong with him?" he heard himself ask in a croaky voice, not sure if he could bear knowing.

Gemma lifted her head—and her chin. "What do you mean? He's perfect."

She'd taken his comment the wrong way. He'd have been offended if he'd had the time. "I'm talking about why he's here in the hospital." The child didn't show any outward signs of an operation except for the hospital gown.

She winced. "Yes, of course." Then she took a breath. "They put tiny tubes inside his ears to drain them. He was getting repeated ear infections and the antibiotics weren't working anymore. Without the tubes, he could suffer hearing loss, and that could affect his speech and development."

As serious as that sounded, Tate felt the tension ease out of him. Thank God it wasn't anything critical.

And then he remembered her lies, and the tension was back. "You didn't think to tell me about it?" he said, keeping his voice low, aware of others in the room.

"Why would I?"

"Because he's mine, dammit."

Her arms tightened around her son. "No, he isn't."

"Don't lie, Gemma. He has my eyes."

Fear came and went on her face. "No, he's got blond hair like me. He *looks* like me. He doesn't look like you at all. And he's only ten months old."

Nathan *did* look like her—except for the eyes. "He's mine. And he's a year old. I know it, and so do you."

"Tate, please," she choked out. "I don't think this is the right time or place to discuss this."

"Gemma..." He had to know this minute. He had to be sure.

She shuddered, then expelled a deep breath. "Yes, he's yours."

Hearing the words out loud was like a wave breaking over Tate. For a moment he couldn't breathe, couldn't get his bearings. And then he looked at his son. He wanted to hold him in his arms and *feel* the moment, but as much as he wanted to hug Nathan tight, Tate figured things had to be taken slowly. A child had the right to personal space.

Gemma looked dismayed. "Wh-what are you going to do now?"

He had to concentrate, and that was hard when he was so damn angry with her. "We'll have a paternity test done first. As proof."

Her eyes widened. "So you're not really sure?"

"I'm sure, but I want there to be absolutely no doubt about this. Besides, it wouldn't be the first time I've been fooled by you, would it?"

He would never forget finding her kissing his best friend. And then having Drake awkwardly confess she'd been coming on to him from the start. The incident had made Tate want to kill both of them. Much to his credit, Drake had been honorable enough not to let her seduce him. It was the measure of the man that he could withstand such a beautiful woman. Sure, out in the corridor Tate had asked her if the infant was Drake's, but the question had been more about covering all bases than believing his friend had slept with her. Drake wouldn't do that. He always kept his word.

Unlike Gemma.

"I've all but admitted he's your son, Tate. There's no need for a paternity test."

"Your word isn't good enough, I'm afraid." His jaw felt so tight he thought it would snap. "We'll talk about everything later."

She straightened. "No, it'll have to wait. I'm taking Nathan home as soon as the doctor releases him."

"We'll be going to my home."

She gasped. "There's no need for that."

"Isn't there?"

She swallowed. "He's already unsettled from being here. I want to get him back in familiar surroundings. He needs the comfort of his own home right now."

Only for his son's sake did Tate relent. "Then I'm

coming with you and staying the night, but tomorrow we'll be going to my place."

"What!"

"Don't worry. I'll sleep on your sofa. We need to talk, and I'm not letting you out of my sight."

"Can't we leave it until tomorrow? It's only just lunchtime. I'm sure you want to return to your office and get some work done today."

"No."

That's all he was going to say. He'd already missed the first year of his son's life, he wasn't missing a minute more. Having his child without telling him was unforgivable. What if something had gone wrong with the operation? What if he'd never gotten to stand here with his own flesh and blood? What if Nathan had needed *him?* Tate's chest constricted with the oddest pain.

Right then the nurse appeared beside them. "Didn't I tell you your baby boy would be fine?" she teased Gemma.

Gemma nodded. "Thank you, Deirdre. You've been wonderful."

"You're very welcome, love," the nurse said. "Now, I see the doctor has just come in, so you should be able to take your little one home shortly."

The younger man appeared at Deirdre's side and glanced from Tate to Nathan, then back to Tate. "So you're the father," he said without question.

Gemma made a sound that could be mistaken for a sob, but all Tate felt was fatherly pride swelling up inside his chest. The doctor's assumption was based solely on the sight of Tate and Nathan together.

Father and son.

Tate cleared his throat. "Yes, I'm Nathan's father."

The doctor accepted that, then turned his attention to the infant.

Tate sent Gemma a look that said it all: There was no going back now.

Two

"Look straight ahead and keep walking to the limousine." Tate's hand slipped around her waist as if he were shielding her from the man standing in the parking lot. Or shielding his son was more likely, she thought, trying to ignore the protective feel of this man beside her as she carried Nathan.

"Who is he?"

"A photographer. He was here for the dedication. I'm not sure why he's still here. Probably just our bad luck he was leaving at the same time as us."

The open car door loomed ahead, and it was sheer instinct that orchestrated their haste onto the backseat in a matter of moments. Then the driver came around and Tate pressed a button to lower the screen as the older man slid in behind the steering wheel. "Go straight home, Clive, but take it easy." He was clearly thinking about Nathan, who now sat between them in the car seat the driver had moved from her car. The screen came back up.

Gemma finished checking that her son was comfortable and had his teddy bear, then she looked up. "I want to go to *my* home, Tate."

"And lead the media straight to you and Nathan?"

"It was only one guy, and he can't know anything," she said, trying not to overreact. "You said earlier you would take me home and have someone collect my car. I'm sure you want to get back to the office. You can come over tonight and we'll talk then." She needed some time to herself to sort things out in her head.

He snorted. "And find you and Nathan gone when I return?"

She blinked. "Where would we go?"

"Your parents' place, for a start."

"You'd find me in next to no time." Not that she would go there. Or even *could*. Her middle-class parents had cut her out of their staid and virtuous lives, but she couldn't tell him that. Apart from it hurting too much, she wouldn't give him that power over her.

And she had no other relatives to whom she could turn. With her parents starting a new life and coming to Australia from England straight after their marriage many years ago, distant relatives were exactly that. Distant.

He picked up his cell phone and began speaking to someone called Peggy, who by the sound of his instructions was the housekeeper. His last housekeeper had been an older lady who'd merely come in to clean the apartment a few times a week, usually during the day when no one was there.

Accepting that she couldn't change anything right now, Gemma tuned him out. Lord, she was still reeling from everything that had happened today, and in her life in general over the past two years. She didn't regret having Nathan—not at all—but her life had changed so much since meeting Tate.

Not wanting Tate to learn she was having his baby, she'd left her job in an architect's office, downsized her trendy city flat and moved into a one-bedroom apartment in the suburbs. But getting to and from work in the city would have become impossible once she'd had Nathan, so she'd taken a job closer to home. At least then she hadn't had to worry about the hour of traveling each way cutting into quality time with her child.

She'd done her best, and it *had* been good enough, but it still hadn't been easy to stop herself from running to Tate and asking him to take them away from it all. She'd been more afraid he would only take Nathan away from *her*. Tate had kicked her out of his life once before. She had no doubt that if he believed he was doing the right thing, he would kick her out again—and keep her son.

Yet all this heartache could have been avoided if only Tate had believed her eighteen months ago. He'd given a party for his best friend's birthday and invited her to play hostess. She'd been so excited. Later in the evening, she'd written a note to Tate, telling him to meet her in his study for a kiss, and asked the waiter to give it to him.

The room had been dark when he stepped inside and she'd thrown herself at him. Only…it wasn't Tate. The real Tate had opened the door and caught her kissing his best friend thoroughly, her arms around Drake's neck. It seemed Drake had followed her into the room, but it had been *she* who looked guilty.

The thought of that night made her feel ill, so she pushed it out of her mind, and a while later the limousine turned into a driveway. A security guard opened two large gates, showcasing a beautiful mansion. Gemma said the first thing that came to mind. "This isn't your apartment."

"It's my home now."

A spasm went through her heart. This was more than big enough for a family. "Were you planning on marrying?"

"One day."

"So there's someone special in your life?"

"Only my son."

She looked away, thankful the car was pulling to a stop. The pain of losing Tate had been made worse by frequently seeing him in the papers with a beautiful woman on his arm. Not that it was any of her business, but knowing he wasn't serious about anyone made her feel better about things.

Everything was a bit of a blur after they left the car. Gemma insisted on carrying Nathan again as they went inside. He was usually a happy child, but his eyes were wide and she could sense he was confused by everything today.

He wasn't the only one!

Tate briefly introduced them to the housekeeper, who beamed at them both. "He's beautiful, Mr. Chandler."

Tate's face softened as he looked at his son. "Yes, he is, Peggy." Then he glanced at Gemma and his eyes hardened before he turned back to Peggy. "So the suite next to mine is ready?"

"Of course." She hesitated. "Mr. Chandler...I was thinking. I have a crib you can use temporarily. It's not an expensive one, but Clive and I keep it in our rooms for when we mind the grandchildren. He could set it up in the suite...until you get your own, that is. We won't need it anytime soon."

Tate nodded. "Good idea, Peggy. Thank you for thinking of it."

Peggy's face filled with pleasure. "You're welcome. I'll get Clive right on it."

Tate put his hand under Gemma's elbow and herded her toward the staircase. "Good. I'll talk to you shortly about what else we need."

Of course Tate would give her and Nathan their own suite, Gemma thought with relief. Tate hadn't wanted her once he'd "discovered" her with Drake. He wouldn't want her now.

As he opened the bedroom door, he indicated his own rooms farther along the landing. The distance was considerable, thank goodness.

Her suite was bigger than her apartment. The large bedroom had a king-sized bed, a sitting room and a gold-encrusted ensuite. It was as one would expect in such a house, except that while the bedroom was suitable for a crawling infant the sitting room definitely wasn't childproof.

"I might need to move a few things out of Nathan's way. And that couch might need a cover." It looked like it was made of velvet. Not exactly safe for grubby little fingers.

"I don't care about the furniture, but I don't want him hurting himself, so do what you need to do. I'll make sure Peggy has everything else in the house childproofed as soon as possible." Tate put the bag of baby paraphernalia she'd brought to the hospital on one of the chairs. "Does he need anything heated up?"

"No. This is fine." Gemma had a bottle of juice in the baby bag. "He'll probably take a nap." He'd been sleepy in the car, though now he squirmed to be put down.

Gemma placed Nathan on the plush carpet with his teddy bear, then closed the sitting room door so he couldn't go in there. He wasn't quite walking yet, but he could crawl like the wind and at least she could keep a firm eye on him in here.

"Clive will bring the crib up, and I'll be back soon. Peggy will need a list of anything Nathan needs. We'll order a crib and other things tomorrow. I want them as soon as possible."

How wonderful to be able to snap your fingers and have things happen. She'd snap her fingers and get her and Nathan out of here if she could. "I've got everything he needs at home."

Arrogance bounced off him. "I intend my son to have the best."

"He has. He's got *me*."

"Of course. And now you won't need to worry about anything else."

Her breath stalled. "What do you mean?"

"We're getting married."

"Ma-married?" She heard the words and thought she might faint. The minute he'd learned about Nathan, she'd known he was old-fashioned enough to insist on marriage, but hearing it out loud hit her hard.

And yet…if she had her son, she had everything that mattered. "So you're *not* going to try and take Nathan from me?"

"No." He allowed a silence. "Of course, if you don't marry me I'll fight for custody. A child should have both parents."

She quickly pulled herself together. To live with the man she'd once loved, knowing he believed she'd cheated on him—wouldn't her life be a living hell? How would that affect Nathan? Perhaps if she pointed this out…

"Even if we don't love each other?"

"Yes."

"Even if you consider me a liar?"

"Yes."

"That won't be a marriage, Tate. That'll be a nightmare, not only for us but for Nathan."

His mouth tightened. "If you care about your son, you'll make it work."

"That's unfair."

"Is it?"

"Perhaps part-time custody," she began, knowing she was in a losing battle now, not even sure why she didn't simply give in. Tate always won.

"No."

"Hear me out. I—"

Just then, the infant babbled something. When she looked, Nathan had pulled himself up by the side of the bed and was hanging on to the quilt, the cheesiest of grins telling them how clever he thought he was. Gemma's heart overflowed with love.

Then something about Tate made her look at him. In his eyes was twelve months' worth of longing for a son he'd never known. "Tate, I—"

"Don't, Gemma," he said tersely. "Don't say another word." He twisted on his heels and left the room.

Tate stood at the living room window, a hard knot in the center of his chest. He still felt shell-shocked by today's events, like he was in a war zone with everything raining down on him.

And then his infant son had smiled and lit up the room, and Tate knew there was a reason he had run into Gemma today. His son might have a mother, but Nathan needed his father. Tate had never felt more certain of anything in his life.

God, how could Gemma have kept Nathan from him? And how could she let him believe—even briefly—that she'd had another man's child? He'd felt physically ill in that hospital corridor. The reminder of her with other men, the shock of thinking she'd had another man's baby, had knocked the breath from his body.

There had only been two times in his life when he'd been this winded. Once when he'd caught Gemma kissing Drake, and the other when he was twelve and his mother had left his father for another man.

Darlene Chandler had supposedly gone away on a trip to visit a sick cousin, but Tate had overheard his father talking to her on the phone. Never would Tate have thought he'd hear his tall, strong father pleading for his wife to come back to him. Nothing had worked, and Jonathan Chandler had seemed to shrink in size, as if he'd lost a part of himself. Not even Tate's young sister, Bree, who'd been too young to know and who was the apple of her father's eye, could get through to him.

A week later, his mother had walked back in the door.

Tate had always felt protective of his father after that. He loved his mother, and somehow his parents' marriage had been better than before, but Tate couldn't forget how loving a woman could tear a man down. He was determined never to let that happen to *him*.

Certainly not with Gemma.

It had been all about sex with them, nothing more. He'd never wanted a woman like he'd wanted her. From the moment he'd set eyes on Gemma, he'd needed her with an ache that had gone right through him. He'd spent every spare second of the next month trying to ease that ache. She hadn't moved into his penthouse, exactly, but they'd spent so much time there, she might as well have.

He'd been confident their affair would eventually run its course. He wasn't fool enough to believe it had been about love. He'd known he'd never give his heart to any woman.

Sure, one day he'd marry, and he'd have kids, but that was in the future. Until then, he thought, he had plenty of time to tire of Gemma and then go back to playing the field.

He just hadn't expected *Gemma* to be the one playing games, and definitely not with his best friend. She may not have slept with Drake, but it hadn't been for want of trying.

Memories flooded back. It had been Drake's birthday, and Tate had asked Gemma if she'd host the party. No wonder she'd agreed so enthusiastically. He'd thought it was because she was finally meeting more of his friends. In reality it was because she'd planned on seducing Drake.

God, he'd been a fool. She'd used him two years ago, making him think she was a woman to be trusted. How could he still want a woman like her? Sure, she was very beautiful, even with those small lines of tiredness under her eyes and a weariness to her shoulders that could not be manufactured. But she would milk his sympathy for all its worth.

He was one step ahead of her this time.

He'd been duped once by her charm. He wouldn't let that happen again.

After Clive delivered the crib and Peggy brought up a tray with a plate of daintily cut sandwiches and a pot of coffee with two cups, Gemma thanked them and settled Nathan down for a nap. In the sitting room and alone at last, she gratefully poured herself a coffee and sat on the couch, not realizing until then how desperate she was to ease the dryness in her mouth. The sandwiches she left untouched. She couldn't eat a thing right now.

As she wrapped her cold hands around the china cup, it was hard to believe how things had spiraled so out of control within a few hours. God, why had she chosen to get involved with Tate Chandler in the first place? Why couldn't she have settled for a simple man? Damn him for being a man of substance in more ways than one. Moneyed or poor, he'd fight to have his son. Of course, that left her with no options at all.

Just then, there was a soft rap on the bedroom door. She hurried to answer it, knowing Tate was being quiet for Nathan's sake. His manner reminded her of how a lover might sneak into her room. But that was crazy thinking. Tate had never snuck into her room or her apartment. He hadn't needed to.

Tate's eyes flickered to his son in the crib then back to her as he stepped inside the door. "Everything okay?"

He meant his son.

"Yes. Coffee?" Not waiting for an answer, she led the way to the sitting room, quietly closing the connecting door. All at once, she was aware of Tate behind her, following her, feeling his eyes on her as he stood and watched her pour.

She handed the cup to him, then gestured to the other chair, giving the impression that this was her territory. At least it made her feel she had the upper hand in here.

That impression didn't last long.

Not with Tate.

He didn't sit. He drained the coffee from the small cup, then went to the window and stood looking out, his back totally immovable and unbending. "By the way, you won't be getting your car."

She'd been about to put down her cup, but her hand stopped midair. "What do you mean?"

He slowly turned around. "They couldn't even start it, let alone drive it out of the hospital grounds. I've told Clive to get rid of it."

The coffee cup wobbled and she almost dropped it onto the saucer. "What!" she exclaimed, keeping her voice low so as not to wake her son. "You had no right to do that."

"You're not driving my son around in that thing."

She ignored the fact that he didn't care that *she* drove around in it. "My car is only five years old. Admittedly, sometimes it can be temperamental in starting, but apart from that it works fine." It had been a good buy at a time when she'd needed to be very careful with money. She *still* needed to be careful with money. "Anyway, I need my car to get to work."

An arrogant brow lifted. "You work?"

"Yes, that's how we mere mortals pay our bills," she snapped sarcastically.

"If you'd told me about Nathan in the first place, you wouldn't need to worry about the bills."

"And then I'd have bigger problems, wouldn't I?"

"You've got them now."

"Damn you, Tate."

There was a moment of stony silence.

"Why didn't you tell me about Nathan?" he demanded, his voice tight with strain.

"I had my reasons."

"You took it upon yourself to keep my son from me. Those reasons had better be bloody good."

There was no way she'd let him see how heartbroken she still was by everything that had happened between them or he'd use it against her. "You already thought the worst of me. I had nothing else to lose by keeping him to myself."

His eyes narrowed. "So this is about you not wanting to share him with me?"

It wasn't that. She would have been glad to share with him, only she wasn't convinced Tate would want to share with *her.* "At least I only had to please myself," she said offhandedly.

His mouth tightened. "He needed both of us, Gemma. He still needs both of us."

"We did all right without you."

Anger flashed in his eyes. "Really?"

She wondered if somehow he knew about her struggle to put food on the table—not for her son but for herself. But then, how could he possibly know that? Was he talking about her car?

Anyway, she'd made sure Nathan had everything he needed, the most important thing being love. Tate may have killed her love for him when he kicked her out, but she'd never had reservations about her love for his baby.

"Tate, think about this. If we marry, do you really want your son living in such a stressful environment? Because it can't be anything but. You know it and I know it."

"He doesn't seem too stressed out right now," he said, directing her gaze to the quiet coming from the bedroom.

"That's probably the anesthetic. It may not have worn off." And she couldn't help but add, "Look, I have no doubt all the attention he'll get from you will be a novelty to him at first, but it can't last. There's more to being a father than claiming a child as your own."

"You say that when you haven't even given me a chance?"

"You were quick to drop *me* like a hot rock," she said, surprised by how cool she sounded.

"The two things don't compare," he said dismissively. "And actually the shoe is on the other foot. I'd say you're the person least likely to stick with parenthood."

That stung. "I'm a very good mother."

"And I'll be a very good father."

Stalemate.

"Who looks after Nathan while you're at work?" he fired at her.

"He goes to a day-care center. And it's a very good one," she said defensively. "I wouldn't leave him there otherwise."

"And the job? I ran into your old boss ages ago, and he told me you'd left."

Clearly he must not have been interested enough to ask where she'd gone. Why did that hurt now? "I work for a courier company. In the dispatch department."

"A bit of a comedown, isn't it?"

"There's nothing wrong with working in a demanding environment. We all work very hard."

"I wasn't denigrating the courier business."

Her top lip curled. "No, just me."

His look said he acknowledged that. "As my wife, you don't have to work."

"I won't leave them in the lurch," she said, then could have kicked herself. She didn't want to hint that she was prepared to give in to another of his decrees.

"I don't think you've thought it through, Gemma. There are plenty of people looking for work, and some of them might not like a rich man's wife taking a job that someone else needs. Would you be comfortable with that?"

She sent him a sour look. Why was nothing going her way today? He was right, damn him. If she kept working there, word might get out, then how would it look to work friends who struggled to keep their jobs and food on the table for their families? And now that she didn't have a car, she could just imagine rolling up in Tate's limo each day.

"Wouldn't you rather stay home with Nathan?" Tate asked more quietly.

There was nothing for it but to admit, "Okay, yes. I miss being with him." She missed every minute she was away from her son. She'd hated leaving him, even knowing it was good for him to be around other people and that he was in good hands.

"There you are then. Problem solved." Tate had a results-driven mind set in everything he did. Nothing had changed there.

"It's all black and white to you, isn't it? There are no shades of gray. No room for error."

"Things are what they are. For now, take the time off to stay home with Nathan and we'll worry about the future later. He needs his mother, and you look like you could do with a long rest from performing two jobs."

Inwardly, she slumped with an odd relief, knowing the one good thing about marrying Tate would be getting help. She was so tired. She'd been responsible for everything, with no one to turn to for so long. There had been the trauma of breaking up with him, then the realization she was pregnant, the acceptance that her parents would be no help. Then she'd had to move to somewhere less expensive, find a new local job that would give her time off to have the baby—all without any real break for herself. She'd do it all again, for her son, but it would be nice to lean on someone else for a change—until she could get back to normal.

"At least I know you didn't deliberately get pregnant," he said, surprising her with the backhanded compliment just as she'd started to relax.

"I could have put a pin in one of the condoms," she quipped, wanting to rock him.

His eyes lasered on to her. "Did you?"

She blinked. "Of course not. Anyway, why would I?"

"Seems clear to me." He looked around the room. "You had a lot to gain."

She was offended by the suggestion. "I don't believe I've asked anything of you. In fact, I don't *want* anything from you. Not a damn thing."

He regarded her, his expression one of mockery. "You know, I look at you and wonder how I could have been such a fool." His gaze slid down, then up. "Of course, you *do* have a great body, and you can certainly charm a man right out of his pants." He paused just enough to be insulting. "But you know that already, don't you? You don't need me to remind you how quickly I took you to my bed…and how quickly you let me."

All at once she knew she was fighting for something more than her son. She wasn't sure what. Perhaps the right to be judged fairly and honestly.

"Tate, no matter what has happened between us in the past, I don't—and can't—regret having Nathan." She angled her chin in defiance. "So do your worst…but do it to *me*."

A dash of admiration entered the depths of his eyes, but a sudden knock at the sitting room door stole it away.

Tate opened the door.

The housekeeper stood there. "Mr. Chandler, there's a phone call for you. It's your father. He says it's urgent."

Tate seemed to stiffen. He turned to Gemma and nodded, before stepping out in the corridor and closing the door behind him. She sagged against the sofa, glad he'd gone. She needed the breathing space…needed *not* to think. Lord, it had been such a long day.

Tate was back too soon.

This time he didn't bother to knock.

And this time his face seemed to be carved from stone.

"What's the matter?" she asked.

"The hospital announced a few weeks ago that my family's going to be the recipient of a humanitarian award. It's for our support of the hospital, especially the children's wing, over the years."

"That's very nice." She didn't have it in her to be enthusiastic right now. She had too much on her mind.

He didn't look happy. "One of the newspapers just called my father. They wanted to know how he feels about being a grandfather." He paused. "They know about Nathan."

"Wh-what?"

"Dammit, Gemma, they wanted to know why I turned my back on my son."

"No!"

"What else would you think they'd make of it?" He shot her a suddenly suspicious look. "Did you tell that nurse anything about us before you left the hospital? It seems strange that a photographer waited for us long after the ceremony ended."

She gasped. "I didn't! Why would I?"

"You knew I wouldn't walk away from my son. Perhaps you thought you could get the public on your side, so they'd think I'm a rotten father. That way, if you tell them what a terrible person I am, you might win any future custody battle."

"No!" She was appalled he'd think she'd do something like that. She'd never do it to Nathan. One day he'd grow up, and she wanted him to respect his father, despite how she felt about Tate personally. "My son is not a commodity to be used like that."

He held her gaze. "I'm glad to hear you say that about *our* son." His brow knitted together. "It must have been someone from the hospital."

He believed her? She wanted to cry with relief.

She forced herself to think. "I can't see it being Deirdre. She was too professional. And the doctor didn't seem to recognize you." She tried to remember everything from the moment she'd run into Tate. "There were plenty of other people in the recovery room. Any one of them could have put two and two together." With the crib being away from the others, Gemma suspected she and Tate had been out of hearing range. "Our body language would have been enough to show something was up."

"True." He expelled a breath. "Dammit, if one newspaper knows, you can bet the rest will, too. It'll crush my grandmother if the hospital decides not to give the award. She and my grandfather worked hard to support them and my parents carried on the tradition."

"Would they really do that? Take it away from your family, that is."

He arched a cynical brow. "My family receives a humanitarian award, yet it looks like we can't even be responsible for a child of ours? What do you think?"

He was right.

"Bloody hell, the timing couldn't be worse."

Her chin came up of its own accord. "I'm sorry if you feel *our* son is an inconvenience."

"That's not what I meant, and you know it." He ran his fingers through his hair, for the first time looking really upset.

It was such an unusual sight that Gemma felt an unwelcome surge of sympathy. "Perhaps you could appeal to the board's better nature?" she asked, but she knew it was a silly suggestion the minute the words left her mouth.

"Do they have one?" he quipped, though his sarcasm wasn't directed at her. "No, as much as I hate to give in to them, I'll have to make a statement acknowledging Nathan as my son and telling them we're getting married as soon as possible."

"But we were getting married for Nathan's sake anyway," she pointed out.

"Yes, but now we're going to put on a real show. I don't want a scandal following our son all his life," he said, his voice low and rough.

Her heart filled with warmth to know he had a vested interest in Nathan's well-being. "What sort of show?"

"We'll say we had a misunderstanding that's been righted, and we'll show them how much in love we are." He paused. "I'm sure you'll have no trouble playing your part. You did it once before, remember? You totally hoodwinked me. I'm sure you can do it again for everyone else."

So it was back to this.

She lifted her head high with dignity. She'd just about had enough. "Please leave."

Clearly no one had ever said that to him before. A muscle flexed in his jaw, then he swung around and grabbed the door handle. "My parents will be here within the hour. They want to meet their grandson."

He was gone.

Their grandson, he'd said.

They didn't want to meet *her.*

Gemma stood there feeling insignificant and small—a nobody who amounted to nothing in the lives of the family she was soon to marry into.

Welcome to the world of the Chandlers.

Three

Ten days later, Tate stood at the end of the red carpet in his family's country estate north of Melbourne and watched a vision descend the sweeping staircase into the old ballroom. He heard the guests' gasps of delight, and pride swelled inside him. Gemma looked so beautiful and elegant, her strapless white wedding gown cascading down to the ground. If he *had* been in love with her, he would have had a lump in his throat right about now. Under the right circumstances, he would have been happy to have her as his wife.

God, this woman certainly knew how to make a grand entrance, even at her own wedding. Was it intentional? Probably. Yet he saw her hand slightly gripping the banister. Perhaps she wasn't as self-assured as she wanted to appear. Nothing was ever as it seemed with Gemma.

Like right now, he mused. Gemma's parents were overseas, and she said she had no other relatives, so his father had offered to walk her down the aisle. She'd thanked him and shocked them all by refusing. And she hadn't budged.

It didn't make a difference to the outcome. They were still going to be married today. Only his immediate family knew they weren't in love. The other guests had to be convinced they *were*. Tate didn't want his son growing up tainted by rumors that his father hadn't wanted him. As far as Nathan was concerned, he would know he was the reason for bringing his parents together. Today was really all about his son. And if Gemma let Tate down, then she'd be letting Nathan down, too. She knew a lot was riding on her performance today, hence her stunning entrance.

Just then, she reached the bottom of the stairs, took a moment to brace herself in an enchanting fashion and started her walk down the aisle.

His heart thumped as she came toward him, her eyes on his, not missing a step. She was most of the way, when her gaze slid sideways to the front row. An extremely cute Nathan in a little tuxedo was being cuddled in his grandmother's arms.

Without warning, Gemma stepped away to kiss her son on the cheek, causing a murmur of approval. Cameras clicked, and just that quickly he wondered if the loving gesture had been just to win the hearts of their audience. If so, it had done the trick.

She stepped back onto the red carpet and continued toward him. Up close, their eyes connected. He could see the nervousness on her face. All at once he found himself holding out his hand. After the briefest of hesitations, she accepted and slipped her palm in his. He brought her to him, lifted her hand to his lips and kissed it. She wasn't the only one who could make loving gestures, he told himself.

The ceremony began and Tate concentrated on that, not letting himself think about more than putting on a show. The vows seemed to be said by someone else, the wedding rings exchanged by another couple. He wouldn't let himself become sentimental. This was how it would be with any other woman.

Soon it was time to kiss the bride, and that's when Tate felt something inside him stumble. He'd *missed* kissing her.

He managed to look deep into her eyes, fully aware everyone would think the stare meant love. Only Gemma would see what he was truly saying.

Kiss like we mean it.

He dipped his head and placed his lips against hers. They were cool, and he could deal with that. He wanted cool between them. This show wasn't the place for passion. This was about sealing their vows with a kiss.

And then her lips quivered slightly, and without warning his mouth took on a life of its own. Her lips parted, her taste burst into his mouth.

A loud noise broke them apart, but it was reluctant on both sides. He caught the same sense of shock he felt reflected in Gemma's eyes before he turned to see that Nathan had dropped his toy car on the parquet floor.

"I think your little boy wants the attention now," the female celebrant said, and everyone laughed.

The ceremony was over.

"Yes, he's a natural," Tate agreed, glad to ignore how the softness of Gemma's lips had clung to his.

For show?

He didn't think so, he told himself, not happy about his part in that kiss either—nor the aftereffects of it. He'd thought he was immune to her. Now he knew he wasn't. How easily he could succumb to her charms again. He'd just have to make sure her lips weren't beneath his too often, if at all. Today was the exception.

"You'd better get used to the interruptions," an uncle said, approaching them with his wife at his side. Then the older man chuckled. "Look, Gemma's blushing already."

Tate saw pink tingeing her cheeks. "My blushing bride," he teased for the benefit of the others as he slipped her arm through his.

The official photographer took a couple of pictures, then others came up to wish them well, and somehow he and Gemma were separated. Frankly, he was surprised so many guests could come at such short notice. On the other hand, everyone liked good gossip, he thought with a touch of cynicism as he glanced through the French doors leading out to the terrace.

The extensive lawn had a large tent set up with tables and chairs as well as a dance floor. The landscaped gardens flowed down to a man-made lake. They'd decided not to have a formal wedding feast, merely the ceremony and as few speeches as possible, but plenty of food and drink and dancing if anyone was inclined.

His mother caught up with him, now minus her grandson. "Where's Nathan?" he asked.

"Bree's showing him off."

He smiled as he caught sight of his younger sister getting Nathan to clap hands for a few of the guests.

"That was a really lovely ceremony, darling."

He dragged his focus back to his mother, and the trace of hardness he always felt for her returned. "Yes, it was very convincing."

Her eyes flickered, noting the change in him, but she ignored it. "I do so wish Gemma's parents could have been here. It would have been nice if her father had walked her down the aisle."

"She was adamant about not interrupting their Mediterranean cruise."

"Hmm," his mother said, a frown creasing her forehead. "Something's not quite right there."

He agreed with his mother's assumption, but he had too much on his mind to worry about something that didn't concern him. "That's what Gemma wanted, so we respected that. It's none of our business."

Darlene sighed. "What a pity Drake couldn't make it either."

Tate stiffened. "Yes," he lied.

He hadn't called his best friend until a few days ago. He'd intended to point out it was best the other man didn't come to the wedding, but before he could say the words, Drake had wished him well and told him he couldn't get away. Tate knew that was just Drake's way of being a good friend, but it had been a relief.

"He's in Japan, you said," his mother continued as Gemma joined them.

"Drake's in the middle of trade negotiations." He felt Gemma freeze.

Tate wanted the subject changed.

Now.

"Still, he's your best friend. He should have been here."

Tate forced a smile for his new bride as he again slipped her arm through his. He wished his mother would shut the hell up. "Everything looks great, don't you think, Gemma?"

For a moment it didn't seem that she would manage a smile, but one appeared, if a little weak. "Yes, you've done a wonderful job, Darlene."

Darlene sent a really warm smile to her new daughter-in-law. "Thank you. I wanted it to be a special day for you both."

Then it was a pity she had mentioned Drake, Tate thought, surprised that his mother and Gemma had hit it off so well. Of course, the two women didn't know it, but they had a lot in common. Both of them had betrayed the men in their lives. Perhaps that's why his mother had a soft spot for Gemma.

And perhaps Gemma sensed it.

It would explain a lot.

Tate was grateful Bree chose that moment to come up to them carrying Nathan. He didn't want to think about what had happened between Gemma and Drake. She was *his* wife now. There would be no opportunity for those two to get together in the future. He'd make damn sure of it.

Gemma went to lift Nathan out of Bree's arms. "Here, let me hold him." She tried to pretend she hadn't heard Darlene and Tate talking about Drake. At least she now knew why the other man hadn't attended. Thank God he hadn't! She hadn't wanted to see him on her wedding day, but she hadn't dared mention him, or Tate might think she was interested.

She wasn't.

Not at all.

Her sister-in-law stepped back with a cool smile. "No, Nathan's fine. Besides, we don't want you to dirty that beautiful dress."

Gemma really didn't care about a dress that was off the rack, in spite of the fact that she and Nathan could have easily lived a year on the same amount of money. "That's okay, Bree."

"No, I insist. Besides, you and Tate need to circulate." It was a reminder of why this wedding was taking place.

"I'm happy to look after my nephew." Bree walked off with Nathan in her arms.

Under different circumstances, Gemma would have gone after her and taken back her son, but Nathan was chuckling as Bree bounced him on her hip, so Gemma let him be.

Anyway, Bree's issues were with Gemma, not Nathan. When she had commented on it, Tate had said his family knew nothing about their previous relationship. He'd said she must be imagining it. But Gemma was aware they all blamed her for keeping Nathan from them—everyone except Tate's mother, who was the only Chandler to show her some sympathy.

And Darlene had paid the price for it. Gemma had noticed some tension in the air. Even Tate showed a hint of reserve with his mother, though it wasn't something Gemma could put her finger on.

Just then two older ladies came up to them. "Oh, it was a lovely ceremony."

Gemma acknowledged that the Chandlers had pulled out all the stops to get the wedding arranged in such a short time. Needless to say, it was amazing what one could achieve when there was money to spare and family honor at stake.

"And so adorable how you gave your little boy a kiss on the cheek," the other woman said. "That was so sweet."

"Yes, that was inspired," Tate drawled, his meaning obvious, at least to her, though she noted Darlene gave him a sharp look.

Gemma ignored him. "Thank you. I wanted Nathan to be a part of it all."

"Well, you did that very well, my dear."

"It's good that he has both his parents now, don't you think?" the other lady said without menace.

Before Gemma could speak, Darlene stepped in, shepherding them away. "There's someone over there I want you both to meet."

"I didn't kiss Nathan for show," Gemma hissed at Tate, "despite what you obviously think."

"Really? You went above and beyond the call of duty with that one."

"It wasn't a duty."

"So you say."

"Drop dead, Tate," she said, the words falling out of her mouth before she could stop them.

He actually looked amused. "You'd like that, wouldn't you?"

"Married and widowed to you on the same day? Sounds good to me."

"You won't be so smart when we're alone later."

Her heart stuttered. "Wh-what?"

He stilled, then looked away. "Nothing," he muttered. "Not a thing."

She had the feeling that, like her, he'd spoken without thought. It had been the kind of thing they'd used to say when they were lovers. They hadn't discussed it, but she knew Tate would not let himself want her again. Their wedding kiss might have felt like a reunion for a few heartbeats, but neither of them would be caught out again.

More guests came up to them, and Gemma tried to act relaxed, but she was glad when Tate excused himself to speak to his grandmother and his father, who were holding court across the room. Bree approached them, and Tate lovingly scooped Nathan out of his sister's arms, making Gemma's heart lilt. She'd been watching Tate with Nathan these past ten days, and she had no doubt he loved his son. Nathan had grown used to Tate, too. They looked relaxed and comfortable together, these four generations of Chandlers.

She was the outsider.

And she'd probably never be a true part of this family. Add that to her own parents cutting her off and she suddenly felt like everyone in the world had deserted her.

Everyone but her son, she reminded herself.

Nathan loved her.

Nathan needed her like no one else.

How she wished it could be different with her own family. For her son's sake, she'd even phoned her parents to invite them to the wedding, hoping they might be pleased. After getting no answer, she'd phoned her father's work to learn they had gone on a Mediterranean cruise. She had to admit now that she was glad they weren't able to come. Her life was one big pretense, and she wasn't sure she could keep up the facade of happiness with them here. They'd hurt her too much.

At least Tate would be a far better parent to Nathan than her own parents had been to her, she thought, pushing aside her momentary self-pity as Nathan started to cry. Her poor little darling was overwhelmed and overtired. The doctor had said there were no complications from the operation, but Nathan could still be feeling the aftereffects.

She excused herself and went to him. "Ssh, Mommy's here, sweetie." She lifted Nathan out of Tate's arms, looking at the others. "It's his nap time. I'll take him upstairs." She was about to turn away when Tate's driver appeared at their side.

"Mr. Chandler, the reporters are here. They want to know when you and Gem—I mean, Mrs. Tate—will come out to see them."

Gemma groaned inwardly. She knew this was part of the deal, but not right now.

"Tell them they'll be there shortly, Clive," Jonathan Chandler said before Tate could speak. Then her father-in-law went to take Nathan from her. "We'll get one of the staff to take this boy upstairs while you and Tate do what you have to do."

Gemma instantly moved her son out of reach. "I'm sorry, Jonathan, but I intend to put Nathan to bed myself." She couldn't call him Mr. Chandler. She wouldn't. She doubted he'd ask her to call him "Dad."

"But the reporters—"

"Can wait," Gemma said quietly but firmly. Nathan needed her more than anyone else. And Lord knows, she needed the break.

"Gemma's right, Dad," Tate said, surprising her. "Nathan's needs are more important. The reporters can wait. They won't go away anytime soon." He gave a slight smile. "Unfortunately."

Jonathan looked from Tate to her and back again, then gave a sharp nod. "Okay, son."

Gemma had to bite her tongue. When *she* took a stand, she was ignored. When Tate took a stand, they listened. She hoped it wasn't going to stay this way her whole life.

Tate squared his shoulders. "I'll go talk to them, while Gemma goes upstairs." His gaze shifted to her. "Come down when you're ready."

Gemma was grateful to escape, but she wasn't sure she'd ever be ready to face them all. If only the day could be over.

Upstairs she gave Nathan a bottle and then changed his diaper in the small bedroom connected to hers.

"There we go, sweetie," she said, putting him in the crib. His eyes were closing as soon as his little head hit the pillow, and she smiled to see him sucking furiously on the bottle. For a few minutes she watched over him with all the love in her heart.

It wasn't until she went to leave the room that she realized she had a dilemma. Tate had bought the latest in digital baby monitors so she could hear Nathan no matter what room she was in, but she wasn't about to leave her son alone in here when a bunch of strangers were crawling all over the house.

Absolutely no way.

She looked out in the corridor, hoping to see someone who could pass a message to Tate, but there was no one. She even used the intercom for the kitchen, but no one answered. They were probably all too busy, maybe not even able to hear it. There was nothing to do but sit and wait it out. Tate would eventually come looking for her, she was sure. He had to. He needed her for the photographs.

About fifteen minutes later, someone knocked on her door and she hurried to open it. Tate stood there, his eyes showing his anger. "Is this some sort of protest?"

She angled her chin at his tone. "I guess it is."

"Not now, Gemma. We've got—"

"I'm not leaving Nathan up here alone."

He stopped and digested the info, then nodded. "I'll get Sandy to come up and stay with him."

Gemma had met Peggy and Clive's twenty-one-year-old daughter, and she was happy to leave Nathan with her. "No one's answering the intercom in the kitchen."

"I'll go get her." Ten minutes later he was back and was soon escorting Gemma down the staircase, her arm tucked under his as if it was the most natural thing in the world. "You made quite an entrance earlier."

She wouldn't let him know she'd been scared to death. "It's what you expected, wasn't it?"

"Yes, it's definitely something I would expect from you."

She hated the way he said that. "Actually, your mother suggested it."

"Did she now?" He remained quiet, but she wasn't sure what he thought about what she'd said.

Gemma was suddenly aware of Clive standing at the large front door, all set to open it to the reporters. When they reached the bottom step, she stopped. "Er…it's only going to be a couple of pictures, right?"

Tate looked at her oddly, then squeezed her arm. "A couple of photographs by the fountain, that's all. I'll answer the questions, but if they ask you anything, just do your best."

"Okay." Would her best be good enough?

He pulled her closer to his side. "Ready?"

She was surprised by his gesture, warmed that he wasn't quite prepared to feed her to the wolves. She cleared her throat. "Yes, as ready as I'll ever be."

Gemma wasn't sure how they pulled it off, but she and Tate managed to look like a loving couple as they stood in front of a spectacular fountain on the front lawn while a group of people took photographs. Hopefully any nervousness on her part was understandable.

And then…

"A kiss for the camera," one man suggested.

Almost imperceptibly, Tate's arm tensed beneath hers. For a moment she thought he would refuse. If only he would. She didn't want to relive the sensation of their last kiss.

Then his head rushed toward her, and he didn't miss another beat as he swept her into his arms like some romantic hero in a movie.

Lights.

Camera.

Action.

Even knowing this was all for show, her breath caught high in her throat. She fought not to let him take anything from her this time, but the kiss went on…and on…and on… Then, just as she started to yield, he released her.

His eyes gave nothing away, but she could see a slight flush to his cheeks. That, at least, made her feel less exposed.

With the practiced ease of someone who'd grown up in the spotlight, he turned to look at the photographers, a confident smile coating his lips. "Is that good enough, people?"

"Terrific!"

"Great!"

"Hey, what does the new Mrs. Chandler have to say about it?" a woman asked.

Gemma struggled to pick up her scattered senses. She had to play the game. If she showed how scared she was of the limelight, they'd chew her up and spit her out.

She gave what she thought was a convincing smile. "Practice definitely makes perfect."

Laughter erupted as the cameras clicked.

"Great quote! Now about—"

Tate put up his hand. "No more. My wife and I have a wedding to get back to." His mouth curved and he winked. "And a honeymoon." He started to lead her back inside.

"But what about the humanitarian award? What do you think about that?"

Tate stopped briefly. "I'm very proud of my family. It's an honor to receive such an award."

"And what about—"

Gemma saw a helicopter coming toward them in the distance.

Tate must have seen it, too, because he moved her toward the front door. "That's all, guys." They stepped inside and Clive closed the door behind them just as the chopper reached the estate.

"You'd better get on that, Clive, or they'll all be swarming overhead soon. They've got enough pictures now."

"Sure thing, Mr. Chandler." The other man hurried off.

Gemma's legs were shaky. "Thank God that's over," she managed to say.

As well as everything had gone, there was nothing quite as daunting as a helicopter overhead and a flock of reporters intent on finding a story. Any story.

Unless it was a comment from her new husband about a honeymoon…

He didn't mean it, she knew that. But still, it had shaken her, reminding her that Tate was a virile man and wouldn't remain celibate for long.

Would he take a lover?

The thought made her feel ill until she hurriedly decided he wouldn't. At least not yet. He wouldn't risk raining more bad press upon his family.

But would he want *her* eventually?

She believed that any sex between them would be full of hostility. Yet his kisses today hadn't been angry. She swallowed hard. That's because they'd had an audience, she told herself. It had all been for show. Nothing more.

Still, she'd started contraceptives last week as a precaution. The doctor had said they would take a month to work and had recommended using other precautions until then. She didn't expect to need them.

"It's not quite over yet," Tate said, bringing her focus back to the present. "We still have to return to our guests."

She forced aside her thoughts. She could handle the rest of the wedding. After that lot out there, it would be a piece of cake!

Perhaps she would rethink that, Gemma mused to herself, when a short time later she ended up alone with Tate's grandmother.

"I hope you'll treat my grandson right," Helen Chandler said, with that same coolness her granddaughter, Bree, showed to Gemma.

For a moment, Gemma thought Helen was talking about Nathan, then realized she meant Tate. "As long as Tate treats me and Nathan right, I will."

Helen inclined her head. "He will. My grandson knows his responsibilities."

"I'm sure." His sense of duty was the reason they were here today, wasn't it?

And then…Helen seemed to hesitate. "Tate takes things to heart. He feels deeply…like his father."

Gemma had the feeling that the older woman was trying to tell her something. After all, there was no question that Tate felt deeply. He thought he'd been deceived. First about Drake and then about his son, and both assumptions had greatly upset him. But was Helen talking about more than that? Was there something Helen knew that *she* didn't? Gemma couldn't think what.

Tate appeared in front of them. "I'm afraid I have to take Gemma away from you, Gran. We're expected to dance."

Expected? There was that responsibility thing again. Gemma suddenly felt like someone's cross to bear.

His cross.

She slipped smoothly into his arms, wishing she could

slip as easily into his life—or *out* of it—but neither was to be. "I know where you and your sister get it from now," she said, tilting her head up at him.

"What?"

"That attitude of yours. They're never going to forgive me, are they?"

"Gran's old."

"And Bree?"

"She's young, but her experience is light years away from yours."

Gemma swallowed her gall. He made it sound as if she'd been sleeping with the local football team. "As long as they don't take it out on Nathan, they can be as cool as they like to me."

"No one in my family will hurt my son."

"*Our* son."

He ignored her comment as they continued dancing, but their conversation got her thinking. The paternity test had been taken, but Tate hadn't mentioned it since. Maybe it took a while for the results to come in. Not that she was worried. Nathan could *only* belong to Tate.

"Your parents will be sorry they missed all this," Tate said, jolting her. She reacted without thinking.

"I'm sure."

He immediately scowled. "Why do you say—"

"Ouch!" she said, needing to change the subject.

"What's the matter?"

"My toe. You stepped on it," she fibbed.

She didn't want to discuss her parents. If they were here, it would only be out of duty, and she'd probably get upset. Why give Tate the chance to be more critical of her?

"I did? Sorry." He actually smiled. "I haven't done that since I was a teenager."

"Perhaps you're going through puberty again," she joked.

He chuckled, and, for a brief instant, they were on the same wavelength.

Like old times.

Only, it wasn't like old times, she reminded herself, quickly looking away.

Far from it.

The music ended and Tate led her over to his parents. Gemma was surprised to hear them talking about building a childproof fence around the gardens and grounds, to keep Nathan from accidentally wandering off or falling in the lake. For that, Gemma couldn't stop her heart from softening toward them, and she now regretted keeping Nathan from them for so long. As painful as it was to be married to a man who hated her, she was glad that Tate had accepted his son and glad Nathan had people around him who would always care for him. That was a huge comfort.

The afternoon came to a close after that, and the guests started to leave. Finally, only Tate's immediate family remained, and they said their goodbyes once the caterers had cleared up. It was an hour's drive back to the city, but everyone had agreed it wouldn't look good "honeymoon-wise" to have the in-laws staying in the house, no matter that it was the size of a football field.

The only people to stay were Peggy and Clive, and they were in separate quarters at the back of the house. Upstairs, she and Tate found Peggy's daughter on the floor playing with Nathan. It was a lovely picture, but as soon as Nathan saw them, he quickly crawled toward them.

Tate met him halfway and scooped him up. "Hey there, little man."

Gemma was happy to see father and son together, but

she couldn't help feeling a little weird. With the whirlwind of a wedding, she hadn't had the chance to think about Tate moving in on her territory. It had always been *she* who had scooped up Nathan. She who had received the first cuddle. Well, the only cuddle, really. There hadn't been any competition before.

Peggy's daughter left them to go back downstairs with her parents, and Tate's gaze flickered over Gemma's wedding gown. "I'll keep an eye on Nathan while you change."

She nodded and left the room. Last week he'd paid for the delivery of a wardrobe of expensive clothes. Thankfully, the sort of things she liked herself. Of course, what woman would say no to a new wardrobe? Especially when her clothes had been starting to wear thin.

Going into the other room, Gemma closed the door between them. Her hands shook as she changed into black slacks and a knit top, the quality of which couldn't be denied. They were so different from the blue jeans and T-shirts she'd always slipped into when she got home to her apartment.

Home was now with Tate.

Lord help her.

All at once she was aware of Tate's deep voice as he talked to his son in the other room. His voice alone used to make her knees wobble. Just as they were wobbling now.

His brief, detached glance didn't calm her nerves when she stepped back into the other room to find the two males playing on the floor.

Tate pushed to his feet and headed for the door. "I've got a couple of things to do. Call through to the kitchen when you're ready for dinner. Peggy will be happy to stay with Nathan if he's still awake."

Cold feet got the better of her. "Wait!" She swallowed

as he stopped. "Thank you, but I'd prefer to eat in my room tonight, if you don't mind."

His eyes turned frosty. "But I do mind."

"Tate, look." She tried to think. "Can't you let me have some time to myself? It's been a hectic day." It was an excuse, but it was a valid one.

"I'd be glad to leave you to it, but my mother arranged for Peggy to cook a special dinner in the small dining room, heaven knows why. So you're going to come down and we're going to eat it together. We start as we go on. Right?"

She could see he wasn't about to relent. She nodded. "Right."

"I'll see you downstairs at seven. If you want anything, call Peggy. She'll make sure you and Nathan have whatever you need." He twisted on his heels and left the room—and left her wondering how she would get through the evening.

At seven, Gemma went down to the smaller of the dining rooms, having changed into a dress for the occasion. Oh, she was going to be such a good little wife...in that respect anyway, she thought with a touch of cynicism. She'd follow instructions as necessary, and in public she'd be accommodating whenever it came to putting on a wifely show, but that was as far as it went. He'd coerced her into this marriage. She wasn't going to pretend to be happy about it.

Tate's eyes reflected fleeting approval, but all he said was, "He's asleep?"

"Yes." It had taken a while to get Nathan settled, but she had the baby monitor with her now and didn't have to worry about him waking up without her hearing. "He settled down. He just needed to have a cry."

"Don't we all," Tate mocked as he held out the seat for her.

Her heart lurched. The newness of her wedding ring suddenly weighed down her finger. She took a quick peek at his ring finger. Did he feel it as heavily?

The heated food warmers held an array of steamed vegetables and roasted meats, and a delicious-looking dessert. "It looks delicious," she said. Soft music played in the background, but it wasn't soothing.

"My mother thought we could do with something substantial after today." He sat down opposite her and poured some champagne. "Clive tells me there was barely any food in your apartment."

The words took her by surprise. She didn't want him to know how little food she had on hand. She'd lived on canned goods and bread. It was amazing what a person could do with a can of beans.

"He only mentioned it in passing yesterday," Tate added.

"He reports everything back to you, does he?" she said, already knowing the answer. "I didn't have time to shop, that's all."

Tate considered her. "You should eat more now. You could do with a little extra weight." He stared a moment more, then lifted his glass to her. "To us."

She could do with a drink of water rather than more alcohol. "You don't have to toast us, now that we're alone. It's not a proper wedding, Tate."

"Isn't it?"

She gave a soft gasp. "You don't mean—"

His face closed up as he put down his glass. "No, I don't mean that at all. I won't be sleeping with you tonight, Gemma. Not tonight, nor any night in the foreseeable future. I don't know if I can."

The ability to speak deserted her. He disliked everything about her and didn't intend to overcome it, not even to exercise the physical desire they'd once shared. Regardless of her fear that she'd be a pushover if they were to make love, a deep hurt rolled through her. It was one thing to know he had a grudge against her. It was quite another to realize the depth of his animosity.

She raised her chin with a cool stare. "I didn't ask you to sleep with me, Tate, but at least leave me with *some* dignity. I may not be the perfect wife, but you don't have to make me feel like I'm something that crawled out of the gutter."

He stiffened. "I'm sorry. I just don't want you thinking I might be tempted, that's all."

She managed a cynical smile. "Oh, believe me, I know you're not tempted. But I'm not interested either. So rest easy, Mr. Chandler. Your virtue is intact."

"I'm glad we've made that clear."

"Perfectly." Willing her hands not to shake, she reached to serve herself some of the vegetables and meat, even though her appetite had disappeared. Tate had said they'd start as they'd go on, and she would make sure she did. Today, tomorrow—it was all about Nathan. She would remind herself of that as often as she could.

They didn't talk much as they ate, except for a few things about the wedding. Tate mentioned giving Peggy the night off after such a long day, but Gemma didn't think for a minute he had any ulterior motives.

It seemed a long meal and one she didn't look forward to repeating night after night. It would only remind her of other dinners during their affair when conversation had been easy and led straight to sex.

Finally they'd finished dessert. She was just about to refuse coffee and make her escape when Tate drew a plain white envelope from his pocket and slid it along the tablecloth.

Her brows drew together as she picked it up. "What's this?"

"The results of the paternity test."

The envelope almost fell from her fingers. Then she saw it was sealed. She looked up. "You haven't read it?"

"No."

Could he be saying he was prepared to take her word that Nathan was his? Her heart thumped as she asked the question. "Why not?"

"I wanted to prove I would marry you without knowing the results and without taking your word for it. *That's* how sure I am Nathan is my son."

"I see." He hadn't married her because he believed her. He'd married her because he'd believed in *himself,* in his gut feeling that Nathan was his son. Nothing else. He was saying he didn't trust her—not even with a truth he himself believed. She'd known Tate felt this way. She'd accepted it. But she felt a fool for doubting it for just this instance.

"Aren't you going to open it, Gemma?"

She hesitated, not because she didn't know what it would say, but because she was still trying to pull herself together.

"It doesn't matter to me if you open it or not," he continued. "The results are still the same."

She had no doubt, but she had to read it—for Nathan's sake. She quickly opened it, scanned it, then passed the sheet of paper to Tate.

He didn't hesitate as he took it from her. Didn't hesitate as he read it and said easily, "He's mine."

It was a statement of fact.

"Yes."

He sat in the chair and nodded, almost to himself, looking

pleased but not surprised. Then he began tearing the paper in half, then quarters.

Her eyes widened. "What are you doing?"

"We don't need to keep any proof." He let the pieces sprinkle down on the tablecloth.

Her forehead creased. "But don't you want your family to know the truth?"

"They already know all they need to know. I've said he's my son, and they can see he is. I don't need to show them proof. My word is good enough."

It must be wonderful to have a family who believes in you, in what you say and do. She was quite envious of Tate for that.

And now Nathan would be part of such a family, she reminded herself. Now more than any other time today, she felt she'd done the right thing in marrying Tate. She may not love Tate madly like she'd once thought she did, but it took a special man to offer marriage for the sake of a child not proven to be his. Tate had even begun to love a son without proof that he was the father. For that alone, a small pocket of her heart would always belong to Tate Chandler.

Four

Gemma wasn't surprised that she woke early the next morning. Nathan had slept through the night, and she'd fallen asleep as soon as her head hit the pillow. She'd probably even snored, so it was just as well that Tate hadn't shared her bed.

Her heart cramped at the thought, as she looked up at a high ceiling as untouchable as her new husband.

She understood that he didn't want to share her bed, but it still hurt. It filled her with despair to know she had to live with a man who wouldn't let himself want her, now nor in the future. She had done nothing wrong!

It wasn't fair.

But did she really want someone who couldn't trust her? To be truthful, deep down she did still want Tate. She wasn't *in love* with him. It was all purely physical. But knowing that didn't change a thing.

Thank God physical attraction was something she could teach herself to ignore.

Starting right now.

She threw back the covers, glad to escape her thoughts, and sneaked a peek at Nathan, who was still sleeping. She showered and dressed, and by the time she was ready, Nathan was awake and hungry. She quickly clothed him, then took him downstairs in search of food.

In the kitchen, Tate was eating a bowl of cereal at the island. Her pulse raced, but she tried to ignore it. She'd seen him each morning for the past ten mornings, though his focus had been on Nathan or the wedding or business.

Today, his hooded eyes told her he had heard her coming.

"Good morning." His gaze moved to his son and lit up, filling with a warmth that had once been for her. "How is he this morning?"

"Hungry." She couldn't be jealous of her son, but Tate's reaction was another reminder that things had changed a great deal between them.

"He's a growing boy, aren't you, sport?" Tate smiled at his son with an indisputable look of fatherly love.

She wrenched her gaze away. This all could have been so different...*should* have been so different.

"Peggy not around this morning?" she managed to say as she carried Nathan into the pantry, where Peggy had put the baby food. More often than not, Gemma fed her son fresh food, but the jars came in handy sometimes.

"Clive was going to drive their daughter back to the city, so I told Peggy to go with him and take the day off." He raised his voice to reach her. "They'll return this evening. I assured her we could look after ourselves."

"I'm sure we can." Gemma was suddenly relieved he

couldn't see her face. This would be the first time she and Tate would be alone—except for Nathan—in the house together since they'd run into each other at the hospital. And they were supposed to be on their "honeymoon," making the situation seem intimate.

Tate looked up as she exited the pantry with the food. He put down his spoon. "Here, give Nathan to me while you heat that up."

"No, that's okay. You finish your breakfast. I'll put him in his high chair."

Tate pushed his bowl aside and came toward them. "I'd really like to hold my son, Gemma."

He met her gaze, boldly showing her his fatherly side. It gave her an odd feeling, sort of squishy inside. She handed Nathan over without a word and went to heat up some milk to go with the oatmeal. At least Tate didn't hold back on emotion where their son was concerned.

"Do you want to feed him?" she asked.

Tate looked up in surprise. "Sure." He cleared his throat. "Thanks."

It was silly to warm to him just because he wanted to feed his son, but she did anyway. "Okay, put him in the highchair first." She waited while he fastened the safety belt, then passed Tate the bowl and spoon. "Now just spoon it into his mouth. You've seen me do it. It's easy."

Tate scooped up the mushy food, then hesitated. Gemma had to smile. It was amazing that this successful businessman, with confidence seeping from every pore, actually looked nervous.

"He's waiting for his breakfast," she pointed out.

That pushed Tate into action. He moved the first spoonful toward Nathan, who instantly opened his mouth. Tate's eyebrows shot up. "Hey, this is easy."

Something lightened in the room.

She gave a soft laugh. "Of course it is."

"Clearly he's an amenable chap," he said, winking at her. "Must take after me."

Gemma wasn't sure who was more taken aback by that wink—her or Tate. She was certain it wasn't something he had done intentionally, especially when he averted his eyes again to scoop up another spoonful of food.

Still, it was nice to have a cheerful mood between them, if only for a few minutes. "Yes, well, he's hungry right now. You should try getting him to open his mouth when he's *not* hungry."

Tate slipped another spoonful in his son's mouth. "I can't believe that."

"You *did* say he took after you," she joked.

Tate's gaze returned to her, one eyebrow quirking, his eyes amused. "So you're calling my son and me stubborn?"

"*Obstinate* is the word I would have used."

"Oh, really," he drawled.

Their gazes linked...

It was like old times...

Suddenly they were talking on one level but aware of each other on another. She stood close enough to see the attraction flare in his eyes.

He was the first to break eye contact, turning back to his son. "What are your plans for this morning?" His voice was neutral, as if the camaraderie had never been.

Disappointment rippled through her, followed by anger at herself. Why be disappointed because their one moment of bonding was over? It couldn't make up for the rest of the issues between them.

The rest of their lives...

And his question made it sound as if he wasn't hoping to share the day with her either, which was a relief. She

could be herself without him around. She didn't have to
defend the person she was.

"I thought I might take Nathan for a walk around the
gardens and down to the lake. It's a beautiful day."

He nodded. "Good idea. He needs fresh air and sunshine. He's a bit pale."

Was there an implied criticism in his words? Was
he saying their son hadn't been getting proper care and
attention because she'd been a single, working mother? If
so, that just wasn't true. He was at a wonderful daycare
while she worked, and every weekend she'd made sure
Nathan got out and about with her. They went to the beach
or a park, or even the local supermarket where she'd do her
weekly shopping. He'd always had fun there, charming the
cashiers with his smile. Gemma had loved showing him
off.

"I know Nathan can't go swimming yet," Tate said,
reminding her that the doctor had said it was best to wait
awhile before putting Nathan in the water, and even then
he would have to wear a special cap to cover his ears.
"But the pool is there anytime for you to use. It's not quite
summer, but it's heated and you won't get cold."

His consideration surprised her. "Thanks. It'll be nice
to have some time to swim by myself." As soon as she said
the words, she held her breath. Would Tate think she had
an ulterior motive? Would he think she was suggesting *he*
join her in the pool?

His eyes closed in on her, but not in the way she might
expect. "Gemma, you realize we have to stay here for the
full week or it won't look right?"

Everything inside her went thud. "I know you don't want
to be with me, Tate. You don't have to keep telling me."

He cursed softly. "You're losing sight of something.
This isn't about us. I'm doing this for my family's sake,

and in the long run for Nathan." He allowed a tiny pause. "I thought you were, too."

How did he manage to turn everything to his advantage? She gave a sigh. "Yes, of course I am."

"Then what's the problem?"

There was an empty ache in the region of her heart, but she ignored it. "No problem. You're the one seeing problems where there's none."

He stared hard, clearly not liking her answer. Then he gave Nathan the last spoonful of food and pushed to his feet. "I'll be in the study all morning."

The chill was back.

And yet as he went to leave, he stopped to ruffle his son's hair in a brief but loving caress. Gemma saw the gesture and realized Tate was right. For a moment, she *had* lost sight of the reason for their marriage. This was about Nathan. She just had to get used to there being nothing for *her.*

Once in the study, Tate tried to concentrate on a thick business report but soon gave up and went to stand by the window. His mind was on Gemma, and he needed to follow his thoughts or they would drive him insane. Just like the woman herself.

As much as he hated to admit it, he wanted her. He wanted her in a big way. And that's what it came down to between them—the *only* thing between them.

Want.

A want like no other.

God, how did he continue to want a woman who'd used him like she had? And how could he exorcise her from his system now that she was a part of his life? By ignoring the wanting, that's how. By refuting it every time it reared its head, like he had last night over dinner, and again this morning in the kitchen. He couldn't forget seeing her kissing Drake two years ago. The memory was tattooed on his brain. Her physical attributes might temporarily block it out, but it always returned, full force. The future looked dark indeed.

It was all her fault, so why was he feeling rotten about it?

Women!

He loved his mother, but she had let his father down badly. And Gemma had let *him* down badly. He hadn't learned to trust his mother again. He wasn't sure he could learn to trust Gemma. Not for a long time, he decided, as he saw Gemma pushing Nathan's stroller along the path toward the lake.

The urge to join them was strong. And it had nothing to do with those long legs of Gemma's showcased by her slim slacks. Heaven help him if she decided to strip down to a swimsuit and use the pool. He knew every inch of her luscious body, remembered every taste of her delicious skin and the husky sounds she made beneath him, the heavenly feel of being inside her.

Remembering was suddenly too much.

He had to concentrate on other things. Things like Nathan. The child who *was* his son. The paternity test had only proven what he'd already known. He couldn't even explain how he'd known the connection between him and Nathan was there.

He'd just known.

Just like he knew that if they were spending the week here, the child would need to be occupied. And what *he* needed to do was concentrate on Nathan's needs and not his own.

Right.

Nathan couldn't swim yet because of his ears, so a

sandbox and some toy trucks sounded like just the ticket. A friend had bought their son one, and the boy had loved it.

After taking one more look to check that Gemma and Nathan were okay as they reached the lake, Tate went to his laptop and searched the internet for a local toy store. It was much more interesting than reading a report.

After Gemma had tidied up the kitchen, she'd changed Nathan into cute little jeans and a T-shirt. Next, sunscreen on them both, she got his stroller and headed out. Tate had insisted they bring the stroller, though she hadn't thought she would need it. But now his reason became obvious. He hadn't intended to spend more time with them—with her—than necessary, and had probably been trying to ease his conscience, figuring she at least wouldn't have to carry Nathan around everywhere.

How caring of her new husband, she'd mused cynically.

Now, as she pushed Nathan's stroller along a side path down to the lake, the sunshine melted her cynicism. It was so beautiful and peaceful out here, with a light spring breeze playing over the rolling countryside, making her feel as if she were walking in a private park.

The lake was even more breathtakingly gorgeous up close, partly surrounded by trees and with a gazebo close by. Along the water's edge, patches of tall reeds partially hid nests of swans, while others quietly glided on the water, creating gentle ripples over the reflective depths.

Gemma decided to take Nathan out of his stroller and carry him to the water's edge to show him the swans, when she heard a noise over in a group of trees. She twisted toward the sound, thinking it was Tate, her heart missing a beat. Only it wasn't Tate. A young teenager came out of the shadows, walking his horse toward the lake.

He jolted when he saw her. "Oh. Sorry. I didn't know anyone else was here."

She stared, not really sure what to say.

"I'm Rolly." He pulled a face. "Roland, actually. My dad works for the people over the rise there. I help him out. They let me exercise their horses."

He looked to be around eighteen and didn't appear threatening, so Gemma relaxed a little. "I'm Gemma, and this is my son, Nathan."

He nodded as his gaze slid to her son then back. "I'd heard there was a wedding here yesterday." He glanced toward the stroller near the gazebo steps. "Tate's not with you?"

She was immediately on her guard and realized that from here she couldn't be seen from the house. The young man didn't look dangerous, but who was to say this Rolly was who he said he was? He could be a reporter, and even if he wasn't, she wasn't about to say too much.

"He had to make a phone call, but he'll be here shortly."

All at once, he seemed to sense her nervousness. "In case you're wondering, I'm allowed to bring the horses here to drink. Mr. Chandler said I could."

"You mean Jonathan?" she said, thinking of Tate's father.

"No, Nathaniel." His expression clouded. "He was a nice old man. We used to play chess together sometimes when he was here."

From all accounts, that sounded like something Tate's grandfather would do. "I'm sure you'll be welcome to keep on doing that." It was the country way, after all.

He fell into a grin. "Thanks."

She smiled back, touched to see a genuine smile for a

change. The past two weeks had been all about putting on a brave face, or a cool face, when she felt nothing like that inside.

The horse wandered to the water's edge and began to drink. "That's a nice horse. He's a lovely color."

"He's a young racehorse."

"I don't know much about horses except that they like to eat hay."

Rolly chuckled. "Yeah, hay and other things. This guy has a particular sweet tooth. I give him an apple sometimes. Not often though." He patted the horse's side. "Do you ride?"

"No. I've been pretty busy." She didn't say she'd never ridden a horse in her life. As nice as he was being to her, she should keep her distance. "Well, I'd best go and see what's keeping Tate. It was nice meeting you, Rolly."

"You too, Gemma." He hesitated. "I come down here most days around this time. In case you want some company."

He seemed to understand more about her than she'd assumed. He was offering a hand of friendship. It was very generous of him, and she appreciated it.

She smiled. "I'll keep that in mind." She went over to the stroller to strap Nathan back in. It only took a few moments. "Stay as long as you like," she added as she straightened.

"Okay. Thanks again."

Gemma headed back to the house with a lighter step. It was silly, but she really did feel as if she had made a friend, someone who had no real connection to the Chandlers and their condemnation. It was a pleasant relief, and one she wouldn't spoil by mentioning it to Tate. He probably wouldn't be interested anyway.

All was quiet as she stepped inside the kitchen, and she

was surprised to see that an hour had passed. There was no sign of Tate, so she made herself a cup of coffee and gave Nathan a biscuit and a drink. They went into the sunroom, where he crawled around on the floor and played with a collection of small plastic containers she'd brought from the kitchen. The items kept him occupied for some time.

When he started to get tired, she carried him upstairs and put him to bed, taking the baby monitor with her downstairs. Now, alone, she finally had time to get her bearings. There were a variety of formal and informal living areas, a conservatory, a room with a pool table, another with a spa. Gemma wasn't surprised Tate hadn't mentioned the latter; they'd made full use of the spa in his penthouse two years ago.

Shying away from the memories, Gemma continued past the study door, now firmly closed, and headed back to the relaxed warmth of the sunroom, where she sat on a recliner and read a magazine. After a while, the warm room made her feel drowsy. Soon she closed the pages and leaned her head back, shutting her eyes for a mere moment…

The next thing she knew, a warm hand on her shoulder shook her awake. Her eyelids flew open and air escaped her lungs as she looked straight into Tate's blue eyes. His intense look made her wonder how long he'd been watching her. In that one split second, what they'd had between them came rushing back—the excitement, the adrenaline rush, the sweet torment of bringing each other to climax…

Her stomach gave a quiver as she hastily sat up. Thankfully he moved back, and the moment was lost.

Forever? She'd thought so, but now she wasn't sure.

"It's past twelve," he said, his voice sounding slightly gruff.

She pushed to her feet and tidied her hair. "You want lunch, I suppose."

He scowled. "Yes, but I'm not asking you to do it. You're my wife now, Gemma, not my servant."

She liked that he wasn't taking advantage of their relationship, and an odd tenderness wove through her even as she chastised herself for being such a pushover. Good Lord. What was she thinking by offering to make him lunch? He had a perfectly good pair of hands.

Dream hands, in fact.

The golden touch.

Oh, yeah, how often she had succumbed to his touch.

She cleared her throat. "I'd better go check on Nathan. He should be awake soon." Taking the baby monitor with her, she left the room.

When she went back downstairs with Nathan, Tate had laid out their lunch on the island in the center of the kitchen. Nathan's high chair was already seated next to it.

"Why don't you feed him, then we'll eat," Tate suggested, and she nodded, liking that he wanted his son's needs met first.

Once that was done, Nathan was happy to play with a spoon while she and Tate ate their lunch of cold cuts and salad. Then Tate surprised her by saying, "By the way, I've got a delivery coming this afternoon."

She lifted a brow. "A delivery?"

"For Nathan. He needs some toys."

She frowned. "But he's already got toys."

"He doesn't have an outside play area, so I've ordered one of those shell-shaped sandboxes, plus a bucket and spade, a toy wagon, a toy lawn mower and some other things he'll enjoy."

"Other things?" Just how much had he ordered?

"A plastic pit with balls and an activity center that will keep him busy. Those are for inside. There are a couple of other things, too." He gave a slight shake of his head. "It's amazing the toys available these days. Very educational, too. I've ordered two sets of everything. One for here and one for when we get back to the city."

"Did you order the whole store?" she joked.

The corners of his mouth quirked upward. "Are you making fun of me?"

His affability was disconcerting, but she hid the feeling behind a small smile. "Never."

His mouth twisted wryly. "You think it's overkill, don't you?"

"Well…yes. I think a little. He's not even walking yet."

"He will be soon though." Tate's brows drew together. "Won't he?"

She nodded, endeared by his hesitation despite herself. "I'm told they usually start to walk about now, but every child is different. It could be a few more months," she warned, so he didn't get his expectations too high.

Tate took that in, then nodded. "He'll be fine. As you say, he'll do it in his own time." For a moment his eyes rested on his son with pride. When he turned back to Gemma, he was all business again. "They probably won't get here until around five. Unfortunately, I couldn't get it any earlier."

"When did you place the order?"

"Not long ago."

And he expected it to be here in a few hours? It always amazed her how fast he could buy things. The world of the uber-rich was certainly different. Her own upbringing in a middle-class family didn't come close to the privilege and entitlement afforded to a family like the Chandlers.

"I'll see Dad about getting the pool fenced off, too," Tate said, drawing her from her thoughts.

She tilted her head. "Will your parents mind about the play area?"

"Not at all. They've probably already thought of it. And they've said they wanted to put a childproof fence around the lake, remember? Anyway, it won't be an issue until he's walking."

She loved that he was so protective of Nathan's well-being.

After lunch, Tate went to clear the table, but she waved him aside. She needed something to do while he went back to his study. She wasn't used to having time on her hands. She'd always been working, and even these past ten days had been full with rushing to get ready for the wedding. Now, she looked down the long stretch of the afternoon with only a toy delivery on the agenda.

Enough! she told herself as she cleaned up the kitchen while chatting to Nathan in his high chair. Spending time with her son was exactly what she'd been longing to do. Now she could do that. She wouldn't waste a moment of it.

Once in the right frame of mind, the afternoon flew by, then just before five, the delivery van arrived. Tate told the man to drive around back, and Gemma let Nathan play on the floor of the sunroom as she watched Tate help unload a large plastic sandbox.

The rest of the items were soon dispensed with, and she watched a few minutes more as Tate asked questions about the other bits and pieces. She couldn't help noticing that for someone born with a silver spoon in his mouth, Tate got on well with people of all levels, even as he kept a slight reserve that was inherent in his personality.

By the time she heard the van depart, Gemma was

sitting on a stool in the kitchen feeding Nathan his dinner. A couple of minutes later, Tate appeared in the doorway.

"Oh." He looked disappointed. "He's eating."

"Sorry, he usually eats around now, and I didn't want to wait any longer." She used to collect Nathan from the day-care center around four-thirty each afternoon, and he was more than ready for his dinner by the time they got home and she had prepared it. Then she used to have an hour of play and bath time with her son. It was wonderful to be able to do it all now without rushing.

Tate nodded. "Yes, you're right." Then he looked down at himself and grimaced at the black streaks on his trousers and marks on his shirt. "I need a shower."

At the mention of water sluicing down his body, she felt her cheeks heat up. She looked away and continued feeding Nathan as she tried to push aside her memories of sharing a shower with Tate. "Um...we can have dinner around seven." A few seconds lapsed, and she glanced up. He was giving her hot cheeks an intense look. "I'll be bathing Nathan after this," she added, trying to cover the awkward moment.

His expression changed. "I'd like to give him his bath, if that's okay with you."

She blinked in surprise. "*You* want to bathe Nathan?"

"Sure." His jaw tightened. "I know I haven't been around as much as I'd have liked these past ten days, but that's going to change."

Why? she wanted to ask, both of them knowing he could have spent more time with his son today, both of them knowing why he hadn't. This was about avoiding spending too much time with *her*. Regret washed over her that Nathan had to unknowingly suffer because she and Tate had personal issues.

"Anyway," Tate's voice drew her back to him, "I got

some last-minute things out of the way, so tomorrow Nathan and I will be able to spend more time together."

Time with his son.

Not with his wife.

"I'm sure he'd like that," she said, keeping her voice neutral.

There was a moment's pause, as if Tate were trying to read more into her answer, but she kept her eyes averted, not letting him see anything on her face. They both knew the score.

"Maybe we'll go for a drive in the afternoon," he said.

Her gaze snapped instantly to him. "You mean you and Nathan?"

He frowned. "You as well."

"Oh." She hadn't expected that. A feeling of joy raced through her, even though she knew she shouldn't get her hopes up.

A shadow crossed his face, then he pivoted away. "I'll go take that shower now," he muttered, and strode through the kitchen to the back stairs.

Gemma waited for him to disappear before she let the tension leave her body. She'd thought her question reasonable under the circumstances, yet it had seemed to surprise him. Needless to say, she couldn't automatically assume she would be included in all the activities he shared with their son. Hadn't she been preparing herself for that reality ever since he'd seen Nathan at the hospital?

But as she continued to feed Nathan, she realized there was something more significant going on here. Tate had willingly suggested they do something together that wasn't for show. It was almost as if he'd offered to go for a drive with her, whether Nathan was with them or not. It was almost as if he wouldn't mind spending time in her company. Could that mean he was beginning to trust her?

And why did that suddenly make her feel so good?

Tate stood under the shower, hoping the water would loosen the knot in his gut. Did Gemma really think he would leave her at home tomorrow and take off with Nathan by himself? How could she think she wasn't invited? She was the mother of his son, for heaven's sake. He wouldn't leave her behind. It wouldn't look right. She was his wife now, and they had to act their parts.

The truth was that it wouldn't *be* right to leave her at home. Just what sort of person did she think he was? He winced. Okay, so he knew, but despite remembering their breakup, he only had to look into her blue eyes to feel like a heel.

He could handle her anger. He could even handle her hurt. She had brought all this on herself. But sometimes he saw more in those enticing depths.

The memory of what he'd once felt for her shook him up. Why this particular woman got to him, he didn't know. He wished to hell he could ignore his desire for her, but he couldn't. In the meantime there was only one thing for it.

Tate blasted his heated blood with cold water until it turned to ice.

By the time he dressed, he was ready for anything—until he went into the other suite, drawn by the sound of running water. He stopped dead in the doorway, watching as Gemma leaned forward and squirted bubble bath while swirling the water with her other hand. She'd kicked off her shoes.

The vision of her very nice rear view made him want to walk lazy fingers over her. Lord, he remembered how well the cheeks of her bottom fit his hands as he'd pulled her naked body against him. Those cheeks were a little more lusciously rounded than before, but she'd had a baby since he'd last known her, touched her...

He coughed, more for himself than to alert her to his presence. Otherwise he could easily stand here all evening appreciating that view.

She looked over her shoulder. "You're back." She put the bottle of bubble bath on the sink, then straightened, a flush on her cheeks.

"And ready for bath time," he said as a joke, only it came out husky.

Her gaze slid down his chest, then back up again.

Their eyes met.

She pushed past him, heading to the playpen. "I'll get Nathan ready."

It wouldn't have taken much to pull her to him. Nor would it have taken much to put her against the door and kiss every inch of that creamy skin. Only, he didn't. He followed her, watching her dart a nervous look over her shoulder as she picked Nathan up. For a couple of seconds, the sexual stimulation of pursuing Gemma called to something inside him.

With effort he put the feeling aside. "He likes a bath, does he?"

Relief that was no doubt due to the change of subject crossed her face as she began undressing the baby. "He loves it. He cries whenever I take him out."

She looked away and placed a special cap on Nathan to protect his ears before swinging him toward Tate, a determined angle to her chin. "Here we go. One little boy." She went back into the bathroom. "I'll just check the water's still the right temperature."

Tate followed her, his eyes drawn once more to her slim figure leaning over the tub.

"Just right," she said, straightening.

Hell, yeah.

"Your clothes might get wet."

"No problem."

A frisson of awareness entered her eyes. It was for the best that Nathan squirmed and insisted on his full attention right then. He eased his son into the warm, sudsy water and got down on his knees on the fluffy bathmat, fully aware of Gemma moving out of touching distance.

But his son wouldn't be ignored. Tate was soon engrossed in games with Nathan. "This really is fun," he mused, half to himself.

"You sound surprised."

He looked up. "I didn't know it could be like this," he admitted, startled to feel his chest squeeze tight with emotion. He quickly looked back down at the water, not wanting her to see just how much this was affecting him.

"It's awesome, isn't it?" she said softly, as if she knew exactly what he was feeling.

"Yeah." He cleared his throat, but he didn't look up. "Awesome."

More playtime followed, and as much as he was enjoying it, he was beginning to realize how tiring an infant could be. It must have been hard for Gemma to juggle a job as well as look after a baby all by herself. In spite of his animosity toward her, he had to admit to a growing admiration for her.

"That water will be getting cool now," she said eventually, unfolding a towel.

Tate felt the coolness of the water and nodded. Then he reached for the plug.

"Don't!"

His hand stopped. "What's the matter?"

"The sound of the water going down the hole frightens him."

He couldn't hold back a small laugh. "That's cute."

"You wouldn't say that if you heard him screaming his lungs out," she teased, holding up the towel.

Tate picked up Nathan from the bath, and she engulfed the child in the fluffy material and then handed him back. "You can finish off the job, while I tidy up in here."

"I'm not sure who's getting the better deal here," he drawled, trying not to show his lack of confidence in his parenting abilities. Her eyes said she was enjoying this.

"You have to learn to dress him sometime."

He looked down at his son then back up at her. "I'll pay you a thousand dollars to do it for me."

She gave a tinkling laugh, and the sound did crazy things to his pulse. "Not on your life."

His eyes locked on her mouth...

And her smile froze...

She twisted toward the bath. "I'd better clean up in here."

He paused before moving toward the bedroom. "I'll shut the door so he won't hear you emptying the bath."

"Thanks."

He closed the door behind him on the way out, took a breath to let his pulse settle, then looked down at his son. "Okay, sport. Let's get you sorted."

And no more thinking about that smile of Gemma's, he told himself, as he carried Nathan to the changing table. He gave the baby a squeaky toy, continuing to talk to him in case he could hear the bath water going down the drain.

He was still standing at the changing table when he saw

the bathroom door open. He looked up at Gemma with relief and conceded defeat. "I need your help."

She came toward them. "With what?"

"Please show me how to put on a diaper. I can't seem to get it right."

Her lips twitched with the amusement of an all-knowing mother. "For a start, that's the wrong way."

"It is?"

"And you've worn the adhesive off the tabs."

"I was trying to get it right."

She ruefully shook her head. "Move aside." In one quick motion, she'd grabbed another diaper from the pack, did a few things with it, lifted Nathan's bottom, removed the old and put the new one under him. "See. This is how—"

Tate was concentrating when something arced in the air and splashed across his chest. "What the—"

Gemma blinked, then giggled.

He looked down at his shirt. It had been damp a moment ago but was now wet. She giggled even louder as she pulled up the front flap of the diaper and covered their son's private parts.

All at once Tate saw the humor, too. "I guess that's what happens when you have a boy."

She held the diaper in place with one hand as her giggle turned to laughter. "Oh, my God…" more laughter, "you should see…" laugh, "the look on your…face."

He had to chuckle. "Stop laughing, Gemma."

"I ca-can't."

His laughter increased, and all at once they were both laughing together. Really laughing. It seemed so long since they'd shared something this funny.

Then, "I've always thought you had a lovely laugh," he murmured, unable to stop himself.

Her amusement stilled, and she moistened her top lip with her tongue. "You did?"

His gaze dropped to the tip of that pink tongue. "I've told you that before, surely?"

Her eyes flickered. "No, I would have remembered."

Suddenly there was something more between them than their love for their son. "Would you?"

"Yes."

Several heartbeats ticked by. He knew his head was lowering toward her. He couldn't stop himself.

Then Nathan squeaked his toy and they both jumped. Gemma hastily turned back to their son, who she was still holding on the changing table with one hand. Tate blew out an unsteady breath.

They'd been getting too intimate. He stepped back. "I'll go change my shirt."

She flicked him a look. "I'll put Nathan to bed, then I'll check on the dinner."

"Fine." By that time he fully intended to be detached again.

Yet, as he went back to his room, he tried to analyze what was happening between him and Gemma. He didn't want to like her, but she kept slipping under his guard. His only excuse was that sharing a bond over their son was getting to him, causing the awareness between him and Gemma to build.

Neither of them wanted this…

Both of them wanted this…

Five

Gemma dreamed that Tate was saying she had a lovely laugh, and—oh, God—he was about to kiss her...willingly...

Then she opened her eyes and deep disappointment ripped through her. He wasn't about to kiss her at all. It was morning. She was in bed. And Tate wasn't with her.

And it was *his* fault she'd been dreaming about him all night. He *had* been about to kiss her last night after they'd bathed Nathan. He *had* been tempted, in spite of his earlier assertions that he wasn't.

Of course, once they'd gone downstairs he'd made it quite clear he wouldn't let her get so close again. They'd eaten their casserole then he'd gone to the study while she'd watched a movie. Alone. The home movie theater wasn't the largest of rooms, but it had felt empty. She wondered if he would keep to his promise of taking them for a drive today.

Right then, she heard Nathan's chuckle from next door. She threw back the blankets and hopped out of bed, slipping on her robe as she hurried to the connecting door. She found Tate on the floor playing peek-a-boo with Nathan, who was in his playpen. Her son looked incredibly adorable standing up, holding on to the rails in his pajamas.

And Tate looked so relaxed and carefree.

The old Tate.

Then he looked at her and the wary new Tate slipped back into place. "Did we wake you?"

"Yes, but it was time for me to get out of bed anyway." She wanted to step into the room to give her son a morning kiss but was conscious of the word *bed* and Tate's gaze on her silky robe. She remained where she stood.

"You were sleeping very peacefully," he said, his eyes lifting back to her face.

So he'd checked on her. The image unnerved her. "I was tired."

He scowled. "Are you okay?"

His concern took her by surprise, and warmed her. "Better for a good night's sleep." And that was something she wouldn't have had if he'd been sharing her bed.

As if he read her thoughts, the words suddenly transported them to last evening—and their almost-kiss right here in this room…right there beside the changing table.

Stop!

She grabbed for something to break the silence. "Er…I should change Nathan's diaper."

"Done."

She couldn't have made a joke about that if her life had depended on it. Breaking eye contact, she mentally scrambled to pull herself together. "If you could mind him a little longer, I'll shower then take him down for breakfast."

"That's okay, I'll take him downstairs with me." Tate got to his feet, all business now. "By the way, Peggy and Clive are back."

"They are?" The other couple must have left the city before dawn to get here.

He swung Nathan up in his arms. "We'll be in the sunroom. Take your time." He crossed to the other door and left her standing in the connecting doorway.

After he left, she took a ragged breath, then she hurried to the shower. It was better that Clive and Peggy had returned. Having others in the house could diffuse the growing tension between her and Tate. If it got out of control again, that is. Not that she expected it would. Tate wouldn't let that happen. He'd been clear about that.

Yet she had to wonder what the older couple would make of their separate bedrooms. Before the wedding, that might not have been a concern. After the wedding, it would be clear that she and Tate were having problems.

Not that it was anyone's business but their own.

Fifteen minutes later, Gemma walked into the sunroom. Nathan sat in his high chair, next to Tate, and the two of them looked so right together that she wanted to rush forward and be part of their family unit. She restrained herself as she kissed her darling son's head, then sat down beside them.

"You've done well," she told Tate, referring to the finger of toast Nathan chewed on.

"I can't take credit for that. It was Peggy's idea."

Just then Peggy came into the sunroom with a pot of coffee, and they chatted for a short time before she left. Gemma poured herself some cereal and crunched on that while keeping an eye on Nathan, and while trying *not* to keep an eye on Tate.

"He's a slow eater today, isn't he?" Tate said, after a couple of minutes.

All at once Gemma realized Tate was restless. She gave him a knowing look. "You're waiting to show him the sandbox, aren't you?"

His eyes filled with wry amusement. "Am I that obvious?"

"Yes," she teased. He chuckled, and the low sound softened the tension between them.

Thankfully, Nathan threw his remaining finger of toast on the floor right then. By the time she'd picked it up and discarded it, she hoped she could blame her flushed cheeks on having to bend down to the floor.

Tate got to his feet. "I'd say he's finished eating, don't you think?"

She needn't have worried about explaining her flushed cheeks. Tate evidently had other priorities. "Just let me take him upstairs and change him out of his pajamas first."

Tate nodded. "I'll be outside. Don't be too long." He sauntered out toward the patio area.

Men!

Her heart actually felt lighter as she changed Nathan into jeans and a T-shirt. Their son may have been the reason for their marriage, but he was proving to be a great leveler, too.

Once back downstairs, Gemma found not only Tate outside at the sandbox, but Clive and Peggy, as well. Tate saw her coming and immediately took his son. The males joined right in with enthusiasm. Soon both men were kneeling on the grass outside the shell-shaped sandbox, not seeming to mind about their trousers, while Nathan sat in the middle of the sand, trying to grab the dump truck that Tate was showing him how to use.

Then Clive said something and Tate laughed. He was totally relishing being a father, Gemma mused, admitting she was seeing a new side to Tate. He treated Clive as a personal friend rather than an employee. He treated Peggy more like a mother figure. Gemma hadn't seen him with other people during their month together, but she'd assumed he would keep his distance because of who he was and especially with the hired help, but that wasn't the case.

"You should join them," Peggy encouraged.

Gemma looked down at her casual slacks and top that would have cost more than her weekly wage. "I'm not exactly dressed for it."

"Neither are they," Peggy pointed out with bemusement.

Gemma smiled. "They're having too much fun playing at being boys. I'll just watch for now."

Peggy nodded. "Well, I think I'll leave them to it. I must clean up the breakfast dishes."

As Gemma watched Tate be so caring and tender with his son, she suddenly felt herself blinking back tears. It must be the strain of the past two weeks, she decided, and turned to go inside.

By the time she entered the kitchen where Peggy was busy cleaning, she was fine. She poured herself a cup of coffee. "Can I pour you a cup, too, Peggy?"

The older woman looked up from stacking the dishwasher. "No, thanks, Gemm…I mean, Mrs. Chandler."

Gemma only now realized the housekeeper hadn't addressed her by name since the wedding yesterday. "Gemma will do nicely, Peggy. Otherwise I may not know who you're talking to."

"But you're Mrs. Chandler now," Peggy said, not looking as if she would be swayed.

"And I was Miss Watkins these past ten days and you didn't have a problem calling me Gemma then." She had insisted right from the start, and while Peggy had been a little reluctant at first, she'd agreed to use Gemma's first name in private.

"I know, but that was then and this is now."

"That doesn't make sense, Peggy," she teased.

"It does to me. Mr. Chandler is Mr. Chandler, and you're Mrs. Chandler."

Gemma laughingly held up a hand. "You're making my head spin."

Peggy wrinkled her nose. "It does seem silly, but please, allow me this."

Gemma remembered how the other woman had mentioned Tate telling them to call him by his first name but they had refused, not because they didn't like him but because they were old-fashioned.

"Okay, I give in." Gemma paused deliberately. "For now."

The housekeeper clucked her tongue with mild exasperation as she continued clearing up. "How are you feeling now that the wedding's over?"

"Relieved," Gemma quipped, then hoped she didn't sound like she was all about getting married to a rich man. "I mean, relieved that the day is finally over. It was quite nerve-racking."

Peggy nodded, her eyes understanding. "Getting married is more wearing on the nerves than not. My eldest daughter was a complete wreck. She even fainted at the altar."

"*Who* fainted at the altar?" Tate said, coming into the kitchen with Nathan on his hip.

"That would be Sonya," Clive joked, following him. "Our eldest daughter. She's a bit of a drama queen."

"Clive," Peggy admonished, easing into a smile. "He's right, though. She *is* a drama queen."

"That girl is never going to change. She's thirty now and still doing it." Clive shook his head as he walked over to the refrigerator. "What's that old saying about a leopard not changing its spots?"

As if he couldn't help himself, Tate's eyes shot to Gemma. He looked away again as fast, but she didn't need three guesses to know he was thinking about her supposed kiss with his best friend.

"And you love her anyway," Peggy pointed out to her husband.

Clive grinned. "Of course."

Peggy returned the smile, then turned her attention to Nathan. "Heavens, what did you two do to that young fellow? He looks like he's been sandblasted."

Tate finally focused on the housekeeper. "He kept trying to eat the sand, so we've brought him in to show him the new activity center."

"They're a handful at this age," Peggy said.

Nathan was the excuse Gemma needed. She moved to collect him from Tate's arms. "I'd better take him upstairs for a wash first."

Tate handed Nathan over without a word and she made her escape. But not before she'd seen the look in her husband's eyes. He considered her a person who would never change for the better. A person worthy of his mistrust. It was just a pity he couldn't see how inflexible he was being himself.

Surprisingly, later that day they did go for that drive, and Tate was polite but remote, as if he'd been reminded

of exactly who his wife was and regretted getting close
to her earlier. He was the same for the rest of the week,
whether they went sightseeing or lazed about on the patio
with Nathan or watched television together after dinner.
The only time he'd said anything the least personal to her
was when she'd been lounging on the deck chair, immersed
in a book.

"Don't stay out here too long in the sun or you'll get
burned," he'd warned, startling her as he'd stepped onto
the patio.

She looked up at the sky, noting the sun was overhead.
"I was in the shade before."

"Yes, but the sun's moved."

He went back inside.

And that was that.

He'd done his duty.

Then, halfway through Friday morning, Gemma was
about to leave her room when she caught sight of the
light flashing on the telephone beside the bed. Nathan
was asleep in his crib. Tate and Clive were in the garage
checking on a problem with Clive's car. The sound of
the vacuum cleaner came from another part of the house
and she knew Peggy couldn't hear the telephone ringing.
Thinking it might be important, Gemma picked up the
handset, almost dropping it again at the sound of the male
voice on the other end of the line.

"Well, well," Drake Fulton's voice said into the black
hole that suddenly swallowed her up. "If it isn't Gemma
Watkins...oops, it's Gemma Chandler now, isn't it?"

He sounded pleasant enough, if anyone had been
listening on another extension, but she knew there
was more than that in his voice. "What do you want,
Drake?"

"Congratulations are in order, I believe. A marriage *and* a son. Well done, Gem."

She clasped the phone tighter. She hated him calling her Gem. He only ever did that in private. "Are you looking for Tate?"

"I was." He didn't acknowledge her abrupt tone. "I wanted to apologize again for not being able to make the wedding, but I thought it best I didn't go. Tate agreed with me that it was the right thing to do…under the circumstances."

Gemma had to bite her tongue. This man didn't know how to do the right thing, under any circumstances. "I'll tell Tate you called."

"No need," he said cheerily. "I'll phone him back another time."

"Goodbye, Drake." She hung up with shaking fingers and sank down on the bed, thoughts milling in her head. Drake hadn't called to talk to Tate at all. He'd called on the off-chance that *she* might answer the phone, otherwise he could have easily called Tate on his cell phone.

Gemma had to get out of the room and out of the house. She jumped to her feet, sick to her stomach. "I'm going for a walk to the lake," she told Peggy as calmly as she could when she passed her vacuuming downstairs. "Would you keep an eye on Nathan? He should sleep for another hour or so."

"Of course."

"Thanks. I just need some fresh air." She needed to get the stink of Drake Fulton out of her mind.

Gemma was still upset when she reached the sanctuary of the lake, where the cluster of trees and the gazebo hid her from view. She sank down on a small bench near the water's edge. There was no way she could tell Tate about the call. He'd accuse her of somehow engineering this so she could talk to Drake. How she could have achieved that she didn't know, but Tate was blind where she was concerned and totally biased about his best friend.

God, she couldn't even confide how ill at ease Drake had made her, or Tate would say she was imagining things or, worse, trying to stir up more trouble. Hadn't she once attempted to tell him how Drake had made her uncomfortable? He hadn't been prepared to listen then and she was sure he wouldn't now. Otherwise he'd already know that this was the way Drake worked, pretending to be friendly in front of others, pretending to be Tate's best friend, while trying to get her into bed.

No doubt if she'd fallen for Drake's charms and slept with him two years ago he'd have dumped her as quickly as Tate had. He hadn't liked that she'd ignored his advances then, and she could tell he still didn't like it. How far would he go now that she was married to Tate and had a child? She suspected he wouldn't stop at less than destroying what she and Tate had. Suddenly her tenuous hold on her marriage was everything to her. She didn't want to lose it.

Right then, a horse and rider came over the rise and Gemma groaned, wishing she'd gone somewhere else. Wasn't there anywhere she could have some privacy in this place? The last thing she wanted right now was company.

Rolly saw her and waved, then brought the horse in her direction. "I didn't think I'd see you here this morning," he said as he got closer.

She rose to her feet and mustered up a smile. "It was too nice to stay inside."

"I'm later than usual. I had to do a job for my dad." He slid down to the ground and smoothed his hand along the horse's flank as he spoke to her. "Where's your son?"

"He's back at the house, but Tate will be bringing him down to see the swans soon."

"Does he like the swans?" he said, looking a bit preoccupied as he dropped the reins and let the horse amble over to the water's edge.

"Yes, he does." There was a momentary lull. "Rolly, is something the matter?"

Indecision crossed his face, then, "My dad wants me to go visit my mother."

She should have known it would be a family problem. There didn't seem to be any other kind right now.

She felt sorry for the teenager. He'd been nice to her, and helping him would certainly stop her from thinking about her own problems. "You don't want to visit her?"

He shrugged. "She married someone else, but I don't like him much."

"Why not?"

"He doesn't want me there. He just wants my mom."

Gemma totally understood not being wanted, and her heart squeezed for him. "I wish I could tell you it shouldn't be like that, but sometimes no matter how much we wish for something, it still doesn't happen." She didn't want him to feel too down about it all, though. "But I have absolutely no doubt you'll get through it."

A spark of hope brightened his eyes. "Really?"

"Really. And think about how happy it will make your mother if you visit her," she said. It would be wonderful if her own mother would be as happy, but Gemma knew that wasn't about to happen.

The teenager gazed at her speculatively. "You know a lot about life and things, don't you?"

"No more than anyone else."

Suddenly, he looked at the top of her head. "Hey, you've got something in your hair." He took a couple of steps forward and reached to pick it off. "It's only a gum leaf. I get them in my hair all—"

"Gemma," Tate's voice snapped behind them.

Gemma spun around at the same time as Rolly did. "Tate!" she exclaimed, feeling her cheeks instantly flush with a heat she had no control over.

A guilty flush, Tate decided, unable to believe this was happening again. Peggy had told him she'd gone for a walk down here, but this was more than that. This was a rendezvous.

No wonder she'd put Nathan to bed. Was no man—no *boy*—safe from his wife? Did she need male attention all the time, no matter what the age of the cohort? Their marriage wasn't a bed of roses right now, but couldn't she at least remain faithful while they were still on their honeymoon?

Clearly not.

"Er...where's Nathan?" she asked, as if she was trying to smooth things over. "I thought you were bringing him down here to see the swans."

Tate knew that was an outright lie, but he leashed his immediate reaction. What was between him and Gemma stayed between him and Gemma. "He's still sleeping."

"Hi, Tate," Rolly said, a slight flush to his cheeks that told Tate more than he wanted to know. "Long time, no see."

Tate gave a short nod in acknowledgment. "Rolly."

The teenager looked at Gemma then nervously back at Tate. "I was just letting the horse drink from the lake. Your grandfather told me I could."

"I know."

"So...you don't mind if I continue that?"

"No, I don't mind." The kid was pretending he was

nervous over bringing the horse here, when they both knew that was just an excuse.

"Great. Thanks." Rolly picked up the reins and scampered up on the horse. "I'd better be getting back or my dad will come looking for me." He glanced at Gemma and gave a quick smile. "Thanks, Gemma."

It was just as well the teenager took off after that. Tate gritted his teeth. God, how could he have been so stupid as to let his guard down with her? Gemma was beautiful, but she wouldn't turn him into a fool again.

"Tate—"

"I don't want to hear it, Gemma." He stepped forward and put his hand under her elbow, intending to walk her back to the house.

She took a couple of steps with him, then pulled away. "You're overreacting."

"Am I?" He didn't think so. How could he forget what had happened with Drake?

"Rolly was merely getting a leaf out of my hair."

He gave her a skeptical look. "Is that what you call it these days?"

"Don't be ridiculous," she said dismissively, sending his blood pressure soaring.

His jaw clenched tight. "How long has this been going on?"

"Nothing's going on," she snapped, but she had turned pale. "I met Rolly by accident the other day when I brought Nathan down here. This is only the second time I've run into him."

"Why did he thank you then? *What* did he thank you for?"

She shrugged. "He's got some personal problems. I was helping him sort them out."

"Yeah, I could see that." Tate let his voice drip with sarcasm.

She drew herself up taller, looking haughty and so darn beautiful. "Don't you dare suggest anything else, Tate Chandler. He's a boy who needed to talk and that's all."

Was she blind? "He's only ten years younger than you. He's a young man with a young man's hormones, and having you close by would be torture for him." Dammit, she was torturing *him*.

"And that's got to appeal to me, does it? A pimply teenager with raging hormones is just what I've been waiting for. Gosh, all my Christmases have come at once. I don't know how I've contained my excitement all this time."

He grimaced. Okay, so she had a point. Perhaps he could admit his reaction had been over the top. But seeing the young man touch her hair—he'd felt as if he was losing her again, as crazy as that sounded. Last time, he'd decided it had been for good, but this time he *knew* it would be forever. Not even for Nathan's sake would he go through that again. Hell, if she had any affairs in the future—and God help her if she did—then it would be *for* Nathan's sake they would split up.

He didn't want it to get that far. "Just stay away from Rolly."

She crossed her arms over her firm breasts. "You know what? I don't have to do a thing you tell me to do."

For some reason the image of her breasts took precedence. And suddenly Rolly wasn't the problem. "You never did do anything I told you to do. But you're my wife now, so perhaps you'd best learn."

"Then perhaps *you* should act like I'm your wife."

The comment threw him. "What does that mean?"

"You figure it out."

Was she suggesting what he thought she was suggesting? "If you're feeling lonely, find another outlet. Don't go turning to someone else."

"Well, it's no use turning to you, is it, Tate?"

Something burst inside him.

He slipped his hand under her hair and drew her hard against his body. She gasped as he held her head still, his lips seeking and finding hers, taking advantage of her open mouth and sliding his tongue straight in and over the top of hers, instinctively wanting to dominate her. Hell, he wanted to erase the kiss of another man—*any* man—right out of her mouth.

Then she came alive and seized control. Suddenly *she* was the one calling the shots, and he was the one being taken over. She made him remember what their kisses had been like—*real* kisses, *no-holds-barred* kisses—as she arched against him and sent the blood storming through his veins, his muscles locking into place, his body tightening with need against her softness.

A buzzing sound interrupted his consciousness.

For a moment he didn't realize what it was, but soon the sound of a small, low-flying plane could be heard coming closer. Breaking off the kiss, he shielded Gemma and moved her a few feet to the side of the gazebo and out of sight. He wouldn't let anyone see them. This was private property.

The plane didn't appear to be scouring the area. It was heading in a direct line north, so it was unlikely to be reporters. He waited until it was past the house before looking at her.

For a long moment, he was riveted by her and what had just passed between them. Had he really ever been convinced he wouldn't let himself be tempted by her charms? Heaven help him, but his body still thrummed with need as he noted the color high in her cheeks and her softly swollen lips. Her eyes were uncertain now, calling to something inside him. Thankfully sanity prevailed. Giving in would be a mistake.

Just like *she* had made a mistake when she'd kissed his best friend, he reminded himself.

"I won't be a substitute, dammit," he said, dragging up the thought of her and Drake together to get him through this moment. He had to. He had to protect himself from his own desires.

She drew in a sharp breath. "Tate—"

"You'd better go back to the house."

"But—"

"Just go."

She looked like she might say something further, but she merely glared at him before hurrying along the path.

Tate ran his fingers through his hair, damn grateful she had gone. The memory of her and Drake kissing might be in his mind, but it was a different memory beating through his body right now. He had to take her to his bed or learn to live with the wanting.

Neither option was acceptable.

Gemma's mind was reeling as she straightened her blouse and hurried back to the house. How could Tate think he was a substitute for any man? No one else had ever come close to him.

And while he had carried on about Rolly, it had been a storm in a teacup. The real issue was Drake. Even when she and Tate had good moments between them, it always came back to the other man. Drake had been the cause of their breakup. Drake was the reason for her walk today, which had resulted in that kiss just now. And coming full circle, Drake was the cause of Tate's contempt for her.

Yet in spite of Drake, there was still something between her and Tate that wouldn't be denied. She was horrified with herself for challenging him to kiss her like she had. She didn't know where the words had come from, but she should have remembered that he always faced a challenge.

Lord, as much as she'd wanted Tate to kiss her, she wished he hadn't. It only made her more aware of what she *couldn't* have and of what she *shouldn't* be wanting. Now every time she was with Tate, and even when she wasn't, there would be this consciousness between them.

Already she ached to be back in his arms.

She didn't expect him to come to her room a short time later and tell her they were going back to the city tomorrow.

"Won't that cause suspicion?" she asked with a frown.

"It's only a day early. I don't think it'll matter." A pulse began beating in his cheekbone. "And we ignore what happened before, right?"

"For how long, Tate?" she heard herself ask.

"For as long as it takes."

"To do what? To convince yourself I'm worthy of your touch?"

"A bit of honesty wouldn't go amiss."

"So if I tell you I kissed Drake on purpose then you'll forgive me and we'll be able to move on?"

His eyes flared with triumph. "I'm not making any promises, but I'll try."

Her heart gave a painful twist. "How noble of you. Sorry, but I'm not telling a lie just so you can feel better about something that's simply not true."

He expelled a raspy breath. "Nothing was ever simple between us, Gemma."

She wasn't getting through to him. So there was nothing left to do but to salvage her pride. "Actually, I thought that's all we ever had between us—*simple* lust."

His mouth tightened. "It was...until you wanted Drake."

He left the room and Gemma sank down on the bed, a sob catching in her throat. It was like talking to a brick wall. What could she do now but keep right on doing what she was already doing, knowing she had done nothing wrong in the first place.

It was the only way to make this marriage work.

Six

Late the next morning, Peggy and Clive left the mansion an hour before them and drove back to Melbourne in their own car. By the time Tate and Gemma arrived, a light lunch had already been prepared.

Nathan had slept nearly the whole way, so now he was a ball of energy and very fidgety as Gemma helped him eat his lunch. He was going to keep her on her toes for the rest of the day, she knew, and perhaps that wasn't a bad thing. Without a doubt, Tate would head to his study and throw himself into his work, or even go into his office in the city. It would be business as usual for him from now on.

The job.

Play with his son.

Ignore her.

"What are you doing for the rest of the afternoon?" he asked, as if reading her thoughts.

"I'm not sure." She could easily have taken a nap, but hopefully she'd get her second wind soon. She hadn't had time for naps when she'd been working, she reminded herself. "I might take Nathan for a walk to the local shops."

Tate frowned. "What do you need? Clive can get it for you. Just ask."

She lifted a shoulder and then let it drop. "I don't need anything really. It's merely something to do to help Nathan chew up some energy."

His lips twisted. "I see. You're sick of all this already, are you?"

"No." Why did he turn her words around? "I merely thought Nathan might like some fresh air, that's all. It's no different from me taking him down to the lake." She could have bit her tongue off when Tate's jaw clenched tight.

"I'll come with you."

Her eyebrows shot up. "Why?"

"Because."

"I see. You think I'll leave Nathan sitting in his stroller while some store owner has his way with me out back, do you?"

Tate cursed low. "I'm coming with you and that's that. We'll go through a side entrance in case any reporters are out front. Put sun hats on you both. And wear your sunglasses."

He was serious about coming with them. "All that for a short walk?"

"A short walk could turn into a nightmare if the reporters discover us."

Thoughts of cameras being pushed in Nathan's face turned her cold. "On second thought, it's probably best not to go."

"We're not prisoners, Gemma. We'll go out and get our son an ice cream if we want. No one is going to stop us."

Understanding dawned. She had to admit, when she thought about it some more, she felt the same. This was Australia, for heaven's sake. Surely they were entitled to some space to themselves? Still, she'd feel better with Tate there to protect them.

After that, considering everything between them, it was quite an enjoyable walk in the sunshine. Tate hadn't worn a hat, but he seemed to relax more with each step, and so did she. They even stopped at a local park next to the small strip of shops so she could feed Nathan some ice cream.

It was Saturday, so there were quite a few people in the park. A couple of children playing with a small puppy caught Nathan's attention, and he started to laugh at their antics. The children, a girl and a boy around seven or eight, heard him and brought the puppy over. Before they knew it, the puppy was licking drops of ice cream off Nathan's T-shirt.

Gemma actually felt happy—seriously happy—as Tate asked about the children's names and the age of the puppy. He was really good with the kids.

A nice-looking man strolled toward them from the direction of the shops, carrying a loaf of bread. "I hope they aren't bothering you," he said, smiling as he approached.

Tate smiled back. "Not at all. They've been keeping us quite entertained."

The man blinked, and Gemma knew he'd recognized Tate. So much for their sunglasses and her sun hat!

"If you want to wear your kids out, just get them a puppy," the man joked.

"I plan on it, when my son's a little older." Tate proudly glanced at Nathan.

A short time later, the other family left and Gemma couldn't help saying something. "Did you mean it about getting Nathan a dog?"

"Sure, why not?" Tate lifted a brow. "You don't want him to have one?"

"No, I think it's a great idea." She shrugged. "It's just such a…family thing to do."

An odd expression flickered across his face. "We *are* a family now," he said, as he turned away to push the stroller.

Her vision blurred and she was thankful for her sunglasses. She didn't want to acknowledge how much his words meant to her, but his comment warmed her all the way home.

On their return, Gemma carried Nathan into the informal living room while Tate put the stroller away. She vaguely heard Peggy's voice, but she didn't take much notice as she placed Nathan down on the carpet and let him crawl around the now-childproof room.

About ten minutes later Tate came through the doorway, sheets of paper in his hands, his face tight. He held them out toward her. "Someone's just posted these on the internet," he said, keeping his voice low. All his earlier softness had disappeared.

She frowned as she read what was in her hands, then gasped, her eyes widening. On one page was a photograph of her old apartment minus the furniture. The place looked like it needed a coat of paint and seemed a little shabby. On another was a picture of Tate's house, with its magnificent gardens and luxury cars parked in the sweeping driveway. Farther, on the next page, someone had put the two together with the caption, "From *This* to *This* in Two Weeks," then there were some derogatory remarks, not about Tate but about her becoming pregnant on purpose so she could marry into money.

She lifted her head in bewilderment, trying to get her head around it all. "*This* is on the internet?"

"Yes."

"But why?" She swallowed hard, her mind whirring. "How did you even know these were there?"

"One of Bree's friends rang to tell her about it, so naturally my sister rang here. She left a message with Peggy." Something brutal entered his eyes. "I printed them up to show you. I'll get my lawyer to investigate the website."

The thought of this being all over the internet turned her stomach. "Investigate?"

"I'll find out who's done this. They'll pay."

She took a shuddering breath. "God, I feel violated." Not only was her reputation being ripped to shreds in a public forum, but the place—the *home*—she'd tried to make for her and Nathan had been held up for everyone to see—and judge.

She felt tears mist her eyes. Could her day—her *life*—get any worse? She was so emotionally drained. As one of the Chandlers now, did she have it in her to take this over all the years ahead?

"Gemma?"

She turned her back on him and blinked rapidly, seeing her son playing on the carpet with his toys but more aware of Tate. She didn't want this man to see her crying. It would be the last straw for her. She had to remain strong, or fall in a heap.

"Gemma?" he said, more softly this time.

She remembered something. She spun back. "The humanitarian award! This might ruin it." A sob escaped her lips. "Oh, God, I seem to be wrecking your family's chances everywhere I turn."

"Screw the award."

"Wh-what?"

"I said screw the award. This attack on you is more important. I won't have your character denigrated in such a personal way like this. You're my wife now, and as such you should have respect." His head at a proud angle, he took the papers out of her hand and strode to the door, purpose in every tense line of his shoulders, his intention obvious.

Don't mess with his family.

Okay, so it wasn't about *her* exactly. It was more about her position and probably more for Nathan's sake than not. But that didn't change something quite remarkable: Tate wasn't blaming her for this.

And that had to be a first.

The rest of the day went by quietly and Gemma wasn't unhappy about that. Except for dinner and time spent with his son, Tate stayed in his study, no doubt checking into this latest mess.

He didn't mention anything more about it the next morning when she went down to breakfast, so Gemma didn't either. Perhaps if he played with Nathan after breakfast, she might go into his study to check online. But, she decided, that would only upset her. Best to let Tate handle it. He had the means and the connections to get to the bottom of it fast.

Then over breakfast he said, "I've given Peggy and Clive the rest of the day off so they can visit their grandchildren." He paused. "And my parents have invited us to lunch."

Gemma groaned inwardly. The one place she *didn't* want to be today was with his family. His mother was nice, but the rest of them hadn't forgiven her for keeping Nathan from his birthright. Now they would have something more to castigate her about.

"They usually eat a late lunch," he continued, "so we won't have to leave until around one. That will give Nathan time for his morning nap."

"Er…did you tell them about the photos?"

"I didn't have to. Bree already told them."

"How kind."

He gave her a sharp look. "My sister was only trying to look after them."

Gemma understood that, but it was at *her* expense. "And?"

"They want to get to the bottom of it as much as we do."

She noticed he didn't say anything about them not blaming *her* for bringing more ill-repute on their family name.

"Let it go for now, Gemma. There's nothing we can do at the moment. I've got someone working on it, and we'll find the culprit as fast as we can."

He was right. She tried to relax. "At least they weren't nude photographs," she quipped, then froze. What on earth had made her say that?

"Should we be worried about that?" he demanded.

"Of course not!" She'd never been promiscuous with her favors. *Except with him.* But she refused to look away. She had nothing to be ashamed of. Not with him, not with anyone.

They glared eye-to-eye, then something lifted in his gaze and she could see he believed her. Before she could shake off the moment, she realized he was mentally undressing her, just like he used to…right down to her bare skin…sending her stomach into a flutter. Then he noticed her noticing, and he looked away, breaking the connection.

Thankfully Peggy came in then, but it took a while before Gemma's pulse settled to its normal pace. After breakfast, she took the opportunity to escape, carrying Nathan upstairs to pick out an outfit for him to wear to lunch while Tate answered a call on his cell phone.

The morning passed surprisingly quickly. She brought Nathan back downstairs, but Tate's study door was firmly closed. She kept busy, playing with Nathan on the carpet.

Then her eye caught sight of a local newspaper. She jumped to her feet, panic spurting through her veins. Could the story have reached the newspapers? She left Nathan to play close by with his toys while she sat on the sofa and combed the pages, shuddering with relief when she didn't find anything. Even so, how long could that last?

Shrugging aside a growing sense of despondency over it all, Gemma eventually took Nathan back upstairs for a mid-morning nap. He cried a little in resistance, but if he was going to be awake all afternoon then he needed some sleep first. A couple of minutes later he was out like a light.

She'd just put on a dress and was finishing her makeup in preparation for the luncheon, when Tate knocked on her door. He always knocked before entering now, except that time the newspapers had called his father and broke the news about Nathan. Tate had been angry enough to walk right in then.

"Your parents are here," he said without preamble.

The closed tube of lipstick slipped from her fingers and onto the vanity. "My pa-parents?"

His gaze sharpened. "The guard rang from the front gate. I knew who they were as soon as I saw them on the security camera. You once showed me a photograph, remember?"

"Oh, my God," she muttered, her mind agog. Her parents were *here*? They were back from their Mediterranean cruise? They *wanted* to see her?

"I told them to wait."

She blinked. "You did?"

"I didn't know if you wanted to see them or not." He left a longish pause. "Do you?"

Did she?

"I'm not sure," she admitted, then realized he'd seen more than she knew when a frown creased his forehead.

"Do I let them in, Gemma? You have to make a decision. I can tell them to go away or—"

She couldn't bear that. "No, let them in."

He stared a moment more as if judging her sincerity, then, satisfied, he walked over to the bedside table and used the telephone to talk to the security guard.

Gemma stood there, still reeling from the news. This didn't seem real. She'd wanted their support for so long… yearned for them to ask to see her and Nathan. She could admit that to herself now.

He hung up the phone. "Right, they're on the way."

The words somehow pulled her together, reminding her that this was her problem, not Tate's. It was best she handle it herself. And she had to admit she was a little ashamed for him to know what had happened with her parents. Was loving a daughter through thick and thin so very difficult?

She veiled her expression. "Thank you, Tate. I'd like to see them alone."

"No."

"Tate—"

"What's going on with you and them anyway? I know there's something wrong, so don't tell me there isn't."

"I'll tell you later. There's no time right now."

"There's time enough to give me the gist of it."

She deliberately hadn't told him what had transpired, not wanting him to tap into her emotions and use her pain against her. Now she knew that was one thing he wouldn't do, at least where her parents were concerned. He valued family too much. And while she didn't want his sympathy, she wanted him on her side. She needed his support right now, if only for this short time.

She took a shuddering breath, the words harder to say than she'd expected. "If you really want to know, they kicked me out when I told them I was pregnant."

Rage erupted in his eyes. "What the hell! God, what type of parents do that sort of thing?"

She wasn't totally sure if the rage was for her or for his son. "They couldn't handle the shame of their daughter being pregnant and unmarried." She tried to sound uncaring, but it still hurt deeply that her mother and father had turned their backs on her when she'd needed them most.

And on their grandson.

Tate's jaw flexed. "Shame on *them*."

Something softened inside her. "Thank you," she whispered, then drew her shoulders back. It was time to move.

"Gemma, look, I'd fully understand if you don't want to see them."

She appreciated the turnabout. "No, it's best this way." Otherwise she'd always wonder why they'd come. Besides, she needed to think about Nathan. If there was a chance they wanted their grandson in their lives, she couldn't deny him that opportunity. Anyway, once they saw Nathan they would fall in love with him. She was certain of that.

For all her self-assurance, when she and Tate reached the bottom of the stairs, she hesitated. She saw their shadows through the glass door and was unable to bring herself to open it. Reminiscent of their wedding day, when they'd had to face the reporters outside, Tate gave her shoulder a squeeze. Then he moved forward.

She quickly grasped his arm. "They're really not so bad, Tate." She didn't want him to think it was *all* their fault. For good or bad, she *had* made some unwise choices.

He nodded but his face closed up. And then he opened the door. Gemma stood where she was as he introduced himself and invited her parents inside. They saw her and hesitated before stepping into the foyer. Her heart staggered beneath her breast. Was it too much to hope that they might have rushed forward and taken her in their arms?

On second thought, perhaps they were simply over-whelmed, she told herself, not willing to let the doubt-devils get to her this early. She went to them and kissed them on their cheeks. "Mom. Dad. It's lovely to see you both." But she noticed her mother had stiffened at Gemma's touch.

"Hello, Gemma," Meryl Watkins said without a hint of warmth. She'd always spoken like that, Gemma reminded herself.

Her father's expression faltered before he cleared his throat. Frank Watkins had always given in to her mother, even if Gemma sensed he didn't always agree with her. "Yes, hello, Gemma."

There was an awkward silence. It was like they were strangers. She waited for them to ask about Nathan, then was disappointed when they simply stood there.

"Let's go to the drawing room," Tate suggested.

"Yes, good idea." Gemma tried hard to relax. "Would you like some coffee or tea?"

"No, thank you, Gemma." Her mother walked through the arched doorway, looking critically around the room before sitting down on the sofa without being asked. "This is certainly very nice, don't you think, Frank?"

Her father nodded as he placed himself beside her mother. "You've done well for yourself, Gemma."

Gemma ignored the tightening of Tate's mouth as she moved to sit opposite them. "I hear you've been on a Mediterranean cruise."

Her father's bushy eyebrows knitted together. "How did you know that?"

"When no one answered the phone at home, I phoned your work. I wanted to invite you to the wedding." Hopefully they would see that as a peace offering.

Frank glanced at his wife. "See, I told you she would have sent an invitation."

Gemma wasn't sure she liked being called "she" in such a fashion. Couldn't her own father call her by her first name?

And were they ever going to ask about Nathan?

"The papers said it was a lovely wedding," her mother said. "Though Gemma," her tone turned disapproving now, "I really don't think you should have worn white."

The criticism stung, but Gemma tried to move past the hurt, for Nathan's sake. "That's a bit old-fashioned, isn't it, Mom?" she teased, trying to lighten the mood.

"And I raised you to be an old-fashioned girl," her mother said, then gave a heavy sigh. "Still, at least you're married now."

Disillusionment ripped through Gemma. She was beginning to see that nothing had changed. It had been hard growing up under constant disapproval. It was the reason she had moved out once she'd found herself a decent job. Her parents hadn't tried to dissuade her, and she'd had the feeling they'd been relieved to get her out of the house. It had been the same when she'd told them she was pregnant. She was too much of a problem for them. They couldn't cope, so they'd been happy to get her out of their lives.

Tate had been standing by the large windows, but now he moved in closer, his eyes narrowing. "So the only reason you came to see Gemma now is because she's married?"

Her mother's face showed that she clearly didn't like Tate's tone. "That and because we wanted to see our grandson."

"Whom you haven't asked about," he pointed out.

"Give us time," her father tried to joke.

Tate came to stand by the sofa, intimidating as he looked down at the older pair. "I'd imagine that would be one of the first things *I'd* ask about."

"Of course you would," Frank said, his tone placating. "He's your son. We're only his grandparents."

Tate's eyebrows shot up. "Only? That about says it all, doesn't it?"

"I didn't mean it like that."

"And that's the real shame of it," Tate said, and a split second later he indicated the door with a brief dip of his head. "I'll see you both out now."

There was a stunned silence.

For a few seconds no one moved.

In spite of everything, Gemma was dismayed by what was happening. She'd didn't want it to end like this. It had hurt so much the last time they'd walked away from her.

"Are you going to let him talk to us this way?" Meryl Watkins demanded of her daughter.

Put on the spot, Gemma's mind stumbled. She'd tried

over and over to stand up to her mother, but she had always felt intimidated. In the end, it had been better to leave home. "Er...Tate has a point," she said, not daring to look directly at him, knowing what he would be thinking. But he had to understand there was something so...final about all this.

The older woman got to her feet. "The only point your husband has made is that he's kicking us out of his house."

"*Our* house," Tate corrected. "Mine and Gemma's house. And our son's."

"Come on, Frank. It's clear we're not wanted here."

Tate's mouth turned sour. "Good God, I don't believe you two. You haven't seen your daughter for more than a year, yet you both came in here without giving her a hug or a kiss. And you didn't even mention your grandson. So I have to ask myself why you're here at all." He scanned the pair, then a steely look entered his eyes. "I suspect you've been shamed into this by your friends. Is that what this is all about?"

As if he'd touched a nerve, her mother reddened. "How dare you!"

"I dare."

Suddenly Gemma knew that's exactly what this visit was about. Their daughter had married into a prominent family, and they were frightened they wouldn't look good in front of their friends. After all, if Gemma could catch a man like Tate Chandler, then perhaps she wasn't so terrible...

"You'll regret this, *Mr. Chandler,*" Meryl said now. "Your family's good name will be mud by the time we finish telling everyone how you stopped us from seeing our daughter and our grandson."

At the threat, Gemma finally found her mental footing.

For the first time in her life, she understood that she had done nothing to deserve the treatment her parents had dished out to her. Just like Nathan had done nothing wrong. Nor Tate. This battleground was all her parents' doing.

"Mom, while you're at it, don't forget to tell them how you and Dad turned your back on your unmarried, pregnant daughter, leaving me alone to fend for myself and my child."

Her mother pursed her lips. "You knew the rules."

"Rules?" Gemma scoffed. "Oh, yes, it's rules that matter to you, not me or your grandson."

Her father was shaking his head as he got to his feet. "Gemma, please, your mother doesn't mean—"

"Be quiet, Frank. I do mean it. Gemma has been nothing but a disappointment to us."

Gemma froze, vaguely aware of Tate's low curse. Just when she thought they couldn't do anything more to hurt her... She'd known she was a disappointment to them, but hearing it out loud like this...

As painful as it was, she wouldn't let them know just how much they'd hurt her. Her chin lifted. "At least I finally know what you think of me. Please leave. I never want to see either of you again."

Her mother's face didn't relent. She spun around and made for the front door, where Tate now stood sentry. Her father looked at her with a glimpse of compassion before he scurried after his wife.

Bitterness rose in Gemma's throat and bubbled over. "And by the way, Nathan is doing very nicely without either of you. So am I."

They left then, and Gemma collapsed on the sofa. She heard Tate close the front door, then heard car doors slam and her parents drive away. By the time Tate came back into the drawing room, she could feel a reaction setting in. This was it. She'd never see them again. The ties were finally cut.

She should feel relief.

She could only feel despair.

"I shouldn't have done that, Tate," she mumbled, hugging her arms around herself, trying to hold the pain in so that she wouldn't fall apart.

Sympathy shone from his eyes. "Don't do this to yourself, Gemma. They've treated you very badly."

She didn't want his sympathy. "Like *you've* treated me badly?"

His head went back.

"They're *my* parents, Tate," she said, getting to her feet, anger bubbling up inside her. She wanted to strike out, at anyone. He would do. "I should have told them to go in the first place."

He remained calm. "So why didn't you?"

She had to stay angry. Anger would get her through this. "I was thinking of Nathan. They're his grandparents."

"Pity they didn't act like it." He tilted his head at her. "Do you really want people like them in your son's life?"

"No, but it should have been *my* decision to ask them to go, not yours."

"I didn't think you would do it."

She lifted her chin. "You were wrong."

A heartbeat passed.

"I was proud of you, Gemma." His voice had softened.

Something wobbled inside her. "Don't say that."

"Why not?"

Tears weren't far away, but she held them back. "I'll cry. And I don't want to cry."

"I'd say you're more than entitled."

All at once she longed to have someone put their arms

around her and tell her everything would be okay. She'd never had anyone to reassure her in such a way.

And now her parents never would.

Through a haze of emotion she saw Tate. He was the only person who had ever made her feel safe. She needed to recapture that feeling. "Tate, make love to me."

Time seemed to decelerate.

"What?"

"Make love to me. Please. I need you."

He stiffened. "Gemma—"

The next second, she knew he would refuse. Her heart squeezed as she put on a brave face. "That's okay, I understand." She stepped past him, intending to rush to her room and lick her wounds. "My parents didn't want me, so I can't blame you for—"

He put his hand on her arm, stopping her. "Don't put me in the same category as them." He tugged her gently toward him. "Do I want you?" His eyes darkened. "Oh, yeah, I want you, Gemma."

The last thing she saw was Tate's head lowering, blocking out the sunlight streaming through the windows. Or was it dark because her eyelids had come down? She didn't know. She didn't care. The feel of his arms around her, the touch of his lips on hers, the raw emotion she'd heard in his voice—all of it cut away their surroundings. A breath caught in her throat.

The taste of him flooded her and she shuddered in pleasure. Her hands slid up and locked behind his neck, clinging to him as she gave him kiss for kiss. She couldn't believe she was finally in Tate's arms, and there was no denying that he wanted her. She could feel his arousal growing, hardening against her stomach.

His lips made their way along her jawline, and she let her head fall back to give him better access. He dallied briefly at her earlobe before his kisses moved to the sensitive skin of her neck. Eyes remaining shut, she felt him place his lips against the base of her throat and hold there for a few seconds. She held still, too.

Then his hand slid under her hair and eased her zipper down. The dress came off her shoulders with a gentle draft of air as he pushed the material down and let it descend to the carpet, leaving her in bra and panties.

Only then did she open her eyes. His gaze traveled over her body like a whisper. "You're even more beautiful now than before."

Her heart bounced. "I am?"

"You've had my baby," he said simply, but there was nothing simple about the way he brushed his fingers between her breasts to her trim stomach, making her quiver in reaction.

Then his fingers slipped inside one cup of her bra and lifted out her breast, holding it up for his pleasure. He captured her nipple with his mouth. She took quick breaths, hearing the sound reverberate inside her throat, growing tenfold as his tongue played with the tightening bud.

He caressed her other breast with his hands then his mouth, and soon her bra disappeared. Everything intensified. Her panties were gone. He pressed her down on the sofa and stretched her out on it. He slipped a cushion under her head, clearly concerned for her comfort, making her feel special even as the pressure built between them.

He moved back and stood looking down at her. "God, I want to take my time with you," he rasped, his blue eyes deepening with color.

Somewhere in the back of her mind she knew they had a luncheon to attend and a child to get ready, but it had been almost two long years since he'd been a part of her. And she couldn't bear it if Nathan were to wake up right now and put a stop to this. Would they ever get back to this moment? Their emotions were high, but nothing between them had been resolved...

"Next time," she whispered, beckoning him to join her, vaguely thankful they were the only adults in the house.

He proceeded to strip off his clothes. Her eyes followed every sinew revealed, every hair on his chest, the darker patch surrounding his full erection. He lowered himself down on her, but not in her. Not yet. They both knew the feel of him against her naked skin was just too much pleasure to sacrifice for the sake of time.

But soon it wasn't enough. He kissed her deeply, adjusting himself more fully, probing now at the top of her thighs. The air grew thick as she opened her legs. She wanted him to be a part of her. She'd missed him so much.

And then he stopped.

"Gemma?"

She looked into his eyes and saw something that would have made her knees buckle, if she'd been standing.

"You are *not* a disappointment to anyone."

Her heart rolled over, the breath locked in her throat. For him to take this moment to say that when he was more than ready to *take* her...

"Thank you," she whispered, grateful that no matter what had passed between them he had given her this.

"And you've *never* been a substitute for anyone else," she said, risking everything in the spirit of the moment, wanting him to remember how it had once been for them. It was important that he knew the truth.

His eyes flared, but she didn't give him time to speak.

She held on to his shoulders and tilted her lower body up to his. "I want *you,* Tate."

He groaned. It was a sound of need, but she wasn't sure if he would push into her or pull away. Did he need to get away from her? Or did he need her?

As if he couldn't stop himself, the next second he thrust between her thighs. Her heart soared and she rose to meet him. He groaned again and she knew she was what he needed, at least right now. He thrust deeper and she clung to him as he took her higher.

"Only you," she whispered, then she shattered around him, feeling him climax inside her.

Tate kissed Gemma hard and quick, then moved away to gather her clothes and hand them to her. He began pulling on his own clothes, needing to keep himself busy and not look at her naked body lying there all delicious and warm from his touch. He could take her again right now.

Easily.

He waited until he was dressed before looking down at her again. "Are you okay?"

She had sat up to dress, and now she gave a small smile. "Sure."

He searched her eyes, but she wasn't giving anything away, and he wasn't about to either. "We'll leave for lunch in an hour," he said, and left the room. He had to walk away before he was tempted to carry her upstairs and tumble her on his bed.

He was growing hard just thinking about it. Her sexual power over him was immense. Hell, he hadn't even given a thought to contraception. They'd deal with that later. There were already too many complications between him and Gemma.

If he were to be truthful, their lovemaking had been

about more than the sexual pull she had over him. A combination of things had been building since their marriage. First Rolly, though Tate had to admit he'd been in the wrong about the teenager. Then the pictures on the internet showing Gemma's threadbare apartment and hinting she was a gold digger. Yesterday, the puppy and Gemma asking if they could have a dog, as if she'd accepted they were now a family.

But all that paled in comparison to her parents' visit. And what a piece of work they were! Learning what they had done to her, seeing how they'd treated her today, had caused a primitive anger to well up inside him. He'd gone hot with rage, then ice cold. Gemma had made him proud that she'd stood up to them.

And him.

And then she'd blown him away when she'd asked him to make love to her. He'd hesitated only because she'd caught him by surprise. God help him, it hadn't been because he hadn't wanted her. But she'd thought he was rejecting her, like her parents had rejected her. An odd pain had ripped through him then—he'd wanted to comfort her.

You've never been a substitute.

If he hadn't known better, he'd have thought she was telling the truth. There was no other man between them. Even now, she made him feel as if he was the only man who could do it for her, the only man to turn her on. Dammit, she'd even said so.

I want you, Tate.

Only you.

But was she just good at pretending? What was he to believe? *Who* was he to believe? The sexy woman who'd been in his arms back there, or the woman who knew how to wind him up like a watch? He had to find the truth, and the only way to do that was to open himself up a little and let her in. She'd either prove her worth…or reveal she was merely a fake.

Seven

When they arrived at his parents' place, Gemma was dismayed to find Tate's whole family there for the lunch. She'd expected his parents, perhaps his sister, but definitely not his grandmother. Helen still lived in her own home, so it made sense that Jonathan would invite his mother. Why Gemma hadn't expected her to be there today, she didn't know.

Of course, now she felt even more self-conscious about what had happened with Tate, as if the all-wise, elderly woman could actually see they had become lovers again. Considering they were married now, it would be a reasonable assumption to make anyway, but it made Gemma more than uncomfortable. What had happened between her and Tate was private.

"So what's happening about those pictures?" Tate's sister asked, before anyone had a chance to say more than a few words of greeting.

Tate's mouth tightened as he let his mother take Nathan from him. "I'm working on it."

"You realize what's out there in cyberspace stays out there forever, don't you?"

"Stop exaggerating, Bree," her father said from the bar in the corner, where he was pouring drinks.

Bree spun toward him. "I'm not exaggerating, Dad. Ask anyone."

"Give it a rest, sis," Tate growled, echoing Gemma's thoughts, and probably everyone else's, too. It seemed as if his sister was deliberately stirring up trouble.

Could Bree have been the one to take the pictures and put them on the internet?

"My, look at this little one," Darlene said in a calming voice as she sat down with her grandson on her lap. "He's such a little man now." It was clear she was trying to change the subject. "He looks like Gemma, but he reminds me of you at that age, Tate."

The words drew Tate's attention to his son, and his face relaxed. "Does he now?"

"Oh, yes. You were a beautiful little boy."

"Gee, thanks," Tate said. He gave her a crooked smile, but there was the usual hint of hardness as he looked at his mother. "Just what a grown man wants to hear."

Darlene's eyes flickered. "There's nothing wrong with a mother thinking her son is beautiful, no matter what his age." She sent her daughter-in-law an encouraging smile. "Isn't that right, Gemma?"

No matter what was going on between mother and son, at least Darlene wasn't holding anything against her. Gemma was grateful for the other woman's support. "I couldn't agree more, Darlene. Our sons will always be beautiful to us."

"Yeah, but thinking it and saying it out loud are two

different things," Tate drawled, giving Gemma a hooded look that made her acutely aware of everything that had happened between them back in their drawing room. His male possession had been totally consuming and irreversibly branding. At one time, she would have reveled in it. Right now all she wanted to do was get those perceptive eyes off her. Would he think she was putty in his hands now, not just physically but in every other way? No, that wouldn't happen. She wouldn't let it.

"Er…what was Tate like as a child?" she asked, dragging her gaze back to her mother-in-law.

Darlene beamed. "Oh, he was—"

"Best to ask Jonathan that question," Tate's grandmother interrupted her, speaking for the first time and not in a friendly tone. "I'd say he knows his son better than anyone."

The animation left Darlene's face and suddenly there was awkwardness in the air. It was as if Helen had been trying to make a point at her daughter-in-law's expense.

Then Jonathan came toward them carrying drinks. "No, I'll let Darlene answer that one, Mother." He smiled lovingly at his wife. "Go on, sweetheart."

Darlene looked at her husband, then nodded gratefully and put on a smile. "Now what was I saying? Oh, yes. Tate was a beautiful child with a sweet nature." She glanced at Bree. "So was my darling daughter," she added, and her eyes filled with motherly bemusement. "Of course, right from the start they both had their moments."

"We wouldn't be Chandlers if we didn't," Bree quipped, and everyone smiled.

Gemma looked at Tate, whose expression had closed up and who now had his hands thrust in his trouser pockets. She realized the awkwardness wasn't only between Helen and Darlene. The tension was between mother and son, a tension that Tate didn't have with his grandmother. The warm feeling between grandmother and grandson was obviously reciprocated. At the wedding, Helen had shown more than a soft spot for Tate. Hadn't the elderly woman hinted at being worried Gemma would hurt him? Helen couldn't be such an unfeeling person then.

So why pick on poor Darlene?

Gemma asked herself that question a couple more times during the delicious lunch as everything returned to normal and the only person Helen appeared to be slightly reserved with now was *her*.

Back to square one.

Or was it? All afternoon Tate watched her, stepping in and changing the subject, or getting her away from his grandmother whenever the woman focused on her in the smallest way. It was as if he was protecting her, now that he knew all she had suffered at the hands of her parents. Offering an olive branch? Okay, so it was more like a twig, but it didn't mean any less.

But on the way home it wasn't the tension between Tate and his family that worried her. It was the heightening awareness between the two of *them*—the feeling that after this morning, an arm's length wasn't enough.

Did she really want it to be?

"About my parents," she said, trying to get back to normalcy. "Thank you for sticking up for me. I really do appreciate it."

Tate gave her a pleased sideways glance. "You're welcome." Then, in an instant, there was something more in his look, as if he was remembering making love to her.

She dragged in a breath and searched for something else to say. "Doesn't your grandmother like your mother?"

Oh, dear.

His hands tightened on the wheel, but he kept his eyes on the road. "Why do you say that?"

She'd been trying to dispel the sexual tension inside the car. Instead, she'd replaced it with another type of tension.

She wrinkled her nose. "Just something in the air when they're in the same room."

"I hadn't noticed."

Her gut feeling said that wasn't the truth. Something was going on here. Yet was it really any of her concern? In spite of being grateful that he'd supported her today, she hadn't wanted him messing in her affairs before now. He wouldn't like her messing with his. She let it be.

It was a relief to arrive home and get out of the car. Inside the house, all was quiet.

Not for long, though, not with a one-year-old in the house. Nathan had been thoroughly spoiled all afternoon by the Chandlers, so it took a great deal of patience to get him through dinner, a bath and in his crib.

"Is he asleep?" Tate asked quietly behind her, making her jump as she backed out of Nathan's room.

She spun around. Tate was right there in front of her. Up close. "Almost."

"I thought I'd order pizza for dinner."

"P-pizza?"

"You used to love pizza."

"I still do." Her stomach fluttered. They had once shared a pizza and then made love. Of course, Tate had grown up wealthy, so delivered pizza had been a novelty for him. As *she* had no doubt been a novelty for him…

"I'll leave a note for Peggy that we don't want to be disturbed."

"Won't she—" She paused.

Amusement lit up his eyes. "What?"

She could feel herself blushing. "You know."

"Think I'm having my 'wicked way' with you?" His gaze roamed her face. "That's exactly what I intend to do. Again and again." Giving her the full force of his charisma, he lowered his head, his lips seeking hers...just as Nathan started to cry. Tate hovered above her mouth. "We could let him keep crying," he murmured.

She hardly dared move. "We could."

The crying got louder.

He inhaled deeply, straightened and gave a wry smile. "You'd better go see to our son." Before she could move away, he put his hand under her chin and kissed her quick. "Then later, lady, I intend to see to *you*. And I intend to take my time doing so."

Gemma had already pictured herself locked against his naked body, but his words reminded her of something she had to say. Nathan could wait a few moments more. His was a tired cry, not a hurting one.

She nervously wet her lips. "I know we didn't use... er...protection this morning, but I am on the pill now. I started taking it a few weeks ago when you said we were getting married. I just thought I'd say so. In case you were worried."

"I'm not." He raised an eyebrow but was watchful. "Are you?"

"No." Having his baby again and sharing in the wonder of it, knowing Tate would be pleased to be a part of it this time, would be wonderful. If only...no, she wouldn't wish for more. She didn't need more to give their children a happy life, she told herself.

He frowned. "There's a problem?"

She couldn't tell him her thoughts. "The doctor did say it may not be fully effective for another few weeks."

His face relaxed. "Then we'll take extra precautions in

future." He ran a finger along her chin. "And from now on we're sharing a bed."

"Are you sure?"

"There's no going back now."

She silently agreed. It would be too cruel to return to a platonic marriage. "No, there isn't."

His mistrust of her hadn't been resolved, but she had hopes they could move past it now that there was a renewed connection between them. Their married life had truly begun. And that was a scary but exhilarating thought.

By the time the pizzas arrived, Gemma had showered and changed into slacks and a knit top, and Nathan was asleep in his crib.

She and Tate ate opposite each other at the breakfast bar in the kitchen. There was no playfulness between them, but there was a definite heat that had been building all evening. This time was too serious, too important, to be messing around about it all. She didn't offer to hand-feed Tate any of her slice, and he didn't offer to lick her fingers clean, but oh, my, she could see he was thinking it, and remembering.

She had just finished washing down her second slice with a soda when she heard a rumble in Tate's chest. "Enough," he said in a strangled tone, dropping his pizza back in the box and surging to his feet. He came around the breakfast bar and pulled her to her feet. "Come on. We're going to bed."

Anticipation thumped inside her. "But I haven't finished," she said inanely.

"Neither have I." He didn't smile. He didn't stop. He led her out of the room and kept right on going until they were upstairs in his bedroom, where he quietly closed the door behind them and flicked on the light.

A hush fell.

His eyes took on an intensity that surprised her. "Now...what was that about taking our time..." He moved slowly closer, standing right in front of her, cupping her shoulders.

Time slowed.

Bending his head forward, he covered her mouth with his and kissed her gently. She'd expected a hungry kiss, but it was none the less potent for its gentleness. She closed her eyes and let herself feel him, feel the moment between them.

After a while he drew back. She missed his lips already and made a sound, but she forgave him when he brought her fingers to his lips. One by one, he kissed her fingertips, then the inside of her palm, next the tender skin of her wrist. He moved up her arm, to the curve of her shoulder.

"I remember that," he murmured, slipping his hand around her nape, looking into her eyes.

Her breath quivered. "What?"

"The little hitching sound you make in your throat when I touch you."

"I can't help it."

"I know." He dipped his lips to her throat, stealing her breath away.

Soon he leaned back and unhurriedly peeled off her clothes—her knit top, her bra...then her slacks and panties—exposing her until she was fully naked.

"Oh, yeah, I remember it all," he said huskily.

Sensations raced along her nerves, making her ache with wanting him. He stroked her breast then bowed his head to it. He circled her nipple with his tongue, then caught it between his lips and sucked.

She heard the hitch in her throat then.

And heard it again when he moved to her other breast.

His fingers started down her belly, heading for the apex of curls, and the hitch turned to a longing moan. She wanted him to touch her there. Oh, how she wanted him to touch her and touch her and keep right on touching her.

And then she wanted to touch *him*.

She put her hand against his chest and when she pushed him away she saw his surprise. "Let me." She brushed her lips over his as she pressed her palms against him, steadying herself and soaking up the feel of muscle beneath his shirt.

She undid his buttons slowly, starting at the lowest.

"You used to be much faster than this," he muttered in bemusement. "Not that I'm complaining."

"I was always in a hurry before." She'd been in love with him and she'd instinctively tried to grab all she could before it disappeared like the wind, which it had. Tonight she would take it slower and make memories. She would keep their future alive as long as possible.

Finally she undid the last button and slid his shirt off, loving the way his heartbeat thumped in his chest. She placed her lips to that beating heart and he groaned.

"You are a beautiful, beautiful man," she whispered. She moved her lips over his skin, swirling her tongue through the wisps of hair, the heat rising off him like a sultry day.

Her tongue prowled down toward his trousers.

All at once she was lifted, thrown over his shoulder. He carried her to the large bed, where he let her down on the duvet. She flopped back against it, her legs dangling over the edge, her naked body his to view.

She rose on her elbows, slightly embarrassed by the way she was positioned, slightly confused by the speed with which he'd changed everything. "I thought you said slow?"

"I didn't say torture," he muttered. He went down on his knees, parting her legs to lick through the dark vault already pre-moistened by her desire for him. She bucked at the touch of him. He began stroking his tongue up and down and soon put his hands on her hips to hold her still, allowing her to rise and fall but not escape. Not that she wanted to.

He tormented her with his mouth, and everything inside her grew to a fever pitch. She held his head to her, one minute gripping tight, then tunneling her fingers through his hair. He was touching the heart of her, and she couldn't hold back for much longer. He was rapidly bringing her to the edge of release, his tongue delightful and incredibly effective.

Then he buried his tongue deeper and she didn't have the slightest chance of staying in control. She willingly jumped into the most glorious oblivion.

By the time she had the strength to open her eyes, he had taken off his clothes and was sliding on a condom. She'd missed her opportunity to repay the favor, but he moved her backward on the bed so he could join their bodies. She didn't mind. She took him inside her, surrounding him, and knew this was just right, just how it should be between a man and a woman.

Excitement raced through her veins, followed by another tumult of emotions. Like a far-off light coming closer, they got brighter and brighter. Then it hit her: saying "Only you" was as close as she could get to saying "I love you."

Oh, God, she still loved him.
She'd never stopped loving him.
He was imprinted in her heart for always.

She looked into eyes that were dark in concentration. It

was Tate who made this special for her. *He* was the reason she was edging toward heaven, storming the gates, pushing them open.

She wanted to tell him.

Oh, Lord, she wanted to tell him.

But from somewhere deep inside, she drew on an inner strength she didn't know she had, somehow managing to hold back the words of love she knew could destroy her if she uttered them.

Yet she needed to say something.

"Only you, Tate," she cried out breathlessly as she felt herself being swallowed up by something bigger than the both of them.

And she knew then that no matter what had gone before, no matter what had been, this time in this man's arms she had truly come of age.

After they made love again, in the shower, Gemma lay in Tate's arms listening to his breathing, which was relaxed by sleep. The knowledge that she still loved him filled her with joy, and fear. There was so much more at stake this time. They'd found a profound togetherness when he was a part of her, but she knew it didn't extend beyond those bonded moments. Not for him anyway.

She wanted so much to tell him of her love, but how could she open herself to more hurt? He didn't love her, and he wouldn't hesitate to hurt her again if he thought she'd done the wrong thing again. She only had to remember how he'd reacted to finding her kissing his best friend. He'd been so angry he'd kicked her out of his life. Could it happen again? Drake was still around, wasn't he? And even if he wasn't, Tate still didn't fully trust her. The littlest thing could bring her world toppling down one more time.

Last time he'd kicked her out, she'd gone because she'd had to. Then she'd picked herself up because she'd had to. But if it happened again and she lost her son and her home and the man she loved all at once, she didn't think she'd recover. No organization, no book, no counseling, no amount of self-help would repair her broken heart. Her love for him would never die. It was inside her. It was a part of her. It was love at its powerful best, and that meant it had the capacity to do the most damage.

No, she wasn't willing to tell him.

Thankfully, right then, his mouth sought hers, and her thoughts were soon silenced by the man she loved.

Eight

"Peggy, I'd like you to move Gemma's things into my room today," Tate said at breakfast the next morning, making Gemma's heart jump.

The housekeeper wasn't quick enough to hide her surprise, though Tate's note about not wanting to be disturbed last night must have given her a clue that this would happen. A moment later, Peggy smiled at them both with clear pleasure. "I'd be happy to, Mr. Chandler."

Somehow Gemma managed not to blush, even as she remembered Tate having his "wicked way" with her last night. Three times in fact—three times where she'd had to work hard at not giving herself away—reminding herself that her love for him was a secret. It was a matter of self-preservation.

"We'll do it together, Peggy," Gemma said, thinking she could make a game of it with Nathan while Tate was at the office.

Her heart was light as she and Peggy moved her things into the other suite. With two walk-in closets, there was no need to move any of Tate's stuff to make room for hers. Of course, she couldn't help but think that her clothes from before her marriage wouldn't have taken up a quarter of this space. And it would have only taken a minute to move them.

She kept an eye on Nathan in his playpen as she and Peggy moved back and forth with the expensive dresses, slacks and blouses, coats, swimsuits, everything for any occasion, including her underwear. She blushed at the memory of Tate stripping the scraps of material from her body with total precision.

"I'll just pop downstairs and get some more drawer liners," Peggy said a short while later. "This closet has never been used, and those are looking a bit faded."

Gemma was pleased that no other woman had shared this suite, this house, with Tate. "Take your time, Peggy," she said, flopping down on the bed and taking a breather.

The housekeeper left the room and was heading down the stairs when the telephone rang. Gemma was closest to the phone, so she called out that she'd get it.

She soon wished she hadn't.

"Hello, Gemma."

Drake!

She stood up. "Tate's at the office, as you must know."

"How would I know that? I thought he and you might still be on your honeymoon."

"You could have called him on his cell phone to find out."

"Then I'd miss talking to you, wouldn't I?"

"Drake, stop it."

He sighed as if she were being unreasonable. "Gemma,

you're my best friend's wife now. I'm merely attempting to make amends."

She'd never believe that.

"Anyway," he continued, "I was phoning to commiserate with Tate about those nasty pictures of your old apartment going around the internet. I thought he might be upset about them."

Her heart lurched inside her chest. "How do you know about them?"

"I was talking to Bree earlier."

More and more, Gemma believed Bree was the one behind all this. "She had no right telling you anything."

"I'm Tate's best friend. She thought I might be able to help in some way."

Or cause trouble.

"You know, Gemma, it's never wise to be complacent about these things."

It was a warning that she shouldn't be complacent about her marriage. Suddenly it hit her. Bree wasn't behind those pictures at all.

It was Drake.

"I could say the same to you," she said, trying to keep her voice from shaking. He wanted to hear how he was getting to her.

"Gem, I don't know what you mean. I'm merely trying to be a friend to you both."

God, she hated him calling her "Gem," hated the smugness in his voice. "You were never a friend of mine, Drake. Or of Tate's, if he only but knew it. One day he'll see you for what you are."

"There's nothing to see."

Gemma opened her mouth to spout something scathing, but she heard a noise in the doorway and her head snapped up to see Peggy standing there. "Er...I have to go now.

Please call Tate on his cell phone if you need to talk to him." She hung up and fought to keep her face blank.

A moment crept by.

Peggy frowned. "Mrs. Chandler, I hope you don't think I'm being forward, but if you need to talk—"

Gemma tried to look casual. "Thank you, Peggy, but I'm fine." She was tempted to ask what the other woman had heard, but she was sure Tate wouldn't appreciate her discussing their marriage with anyone, much less their employee. Besides, she didn't want Peggy thinking she had heard anything of importance.

"I thought you might need a friend."

"Thank you." Gemma gave a half-hearted smile. "I can always do with more friends."

Peggy didn't look convinced, but she was professional enough to leave things be. Gemma took advantage of that and remained close-lipped about it all, acting as if nothing out of the ordinary had happened.

Still, she was relieved once they'd finished moving and Peggy had gone back downstairs. With Nathan taking a small nap, she had some time to think about things away from prying eyes. She couldn't contemplate the phone call before now, in case Peggy read her face and related her worries to Tate. As it was, Gemma hoped Peggy would keep her own counsel.

Damn Drake for this. He knew he had her running scared and that she wouldn't say anything to Tate. If only Tate had heard the conversation, then he'd believe her. Perhaps she could record Drake's call next time, she thought with a flash of hope.

On second thought, there wasn't any guarantee that Tate or anyone else would hear the same smugness that she'd heard. She wasn't imagining it, but Tate might not believe that.

God, this was like navigating around quicksand, in the dark, with Drake hot on her tail. She dare not even reach out a hand to Tate and ask him to help her. If she did, she might find the man she loved wasn't prepared to save her while sacrificing his best friend.

Not even for Nathan's sake.

Mid-afternoon, Gemma took Nathan to the kitchen for a snack and found Peggy at the island, chopping food. With thoughts of Drake filling her mind, and on edge about all he was capable of doing to her marriage, Gemma hesitated in the doorway. She was still afraid that the housekeeper might say something to Tate, however inadvertently.

Peggy looked up and blinked. "Oh, Gemma, you startled me. I was miles away."

Gemma put aside her worries. "Sorry." She stepped into the room with Nathan on her hip. "What are you making?"

"Apple pie for tonight's dessert."

"Homemade? Yum. I love apple pie. My mother used to make them," she said, not thinking. Her heart wrenched at the reminder of her parents and yesterday's events. She tried to ignore it. "Can I help?"

Peggy must have seen something on her face. The housekeeper wouldn't know about yesterday's visit, but she would certainly remember her parents hadn't been at the wedding. A touch of concern filled the older woman's eyes and she gave a kind smile. "Why not?" She held up a slice of apple. "Would Nathan like a piece?"

"Sure."

Gemma strapped Nathan in his high chair and gave him the apple, and soon she was busy slicing and rolling out the pastry. The fruit cooked on the stove, the sweet smell of apple and cinnamon wafting in the air. They had an enjoyable time and ended up making two thick, delicious-looking apple pies.

"We'll never eat all this," Gemma said ruefully as they surveyed their handiwork.

"You don't know my Clive. He'd eat a full one himself."

As Tate walked into the kitchen, the sound of Gemma's soft chuckle sent his pulse hammering. She stood with her hands on her slim hips, her blond hair slightly mussed, her gorgeous mouth curved in a smile. She was certainly a picture to come home to. In fact, the whole scene made him feel good about his life. A beautiful wife, a handsome son and a motherly housekeeper who had adopted them as if they were her own.

A sense of satisfaction filled him. This was his family. He'd been sitting at his desk and hadn't wanted to work. He'd wanted to see Gemma and Nathan. He'd actually missed them. It was a strangely powerful feeling that, surprisingly, gave him more pleasure than the corporate world he loved so much. He hadn't realized what had been missing from his life before this.

Gemma suddenly saw him, and panic flared in her eyes. "Tate! You're home early."

He scanned her face. Did she expect him to be the bearer of bad news? He supposed he couldn't blame her for jumping to conclusions. It always seemed to be bad news for her lately.

"I thought we might take Nathan for an ice cream and a walk to the park," he said, putting her mind at rest. He glanced at his son in his high chair. "But he looks pretty happy here with the measuring cups."

Her whole body visibly relaxed. "Oh, yes, that would be lovely."

"It's a glorious day outside," Peggy said encouragingly.

Just then, Nathan let out a wail. There was a small red mark on his forehead where he'd obviously hit himself. Gemma swung their son up in her arms, cuddling him until the crying subsided.

"Is he okay?" Tate asked, an odd feeling in his chest as he watched her mothering his child.

"Yes, he's fine." She rechecked the fading mark on Nathan's forehead, then smiled at the adults. "But I'm sure an ice cream will make it much better."

Peggy laughed. "I'm sure it will."

Tate remembered how he'd been looking forward to taking them to the park. "I'll just go change out of this suit." He glanced at Gemma. "When can you be ready?"

Gemma looked at Peggy. "Do you need any more help?"

The housekeeper shooed her on. "No, we're finished here. I'll clean up."

"Thanks, Peggy. I had fun."

"Me, too, Gemma." Peggy darted a guilty look at Tate, before spinning away toward the sink. He was tempted to invite her to call him by his name again but it would be a waste of breath. Neither she nor Clive would budge on this.

"I'll come upstairs with you and change Nathan's diaper before we go," Gemma said.

Tate waited for her in the doorway. "Let me carry him. He's heavy." He lifted Nathan out of her arms and they left the kitchen. "I'm still amazed at your accomplishment," he said, as they headed for the stairs.

One finely shaped eyebrow rose. "What accomplishment?"

"Getting Peggy to call you Gemma." He grimaced

ruefully as they stopped at Nathan's room. "She still calls me Mr. Chandler."

Gemma flashed him a smile. "We women have our ways."

His eyes dropped to that mouth. "That you do."

Gemma's cheeks held a soft blush. Her reaction filled him with pleasure and stirred his blood.

"You've got flour on your ear." He reached out and ran the pad of his thumb over her earlobe, making her jump. "By the way, I'd ask you to join me in the shower but—"

Her blush deepened. "Don't say that in front of Nathan."

He was amused. "He doesn't understand what I'm saying."

"I know, but—"

He took pity on her and cut her off with a quick kiss. "Go change him."

They would have tonight.

The walk to the park was companionable and leisurely. They enjoyed sitting on the bench and eating their ice creams. There was no sight of the children and the puppy from the other week, but the playground was busy with kids ridding themselves of energy built up in the classroom.

Tate realized Gemma was staring off into space, chewing her lip. "You seem distracted."

She blinked. "Do I? Sorry, I was just thinking about something." She turned away to drop Nathan's now-empty ice cream cup in the bin nearest her.

Tate didn't know why, but Drake slashed through his mind. The thought turned his blood cold, making him glad of his dark sunglasses.

Yet for once he pushed thoughts of Drake aside, not wanting to jump to conclusions. He didn't want the other man spoiling this moment between him and his family.

She attempted a smile. "It's good to get out like this, don't you think?"

"Yes."

She picked up after that, but during the evening, as they ate dinner, then watched a movie together before making love, he couldn't shake the feeling that something still wasn't right. She was pretending it was, but it wasn't.

It could be about her parents, he told himself as he lay in bed in the dark with Gemma asleep in his arms. It was only yesterday they'd been here causing havoc and heartache for their daughter. God, they had a lot to answer for.

And then another thought hit him.

Perhaps *he* had a lot to answer for, too.

As quickly as it had come, he dismissed that thought, not liking the guilt that rose inside him. He'd had a right to be angry about Drake, and a right to be angry about Gemma not telling him about Nathan. Just because he felt sorry for her now didn't mean *he* was at fault.

Even though it felt like he was.

Nine

So many times over the following week, Gemma wished she could tell Tate she believed Drake had posted the pictures of her apartment. But despite her husband making love to her every day, despite him coming home early on a regular basis, she was very much aware of how fragile their marriage was.

Then, at the end of that week, Tate finally volunteered the information that every trail seemed to lead to a dead end, though the investigator hadn't given up. She could have pointed him in the right direction, of course, but at what cost? At least Drake had not called back.

Thankfully, her marriage had slipped out of the media's radar for the moment, and with the awards dinner only a few days away, she began to relax. Time would dull the pain of Tate thinking she'd kissed Drake, and the pain of Tate not believing her denial. She wished she could talk to him about Drake as easily as she'd talked to him about her parents. How she wished he would be equally as understanding. Unfortunately, she knew that wouldn't happen.

And then…life rolled onto the next crisis.

One evening after Nathan was in bed, Tate flicked through the television channels. Out of the blue, an older couple appeared on the screen.

"What the hell!" Tate exclaimed, sitting forward.

Gemma's heart rose in her chest. "Th-that's my parents!"

He darted a look at Gemma. "I'll turn it off. You don't need to hear this." He went to press the remote button.

"No!" She swallowed. "Leave it on."

He paused. "Are you sure?"

She nodded, her eyes already returning to her parents' interview on one of those current affairs programs. To say she felt betrayed was an understatement. She felt like she'd been speared right through the heart.

It only got worse. They talked about being unable to control her as a teenager, about how she'd left home too young, breaking their hearts. How they'd let her come back home, single and pregnant, but she'd walked out again.

"That's not true," she whispered in disbelief, trying to accept that they could hurt her even more than they already had. "They've twisted it all around." She'd left home at twenty because of them. And they'd *asked* her to leave when they learned she was pregnant.

"It's a sob story, that's all," Tate growled.

And everyone would believe it.

Then they said how they hadn't been invited to their own daughter's wedding, and when they'd come to see Gemma and their grandson, they'd been asked to leave.

"But they didn't even ask to see Nathan," she cried.

Tate's eyes were hard. "I was there, Gemma. I saw what they were like."

"I never thought they'd do something like this. I know they had to save face, but this—"

"You're being too generous, as usual."

Her mind swirled with confusion. "Why now? It's been nearly two weeks since we saw them."

"My guess is it's about the awards dinner on Friday. They're probably trying to put a stop to my family getting the award because they're jealous that you and Nathan are Chandlers now."

"But they didn't want me…or Nathan," she choked, jumping to her feet, trying to shake off the anguish.

Tate stood up and pulled her into his arms. "I know, sweetheart."

She buried her face against his chest, the endearment warming her before another thought kicked in. She jerked her head back to look up at him. "Your family won't be happy about this, Tate."

He didn't hesitate. "They won't hold this against you." His jaw clenched as he looked past her to the television. "Your family will be retracting this, I promise."

"But it'll be too late for the award. They've already done a lot of damage."

"No, they're wrong. It's related to the award but it won't affect it at all. If the board was going to withdraw the honor, they would have done it before now."

She supposed that was true. Part of the reason they'd married in a hurry was to protect the family name.

He put one hand under her chin. "You'd better stay home tomorrow. And don't answer the telephone. I'll beef up security."

She hadn't planned on anything but a lovely, relaxing

day with her son, but now… "They're not nice people, are they?" she said on a ragged breath.

Tate gave her a soft kiss. "No, they're not. And you're not like them at all," he said, meaning it.

Gemma didn't sleep well, and she knew Tate hadn't either. He offered to stay home with her the next morning, but she thanked him and told him no. She was in danger of throwing herself a "pity party," and she needed to do it alone.

Of course, once their son was up and about, Nathan's smiling face put things into perspective. How could she mope about when she could be with her child? Every moment with him was precious.

As was every moment with Tate, she thought, as he kissed her goodbye on his way to the office. And a tender kiss it was, too. Loving him might be one-sided, but having this man in her life was more important than anything her family could do to her.

Her head was in a better place, but she was still startled when Peggy showed her mother-in-law into the sunroom just after lunch. Had Darlene been sent to find out more about Gemma's parents? Or was she here to take Gemma to task for bringing further disrepute on the Chandler name?

Gemma gestured for Darlene to sit on the sofa, then she sat, too. "It's nice to see you, Darlene," she said warily, once Peggy went off to get them refreshments.

"It's always lovely to see you, Gemma, but I thought you might need my support today."

Gemma's heart warmed. "That's very sweet of you."

Darlene looked around the bright and airy sunroom. "Where's my grandson? Asleep?"

"Yes, I'm trying to get him to nap after lunch instead of in the late morning."

As if by silent agreement, they spoke about general things until Peggy brought refreshments and left them to it.

"Tate dropped by the house this morning to explain about your parents," Darlene said, once they were alone again. Sympathy filled her expression. "I can't believe what they did to you, not just now, but in the past. It must have been devastating when they turned their backs on you."

Gemma swallowed. Her mother-in-law was a kind person, but Gemma hadn't expected actual compassion. "It was," she murmured with a catch in her throat. Then, in case Darlene couldn't say what she might need to say, Gemma took the bull by the horns. "I'm really sorry to bring your family into this."

"We're your family now, too, you know."

Gemma blinked. She wanted to cry in gratitude. "Thank you. That means a lot to me." She released a shuddering breath. "Being a part of a family again is wonderful, and being a part of your family is terrific." She wouldn't mention that she hadn't felt quite at home with the other Chandlers.

There was a short silence as Darlene nodded. "I know they're not perfect but…" Without warning, her mother-in-law burst into tears.

Gemma stared for a moment. "Darlene?"

Darlene tried to speak but cried even harder as she grabbed for a hankie from her handbag. Gemma could only watch with concern until the woman got herself partly under control.

"Forgive me, Gemma," Darlene sniffed. "I didn't come here to talk about my problems."

Her mother-in-law had problems? "If you want to talk,

I'm here to listen. And I promise I won't say anything to anyone. You can trust me."

The older woman looked at her. "Yes, I think I can. I haven't known you very long, but I feel close to you, Gemma." She paused. "I'm talking about your parents but…" She gave a small sob. "I've not been such a good parent myself. You see…" Sob. "I had an affair years ago."

Shock rolled through Gemma. "*You* had an affair?"

"Yes. And please don't think too badly of me," she said quickly.

"Of course not. I'm just really…surprised. You and Jonathan have such a great marriage."

Darlene nodded and wiped her wet cheeks. "We do now. We didn't then." She winced. "You see, Jonathan was never one to show his feelings. I hope I don't embarrass you by saying this. He's a passionate man in the bedroom, but not even after we were married did he once tell me he loved me." She took a shaky breath. "Oh, I knew he did, but it's not the same as hearing the words."

Gemma understood only too well.

Darlene's eyes started to fill with tears again, but she rapidly blinked them back. "We'd been married about fifteen years when I finally realized I would never hear those words from Jonathan. He was working hard and it seemed he needed me less and less. I was starting to feel not only like less of a woman but like less of a wife."

Gemma reached out and patted the other woman's hand. "That's understandable."

She took a breath. "And then one day I met this man. I was shopping in one of the department stores. I dropped my bag and he picked it up and we sort of clicked. He asked me to have a coffee with him. I knew I shouldn't, but I was feeling low. Jonathan hadn't made love to me for months. Just the night before I'd tried to make the first move in bed, and he'd said he was too tired."

"Was Jonathan having an affair?"

"Oh, no, that wasn't the problem. He was just so focused on work and making money. He had some pretty big shoes to fill. His father was such a force, you see." She gave a quiet sigh. "Anyway, this man and I started to meet for coffee. His marriage wasn't very good either. I was still desperate to get Jonathan's attention, but one thing led to another and I decided I was in love with the other man. I couldn't take my marriage anymore, so I packed my things and left."

Gemma's eyes widened. "You *left*?"

"Yes. I planned on going for good. I told myself the children didn't really need me and were probably better off without me in their lives. I knew Helen would step into the breach, you see. Of course, I was just making excuses for myself." There was a tiny pause. "I was back a week later."

"Only a week?"

She nodded. "Jonathan was shattered, and he begged me to come home. By that time, I realized I'd made a mistake. I regret what I did, but it's been the making of our marriage. It seemed to open up something inside him, and he's been a loving husband and father ever since."

"How old were Tate and Bree?"

Her face crumpled again. "Tate was twelve and Bree seven. Oh, God, I felt so terrible about that." She stopped and took a moment to control herself, then she managed to speak further. "Bree was too young, but Tate knew. He was colder to me when I came back, and he's been reserved with me ever since." Deep regret was etched in her face. "I couldn't bring myself to explain it to my son. Sometimes I wish I had."

Gemma's heart squeezed for the young teenage boy whose world had turned upside down. Suddenly, she realized this explained why Tate had reacted so strongly when he thought *she* was cheating with Drake. After all, they'd only been together a month when that accidental kiss between her and his best friend had happened. Another man would probably have brushed her off like a fly and never looked back. Tate had held a grudge because of the memories of his mother betraying his father. She certainly didn't think now that it was because *she* personally had hurt him. It wasn't possible to hurt someone if there was no true emotional involvement between them.

"Unfortunately," Darlene continued, bringing Gemma back to the discussion, "Helen and Nathaniel never forgave me."

And that explained the coolness Helen showed for her daughter-in-law, a coolness that had been extended to *her* because the matriarch thought Gemma had done wrong by her grandson.

And yet… "Maybe I should keep quiet about this, but shouldn't Helen and Nathaniel have taken some responsibility for putting such pressure on Jonathan in the first place?"

Darlene looked surprised, then gratified. "I've always thought so, too." She sighed. "It's too late now. Nothing's ever going to change with my mother-in-law. I hurt her son, and that's all that matters to her."

"It's a pity you never had it out with her," Gemma said, thinking out loud.

"Oh, I couldn't." She seemed to catch herself. "Could I?"

Gemma hadn't meant to get involved at all, but it wouldn't hurt to support Darlene. Her mother-in-law had supported her in everything so far. "You don't have anything to lose now by talking to Helen, do you? Your marriage to Jonathan is rock solid."

"Yes, it is. And it *is* time to clear the air. She's always been snippy with me in private, but lately…" A determined look crossed Darlene's face. She rose from the sofa. "Thank you, Gemma. I'm going to do it right now."

Gemma got to her feet, suddenly not sure she should have encouraged the other woman. Perhaps she should have let things lie.

Yet the comment about Helen no longer keeping her animosity private worried her. Was Helen becoming bolder because Gemma had joined the family? Did the elderly lady feel she could now openly attack the two women who were "outsiders?" How far would this go? Perhaps it *was* time someone stood up to Helen, before things got worse.

"I guess you need to do what you need to do, Darlene. If I can help in any way, please let me know."

Darlene kissed her cheek. "I will. Thank you." She smiled. "I'm really pleased you don't have to go through all this with Tate. He's so caring and concerned about you. Jonathan was never like that with me."

Gemma was glad the other woman turned to pick up her handbag from the sofa right then and didn't see her reaction. Caring and concerned? Gemma supposed that was true. But Tate didn't love her. It made her wonder if the same thing might happen to them that had happened to his parents. If Tate's care and concern lessened over the next fifteen years, would *she* be tempted to take a lover? She didn't think so. She couldn't imagine ever wanting to be in anyone's arms but his. He was the only man she wanted.

The only man she'd ever wanted.

* * *

Gemma waited until Nathan was in bed before speaking to Tate about Darlene. She'd spent all afternoon thinking about his mother's visit and had decided she couldn't bear having the same thing happen to her marriage that had happened to her in-laws. The only way to prevent such a thing was to bring his mother's affair out in the open. But she was acutely aware that she needed to tread warily.

When they were sitting on the terrace having an after-dinner drink, watching the sun lower on the horizon, she said, "Your mother came to see me today."

Tate's brow lifted. "Did she?"

"She wanted to make sure I was okay."

"Good." He looked pleased. "I know she was concerned about you."

"She's a very caring person, isn't she?"

His eyes turned inscrutable as he paused to take a sip of his drink. "Yes."

Short.

Abrupt.

She took a deep breath, then, "She told me about her affair all those years ago."

He bolted upright, almost spilling his drink. "Jesus!"

She forged onward. "I understand where you're coming from now, Tate."

There was a flicker of raw emotion in his eyes. "If you breathe a word of this, I swear—"

Her eyes widened. "How could you think I would say anything to anyone? I wouldn't repay your mother that way."

"Damn it all," he muttered, setting his glass down on the table.

"You've never forgiven her, have you?"

The rawness in his eyes was replaced by a glower.

"That's none of your bloody business." He pushed to his feet.

"It is when you're making *me* pay for her mistake."

He stared down at her. "Did you tell her about us?"

"Of course not!" She was glad she hadn't mentioned Darlene's coming confrontation with Helen. She wouldn't give him any more ammunition to use against her.

He raised an eyebrow, cooler now and in control again. "Why so affronted? You can't deny you and my mother have a lot in common."

Her chin lifted a notch at his tone. It hadn't taken him long to return to his arrogant self. "I was never unfaithful to you, Tate."

"That's only in the truest sense, since we weren't married at the time. You can still be unfaithful in a moral sense." His mouth tightened. "And you were."

"A kiss is not the same as having sex," she snapped, then she could have bit out her tongue. He thought she had admitted to wanting Drake.

"It was two-timing, Gemma. Make no mistake about that."

Her gaze sharpened as she got up from the chair. "You always were quick to believe the worst of me. Now I'm wondering if you'd decided my time was up. You wanted to be rid of me, and believing Drake's lie was the easiest way to go about it."

He flinched. "That's bloody ridiculous."

"Is it? I'm not so sure."

"I caught you kissing him, dammit."

"I thought I was kissing *you*," she said, not for the first time and probably not the last.

He made a dismissive gesture. "I'm not going over this again, Gemma. Just know this. If I ever catch you kissing

Drake—or any other man for that matter—I'll take Nathan from you so fast your head will spin."

Underneath she shook, but Darlene's revelation allowed her to see beyond this old argument. For the first time, she could see the hurt beneath his stance. A hurt he masked with pure anger.

And with her understanding came a new outlook on how to manage him. "Then I have nothing to worry about," she said quietly and confidently. "I don't intend to kiss any other man except you."

As if bowled over by the statement, he stared at her for a long moment as if searching for the truth. Then his face underwent a subtle change, and she knew he believed she meant it. He gave an almost imperceptible nod before twisting on his heels and heading back inside through the patio doors.

She heard him leave the house soon after, and only then did she let herself slump down on the chair and think about what had just passed between them. In one way, it hadn't gone well. In another, it was a complete eye-opener.

Tate Chandler needed as much reassurance in his life as the next person—even if he would never acknowledge it.

Tate returned home late that evening. He'd spent a few hours at the office trying to work but hadn't succeeded. He'd been unable to concentrate after Gemma challenged him and his beliefs.

Had he forgiven his mother? she'd asked.

Short answer, no.

So he was blaming Gemma for his mother's mistake?

Gemma had made a mistake on her own. He didn't need his mother as an excuse.

He was quick to believe the worst, she'd said.

He'd seen what he'd seen.

He'd wanted a reason to end their relationship.

Actually, he'd felt more for her back then than for any other woman he'd ever known. Why he would want to—

Stop.

Rephrase.

His feelings hadn't come into it at all. He'd *wanted* Gemma more than he'd wanted any other woman, that's all. The reason he'd ended their affair was because he'd caught her kissing Drake. She'd betrayed his trust. She was grasping at straws by bringing his mother into it.

So why the hell had he believed her when she'd said she didn't intend to kiss any man but him? It was incredible that he could accept her statement as truth.

And yet, he did.

One thing was apparent. Over the past few weeks he'd seen a side of Gemma that went beyond sex. He'd seen her as a loving mother, a hurt and betrayed daughter. She was kind to everyone whether they were employees or people at the park. She cared about a teenager's personal problems, even though she had enough problems of her own. She was charming and beautiful, and she found his antics with his son amusing. She was someone he wanted to *be* with, in and out of the bedroom. That was quite an admission. For the first time, he felt hope that maybe their marriage might have a chance.

He had a lot to think about, was even now still thinking about it, as he came out of the shower and slipped into bed beside his wife. He pulled her against him so she could pillow her cheek on his chest. She fit so right against him.

Then, out of the blue, she half twisted on top of him, sliding one leg across his thighs as she stretched up to kiss him. He took the kiss, reveling in the feel of her against his thighs, but he could tell she was trying to tell him something.

He broke away from her mouth. "Gemma?"

"I'm here, Tate." She leaned her palms on his chest, deepened the kiss and adjusted her body, making him growl in his throat. She slid her hand down to where he was hard for her. "And I'm not going anywhere…"

She kissed the length of his throat, down the center of his chest. By the time she'd finished with him, they were both satisfyingly exhausted.

And he knew what she'd been trying to say.

She was staying with him, and nothing would stop her.

Ten

By the time the awards dinner rolled around on Friday night, Gemma was pinching herself. Something had changed between her and Tate. Something subtle but good. It was almost as if he actually trusted her.

Of course, he was still convinced she'd wanted Drake two years ago, and that continued to hurt her, but at least he seemed prepared to put it behind them.

She was praying Drake didn't turn up tonight to spoil things. After a while there didn't appear to be any empty chairs at their table, or any of the other tables. Once the room was full, she finally let out a slow sigh of relief.

Able to relax now, she noticed that Darlene and Helen seemed to be getting on well together and were talking like old friends. Thank heavens that had worked out. She'd worried she might have caused more friction between them. If Tate had found out, it might have damaged the thin trust between them.

"Did you have something to do with this?" Tate murmured in her ear, making her realize he'd been watching his mother and grandmother with a slightly confused look.

Gemma lifted a slim shoulder and shrugged. "I merely listened." And really, that's all she'd done.

An odd gratitude flared in his eyes, and she wondered if he was starting to look at his mother in a more forgiving light. There was a ways to go, but still…

"Thank you, Gemma." He kissed her softly on the lips.

The kiss took her by surprise, and love for him filled her up and threatened to overflow. Dare she believe his affection was developing into something more?

When she looked again, the others were smiling at her. Darlene and Jonathan looked pleased by the kiss, and Helen looked thoroughly delighted. Only Bree seemed puzzled, as well she should. Things in the Chandler family had changed for the better, but Tate's sister hadn't been told anything yet.

Gemma herself had been surprised by the warmth Tate's grandmother had shown her on arrival tonight. At first, she'd thought it was for show, but as Helen had spoken to her as if she was actually welcome in this family, she knew the elder woman had changed her tune. Thankfully, the others appeared to be following her lead.

Just then, the awards presentation commenced and there were speeches about the good things the Chandler family had done over the years. Finally, Helen was asked to center stage, and Jonathan walked his mother through a standing ovation.

The older woman waited until everyone was seated before speaking. "It's a great honor for me to be standing here tonight, accepting this award. As you know, my dear husband, Nathaniel, passed away only a couple of months ago, but he would have been thrilled to know…"

Gemma listened with a light heart. The Chandler family really did deserve this award, and she was so glad that nothing had stopped them from receiving it. She would never have been able to forgive herself if the award had been taken from them because of her actions…or because of her family's actions.

"And Nathaniel was all about family," Helen was saying, bringing Gemma back to the speech. "It's something my son has continued, and now, I'm pleased to say, my grandson, as well. As many of you know, Tate recently married, and his new wife and son have brought great joy to this family."

Gemma's heart lifted in surprise. How lovely of Helen to…

"Gemma is proving herself to be a valued member of our family. She joins my daughter-in-law, Darlene, and my granddaughter, Bree, in being women determined to make life better for their loved ones. Gemma had no decent example to follow growing up, so it's a measure of her as a person that she's so giving and strong."

Gemma sat there stunned, only vaguely aware of Tate picking up her hand and squeezing it. Helen was supporting her in public? She was telling everyone that Gemma's parents were in the wrong? Telling everyone not to believe what was on the internet or the television? Gemma hadn't expected such wholehearted support.

"And then there's my great-grandson," Helen continued. "Nathan joins us as the littlest member of my family, but certainly not the smallest in value."

Gemma was still trying to take it all in.

"Nathaniel would have been so proud to receive this

award for his family. I can see him sitting up in heaven, smiling down at us tonight. God bless."

The sound of applause was almost deafening. Jonathan escorted Helen back to the table, but before she sat down she kissed Gemma on the cheek in a display of public affection. The cameras clicked like wild things. Tears pooled in Gemma's eyes. This meant so much to her. Helen wasn't just being nice for the sake of the media. She was just being sincere.

All at once, Gemma needed some time to herself. "Excuse me for a minute." She got to her feet and grabbed her purse.

Tate put his hand on her arm. "Are you okay?"

She blinked back the tears and gave him a small smile. "Yes." But in case he thought she wasn't, she added, "Yes, I really am fine...now."

He smiled in understanding, and with that smile in her heart she hurried off to find the ladies' room. She didn't stop to talk to anyone as she weaved her way through the maze of tables, her eyes still watery from emotion.

It was a relief to get outside the ballroom. She tottered after a couple of women ahead of her down one of the corridors, figuring they were probably going to powder their noses. She couldn't help but marvel how things had turned around. It was a miracle come true. Tate's family had forgiven her. Now all she needed was for Tate to do the same.

Someone stepped in front of her and put his hands on her arms, forcing her to stop. "Hello, Gemma."

For a moment, Gemma didn't recognize the man in the dark dinner suit. Then her mind screeched to a stop. "Drake!"

"You sound surprised to see me."

She flinched and tried to draw back, but his hands

tightened on her upper arms. "Let me go," she said anxiously. She wanted to sound firm, but her emotions were high and the words came out like a plea.

Satisfaction entered his eyes. "Is that any way to treat an old friend?"

A flashback rolled over her. Dear God, if Tate saw them like this… "Drake, look—"

"I'm looking, sweetheart."

She found the strength to lift her hands to his chest, intending to push him away. "Please leave me alo—"

"Gemma?"

Oh, God.

The sound came from behind her and she twisted around to see Tate standing a few feet from them. The look in his eyes said it all. She could see his trust in her shriveling up, like a flash fire of betrayal had swept over him. He was disbelieving, angry, hurt… It was written on his face.

Gemma couldn't take any more. She'd lost Tate. Lost the man she loved. Again. All that was between them was no more.

And this time she would lose her son, too.

She felt herself slipping down to the carpet.

Tate stood for a moment in a no-man's-land, unable to move as his wife fainted in front of him. He felt sick to the stomach. He'd caught them again. They must have arranged to meet here, however briefly. They probably thought it was safer to meet in public.

Then something strange happened. He caught a glimpse of satisfaction on Drake's face. Suddenly, Tate wasn't sure about anything. He hadn't heard from Drake since before the wedding, and he hadn't contacted him about tonight either. He'd even felt guilty about it.

And Gemma needed him.

He started forward as an odd emotion rose up inside him like bile. She was *his* wife. No other man should be touching her. If Drake truly cared for Gemma, he'd already be on his knees beside her.

Hell, someone who truly cared wouldn't have let her hit the ground. Tate jumped the distance between them, pleased to see her eyes open as she tried to sit up. It was as well that Drake moved out of the way or Tate might have knocked the other man's head off for letting her fall.

"Gemma?" He half sat her against his body, allowing her to lean against him.

"I'm okay."

Looking down at her face, he saw the color coming back into her cheeks, though not in a good way. "You need a doctor."

She tried to get to her feet, but she looked agitated. "I'm fine."

Tate's arm tightened around her shoulders. "No, stay here for a moment."

"I'm sorry, man," Drake said quickly. "I didn't mean to run into Gemma like this."

Gemma's whole body tensed, and, for the first time, Drake's words didn't ring true to Tate. They matched the satisfaction he'd glimpsed on his best friend's face just moments before.

Yet he didn't want Drake to know even a hint of what he was thinking. He struggled to get his emotions under control. By the time he looked up, he knew no one would guess what was going through his mind. "I can handle it from here."

"Is there anything I can do?" Drake asked.

Tate felt a shiver run through Gemma. It wasn't about her wanting the other man. It was the opposite, in fact.

"Can you tell my family what's happened? They're in the ballroom." That at least would get Drake out of the way. "I'll call Clive to come collect us so I can take Gemma home."

"Sure. I'll go tell them right now. No need for you to worry." Drake walked away.

Tate followed him with his eyes. There was a definite swagger to his friend's back that sent a chill through him.

"Tate, it's not what you think."

He looked down at Gemma's anxious face and could see she thought he was upset with her. Hell, he couldn't be sure he *wasn't* upset with her. Deep down he was definitely upset with *someone*.

Then she flinched and something punched him in the chest. She looked like an injured animal expecting to be hurt. Had Drake done this to her?

Or had *he?*

"Come on," he said, helping her to her feet. "We'll go find somewhere for you to sit down until Clive gets here."

A couple of women came upon them and offered assistance. Tate didn't like others seeing this, but they were in a public place and it couldn't be helped. He took up their offer to show him and Gemma to a small sitting area down the next corridor. Once satisfied they were no longer needed, they went back to the ballroom.

Tate called Clive on his cell phone, explained the situation and was thankful the older man was only about five minutes away from the hotel. Clive usually liked to arrive early and chat with some of the other drivers.

The next minute, Bree came racing toward them. "What happened? Drake said Gemma fainted."

"She did, but she's okay now."

"Oh, good," Bree said, looking relieved.

Tate had to admit he was surprised by the concern on his sister's face. She hadn't exactly been friendly toward Gemma these past few weeks.

"It was probably too much excitement tonight," he excused, keeping Drake out of this. With his grandmother putting Gemma in the spotlight a short while ago, and after everything with her parents on television, it was understandable that Gemma's emotions would be running high. "I'm taking her home soon."

"Do you want me to come with you? Mom and Dad are dancing, and Gran's having a great time with some old friends, but I don't mind leaving early."

"Thanks, sis, but we'll be fine. Tell the others, will you? I don't want Gemma disturbed once we get home. She's going straight to bed."

"Sure." Bree went to walk away.

"Bree?" Gemma said, stopping his sister. "Er…thanks."

Bree's eyes softened. "You're welcome, Gemma," she said, before hurrying away.

Tate was startled at the pleasure he felt that these two women now had the chance to be friends. He hadn't realized before how unsettled it had made him, having his sister hold a grudge against his wife.

His eyes met Gemma's and a moment of connection passed between them, but turbulence soon rushed into her eyes and she looked away. He was grateful Clive rang on his cell phone right then to say he'd arrived. And, thankfully, no one appeared to notice anything out of the ordinary as they made their way through the foyer and out to the limousine.

Clive held the back door open for them. "Is Gemm—I mean, Mrs. Chandler okay?"

"Yes, but I'm glad you weren't far away."

"So am I," Clive said, looking pleased to have been needed.

Gemma climbed on to the backseat. "I'm fine, thank you, Clive."

They were soon driving off, the partition in front affording them some privacy.

"Tate, I—"

"Ssh. You should rest up." He had things to think about. Serious things.

She turned her head to look out the side window, then just as fast turned back at him. "I won't give up Nathan," she said in a suddenly choked voice.

Everything rolled on its head. He'd been giving her the benefit of the doubt, but perhaps that had been a mistake. His jaw set as he ignored the stricken look in her eyes. "That sounds like a threat to me."

"I don't care what you do to me, Tate. You're not having my son."

He decided pity was overrated. "I won't have *my* son living with another man."

Her face went blank. "Wh-what?"

"If you go to Drake, Nathan stays with me."

She gaped at him. "But…but I don't want to go to Drake. I don't want to go anywhere."

The comment threw him. "You don't?"

"No."

So what was all this about then?

And then he knew. He'd told her he would take Nathan from her if he caught her with Drake again. And he would have done it—if he still believed she wanted the other man.

"Then we're staying married," he told her, getting back to what was important.

Her eyes widened, her mouth dropped open. "We are?"

"Nathan is ours. We stay together." He wasn't about to tell her this just yet, but for the first time their marriage wasn't only about their son. *He* wanted her to stay.

"Oh." She swallowed hard, then released a shaky breath. "Well, that's okay then."

"Yes, Gemma, it is."

They completed the rest of the journey in silence. Peggy had been minding Nathan for the evening, but she was at the front door as soon as the car pulled up, her concern obvious. "A nice cup of tea will do you good," she said, once they were inside.

Tate led Gemma up the stairs and waited until she was bed. Once Peggy had brought up the hot drink and left the room, he moved to leave, too. "I'll be downstairs in the study if you need me. Just call me on the intercom." He took a couple of steps toward the door.

"Tate, about Drake—"

"Just let it be." He didn't want to hear the other man's name right now. He was beginning to realize his best friend wasn't all he appeared to be.

Gemma couldn't describe the joy in her heart as Tate closed the door behind him. He might have left her by herself, but she didn't feel in the slightest alone. How could she feel alone when she would be staying married to the man of her heart *and* keeping the son they had made together? Perhaps even with time and understanding would come love?

Then she remembered Drake Fulton, and her throat convulsed. God, Drake had put all that at risk for his own malicious purposes. He'd made her think she'd lost the two most important people in her life. She couldn't have endured losing Tate again. And thinking about losing custody of Nathan was debilitating.

Yet somehow Tate believed she *hadn't* engineered the meeting with Drake. She didn't understand why, or the reason he seemed to have mellowed. Could it be that he was finally seeing his best friend for the person he was? Or was it more that Tate was learning to trust *her*?

She prayed it was both.

Eleven

The next morning, Tate left Gemma and Nathan still sleeping and went down to the kitchen early. He'd had a restless night, his mind trying to figure out if his best friend had been full of lies all along. Drake had convinced him that Gemma was the one in the wrong, but suddenly Tate could accept she hadn't been a party to that kiss.

Or was it merely that he *wanted* to believe in her? Was her innocence simply more palatable, something that would not only allow him to stay married to her but to sleep with her as well? But if that was so, why couldn't he shake the image of that smug look on Drake's face?

In the kitchen, Peggy passed him a cup of coffee, waited for him to take a couple of sips and then handed him the morning newspaper. "I think you'd better see this, Mr. Chandler."

The headline screamed out at him.

Chandler's Baby?

"What the hell!"

Newlywed Gemma Chandler faints at the Humanitarian Awards Dinner last night…

It went on to describe an eyewitness account of Gemma in a heap on the floor in the corridor.

Does the Chandler family have more than their award to celebrate? Will matriarch Helen Chandler soon have another great-grandchild to show the Australian public?

"Damn them!" Tate threw the newspaper back on the bench after reading a rehash of his recent marriage and the reason behind it.

"I see Drake Fulton was at the dinner, too," Peggy said, indicating the article.

Tate scowled and took another look at the front page. He hadn't taken much notice of the photograph, which showed his family leaving the hotel. Drake walked beside Tate's mother, smiling down at her as if he was enthralled by what she was saying. It was the way Drake smiled at all women. Nothing unusual there.

Tate nodded. "That's right. He turned up late."

A frown appeared on Peggy's face. "I see."

Something made him look harder at his housekeeper. "Why, Peggy?"

She hesitated.

"Peggy, is there something you're not telling me?"

She gave a tiny pause, then, "Did Gemma faint before or after Mr. Fulton turned up?"

It was his turn to frown. "After. Why?"

"Well…"

"Tell me," he said, his tone firm, allowing no argument.

"He telephoned here about two weeks ago and spoke

to Gemma," she said, sending shock through him. "It was the time we were moving her things into your room."

"Go on."

"I heard Gemma tell him that he was never a friend of yours and that one day you'd see him for what he was." She grimaced. "I'm sorry, Mr. Chandler. Perhaps I shouldn't have said anything, but I really like Gemma and I didn't like how upset Mr. Fulton made her. I know this is presumptuous of me, but I have to say it even if I lose my job. I think Gemma's right to be wary of your friend."

Tate felt like his eyes were being pried open. Wide open. Wasn't it around that time Gemma had seemed distracted? It must have been because of Drake's phone call. His blood boiled as he thought about Drake saying something to upset her or, worse, doing something.

"I appreciate you telling me, Peggy. And no, you're not going to lose your job for speaking your mind."

Relief swept over her face. "Thank you."

His grip tightened on the newspaper in his hand. "I'll take this upstairs. I don't want Gemma seeing it."

Peggy's eyes softened. "She's lucky to have you looking out for her, Mr. Chandler."

An odd sensation flowed through his chest. "I'm beginning to think *I'm* the lucky one, Peggy."

And he meant it.

He left the kitchen and went back upstairs. Gemma was on their bed in her nightgown looking gorgeous, playfully tickling Nathan's tummy. He watched the pair of them, loving the moment and the sound of their giggling. His throat squeezed with a deep tenderness.

She looked up and an unusual warmth entered her eyes. "Tate, I didn't see you there."

"You two are having fun. I didn't want to disturb you."

He wanted to extend this moment. Nathan saw him then and tried to get down off the bed. Tate strode forward and swung his son off the mattress and up into his arms. "Hey, buddy," he murmured, cuddling him close. He smelled so...*his*.

Tate's eyes met Gemma's.

Theirs.

In danger of becoming too emotive, he was thankful that Nathan squirmed to get down on the floor. He placed the baby on the carpet just as Gemma said, "You've brought the newspaper."

His head snapped up, not realizing he'd thrown the paper on the bed when he'd picked up Nathan.

She was unfolding it. Her eyes casually flicked over the front page...then went wide. "What's this?"

There was no easy way to say it. "You made the papers last night."

The blood drained from her face as she began to read more. "They're suggesting I'm pregnant."

"Yes."

"But I'm not. I'm on the pill. And I didn't faint because of—"

He didn't want her saying Drake's name. "Would being pregnant again be the end of the world for you?"

"Of course not!" she exclaimed, falling for the diversion. "I'd love another baby someday." A blush spread across her cheeks even as she lifted her chin with a sort of dignity. "But I want it to be something private."

He more than identified with what she was saying. "We're in the public eye now, so we'll be news whatever we do, I'm afraid."

She let out a breath and threw the paper aside as she got out of bed. "I know."

"But that doesn't mean we can't remain private people at home," he said, sharing what his grandfather had once told him. "They don't, and can't, know everything."

She considered the words. "That's true."

"So don't let it—"

"Tate! He's walking!"

"What?" He felt his son grab hold of his leg.

"Nathan walked! It was only a couple of steps from that chair to you, but he did it."

Tate looked down at his son, who was now standing pressed against his trouser leg. A lump rose in his throat.

Gemma crouched down a few feet away and spoke to Nathan. "Darling, walk to Mommy."

Nathan looked across at his mother and hesitated.

"Come on. You can do it, darling. Come to Mommy."

Nathan let go of Tate's leg, wobbled and then took three steps in a rush to his mother, who scooped him up, tears in her eyes, sheer pride written across her face. Tate could feel that lump rise farther in his throat and choke him up. At that moment he knew he'd never give up Gemma or his son. He'd fight to the death for them.

Their son had walked.

Gemma couldn't believe how wonderful it felt to see Nathan take his first steps, and how perfect that Tate had been there to share the special event with her. Not even that invasive article about her being pregnant could dull her excitement.

Their son had walked.

Then, after breakfast, Tate said he was going out but wouldn't be long. It dampened her spirits a little. He'd been quiet while they'd eaten. At times she'd seen tension etched around his mouth, yet she had the feeling it wasn't directed at her.

On his return, he appeared more relaxed, but he still had a hard look on his face. He was angry at someone. Her parents? Surely Tate would tell her if it was something to do with them.

Or could this be about Drake Fulton? Her heart lifted. As far as she knew, no one else had done anything to cause Tate anger. Oh, she did so hope that Tate was finally seeing Drake's true colors.

"Gran's decided she wants to hold an impromptu party tonight," Tate told her now, as she and Nathan sat on the sunroom floor building a tower with wooden blocks.

"Tonight?"

He got down on his haunches, ruffled his son's hair and added a block to the tower. "I think she's feeling bereft that my grandfather isn't around to share the award, and this is her way of keeping busy. She and Bree have been on the phone all morning inviting people."

Gemma remembered how nice Bree had been to her last night. Would it continue? "It's short notice, isn't it?"

"Yes, but it's only for family and close friends. Whoever can make it, really."

Her heart gripped with an insidious fear. She couldn't bring herself to mention Drake. And then she remembered something. "People will be curious…about me, I mean. They'll be speculating that I'm pregnant."

"We can't stop them, but I'll be there with you anyway."

His reassurance meant a lot to her.

"Peggy's agreed to babysit again." He got to his feet. "I'll be in the study for a while. I promised Gran I'd make a couple of calls for her."

He left them to their tower.

At the party that evening at Helen's house, Gemma took a quick look around as they entered the large entryway, grateful not to see any sight of Drake. She was amazed at the number of guests. "Family and close friends, I believe you said," she teased Tate. It was standing room only.

His firm lips quirked with wry humor. "Gran's been around a lot of years. She's made many close friends."

"There's got to be at least sixty people here."

"Eighty, actually," Helen said, coming to welcome them with a kiss on the cheek for both of them. Gemma couldn't help but be relieved she was still in the older woman's favor. She wasn't sure the awards dinner hadn't been a dream.

Or a nightmare, where Drake was concerned.

And then the nightmare arrived.

"How's my favorite grandmother?" Drake said, bestowing a kiss on Helen's lined cheek.

Helen tutted. "If your grandmother was here she'd have something to say about that, young man."

He chuckled, then nodded at Tate, before his gaze slid to Gemma, his practiced smile fading with concern. "I hope you're feeling better now, Gemma. You could have hurt yourself fainting like that last night."

Gemma felt the slightest stiffening in Tate's body and knew he wasn't comfortable with Drake. But surprisingly, she felt Tate's hand squeeze her waist, as if he was trying to bolster her spirits. It gave her the courage to put on a fake smile. "Thankfully, Tate was there for me."

There was a flash of something vicious deep in Drake's eyes, before he turned to Helen with an easy smile. After that, he was all false charm with the other woman and buddy-buddy with Tate, then Darlene and Jonathan joined them, followed by Bree. Tate's sister was friendly to Gemma before she took off again, and eventually Drake moved to another group of people.

A while later, Tate mentioned wanting to talk to a business acquaintance across the room, and Helen waved him off, saying she would look after Gemma. Gemma nodded at him that she would be fine, but she was warmed by his concern about leaving her alone.

After a while, Helen put her hand on Gemma's arm and drew her aside. "Darling, I wonder if you could do me a big favor?"

"Of course, Helen."

"I'm expecting a friend of Nathaniel's to call me at eight. Dougal's old and he's in a home, and if I don't answer the phone he won't call back. Do you think you could go to the study and wait for his call, then come and get me? I don't want to leave my guests just yet."

Gemma was a little confused by the request, especially as Helen seemed to have so many staff helping out tonight, but if that was what she wanted... "Sure. I'd be happy to do that."

"Thank you," Helen said, looking pleased. "I thought you might like a little time to yourself, too. I know it's been stressful for you lately."

That was really nice of her. "Yes, it has."

Helen glanced at her watch. "It's fifteen minutes to eight. The study is down the hall on the right. Just go in there and wait and come get me when Dougal phones."

"Okay." Gemma went to step forward, then stopped. "I'd better tell Tate." She didn't want him worrying if he couldn't find her. Then she saw that Tate had moved away from the business acquaintance and was now talking to Drake. Her heart sank.

"No, I'll do that," Helen said, shooting relief through Gemma. "You go put your feet up. The party won't finish for another couple of hours, and there are plenty of guests who still want to talk to you."

That was enough for Gemma. The thought of everyone asking questions almost had her running for the study.

By the time Tate saw Gemma leave the room, he'd already positioned himself next to Drake. He was in the middle of a discussion with him when his grandmother approached.

As planned.

"Tate, darling," she said, reaching them. "I'm expecting a phone call from Dougal. He's your grandfather's old friend, if you remember. I hope you don't mind, but Gemma's gone to the study to wait for the call for me. I thought she looked a little peaked, so it will do her good to get away from the crowd."

Tate put on a frown and went to move. "I'd better go see how she is."

Helen placed her hand on his arm. "No, don't, darling. She really is okay and just needed a moment to herself. She said for you not to worry. She'll be back in no time." Helen squeezed Drake's arm. "It's so nice to see you here, Drake." Then she walked away.

"Your grandmother's fantastic, Tate."

"She certainly is."

Drake considered him. "Go to Gemma if you want."

"No, Gran's right. It'll do Gemma good to have some time to herself."

He hated using Gemma as bait to lure Drake into showing his hand, but he had to put an end to this for everyone's sake, especially Gemma's. He now believed she had been telling him the truth all along. God, he wasn't sure how he was managing to even talk to his so-called best friend.

Drake's brows drew together. "Maybe Gemma is feeling stressed because I'm here." He paused. "Sorry again that I couldn't get out of coming tonight, man. Your grandmother insisted."

"That's okay. It's all water under the bridge."

Drake's eyes looked more calculating than not. "You seem pretty confident about Gemma now."

With his own eyes wide open, Tate could see that his friend was getting desperate. It was now or never. "I am."

There was a moment of stony silence.

"I guess if Gemma's pregnant…"

Tate knew the other man was fishing, trying to get a handle on how he could best do damage to the marriage. But why? What was this all about? It had to be something damn significant if his friend was trying to do this to him and Gemma.

Could Drake even be behind the newspaper headline this morning about Gemma being pregnant? Hell, could he even have had something to do with the internet pictures? The thought clenched tight and wouldn't let go.

"We're both hoping for more children," Tate said deliberately, hoping to spur the other man into action, knowing he'd hit the mark when he saw Drake's jaw clench. Tate scratched his earlobe, giving his grandmother the signal.

"Tate, can you come here for a minute?" his grandmother called out to him from where she was holding court with some friends.

Tate looked back at Drake and feigned a wry smile. "I'd better go see what Gran wants."

Drake's answering smile was tight. "Yeah, don't keep the lady waiting."

Tate walked away, but before he'd even reached his grandmother, she gave him a slight nod.

Drake had left the room.

Gemma sat on the leather executive chair behind the large desk and saw the clock ticking toward eight. She had to admit that Helen had done her a favor by asking her to come in here and wait for the phone call. She'd badly needed to get away from Drake's presence, hovering like the snake he was, ready to strike.

She was surprised that Tate didn't seem more upset about it all. Oh, he had that small tightness around his mouth telling her he wasn't happy having Drake here, but he still didn't seem to be accusing her of anything. And that was gratifying, if somewhat confusing.

The opening of the study door broke into her thoughts. The sound of the party rushed in as she saw a tall figure step inside and close the door behind him.

This time she didn't get the man wrong.

Drake.

A sense of déjà vu washed over her.

"So this is where you're hiding?" he mocked, remaining in front of the door, barring her escape.

"This is a private room, Drake," she said, trying not to look like she was frozen in her chair.

He started toward her, "All the better."

"What do you mean?" Her stomach churned. She knew there was a door leading out to the terrace, but the heavy drapes had been pulled across it, and she doubted she'd get to it before him. If only the telephone would ring.

It remained silent.

"You didn't think I would give up, did you?"

"Give up what?"

He stopped right in front of the desk. *"You."*

Her brain stumbled then righted. Was he going to take her at any price? She couldn't let him. Everything she had, everything she loved, was at risk here. She couldn't let him take it all away. Not again.

Somehow she managed to get to her feet and pull back her shoulders, making herself taller, though she wasn't foolish enough to move from behind the desk. If she did, he would attack.

"Why are you doing this, Drake?" she said as calmly as she could. "I never encouraged you."

His eyes narrowed. "Maybe that's the attraction."

In that split second she realized he was used to intimidating her. He wasn't used to her fighting back. She might have disagreed with him on the telephone every time he'd called, but there hadn't been a chance to stand up to him in person. Why, even at the awards dinner last night she'd pleaded with him to let her go.

No more.

"You knew I thought it was Tate I was kissing two years ago," she said, determined to make him accountable.

"Oh, yeah, I knew, Gem."

He was a bully. "Yet you're Tate's best friend. Why would you risk your friendship like this?"

"Am I risking it? I don't think so." He paused, his confidence returning. "You know, it's a pity about your upcoming divorce. Your marriage really was over so quickly. But hey, that's the way with these high-profile marriages."

Inside she gasped, outside she didn't flinch. "What do you mean?"

"Once I make you mine, I'll have to tell Tate how you finally succeeded in seducing me."

She held her ground. "He won't believe you."

He rubbed his chin, cocky and obnoxious. "Oh, I think he will."

"Actually, Drake, I know I won't," Tate growled, pushing the drapes aside and stepping in from the doorway to the terrace.

This time Gemma did gasp out loud.

And so did Drake Fulton.

Twelve

Looking across the room at the other man, Tate had never felt a deeper sense of cold triumph. How had he ever thought Drake was a man of his word?

"What *is* this?" Drake demanded, recovering quickly.

Tate moved farther into the room. "I set you up, you son of a bitch."

"And I helped him," Helen Chandler said, stepping in from the terrace.

Drake winced.

Anger rolled through Tate. "All I want to know is why, Drake?"

Masking his face now, the other man gave a careless shrug. "You took my girlfriend all those years ago, so I decided to take yours."

Tate blinked, then blinked again in disbelief. "Good Lord! You mean *Rachel?* That was back at university."

He shook his head. "And she made a play for me, not the other way around. You said it didn't matter anyway."

Drake's face turned rigid. "I lied. She mattered to me, Tate. Just like Gemma mattered to you. I could tell that, you see. It made my vengeance all the sweeter."

Tate glanced at Gemma and their eyes collided. His heart raced as he saw hope flare in those blue depths. She *wanted* him to care for her.

He did, he promised in return.

His gaze returned to Drake. "You're right about that, Drake. Gemma *does* matter to me," he said out loud. "More than you know." He heard her make a soft sound, but it was Drake's harsher rasp that kept his attention fully focused on the man.

Like a spoiled child, Drake burst out, "I was behind the internet pictures and the newspaper story about her being pregnant."

Rage sliced through Tate. Drake's confession only confirmed what he'd already suspected, but didn't lessen his anger. "I want you out of this house and out of my life. If you ever come near my family again, you'll be sorry."

"Fine with me," Drake snapped. "I achieved what I wanted to do anyway. I split you up for two years. You missed your son's birth and his first year of life." A gloating smile stretched his lips. "That can't be replaced, can it, Tate?"

"Why you—" Tate stepped forward, fist clenched, his chest squeezed so tight that—

His grandmother put her hand on Tate's arm, and he let her stop him. She glared haughtily at Drake. "I'll see you out, Drake. And I suggest you head back overseas as soon as possible and never show your face here again. I'll destroy you if you do." Her tone said she would do what she said. She might be small, but she was a formidable woman. Drake couldn't fail to recognize that.

"Good riddance to you all," he barked, twisting away and stalking out of the room. He almost took the door off its hinges as he slammed the wood shut.

For a few seconds no one moved.

Then Helen went after him, her beautifully aged face easing into a smile as she blew them a kiss before leaving.

And then there were two.

The clock ticked.

Tate's gaze slid back to the woman he loved. Oh, yes, he *loved* Gemma. The knowledge of it had hit him hard when he'd stood outside on the terrace and heard Drake threaten her. The instinct to protect this woman had risen from the very core of him. It had been about more than saving her from harm, more than shielding her from a vengeful, vindictive traitor-of-a-friend. The groundswell of emotion inside him made him want to protect her, to honor her, to share with her the happiest life possible. No one would stop him. Nothing would break them apart. Not again. Never again.

He moved to her, and she was already coming around the desk and flying into his arms. He hugged her tightly, welding her to him. She felt so good, so right. She had to feel something for him, too. Could it be *love?*

"It's over now, darling," he murmured, kissing her eyes, her ears, burying his face in her hair and inhaling the scent of the woman he loved. She was everything to him.

Gemma relished having Tate's arms around her, but she was having trouble believing what had just happened. There had evidently been no phone call expected from

Dougal. Tate had planned this to catch Drake. That meant he finally believed she was innocent.

Thank you, dear Lord.

She leaned back and lovingly looked up at her husband's strong face in wonder. "No, Tate, you're wrong. It's not over."

He frowned, but she could see he wasn't too worried. "It's not?"

Her hands slipped up and framed his face. "It's only just begun, my darling. I love you, Tate Chandler. I love you so very much."

He drew in an unsteady breath. "Oh, God, I love you, too, Gemma. More than life itself."

Their lips and hearts met for timeless minutes. This was love at its finest. It didn't get any better—any more genuine and absolute—than this.

Eventually they eased apart and Tate smiled at her with a love she would cherish forever.

A moment later, deep regret seeped into his eyes. "Forgive me, darling, for all I've put you through. I don't know how I didn't see the truth before. You're a good, kind person, and I don't deserve you at all."

Forgiving him was easy. "There were a lot of things in the way," she excused, knowing that walking through fire had made her appreciate their love. Later, she would tell him how she had loved him from the beginning, but not here, not now.

"Thank you." He kissed her. "Let's make our life a blank sheet of paper from this moment on."

She opened her mouth to agree, then tilted her head at him, her brow wrinkling just a little. "But our pasts have made us who we are, Tate. We've earned our right to happiness. I don't ever want to forget that."

His smile was full of admiration. "See, this is why I

love you so much. You're right, of course. But hey, I don't think we should remember it *every* day."

"Agreed." The sound of laughter erupted in the distance. Clearly Drake hadn't been allowed to spoil the party. "Your grandmother is awesome."

He nodded. "When it comes to protecting her own, she is."

"You didn't do too badly yourself," she teased, forever grateful he had followed his gut instinct. Then she sobered. "I'm sorry I don't have any decent family to share with you."

A part of her would always ache for the love of her parents, but being an adult meant accepting what she couldn't change and living her life to the fullest. Yes, somewhere along the line she'd grown up, too.

"You and Nathan are all the family I need," Tate said, the look in his eyes open and honest. "And let's not forget the two of you have already brought happiness to my family. If you don't believe me, I'm sure my grandmother would be only too happy to confirm that. You brought us back together, Gemma. I'm indebted to you for that."

Gemma buzzed with sheer bliss. "So you've forgiven your mother?"

"We all make mistakes," he said with a self-deprecating smile. "And none more than me."

"She'll be thrilled to have her son back," Gemma said with certainty. "You know, I suspect you couldn't forgive her before because your grandmother couldn't forgive her. I think your loyalties were divided between the two women in your life. In the end, you followed your grandmother's lead. She's a strong woman. Though no less strong than your mother," Gemma was quick to add. "It took guts for Darlene to return and admit she'd made a mistake."

For a moment, a hint of regret filled his expression. "I

know." Then it disappeared and he was back to being the confident man she knew and loved. "Come on. I want to go home and see our son."

His words warmed her heart. "I want another baby with you, Tate."

Something dark flared in his eyes. "So do I. As many as you like."

"I'd like at least three." It was hard to believe this was a possibility now, and that she could share it with the man she loved.

His mouth curved sensually. "Didn't you once say practice makes perfect?"

She went on her toes and kissed his cheek. "I believe I did."

Tate slipped his arm around her shoulders. "Then we'd better get started."

Together they left the study by the terrace door and strolled through the landscaped gardens around the side of the house, heading for the limousine. A night breeze softly traced over their skin, and the brightest of stars twinkled down on them.

Love was definitely in the air.

* * * * *

MILLS & BOON®
Book Club
2 Free Books!

Get your free books now at
www.millsandboon.co.uk/freebookoffer

Or fill in the form below and post it back to us

THE MILLS & BOON® BOOK CLUB™—HERE'S HOW IT WORKS: Accepting your free books places you under no obligation to buy anything. You may keep the books and return the despatch note marked 'Cancel'. If we do not hear from you, about a month later we'll send you 4 brand-new stories from the Desire™ 2-in-1 series priced at £5.30* each. There is no extra charge for post and packaging. You may cancel at any time, otherwise we will send you 4 stories a month which you may purchase or return to us—the choice is yours. *Terms and prices subject to change without notice. Offer valid in UK only. Applicants must be 18 or over. Offer expires 28th February 2012. **For full terms and conditions, please go to www.millsandboon.co.uk/termsandconditions**

Mrs/Miss/Ms/Mr (please circle) _____

First Name _____

Surname _____

Address _____

_____

Postcode _____

E-mail _____

Send this completed page to: Mills & Boon Book Club, Free Book Offer, FREEPOST NAT 10298, Richmond, Surrey, TW9 1BR

Find out more at
www.millsandboon.co.uk/freebookoffer

Visit us
Online

0611/D1ZEE

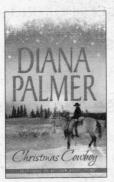

Mills & Boon® Online

Discover more romance at
www.millsandboon.co.uk

 FREE online reads

 Books up to one
month before shops

 Browse our books
before you buy

...and much more!

For exclusive competitions and instant updates:

 Like us on **facebook.com/romancehq**

Follow us on **twitter.com/millsandboonuk**

Join us on **community.millsandboon.co.uk**

Visit us Online | Sign up for our FREE eNewsletter at
www.millsandboon.co.uk

Have Your Say

You've just finished your book.
So what did you think?

We'd love to hear your thoughts on our
'Have your say' online panel
www.millsandboon.co.uk/haveyoursay

- 🌹 Easy to use
- 🌹 Short questionnaire
- 🌹 Chance to win Mills & Boon®
  goodies

*Visit us
Online*

Tell us what you thought of this book now at
www.millsandboon.co.uk/haveyoursay